dark hearts

USA TODAY BESTSELLING AUTHOR
MICALEA SMELTZER

dark hearts

© Copyright 2017 Micalea Smeltzer
All rights reserved. This book or any portion thereof may not be reproduced or used in any manner whatsoever without the express written permission of the publisher.
This is a work of fiction. Names, characters, businesses, places, events and incidents are either the products of the author's imagination or used in a fictitious manner. Any resemblance to actual persons, living or dead, or actual events is purely coincidental.

Original Song Lyrics for Supernova & Dark Hearts by Jordan Janson

Cover design by Emily Wittig

Models Alex Nelson and Libby Yost
Photography Regina Wamba

Edited and Formatted by Wendi Temporado of Ready, Set, Edit

one
. . .

nova

"I FUCKING HATE WEDDINGS."

I glance up in time to see my friend Jace drop down into the seat beside me. He fiddles with his tie, loosening it, and then undoing the top button of his white dress shirt.

"I *never* want that to be me," he continues, waving his fingers lazily to where our just married friends dance, their smiles blinding and their laughter nearly louder than the music.

"Allergic to love?" I raise a brow.

His top lip curls. "No—it's just that love makes you weak. Look at them. They've willingly handed their heart to the other person, giving them permission to break it at any time." He shakes his head and rolls up his sleeves, revealing the intricate tattoos that snake around one forearm. "It's not for me." He makes a face like something tastes bad.

"Can't say I don't agree with you," I mutter.

He raises a brow. "Really? You're a girl, so I can't believe you're not about to give me some spiel on true love and how love conquers everything." He pulls his cigarette pack out of his pocket and taps the box against the white-tablecloth-covered table.

I sigh. "I believed that once, but in my experience, it's not true. Love doesn't conquer everything, it destroys you instead."

Jace looks at me seriously, and I swear it's like his eyes see right through me. "Huh."

"Huh?" I repeat. "What does that mean?"

He shrugs. "Nothing."

"What?" I prompt again. "You're thinking something."

He shrugs, and the motion stretches the shirt tight across his shoulders. "Just that you and I are so alike it scares me sometimes."

I smile at that, and he chuckles. "I didn't think anything could possibly scare you."

He slips the cigarette pack back into his pocket without ever grabbing one. He stands then and holds his hand out to me.

"Dance with me?"

"You dance?" I eye him.

He grins, and I know I'm in trouble. Jace doesn't smile much, but when he does, it means trouble.

"I have sex. Dancing is practically the same thing. You just have your clothes on."

I roll my eyes.

He wiggles his fingers. "Come on, little star, dance with me."

I sigh, slipping my hand in his as I stand, and he guides me onto the dance floor. He towers above my short frame, and I place my hands flat on his chest since I can't wrap them around his neck.

Xander and Thea—who had a quickie wedding in Vegas and are now having this wedding so all of us could attend—twirl around us.

Jace might mock them for what they have, but I can't help but feel a slight sting of jealousy.

I thought I had that once. A love that was impenetrable and everlasting. I was young, though, and so naïve.

Jace's hands cup the small of my waist, and he moves us effortlessly around the dance floor. There's only a handful of people dancing, but everyone seems to be having a good time. Xander and Thea chose to keep the wedding small and only had their closest family and friends come.

"You actually *can* dance," I comment, unable to hide the surprise in my voice.

Jace chuckles. "Confession, I took dance lessons as a kid."

My eyes widen and nearly pop out of my head. *Dance lessons.*

"Confession, I took ballet for five days before quitting much to the dismay of my parents. I have no rhythm," I whisper like it's some sort of secret.

Jace's lips quirk in a smile.

I've been staying with him since the beginning of summer. I didn't want to head home, back to Texas and that God-forsaken small town, and Jace's roommate happened to be moving out so it worked out perfectly. Since then, we've developed a game we've simply dubbed *Confession*. That's all it is. A confession, something we've never shared with another person but we've chosen to share with each other. Some of our confessions are silly and others are more serious. I love all of them. Each one gives me one small piece of the puzzle that is Jacen Kensington.

"You're not so bad."

"And you're a liar," I say, stepping on his toes. He doesn't comment on my clumsiness and moves us easily around the dance floor. I'm light enough that he can hold me and guide me while I do nothing.

The song ends and bleeds into another. I expect him to stop, but he keeps going.

We dance to three more songs before returning to the table.

I pick up my camera and take a few photos of the bride and groom while they're oblivious. There's something about candid photos that leave a more lasting mark in your memory than something posed so I want to make sure they have plenty of those.

Xander and Thea had tasked Rae—another friend of ours—and me with taking photos at the wedding. Rae and I are both going to college for photography. I think they asked both of us to take photos because they didn't want either of us to feel bad for not being chosen. I would've been fine if they only went with Rae, though. Weddings aren't my thing. Don't get me wrong, I knew I could and would get some amazing shots, but it wasn't my passion. Rae liked to take photos of everything. <u>But</u> me? I preferred to make mine into something else. *Conceptual* photography was my go-to, but lately, something else was catching my eye and getting my wheels turning.

Jace.

God, I itched to photograph him.

He made the most mundane things look like the most exciting thing ever.

Like every morning, when he drank his coffee and read the newspaper still wearing his glasses since he never puts his contacts in first thing.

He fascinates me. I can't think of any other twenty-three-year-old guy who still reads the physical newspaper. Let alone *any* kind of newspaper.

I'm sure if I asked him he'd let me. Jace isn't a shy guy. But he is my best friend, and I don't want to make things weird. I haven't had a friend like him in a long time, and I'm not willing to mess with what we have for a few photos.

Click. Click. Click.

The sound of the shutter on my camera is music to my ears.

I feel that *love* is an understatement for what I feel for photography. It is my art. My life. My escape. My *everything*. Without it, I can't breathe.

After I've taken a million photos of Xander and Thea, I move on to taking pictures of the cake and décor. I focus on the little things—zooming in on the turquoise flowers frosted on the cake and the crisp lines of the napkins folded on the table.

I decide to take a break and head back to the table Jace occupies. He sits with his legs taking up as much space as humanly possible. He's now ditched his tie completely and it sits as a crumpled gray pile on the table.

He lifts his gaze to me as I place my Canon 70d on the table.

"You look like you could use a drink," he comments.

I laugh and push my magenta-colored hair away from my eyes. "Is that your way of saying *you* need a drink?"

His green eyes twinkle. "Yes. I'll be back."

He hops up and heads to the bar.

I kick my heels off beneath the table and swear my feet sing halle-fucking-lujah at being free of those death traps.

Thea Montgomery—Kincaid, now, I correct myself—thinks there's something wrong with you if you don't wear heels, but I think she's the one that's not okay in the head because those things are painful.

I lift one aching foot to rest on my knee and begin massaging it.

Jace returns and places a beer in front of me before taking his seat again.

"Feet hurt?" he asks.

Before I can answer, he grabs my legs and tugs my feet into his lap.

He begins massaging the arch of my right foot before I can protest, and I nearly moan because, *Oh, my God that feels amazing*.

He rubs with expert precision, and I wonder where he learned to do it.

My head lolls back and my eyes close. "Feels good?"

I nod and don't open my eyes. "I'm never wearing heels again," I mumble.

He moves to the other foot, and I suppress another moan.

"On second thought, maybe I should wear heels every day if it means you'll rub my feet."

He chuckles, and the sound is warm and husky and perfectly Jace.

He finishes rubbing my feet, and I reluctantly drop them to the ground again.

"It's time for the bouquet toss!" someone calls out.

I groan.

Jace nudges my shoulder and waggles his brows. "Don't you want to catch the bouquet?"

"Yeah, and be labeled as the next one to get married? No thanks."

"Come on," he coaxes. "It'll be fun."

"Are you going to be a part of the garter toss?" I challenge.

He tilts his head and smirks. "Of course."

I sigh. "Fine. I'll do it."

I place my hands on the table and push up as I stand. I

don't bother putting my heels back on. I'm burning those things first thing tomorrow morning.

It's a small group for the bouquet toss since the wedding was so intimate.

I turn around and point at Jace and then my camera. "Take photos," I mouth.

Rae is participating too, and I want to make sure there's at least *one* photo of this for Thea and Xander to look back on. Jace might not be a photographer, but I think he can manage at least one or two photos.

"Me?" He points to himself.

"Yes, you." I point again, and he picks up my camera, looking at it stupidly. "It's that button right—"

Whack.

The bouquet hits me right in the back of the head.

I turn around and glare at the offending flowers now lying pathetically on the ground. Jace laughs uproariously in the background along with a few other people.

Thea turns around from her perch, confused by the laughter. "Who got them?" she asks.

"Apparently, Nova." Rae bends and picks them up and hands them to me. My lip curls in disgust. I didn't want to catch them, and I would've side-stepped it if I'd been turned that way. Instead, I was arguing with Jace over taking a photo and he didn't even get one. "Don't look so disgusted." Rae laughs. "It's funny."

I sigh and shrug. It's only a silly tradition, after all, and means nothing. I force a smile and say, "Yeah, it is pretty funny."

Thea heads over to us, smiling from ear to ear. I don't think I've ever seen her happier.

"They didn't hurt you, did they?" she asks, concerned.

I shake my head. "They're flowers. They can't do much damage."

She rests her arm casually on my shoulder and leans into me. "I didn't mean to hit you in the head with them."

"S'okay." I wave away her concern. "You weren't even looking where you were throwing. It's my own fault. I was trying to get Jace to take a picture of it and he was being an idiot."

"Hey, I take offense to that," he remarks, striding over to us with my camera in hand.

"What would you prefer?"

"Lovable." He grins and holds out my camera. I trade him the flowers, and he looks at them like they're diseased. "Here, you want these back?" He holds them out to Thea.

She rolls her eyes as Xander comes up behind her, fitting his hands around her waist. "Nova caught them. They're hers now."

Jace looks at the flowers again and then me. "Does this mean you're getting married next?"

I gag. "Never."

He chuckles, and I lift my camera to get a shot of Xander's hands around her waist. Then another of him dipping his head into the crook of her neck.

Cade joins our group, standing next to Rae with a smile on his face. She leans into him, and I don't think she even realizes she does it.

"Come on." Xander tugs on Thea's waist. "Garter time."

"Oh, no ..." She laughs as he drags her away. "I don't like the look in your eye."

I must admit, she's right. Xander has a mischievous glint in his eyes that promises trouble. He leads her to the chair that someone's already placed in the center of the dance floor.

The guys at the wedding all reluctantly head that way and gather around the bride and groom. Rae grabs her camera, and the two of us start snapping photos. I can't help but get one of the irritated expression on Jace's face. He looks absolutely disgusted to have to be standing there.

Payback's a bitch.

"Are you going to give me a lap dance first?" Thea asks as Xander gives her a slight push into the chair.

He bends forward so they're eye-level. "You want me to dance, sweetheart?"

"I want you to take your clothes off."

Laughter explodes out of him. "I love you," he says when he regains control of himself.

He kneels on the floor then and lifts all the layers of tulle of her dress and dives under. Her eyes widen in surprise, and we all try not to laugh, but it's hard not to when it looks like Xander is ... well ...

His head moves around and then back down and he comes away with the garter belt between his teeth and Thea's cheeks successfully a bright red color. She doesn't get embarrassed much, so it's nice to see her feathers get ruffled.

Xander tosses the garter belt and we all watch to see who catches it.

"Fuck me."

I can't control my laughter at seeing Jace clutching the garter belt.

"Here, take it." He tries to hand it to Cade.

Cade refuses it and shakes his head. "Nah, man. It's all yours."

Jace dangles the garter belt from his finger and looks right at me. I snap a picture and then a few more as he flicks it at me. I manage to get a shot of it flying through the air.

Perfection.

I bend and pick the garter belt up off the floor and carry it back over to him. "If I have to keep the flowers then you have to keep this."

He grabs it and crumbles it in his fist before shoving it in his pocket. "Traditions are silly," he mutters, but I can tell he's secretly amused by the whole thing. After all, the irony of me "catching" the bouquet and him the garter belt is laughable. Both of us are the ones most likely to *never* get married. "When are we getting cake?" he calls out to Xander and Thea who are completely lost in one another again.

Thea glances over and then up at Xander. "Wanna cut the cake?"

He shrugs. "Sure."

"Cake's happening now," she calls over to Jace.

"Confession," Jace whispers, "I love cake."

I watch as he turns and heads back to the table he was sitting at before. I notice one of the girls Thea has class with eyeing him, and I'm not surprised when she moves from her table over to his to sit beside him. He smiles and leans into her when she says something.

I sigh and avert my eyes.

I have pictures to take and watching Jace flirt is not part of that job.

Xander and Thea cut into the cake, and I'm not surprised when she nails him right in the face with cake. Xander ends up chasing after her to get her back and she makes it all the way to the other side of the dance floor before he catches her. He loops one arm around her waist and swings her around. His other hand with the cake comes toward her mouth. She pleads with him not to do it, but he doesn't listen and she gets a face full of cake. They both can't contain their laughter.

"Look at us." Thea laughs. "We look ridiculous."

He reaches up and tenderly clears her face of cake. "Ridiculous is good."

"Does this mean we can eat the cake now?"

I jump at the sound of Jace's voice right by my ear. "Jesus! Where'd you come from?"

He raises a brow and points to the table. I notice the girl is gone.

"I want some cake."

"Let me guess, you want a middle piece too?"

"Well, it's a circle, so it doesn't really matter." He shrugs.

I glance back at Xander and Thea who are now cleaning their faces with napkins.

The caterer is already cutting the cake and placing slices on plates.

"Looks like your cake is ready," I point out.

Jace rubs his hands together and licks his lips. "*Cake*," he hums. "You want a piece?"

"Sure."

He heads off to get the cake, and I head back to our table.

My heels are still on the ground, and I kick them out of my way.

Heels are the work of the devil. I'm sure of it.

Jace returns a moment later and hands me my slice of cake with a flourish. It's chocolate and covered in icing—and the more icing the better, in my opinion.

He pulls out his chair and plops into it. I notice he has *two* slices of cake on his plate and he's already eaten half of one.

"This is so good." He shovels a forkful into his mouth.

I stifle a laugh. I don't think I've ever seen Jace this animated over anything ever, except maybe his music, and even then, he's a little more subdued than he is now.

It is good cake, though.

He finishes his one slice and starts in on the second.

I've barely made a dent in mine.

"When is this thing over?" he asks after he swallows his next bite.

"It's a wedding. It could last until the end of time."

"Fuck me," he mutters.

"Oh, honey, I'd love to," someone says, but when I look around the only person I see is a little old lady that's maybe eighty who I think is an aunt of Xander's. She notices me looking and winks. *Oh*.

I quickly divert my gaze back to my plate.

Thankfully, it doesn't last until the end of time and after another hour everyone starts to disperse.

Jace and I head to his car together. I have a car of my own but since we live together now we carpool a lot. It's easier that way.

He drives an old black Chevy truck. It looks brand new, though, with the way it shines and the engine doesn't sound ancient. The only thing I have against it is the stench of cigarette smoke that clings to the interior.

None of our friends notice us leaving together, for which I'm thankful.

I haven't told Rae and Thea that I'm living with Jace, and as far as I know, he hasn't told the guys, either.

It's not that I don't want them to know I'm living with Jace it's that ...

I don't want them to know that I'm living with Jace.

I know Thea and Rae will try to make a big deal out of it. They'll think Jace and I are secretly dating or simply hooking up and they'll pester me endlessly and that's not it at all.

Rae and Thea are my friends.

Jace?

He's my *best* friend.

From the moment we were introduced to each other it's like some part of me woke up and said, "Hello, I know you."

We're so similar and we just ... *click*.

He's easier to talk to than them and he gets me.

Most people don't *get* me.

They see what I want them to see.

But not Jace.

He sees it all.

"Still haven't told them?"

See? He reads my mind.

I turn away from the truck window and look at him. It's almost dark now and his gaze is zeroed in on the road.

"No," I admit.

"Why?" he asks.

I shrug. "No reason."

He grins. "If that was the case then you would've told them."

I sigh. "I don't need everyone to know all of my business."

"But it's okay for me to know all your business?" he counters.

"You're different."

"Ah, I see." He turns away with a little smirk.

"Oh, you do, huh?"

"It's because I'm your favorite."

I laugh and look out the window at the moon illuminating the sky. "Can't argue with you there."

"I am pretty great." Sobering, he says, "Seriously, though, why haven't you told them?"

"Because they'll think it's more than what it is," I admit. "I'd rather avoid their pestering. Why haven't *you* told the guys?"

"Same reason."

"We're too alike," I mutter.

He grabs a cigarette and lights it at the next stoplight. We're not far from his apartment. I still can't seem to think of it as *mine* too. Probably because he won't let me pay rent. Well, he takes the checks, but he never actually cashes them. I continue to write them, figuring if he needs the money he'll eventually cash some of them.

The cab of the truck grows quiet—me lost in my thoughts and him ... lost in his cigarette, I guess. Though he always gets this disgusted look on his face when he smokes, almost like he doesn't truly like them.

He blows out a puff of smoke toward his open window.

When we arrive at the apartment he parks on the street behind my beat-up Toyota Corolla.

Neither of us moves immediately to get out of the car.

Darkness has descended completely upon the city, and the barest hint of moonlight peeks out between the buildings. Streetlights illuminate the cab of the truck, bathing Jace's face in a white glow, making him looking almost ghostly.

He extinguishes his cigarette and tosses it out the open window before rolling it up.

I put my hand on the door handle and move to open the door, but he stops me.

"Wait," he pleads, grabbing my arm. I glance back at him. "Sit here for a minute."

I release the door and straighten in my seat.

He rubs his fingers over his lips, a telltale sign he's

thinking deeply. I notice he does it a lot when he's writing songs and he ends up with smudges all over his face.

"Confession," he starts, and I sit quietly waiting. "This is my favorite moment of the day. The time when the sun has completely descended and night takes reign. Night," he muses, a slight smile tugging at his lips, "the dark and misunderstood beast. People are afraid of the dark, but not the light—but it's the light they *should* fear. The light is where the real monsters are."

He's right. The real monsters are right in front of us, and we never even notice it. They slip by unnoticed, masquerading as normal people, but they can't mask their true colors for long.

The evil always slips through in the end.

He taps his thumb against the steering wheel, staring down the street. It's not late so several people are milling around and darting in and out of the stores and restaurants that line the street.

A few more minutes of quiet pass before he reaches for his door.

"I guess we better head in," he says, somewhat reluctantly.

I nod and follow suit.

The apartment building is an old warehouse that some developer came in and renovated. So, it's nice with a lot of old and quirky touches like exposed metal beams and concrete floors on the main level.

Jace's apartment is on the fourth floor and the view is

nice. It's not the best, since it's not a tall building, but it's good enough. It overlooks the park on the block behind us.

We take the elevator in silence. It's not late, but I think we're both tired regardless.

Weddings are exhausting.

When the doors slide open, I follow him down the hall to the apartment door. He slips his key inside the knob and turns, swishing his arm in a flourish.

I laugh and head in first, flicking on the light.

His apartment walls are all white, except one that's black because it's actually chalkboard paint. That wall is currently covered in "graffiti" from our friends. I think Thea is the one who drew FUCK really big and then drew flowers in the bubble letters. The rest of the apartment is a mix of black, white, and gray. When I moved in, Jace told me I could add some things of my own as long as it wasn't *too* girly, but I reminded him there's nothing girly about me at all, and the way he had it suited me fine. I'm not fussy; I enjoy the minimalist look.

I drop my shoes on the floor and collapse on the couch face first.

"Wake me never."

He chuckles, and I turn my head, watching him step onto the platform behind the couch where his mattress sits. There's only one bedroom closed off from the rest of the apartment, which belonged to his roommate and has since become mine. It's small, more like a closet, but it's a room, and that's all that matters to me.

He unbuttons his shirt and drops it on the bed. I hastily look away.

I force myself to sit up and head over to the bathroom, closing the door behind me. I shower quickly and as the colored water swirls down the drain, I decide I'm going to dye my hair again tomorrow. It's time for a new color. This one's becoming stale.

I step out and wrap the fluffy gray towel around my body before wiping the condensation from the mirror.

My reflection stares back at me. The same person I've seen every day for my entire life—minus the ever-changing hair color. I tilt my head to the side, and my reflection follows suit.

Hate.

That's what I used to feel when I looked at myself.

Now?

Now, I feel numb, and I don't know which is worse—hating yourself or not caring anymore.

With a sigh, I open the door and step outside. The cooler air feels like heaven against my skin.

I look up and see Jace sitting in his bed. His chest is bare, the sheets pooled at his waist. His glasses are perched on his nose and he's reading.

The first thing he said when I moved in was, *"Tell anyone I read and you're out of here. I have to keep my cool factor."*

I didn't tell him, but the fact that he reads makes him infinitely cooler in my eyes.

After all, what's hotter than a guy that reads?

Not that I think Jace is hot.

"Night," he says, without looking up from his book.

"Goodnight," I mumble back, ducking my head so damp magenta-colored strands of hair hide my face as I scurry across the hall to my room.

I swear I can feel his eyes on me, but when I look back before I close my door, his eyes are once more on his book, and I can't be sure if he was really looking or if I simply *wanted* him to look.

two
...

jace

"YOU'VE BEEN in there for like two hours. You're not dead, are you?" I rap my knuckles on the door to the bathroom.

"No," she says back, "but it does look like I murdered a Smurf in here."

"I have to go to work," I tell her.

"Do you need the bathroom?"

"Nah, I'm good. Just wanted to let you know I'm heading out. Stop by the bar later. I want to see your hair."

Her laughter trickles through the door. "You should let me dye your hair."

I make a face of disgust but she can't see it, of course. "No, thanks, I'm good. I like my boring blond hair just fine."

"Your loss."

I start to walk away and then step back. "What *is* your natural hair color?"

She laughs again. "Wouldn't you love to know?"

I would. I so would.

Novalee Clarke might be the only girl in the world that I actually *want* to know. She's mysterious and alluring, and I love learning about what makes her tick. She's fascinating. It's probably sick just how much I'm enraptured by her, but I can't help but be drawn to her. She's like a shot of tequila and I'm an alcoholic—I just want one sip, but I know it won't quench the thirst.

I've always only been interested in sex when it comes to girls. I wouldn't say I'm a jerk about it, I'm always up front about that with whoever I'm hooking up with that I don't do relationships, so the fact that Nova is my *friend* says a lot.

I know Cade and Xander are convinced that I've slept with her, and I can't blame them for thinking that, because that's my usual MO but it kind of pisses me off at the same time that they can't see that she's different.

That *we're* different.

I shrug my leather jacket on and call out, "See you later."

I hear something fall on the floor in the bathroom and she curses. I shake my head, fighting an amused smile.

Grabbing my keys off the console table, I head out. I don't pass anyone in the hall or elevator, and, for that, I'm thankful.

I fucking hate small talk.

Outside, I head down the street, smoking a cigarette as I go.

The bar where I work is just down the street from the apartment so driving is stupid. One of the perks of living in the city is that I don't have to drive most places. I like getting out and walking. It gives me time to think.

The front of the building comes into focus, and like always, I can't help but be amused.

(Did you think we meant something else) Restaurant & Bar
Est. 2013

Yeah, I work at a restaurant/bar called W.T.F.

The owner, Eli, can only be described as flamboyant. He's young, a little crazy, but a whole lot of smart.

W.T.F. has become one of the hottest restaurants and bars in the Denver area, and I'm lucky enough to be the head bartender.

Four years of studying music in college and I work at a bar. It's not ideal, but as far as jobs go, it's not the worst. Eli is cool and so is everyone else I work with.

I finish my cigarette and toss the butt on the ground, extinguishing it with the toe of my boot.

Inside, chaos ensues. It's *loud*, packed, and fucking insane. Just a typical night at the bar.

I head straight to the back and clock in before heading behind the bar.

The bar is a giant wood U-shape in the middle of the

restaurant. Eli had it built that way on purpose so that, in his words, it makes a statement.

The whole place is nice but not stuffy—so, thankfully, that means I get to wear jeans and t-shirts to work.

My favorite part of the whole place, though, is the stage straight across from the bar. It's fairly large—large enough for a whole band to fit on it—with stage lights. On the wall above it hangs a cartoonish-looking fork.

Forks are a recurring theme in the whole restaurant.

Like above the bar, thousands of forks hang from the ceiling. Okay, so it's probably more like a couple hundred and not thousands, but it looks cool.

"Hey, *Jacen*," my co-worker Matilda slurs from behind the bar as I join her.

"Matilda," I say curtly.

She's been bitter ever since a month ago when she tried to hook up with me and I turned her down.

I don't know why she took it so personally. So what, I didn't want to fuck her—big fucking deal. There are plenty of other guys in the world she can fuck. We work together, and I don't fuck my co-workers, even though she tried her hardest to get me to break that rule.

Now, because I turned her down I have to deal with her attitude.

How is that fair?

I get straight to work making orders and cleaning dishes.

There's almost always something to do at W.T.F., and I love that fact. I hate sitting around idly. I get bored easily. I need to be doing something.

Eli breezes in at some point, leaving a trail of glitter behind him as he goes.

"What happened to you?" I ask, wiping down the wood bar top. "You look like a fairy sneezed on you."

Eli shakes his head, spraying more glitter across the clean counter. I groan. That glitter is going to be here until the end of time.

"It's just my fabulousness manifesting," he responds.

"Mhmm," I hum, wiping the glitter away with a damp rag.

Eli slides onto one of the barstools. "Get me my usual."

"Drinking on the job?" I raise a brow as I grab a glass.

"I own the place. I can do whatever I want," he objects.

I slide his drink across to him and he slurps it down like it's water on a hot summer's day and not whiskey.

"So, I was thinking," he begins, and I suppress a groan. *Thinking* and Eli never go well together. "Maybe we should have theme nights."

"Theme nights?" *This can't be going anywhere good.*

"Yeah, like one night is boa night."

"Boas?" *Like the snake?*

"Like the pink feathery boas," he says, exasperated. "You come in wearing one and get a free drink. Another night could be …" He taps his lip as he thinks, and I notice his nails are painted yellow. "Silly hat night and—"

"You wear a silly hat," I finish for him, suppressing the urge to roll my eyes. "I got it." I lay my hands flat on the bar. "Those are all dumb ideas and you know it."

His shoulders sag. "I know. But I'm trying to get new people in the door."

"Maybe you should start hiring bands and local artists." I point to the stage. "Open mic Friday nights are a hit."

"A band might be cool," he agrees. "But I don't think anyone is going to want to watch someone paint. That's boring."

"That's not what I meant—"

"But that might work. Yeah, it just might. Thanks, Kensy." He salutes me before sliding off the stool and heading to his back office.

"It's Jace!" I call after him, but he's too busy mumbling to himself to hear me.

I know that he knows my name is Jace but instead he insists on calling me Kensy—a nickname he's given me based on my last name.

I like to pretend I'm not a Kensington so his constant reminder of my heritage is like a slap to the face.

I know he doesn't mean it that way, but that fact doesn't ease the sting.

"Your girlfriend is here," Matilda huffs, purposely bumping into me as she passes.

"I don't have a girlfriend," I hiss. As I say the words, I look across the bar and my eyes connect with Nova's brown ones as she takes a seat. Her hair is a vivid Smurf blue as she called it.

And I fucking love it.

I stride across the bar and lean across to face her.

"Confession, I love the blue hair."

Her lips quirk the slightest bit as she fights a smile.

"You do?" She fingers a piece of it. "I haven't decided what I think."

"It's different," I agree. "I've only seen you with purple and some variation of red, but I like the blue a lot."

"I figured it was time to mix it up and do something *really* crazy. I'm thinking green next."

"Green," I muse. "That could be cool."

"Stop flirting and do your job." Matilda bumps me again as she passes.

Nova wrinkles her nose. "What's her problem?"

"What's *not* her problem?" I counter. "Do you want a drink?" I ask.

"Yeah and a turkey club. I forgot to eat because I was focused on not fucking up my hair."

I chuckle and grab her usual drink and hand it to her. "I'll put that in."

I enter her order into the system and tend to the other people at the bar before circling back to her.

"Ready for class tomorrow?" I ask her, wiping down the bar nearby her so that if Matilda comes by I have the excuse of doing something. Nova started her sophomore year at Huntley University this past Thursday.

"Yeah." She nods, setting her beer bottle down and toying with the label where the corner has peeled up. "It does get a little boring at times since I've already self-taught myself most of it. But it's not so bad."

"I can't believe I'm finally done with it," I admit. "I was beginning to think college was going to last forever."

She laughs. "Yeah, sometimes it feels that way."

"Loverboy, move your ass out of the way." Matilda pushes by me where I'm leaning over the bar toward Nova.

I growl. "If I was a girl I'd pull her hair," I whisper to Nova.

"I might do it for you. She's being a bitch."

"I'm going to check on your food," I tell Nova, holding up one finger to signal to her to give me a minute.

The kitchen is a chaotic symphony of people yelling and dishes clanging.

Nova's turkey club comes up into the window just as I approach, so I grab it and another order for the bar and head back.

I drop the one order off first before taking Nova hers. Her eyes light up when she sees the food and she's grabbing for it before I can even put it down.

I know I can't linger so I head off to mix more drinks and take orders.

I might also "accidentally" splash Matilda with water while I'm cleaning dishes.

Nova sees it and busts out laughing, which only serves to piss Matilda off more, but I can't bring myself to care.

Matilda flounces off and Nova shakes her head as I make my way back over to her.

"I don't know how you can work with her."

"I have to." I shrug. "Want anything else?" I take her empty plate from her.

She shakes her head. "No, I better head back home. With

class in the morning I need to be responsible and get some sleep."

"Thinking ahead. Smart move. I've never been good at that." I start to back away. "Well," I say awkwardly, "since I probably won't see you again tonight ... goodnight."

She looks slightly queasy at my words, which I can't understand. "Yeah, goodnight," she says, laying some cash on the bar.

I watch her head off, wondering what's caused the sudden stiffness in her shoulders.

Fuck, girls are weird complicated creatures.

three
...

nova

SINCE I PROBABLY WON'T SEE YOU *again tonight ... goodnight.*

What does that mean?

Does it mean what I think it means? That he's not planning on coming home? That he's going to spend the night banging some random girl? And if it does mean that, then why do I care so much? Jace can do whatever he wants. He's my *friend*. Nothing more, nothing less. So why does my chest feel so hollow, like my heart has been carved out, at the thought of him with another girl? He's not mine. He owes me nothing.

Get it together, Nova, I scold myself as I walk through the chilly air toward the apartment building down the block.

This freak-out of mine needs to stop.

I'm beginning to think moving in with Jace was one of

the worst decisions I've ever made—and that's saying something. But ever since then, my feelings for him have grown a bit more every day. I don't understand it.

I keep reminding myself that we're *just friends* but those words are doing nothing to assuage my attraction.

I reach the building and push the door to go inside.

I head straight up to the apartment and into my room where I change into my pajamas and flop onto my bed staring up at the ceiling. My room is barely big enough for a full-size bed, a dresser, and a desk which also serves as my night table. On the ceiling, I've hung swatches of black fabric, creating my own canopy, and it has wire star lights dangling down. The great thing about high ceilings is there's an endless list of possibilities of things you can do.

I stare up at the twinkling lights for a few minutes before reaching over to my desk and grabbing my notebook.

Per my usual nighttime ritual, I begin to write.

Dear Owen,

I dyed my hair blue today.

I wish you could see it. I bet you'd love it.

Not much else happened today that I have to tell you. My life is so boring without you. Tomorrow is my first Monday of classes. I can't believe I'm a sophomore. Where'd the time go? I feel like I blinked and became an adult and I guess it feels even weirder because in so many ways I feel like I'm still such a child —like I have so much left to learn.

I guess that's the thing though—we're always learning.

I miss you.
Every. Single. Day.
You're always in my thoughts.
Always.
Love,
Nova

I tear the piece of paper out and fold it up then I stuff it and the notebook back in the drawer. I draw my knees up to my chest, wrapping my arms around them, like the gesture alone can help seal the gaping wound in my chest.

I don't know why I bother.

Some wounds never heal.

Sometimes you have to feel pain to remind you that you're alive.

I allow myself one more minute of wallowing in misery before I shuck off the pain and climb beneath the covers.

My thoughts venture back to Jace and what he might be planning to spend his night doing and I feel queasy again—which in turn makes me angry at myself because I have no right to feel that way.

But the heart doesn't really have control over what it feels. It's on a constant rollercoaster of emotion, and we're just along for the ride.

I count backward from one-hundred, and when that doesn't work, I count sheep.

I'm still awake when Jace comes in a little after one in the morning.

I hear the front door creak open and he tiptoes quietly across the floor and into the kitchen. I hear him rummaging around in the refrigerator, and I breathe a sigh of relief because it's obviously only him.

Exhaustion takes over then and I fall straight to sleep.

"Could you stop smiling? It's weird," I tell Rae as we head across campus together toward class.

"I'm sorry," she says, but she's still freaking smiling. "I'm just so happy."

I shake my head back and forth in disbelief. "It's like invasion of the body snatchers," I mutter to myself.

Last year, Rae kept to herself, barely spoke to anyone unless forced, and always sported a severe case of resting bitch face—all things much like myself, which is why I always liked her.

But then she had to go fall in love and become a ray of fucking sunshine all the time.

I prefer clouds and rain.

"You know what you need—"

"Not a boyfriend," I interrupt. "If you say boyfriend I will drop kick you."

She laughs. "I wasn't going to say that. I think you need a night out. You stay in too much."

"I went out last night," I object.

She rolls her eyes. "Going to the bar Jace works at does not count as *going out*."

She has me there.

"What would you suggest then?"

"It's time for another girls' day."

I try not to cringe. "I don't know if I can handle Thea for that long."

Rae frowns. "I know she can be a bit of a spaz, but she's so sweet. Her heart's always in the right place."

"I know that. I like Thea, I do ... Just in small amounts of time. She's kind of a lot to take in."

Rae mumbles in agreement. "We'll just do dinner then. How does that sound?"

"Equally as boring as staying home—only staying home is better because I can wear my pajamas."

"Nova," she whines. *Yes, whines.* "You never want to do anything. You hang out with Jace and go to school, what kind of life is that?" Her brow furrows and she stops in her tracks, grabbing my arm so I'm forced to stop with her. "What exactly did you do all summer? Cade and I were busy most of the time, and Thea was all wrapped up in Xander, and we barely saw you."

"Um ... I worked and ..." I rack my brain for something I did that didn't involve Jace, but seeing as how I moved in with him after classes ended, pretty much everything I did this summer involved him in some way. "Took pictures and stuff."

"And stuff?" She latches onto the word. "Did this *stuff* involve Jace?"

"Well, sometimes."

"I knew you guys were having sex." I half-expect her to break out in a victory dance.

"Wrong," I inform her. "He's my friend. That's all."

She stares me down—looking for any sign that I'm lying. "Whatever you say," she replies after a moment. She starts walking again, and I assume that means the conversation is over.

It feels good to be back in class.

Unlike most people, I've always loved school and learning. It was my home away from home growing up. My safe place.

Rae and I grab seats side by side, and I drop my backpack between my feet.

Rae's phone vibrates on her desk and she gets a goofy smile on her face—a text from Cade, I figure it's safe to assume.

More students trickle in, and I recognize most people from last year. My photography and graphic design classes are all relatively small. Huntley is better known for its athletics than its arts—but I didn't choose to go here because of what it had to offer but because it was the farthest school away from my family. I wanted the excuse of distance for not going back.

A guy drops into the seat beside me, his bag bumping mine.

"Sorry," he mutters.

"It's okay," I say, not even bothering to look at him.

I bend down and pull my laptop from my backpack so I'll be ready to take notes when the professor gets here. If today's class is anything like the ones I experienced last week, they'll jump right into the lesson and that's that. We're sophomores now so the way the professors see it, we're adults and shouldn't need to be coddled, and that's just the way I like it.

"I'm Joel."

I bend back down, looking for a pencil and my notebook just in case my laptop dies or something else happens. I like to be prepared for all things.

"What's your name?"

My head snaps up, and I look at the guy sitting beside me. "Are you talking to me?"

He laughs. "Yeah."

"Why?" I snap.

Beside me, Rae snickers. I resist the urge to elbow her in the gut.

"I don't know, because you're sitting beside me and we're going to be in classes together for the whole year. I recognize you from my web design class too."

"I'm here to learn. Not make friends."

"She's your friend," he points out, leaning forward to look at Rae.

"He's good," she whispers under her breath.

"I'm new here," Joel continues. "I could use some friends."

"You could also apparently use my foot up your ass," I mutter and Rae snorts.

He smiles—and I'll give him credit, because it's not a smarmy smile. "I like you."

"Well, I don't."

"Like me? You don't even know me yet," he responds.

"Like *me*." I turn back to face the front of the room and let me him think what he wants with that information.

"Remind me to never piss you off," Rae says. "You're vicious."

"Gotta keep you on your toes," I tell her as Professor Hawthorne comes into the room.

four
...

nova

"THIS IS WEIRD. This is so weird," Thea mutters, barely picking at her lunch. "The guys should be here. I can't believe I'm saying this, but I miss them. Especially Xander."

Rae peers at Thea over the top of her sandwich. "You just saw him this morning."

"I know," Thea sighs. "But I love him, and I miss him." She takes a reluctant bite of her sandwich. "I know, I know," she continues before we can say anything. "I've become one of *those* girls—but have you see the boy? He's lucky I don't have him naked and flat on his back all day while I go to town."

Rae covers her face with her hands and groans. To me, she whispers, "Be so glad you don't live with them."

I am. I *so* am.

Although, Rae doesn't see it, she's equally as bad with

Cade. She's mellowed out *some* since they've been together almost a year, but she still has that new relationship glow about her and she turns into mush any time she sees him.

Thea sighs and abandons her sandwich. "Xander's first NFL game is this weekend. You and Jace are still coming?" she asks me, nervously fiddling with the collar of her shirt.

"Um ... yeah," I say, racking my brain for any reason that might have come up that will prevent me from going.

Football isn't really my thing, and I only attended a few college games last year. It wasn't exactly what I'd call a good time. I don't like sports, and I don't understand them, so spending my whole day at a professional game sounds even worse. People get so bent out of shape over the teams they love, and when they lose, they act like miserable little shits.

But I can't tell Thea that.

And I do like Xander and want to support him as his first professional game is a big deal.

Thea asked all of us to go about a month ago, and even though it requires being gone the whole weekend and flying, we all said yes. There was no way any of us would say no.

"He probably won't get any playing time, but I want us to support him," she rambles. "I know it'll mean a lot to him."

Then she's moving on to another topic. She reminds me a lot of a hyper puppy. She can't focus on one thing for more than a few seconds, but it's part of her charm. "I can't believe I'm married, guys," she muses, resting her elbow on the table and her head in her hand. "Not only that, but I married him twice. That's insane."

I still can't wrap my head around the fact that Xander and Thea went on a business trip at the beginning of the summer and ended up married. I mean, everyone except maybe her brother—who also happens to be Xander's best friend—knew those two were going to end up together. Every time they're in a room together their chemistry knocks you down. You can't deny something like that. It's impossible.

"I knew you two would probably end up together," Rae speaks up. "But I didn't expect a Vegas wedding—props to you for being such a go-getter."

Thea snorts. "Still can't believe *I* proposed and he said yes."

"It was meant to be," Rae responds.

I finish my sandwich and wad up the Saran wrap. "While this conversation is super fascinating, we need to get to class," I remind them.

"Crap." Rae drops her half-eaten sandwich down and looks at the time on her phone. "You're right—and our class is all the way on the other side of campus."

She hurriedly gathers her trash, and I do the same.

"See you later," I say to Thea. She looks like a wounded animal at the fact that we're leaving.

"We should all have dinner tomorrow since Xander's still home. He leaves Wednesday and is gone for a few weeks since he has only away games." She looks *really* sad now. I'm sure it must be hard for them, newly married, and a new relationship at that, with him traveling for work and her still in college.

"Yeah, I'm in," I say. I'd say anything to get that sad look off her face. I might come across as rough and hard to like, but with my few friends, I care about how they feel, and I don't like seeing Thea sad.

She brightens a bit. "Good—talk to Jace about that too, please."

"Sure thing."

I salute her and then follow Rae out of the cafeteria where she waves impatiently for me, as if I wasn't the one who reminded her that we needed to go.

We hurry across campus together and into class where I end up forced to sit beside Joel because we're late.

"You've got to be kidding me," I hiss.

Joel looks up with a smile. "We meet again."

"Bite me," I snap.

My anger is uncalled for, I know, because he hasn't been a total dick, but I can't help it. It's like the world is conspiring against me and is going to insist on shoving the new guy down my throat just to spite me.

He chuckles. "You'd probably taste sour, and I prefer sweet, so no thanks."

I'd think maybe I'd finally pissed him off, but he's still smiling and looking at me like I'm hilarious.

I sigh and set my backpack on the floor by my feet. The desks in this classroom are built for two people, much like the ones I remember having in our science classrooms in my old high school.

Professor Blake breezes into the room. "Morning class, and welcome to advanced photography. I recognize many of you from last year—it's good to see you back. We'll be working on lots of different things this year and several of those projects will be with a partner. And lucky for you, you've already picked your partners." *No.* "The person sitting beside you will be your partner for any and all projects. No exceptions," she says, like she knows I'm having an internal freak out.

I look beside me at Joel and he smiles over at me. "Howdy, partner."

Kill me now.

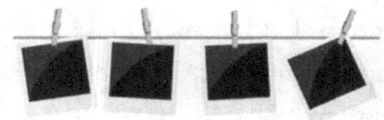

jace

"You look pissed," I comment as Nova takes a seat at one of the barstools.

"I need a drink," she pleads, flicking her fingers for me to get a move on.

I grab her usual and slide it onto the bar top. I half-expect Matilda to magically appear and bitch at me for speaking to Nova, but, thankfully, today is her day off.

"What happened?" I ask, because it's clear *something* happened. Nova doesn't act irritated for no reason.

She shakes her head. "Just some guy that's in almost all of my classes."

I stiffen. "Did he ... try something?"

She looks up at me, her eyes wide with horror. "Oh, God, no. I mean, he flirted a bit, sure, but nothing like that. I just don't like him."

"But he likes you?" *And why the fuck do I feel mad about that possibility?*

"I guess." She shrugs, taking a sip of her beer. "I was pretty blunt that I'm not interested, but something tells me that didn't faze this guy a bit." She sighs heavily. "Then, I got stuck beside him in my advanced photography class and Professor Blake says whoever you sit beside is your partner for the year on any projects she doubles us up on. *No exceptions,*" she mimics what I assume is her professor's tone. "I can't work with this guy *all* year—because yeah, of course *this* class lasts all year and isn't just a semester." She covers her face with her hands and groans. Letting them fall, she continues, "I know I shouldn't let this make me so mad, but I can't help it."

"We're all allowed to get mad. It's what makes us human."

"I guess so." She sighs again, and I can tell she's unconvinced.

"You want something to eat?" I ask. Maybe if she gets food in her stomach she'll be less grouchy. I always turn into an asshole when I'm hungry. Food makes everything better.

"Yeah, I'm hungry," she admits. "And drinking on an empty stomach isn't smart when I have class in the morning."

"What do you want?" I ask. Nova spends a lot of time at W.T.F. with me, so she orders a variety of menu items.

"Surprise me," she pleads.

"What if I get it wrong?"

She waves her hand dismissively. "You won't. I'm not in the mood for any certain thing so you'll be fine."

"Suit yourself," I say, and flip around to place her order.

I order myself something too, since I can take my break any time—perks of days I come in earlier. Most days, I work the late shift and there's no time for a break.

While I wait for our food to be done I tend to the other people at the bar and get caught up on drinks I need to make for the other tables in the restaurant.

Every time I glance at Nova she has a sullen expression on her face. Something tells me it has nothing to do with that guy, but I can't be sure of what it might be. Nova is a hard nut to crack—harder than me. I know she's told me more about herself than she has the girls, but I still don't know much other than she's from Texas and her family was really strict. She doesn't talk about them much, though—at all, honestly. Like, I don't even know if she has any siblings, and I don't like to pry, because if I pry then she'll think she has the right to know more about me, and I'm not going down that path.

Our food comes up and I grab it, telling my manager, Bethany, that I'm taking my break. She waves me off, unbothered since we're not that busy now and she knows I wouldn't be taking a break if we were.

I come out of the kitchen and around the bar, setting

Nova's food down in front of her—the grilled chicken sandwich—and mine at the empty spot beside her. I slide pull out the stool and sit down.

"You're eating with me?" She sounds surprised, because it's not often that I do this.

"Yeah," I say. I point to my nachos. "Have some if you want any."

"That's your dinner?" She raises a brow.

"Yup." I grin, shoving a nacho into my mouth.

She shakes her head. "How you're skinny as a rail is beyond me."

"Height, genetics." I tick them off on my fingers. "And gym time."

"You go to the gym once a month when Xander and Cade force you to go," she snorts.

"I know." I grin back. "And I look this good already. Imagine if I went every day. I'd blow minds."

She shakes her head and picks up her sandwich. She takes a bite and lets out a soft moan. I don't think she even realizes she's made the sound.

"That's good," she says, wiping a bit of the sauce from the corner of her mouth. She takes another bite and then reaches for one of my nachos, dipping it in sour cream.

"So ..." I begin, and then trail off. I want to ask her about what else is bothering her, because it's obvious something is, but I can't pry. Instead, I ask, "Football game this weekend?"

"Yeah," she says forlornly. "Confession ..." Her voice grows quiet, and I tense with anticipation at what she's going to say. "I hate flying," she admits. "I vowed after I flew from Texas to here that I would never fly again."

I chuckle. "I would've never guessed that the great Novalee Clarke would be afraid of flying."

She shrugs, unbothered by my poking. "We're all afraid of stupid things." She's right. Of course. "What stupid thing are you afraid of?" she asks. "There has to be something."

"Rodents," I answer without a second of thought. "Mice, rats, that kind of thing."

Her lips twitch with the threat of laughter. "And you made fun of *me* for being afraid to fly."

"In my defense, I had a friend growing up with pet mice—they got out of the cage, and it was a fucking nightmare trying to catch them. I got bit so many times I was convinced I was going to get rabies. My mom had to take me to the doctor because I was so freaked and nothing she said would calm me down."

"You don't talk about your mom or dad much," Nova remarks, with wide open eyes, begging me to open up.

"Neither do you." My voice is firm and rather rude, and I flinch because I sound exactly like my father—a man I vowed to never become.

"Touché," she mutters and lets the conversation drop, wiping her hands on a napkin.

"How long is the flight?" I ask.

"I don't know," she admits. "We're flying to Florida, so I figure it's a long one. I haven't checked for sure because I don't want to know yet. It's best if I'm kept in the dark until we're in the air."

I laugh—for some reason finding that hysterical. "I'll hold your hand," I tell her, half-joking and half-serious. If she's that scared and wants to hold my hand, she can consider it hers.

"Thanks. I might take you up on that."

And that's when I know that Nova really is afraid of flying. I mean, I didn't doubt her before, but now it's obvious just how bad her fear is. Nova avoids physical contact like it's the plague. At least with me.

"Are you mad about missing class Monday?" I ask her. Xander's game is Sunday and we're flying in Friday night, but our flight out isn't until Monday morning. I know how Nova feels about attendance. For someone that screams *rebel* with her appearance, she really hates breaking rules.

"I'm a little irritated, but it's the beginning of the semester so it should be fine." She finishes her sandwich and starts on the fries. That's one thing that fascinates me about Nova. She has to eat everything on her plate one at a time. So, she'll eat her whole sandwich first and then eat her fries or whatever else might be there. I, on the other hand, go after everything like I expect someone to snatch the plate out from under me.

"Florida," I repeat. "Should be fun."

Hot girls. Bikinis. Ass. Boobs. *Skin*.

She shrugs. "I suppose so."

I glance over at her, and in that moment, I make it my mission to make sure she has the best damn time of her life.

five
...

jace

"I CAN'T FEEL MY HAND," I hiss.

"Do I look like I fucking care?" Nova snaps back. She's white as a sheet. So white that I can count each individual freckle speckled across her cheeks and nose.

We took off two hours ago, but it's been a bumpy ass flight and poor Nova looks like she wishes she could jump out the window to her death. She's that miserable.

"We're almost there," I lie.

"Liar," she hisses immediately.

I sigh. I tried.

Behind us is Cade and Rae and then on the other side of the aisle beside us is Thea and Xander's mom. His dad wanted to come, but couldn't make it work today so he's flying in tomorrow with their daughter—Xander's older sister.

Xander still doesn't know that any of us are coming.

I *think* he'll be happy, but on the other hand it might make him more stressed.

Guess we're going to find out.

We hit another bout of turbulence and Nova turns green.

"I'm going to be sick," she cries suddenly, wrenching her hand from mine. My hand immediately goes numb from the sudden return of blood flow.

I watch Nova hurry down the aisle to the bathroom instead of reaching for a barf bag.

"Go after her," Thea hisses. "Make sure she's okay."

"You do it," I snap.

She shakes her head. "She likes you more. She'll bitch at me if I go."

She's probably right.

I sigh and push out of my seat following Nova to the bathroom.

I can hear her inside, running water.

I knock on the cheap door. "Nova? Are you okay?"

The door slides open, and I find her leaning against the small sink with her face damp like she's splashed it with water.

"I thought I was going to throw up," she states the obvious, "but I didn't. I think I'd feel better if I did, but my body is rebelling against me."

I chuckle. "Or maybe the sickness is in your head." I tap the side of her forehead.

"I *wish* it was made up." She inhales a deep breath. "Can we drive home?"

I chuckle. "Nice try, Clarke. I like you but I don't want to take a whole week to get home. Besides, think of all the classes you'd miss."

She crinkles her nose. "Yeah," she mutters. "I suppose flying *is* better. I still hate it, though."

"Can we go back to our seats?" I ask her. "Or are you still worried you might get sick?"

She hesitates for about ten seconds, gauging the way she feels. After a moment, she nods. "Yeah, I think I can."

I guide her back to our seats, and on the way, I ask the flight attendant for a ginger ale, or something like it, and crackers. She takes one look at Nova and hurries off. I'm sure the last thing she wants to do is deal with a sick person on the flight.

I take the window seat again, since Nova most definitely didn't want to sit by the window, and then she sits down beside me.

The flight attendant drops off the soda and crackers and is gone before I can even say thank you.

I open the soda and hand it to Nova. "Drink," I command, and then open the crackers.

She takes slow sips and smiles gratefully. "Thanks. This helps."

I nod in acknowledgement and hand her a cracker.

She takes small bites of the cracker in-between sips of soda and the color slowly begins to return to her cheeks. I think if anything it's helping her by focusing on the task of eating and drinking instead of thinking about being however many feet in the air.

I spend the rest of the flight distracting her in any way I can. I tell her stories about the guys and me in high school which are mostly stupid and funny and then I move on to singing softly under my breath so I don't disturb anyone else on the flight.

I think Nova likes it best when I sing, which fills me with some sort of sick satisfaction, because for some strange reason I love singing for her.

When the flight lands, we all grab our bags from the overhead compartments—we all only brought carry-on since we're not staying long—and head outside to grab taxis to the hotel.

It only takes us twenty minutes to get to the hotel, even with traffic.

It's already grown cooler back home, even though it's late August, but not here. Even at night it's hot enough that guys walk around shirtless and girls are in bikini tops and shorts. The palm trees blow in the slight wind and a guy passes us on his skateboard.

It's been years since I've been to Florida. My dad preferred to vacation in exotic locations, like Bora Bora and Costa Rica. My mom brought me to Orlando once, when I was about eleven, because I'd been begging forever to come to Disney World and we'd never gone.

It was just me and her, and for a while, it was the best trip of my life.

Until the last day, when she sat me down and told me she was dying and only had six months max left to live.

I've hated anything to do with Disney since then and I guess this place too.

I haven't been back to Florida since and until now I didn't realize the disdain that had grown in my heart to this place.

It's funny how the human mind attaches certain emotions and feelings to a place or object.

For me, Florida will always represent the loss of my mom, and that's not something I ever like to think about.

We arrive at the hotel and file out of the car.

We're responsible for our own rooms so Nova and I decided to bunk together to save money and we have an unspoken agreement not to tell the others.

We head inside to the front desk. Nova and I purposely choose to be last in line, in the hope that the others will get their room keys and go on up.

Sure enough, our plan works and the others head off to the elevators once they have their room keys.

"Name?" the receptionist asks, smiling pleasantly even though she's probably bored out of her mind. I would be bored if I had to do her job.

"Kensington," I respond.

She types a few things and hands me two keys. I promptly hand Nova the extra one.

We head up to our room, and as soon as our bags are placed on the floor, I announce, "We're going out."

Nova's halfway to one of the beds, and she turns back to glare at me. "No."

"No?" I repeat with a laugh. "Come on. We need a night out. We're in Miami. There are clubs on every block."

"I just want to go to bed," she grumbles.

"Nuh-uh." I shake my head. I refuse to let her mope. "We're going out, for at least an hour."

She groans, and I know I'm wearing her down. "I just want to shower and go to bed. Aren't you tired?" she counters.

"I am," I agree. "But we're here and we only have tonight and tomorrow to do something for ourselves and we'll probably have to do something with everyone else tomorrow, which leaves right now for me and you," I ramble.

"All right," she agrees. "Let me change, though."

"As you wish."

I step out of the way as she grabs her bag again, her messy bun bobbing, and locks herself in the bathroom.

I flop on the one bed and turn on the TV.

Twenty minutes later she steps out of the bathroom with her hair down and changed into jeans, a black and white striped top, and a leather jacket. She looks bad ass, like she's ready to take on the fucking world, and I find myself licking my lips.

Down, boy.

I'm attracted to Nova, I can't deny that, and I'm not stupid so I know she's attracted to me too. But I think we both know we're different ... damaged ... and that makes a relationship impossible. Nothing good can come from something so broken.

"Ready?" I ask her, and I hate how annoyingly high my voice suddenly sounds.

She nods, slipping her feet into a pair of boots.

I'm sure ninety-nine percent of the girls at the club will be half-dressed and in high heels, and there's nothing wrong with that, but I find myself intrigued by how different Nova is. She doesn't try to be like everyone else. She is who she is.

I shove the room key in my jeans pocket and tug on her blue hair as I pass.

"Let's go, Clarke."

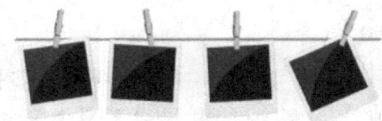

"You look miserable!" I yell to be heard above the music.

"I *am* miserable," she shouts back. "This isn't my thing!"

I take her hand and drag her to the bar, trying not to be blinded by the flashing lights.

I haven't been to a club in nearly a year. I was busy finishing school, working, and playing my music anywhere I could.

Now I'm realizing why I haven't missed this scene. It seems that I've outgrown it.

Regardless, we're here, and I want to do what I can to

make sure Nova has a good time—which means, not letting on that I'm just as miserable.

We reach the bar, and I guide her to the lone empty stool. I motion to the bartender that we want to order and then wait for him to have time.

Which might be never, since everyone is clamoring for a drink.

Nova huffs out a breath and her hair swirls around her face.

"Hi," the guy beside her says, leering at her.

I lean around her and give him my best glare. "Goodbye."

"Sorry, didn't know she was taken." He raises his hands in defense.

Nova lets out a soft laugh. In fact, I can't even hear it, but the shaking of her shoulders gives her away.

The bartender finally makes it over to us and I shout my order. He returns with two beers and plops them down, some of the liquid sloshing out and onto the counter.

I hand him cash. "Keep the change."

Nova sips at her beer, looking more miserable by the second.

Fuck this.

I down my beer and let her finish half of hers.

"Come on." I tug her off the stool.

"Wha—?" She gets out as I drag her onto the dance floor.

Dancing with Nova is probably a very bad, *bad* idea, but bad ideas are usually the most fun.

The music changes and the song oozes sex.

I don't allow myself to care.

Nova looks up at me with wide, shocked eyes, picking up on the tone of the song.

I lower my head so my lips graze her ear when I speak. "Dance with me."

It's not a question, or even a command, simply a statement.

She's dancing with me.

She shivers as I draw away.

I lead her into the thick of the people and then wrap her arms around my neck, my hands fall to her waist, my fingers grazing her ass.

She has a nice ass. Fucking sue me.

She looks up at me nervously, and I can tell she's out of her element.

But that's okay, because I can lead.

And leading is what I do best.

"Feel the music," my voice hums against her ear. "Let your body move to the rhythm."

She breathes out a shaky breath and begins to move.

My lips twitch with the threat of a smile.

This is a whole different kind of dancing than what we did last weekend at Xander and Thea's wedding, and I love it. I can tell she's nervous, but this is *me,* and she trusts me.

I move my hips against her, and I don't miss her shaky inhale of breath.

I lower my lips to her ear and sing the lyrics softly. She shivers and her fingers flex around my neck.

The lights flash chaotically around us, creating the illusion that we're more alone than we actually are.

I skim my thumbs slightly under her shirt, grazing her bare skin, and her dark eyes flash to mine.

I'm playing with fire but I'm not worried about getting burned.

Her eyes reflect desire back to me, and I know she sees the same in mine.

Kiss her. Kiss her. Kiss her.

Every beat of my heart chants the words.

Kiss her. Kiss her. Kiss her.

I fucking want to. So bad. But I'm scared to go there.

Nova's different.

A kiss would lead to sex, I know it would, and then what would happen? She's my friend. She's not a girl I can walk away from after the deed is done with no hard feelings.

Her hips sway to the music, grinding against me, and I bite my lip to stifle my groan. When she looks up at me with surprise in her eyes I know she hasn't missed the hardness straining against my jeans.

Fucking hell.

If this was any other girl I wouldn't hesitate to go in for the kill.

But this is Nova.

My heart pounds like thunder in my ear and sweat breaks out across my skin as I fight the urge to kiss her and drag her out of this club so I can fuck her and show her what she does to me. How fucking *crazy* she makes me.

But I can't do that.

I won't do that.

I tear away and leave her in the center of the dance floor.

I push through the people and I'm gone.

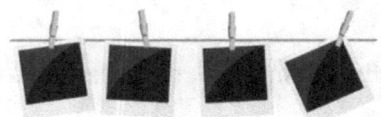

nova

My body feels cold at the sudden loss of Jace, even though I know there's no way I can actually be cold. Not with this many bodies packed so tightly together.

I watch his tall body push through the crowd as he gets further and further away from me.

He was turned on. I know what I saw and felt, and I can't believe he'd just *leave*. Probably to grab some random chick and fuck her in the bathroom—I've heard stories from Cade and Xander about things Jace has done, so it's not a stretch of my imagination.

I blow out an exasperated breath.

I don't know whether to keep dancing, get a drink, or leave.

I settle on getting a drink. I push my way over to the bar and order a beer. There's no stool available but I catch a guy getting up so I dash over and grab it.

The bartender hands me my drink, and I down it like I've been stuck in a desert and it's the only drink I could find. I motion for another.

Fuck Jace.

The bartender replaces my drink and I sip at this one slower—and by slower, I mean it takes me a full five minutes to drink it and not one.

"Did you break up with someone?" the guy beside me asks, his drink halfway to his lips. He looks as miserable as me.

"Something like that," I mutter.

"Feelings fucking suck," he grumbles. "Cage." He holds out a hand.

"What about a cage?" I ask, taking his hand.

He chuckles. "No, that's my name. Cage."

"Oh, I'm Nova," I say.

"Nova," I hear an angry growl behind me and turn to see Jace with a stormy expression. He looks like he wants to rip poor Cage's arms off. Cage could probably take him, though. He looks like he's tall, even sitting down, and he's muscular.

"Cage," I drawl his name. "This is Jace—he likes me but he won't admit it." I hiccup. *Fucking beer.* "So, he probably just went and fucked someone in the bathroom, or even better in the back alley, all because he's my *friend* and he won't touch me."

"Nova," he warns.

I turn to him. "You don't have to say it. I'm not stupid. I know you won't touch me because we're friends." I spin on the stool. "It's okay. I'm sure Cage would be happy to fuck me if I asked him to."

"Don't fucking touch her." Jace glowers at Cage, pointing at him in warning.

Cage raises his hands in defense. "Fuck, I was just making conversation with her. I didn't mean to get into something."

He quickly abandons the stool like his ass is on fire.

"Thanks a lot, Cage!" I yell after him.

"We're going," Jace says, his voice gruff with irritation.

"I still have more to drink." I lift my beer by the neck and wiggle it so the liquid inside sloshes.

"Leave it." He pulls out his wallet and slaps some bills on the counter to cover my tab.

"I can pay for my own drinks. This is the twentieth century."

He rolls his eyes. "It's the twenty-first century, Nova. How many drinks have you had?"

"Um ..." I count. "Three. Four?" I hold up five fingers. "I don't know."

Jace covers his face with his hands and mutters something. When his hands fall, he has a determined look in his eyes.

I squeak when he picks me up and tosses me over his shoulder like I'm a sack of potatoes. I feel slightly disoriented and my stomach churns.

Please do not throw up.

"Put me down," I plead as he carries me out of the club.

He ignores me or maybe he doesn't hear me—which is possible with as loud as it is in here and seeing as how I'm basically speaking to his knees.

When he exits onto the street I shiver from the sudden temperature change.

"Put me down," I say again, knocking my fists against his legs.

"No."

"Ugh," I groan.

He walks a block or maybe two when I cry out in panic. "Put me down."

He must hear the panic in my voice because he obliges. I stumble over to a bush and try to empty the contents of my stomach but nothing will come up.

His cool fingers touch my neck as he pulls my hair away from my face.

I feel like crying. Reality is creeping back in and I realize what a fool I looked like back there. He probably thinks I'm pathetic and stupid, and I don't blame him one bit for thinking it.

His other hand rubs against my back, trying to offer me some small smidgen of comfort.

It's not working. If anything, it only makes me feel worse.

I stumble away from him when it becomes obvious I don't need to throw up. Tears wet my face, and I hadn't even noticed I'd started crying. I wipe at my cheeks and walk away from him.

"Nova—" he pleads.

"Leave me alone," I mumble, crossing my arms over my chest as I walk.

A breeze blows my hair around my shoulders and the coolness feels good against my heated cheeks.

I hear him groan behind me and I snap. I've already made a fool of myself—might as well make it a homerun.

I turn sharply on my heel and face him, shoving a finger into his stupidly muscular chest. It's stupid because I like the way it feels beneath my touch. I'm a goner when it comes to him.

"How dare you dance with me like *that* and make me feel like ..."

His green eyes flash with a flicker of ... annoyance? Desire? Confusion? "Like what?" he prompts.

"Like you feel it too," I finish on a whisper. "Like the attraction between us isn't just one-sided. That you want me as much as I want—"

In a flash, he has my face clasped between his large hands.

In a breath, his lips touch mine.

In a heartbeat, I fall into him.

His large body shields mine, clinging to me like I'm the only thing centering him to the world.

I forget that we're standing on a street in Miami. Instead, all I can think about is the fact that he's kissing me.

Jace is kissing me.

I'd pinch myself but my hands are otherwise occupied as they skim up his chest and latch around his neck.

His tongue presses against the seam of my lips, and I gasp softly.

I keep waiting to wake up back in my bed, but instead, the kiss continues.

I've never been kissed like this before.

I know it sounds cliché, but it's true.

He kisses me like I'm everything he's ever wanted and

hoped for. It's a different kind of kiss. One full of fear, and longing, and regret, and *passion*.

I never want it to end.

I stand on my tiptoes so he doesn't have to strain to my lower height as much.

He groans, his fingers digging into the skin of my back where his hand has found its way under my shirt.

My breasts push against his chest and my body aches all over.

More. I need more. So much more than he's willing to give—and me too, for that matter.

I don't want a relationship.

Been there, done that, never going down that road again.

But Jace?

I want him like I've never wanted anything or anyone before.

We're both complicated people, and maybe that's why we've been drawn to each other from the start.

We're made of the same stuff.

Pain.

Loathing.

Anger.

Betrayal.

He's my mirror.

My fingers wind into his shirt, wrinkling the fabric as I try to get impossibly closer to him.

I'm sinking inside him.

Lost.

Lost.

Lost.

I'm lost in him, and I don't want to be found.

His hands move higher, settling just below my breasts. I shiver from his touch, my lips moving against his, perfectly in sync.

I don't know who pulls away first, but the moment the cool air touches my lips, I duck my head down, burrowing against his shirt so he can't see my face.

I don't want him to look into my eyes and see the swirl of emotion and confusion. He'll panic, I know it, because *I'm* panicking.

I don't want to feel for him what I do, but I'm helpless to stop it.

I'm falling, and I don't see the end—which terrifies me, because I could crash land and never even know it's coming.

I like to be prepared and ever since Jace stepped into my life I've been completely *un*prepared.

I inhale a shaky breath and step away, glancing up at him.

His eyes are shuttered, his jaw tight, hiding his true emotions.

I step away and force a smile, figuring it's best to pretend he didn't just give me the best kiss of my life.

"So, I guess we should go back to the hotel?"

Normal. Act normal.

He nods and shoves his hands in the pockets of his jeans, striding forward and away from me with his shoulders hunched.

I follow, glancing up at the twinkling night sky.

The cool air brushes my heated cheeks, and I pause, closing my eyes.

I hear Jace's footsteps stop and then start again, coming closer to me.

"What're you doing?" he asks.

"Living," I answer simply.

I learned a long time ago that moments like this are precious. Times when everything might seem like a mess, there's that single moment where time stops, and it feels ... *perfect*. I don't know what our kiss means, and I don't want to overanalyze it, but I also know I never want to forget it.

six
. . .

jace

I LIE in bed staring at the ceiling.

Sleep evades me while Nova sleeps peacefully in the other bed beside me—if her steady breathing is any indication.

I keep replaying our kiss over and over again in my mind.

It shouldn't have fucking happened.

I shouldn't have let it.

I shouldn't have gone there.

So many fucking *should nots*.

Yet, I have no desire to take it back.

It shouldn't have happened, but I don't regret it.

Kissing Nova was everything I expected and more—somehow better than every fantasy I've played out in my mind over the last year we've known each other.

I turn my head, looking over at her. She's clearly not torn

up about this like I am. Or maybe her way of dealing with things is different.

Tonight went in a whole different direction than I'd anticipated. I only wanted to cheer up, show her a good time, and then when we danced ... fuck.

I've never been more turned on in all my life.

So much so that I found myself jerking off in the club bathroom. I've never had to do that before, but I shouldn't be surprised about anything when it comes to Nova.

Her breaths are even, her blue hair fanned around her shoulders.

I wish I could find a similar peace, but I can tell this is one of those nights where sleep is never going to come.

I ease from my bed, stepping carefully across the floor so I don't wake her.

I bend down and rifle through my bag until I find my leather-bound journal.

It's where I write all my songs, and on nights like this, it's my best friend.

I walk back to my bed and sit down slowly so the bed doesn't squeak.

Undoing the spiral cord that holds the notebook closed, my pen falls out onto my lap. I flip the pages until I land on a new page.

I pinch the cap of the pen between my teeth, writing with only the small light filtering in from the curtains, but I don't mind.

The words flow from me like water from a tap, and I instantly feel better.

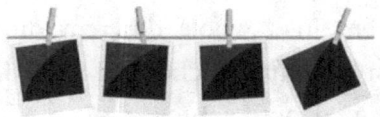

nova

I wake up before Jace. I glance at the clock, and it shows that it's only a little after six. It seems my body is already on school time, seeing as if I was at home I wouldn't have to be at work until ten.

I work at a record shop a few blocks from the apartment. It's a little hole in the wall place. Dark and grungy with exposed brick walls and piping on the ceiling, but I love it. Records line cardboard boxes and hang on the wall along with instruments.

I stumbled upon the place walking with Jace in the early summer. There was a HELP WANTED sign in the window and the rest is history.

I'm lucky that Paul—the shop's owner—is really chill and understands that school comes first.

Granted, school isn't why I'm in Florida this weekend, but he understood that too.

I was surprised by how easily I fell asleep, but I guess it was easier to sleep than to face what happened last night.

But in the harsh light of day there is no denying it.

I kissed Jace.

Actually, he kissed me first, and I kissed him back.

But the logistics of who kissed who first don't matter, because at the end of the day, we still kissed.

I groan and the spray of the shower stifles the sound.

I don't know what this means, and I hate not feeling on solid ground. Jace has been my rock since I met him, and last night might have changed that.

There's no point in dwelling on it, because I have no idea what he's thinking and feeling.

I'll follow his lead.

Yeah, that's what I'll do.

I get out of the shower and wrap the towel around my body.

My hair drips on the floor, leaving behind little droplets of blue. When I had my hair dyed red it looked like someone had been murdered in the bathtub every time I showered.

I wipe the condensation from the mirror and startle when there's a light knock on the door.

I open it and find Jace standing there sleepily. His blond hair sticks up wildly around his head and he's wearing his glasses.

I fucking love those glasses.

His tall frame takes up the whole doorway and since he's shirtless I get an eyeful of his muscular chest and washboard abs. My eyes stray to the colorful tattoo covering one whole arm. It's a kaleidoscope of color that is at odds with his overall more serious personality, but somehow it still manages to suit him.

When I continue to stand there gawking like an idiot, he motions with his finger to the bathroom.

Right.

"Sorry," I mumble.

I grab my clothes and he steps out of the way as I pass.

The bathroom door clicks shut, and I exhale a shaky breath.

He's turning me into a mess, and I don't know whether I love or hate it.

I change into my clothes—jeans and a gray t-shirt that says CAN'T. ADULT. EVER. There have never been truer words.

I gather my damp hair up in a messy bun and then clean up the room.

Seeing as we didn't spend much time in our room other than sleeping that means I only make our beds, but keeping busy makes me feel better.

I open the curtains all the way and gaze out at the city. The sun is just beginning to rise and the streets are empty. It's quiet. Serene.

I sit on my bed and check my phone for any texts from Rae or Thea.

There's nothing—which means I have *nothing* to do.

I flop back on the bed with a groan.

I grab my phone again and shoot Thea a text.

Me: Are you up?

Thea: It's six-o-fucking-clock in the morning! What do you think?!

Me: ...Sorry

Even though she's not in the room I swear I can hear her sigh.

Thea: I'm up now. What do you need?

I bite my lip. I don't *need* anything from her, I just needed to do something to keep myself busy before I lost my ever-loving mind.

Me: Are we eating breakfast here or going out?

Thea: I'm not sure yet.

Me: When are you telling Xander we're here?

I know there's no way she's waiting until tomorrow.

Thea: I don't know. I'm thinking about taking taxi over to the hotel the team is at and sitting all stalker like in the lobby and then when he comes down running after him screaming his name. I know him and he won't realize it's me at first and his reaction will be priceless.

A second later another text comes through.

Thea: I hope he screams like a little girl.

I snort.

Me: I'm glad your husband's pain brings you joy.

Thea: Oh it does. It so does.

Thea: Gotta keep things interesting.

Thea: If I don't keep him on his toes he'll get bored. Can't have that.

I shake my head.

Me: You're a nut.

Thea: I know it. ;)

I lay my phone on the bed and sit up. The shower has cut off in the bathroom, and I can hear him rummaging around in the bathroom.

My palms begin to sweat.

I'm itching to talk to him about the kiss, to understand his motives, and if it was a one-time thing or if he wants it to happen again as much as I do.

I know I won't talk to him about it, though.

I can't, because if his head isn't in the same place as mine then I'll be devastated.

Besides, I don't know what I think or want.

Lie.

Yeah, such a fucking lie.

I've known for months that my feelings for Jace were growing, and I've tried to pretend that they didn't exist. But in pretending I've only allowed it to get out of control.

And now ... Now it's all a mess.

The small hotel room suddenly becomes too much to bear, and I jump from the bed and scurry for the sliding glass door that leads to the balcony. It's barely big enough to stand on, but it's something, and that's all that matters.

I lean against the metal railing, inhaling a lungful of air.

The cool morning air tickles my skin and helps to calm me. On the street below, a car passes by and the palm trees sway in the wind.

Everything is peaceful and calm, not at all like the roiling chaos inside me.

The door slides open behind me, and I jump like I've been shot.

"What are you doing out here?" Jace asks. His brows are drawn in confusion and his hair is damp from the shower, looking more brown than blond for the moment. He's changed into a ratty pair of jeans, white t-shirt, and boots.

"I needed some air," I reply, and I hate how breathy my voice sounds.

He looks me over and steps out fully, closing the door behind him.

"I could smoke," he mumbles.

I suddenly feel like I can't breathe. The balcony is already small as it is, and with Jace's tall and looming presence it's downright suffocating.

Although, it's probably less to do with the small space and everything to do with him.

He leans his hip against the railing beside me, watching me with narrowed eyes as he taps out a cigarette. He puts it between his lips and cups his hands around it as he lights it.

He inhales a lungful of smoke, holds it in for a second, and then turns to blow it out away from my face. His gaze drifts back to mine and his lips quirk up a bit at the corners.

"Why are you looking at me like that?" The words leave me before I even know what I'm saying. Once I realize what I've said, I want to kick myself.

"Like what?" he prompts. "I'm not looking at you in any particular way, am I?" He looks me up and down, his eyes leaving a trail of fire.

"Stop it," I hiss. "You know exactly what you're doing."

A smile flashes across his lips so fast that I can't be sure it was real.

"I'm not doing anything," he drawls.

I shake my head and look down at the street below.

He sighs and smoke drifts through the air. Another

minute passes and then he mumbles, "I suppose we should be adults and talk about last night."

I stand up straight, suddenly alert. His eyes are dark, shadowed with an emotion I can't decipher. I feel the need to protectively cross my arms over my chest, but I resist the urge. The last thing I want to do is look defensive. I need to appear relaxed and unaffected.

He continues to stare at me, neither of us saying a word.

"Jace," I start and look away. I don't know what to say.

I loved the kiss.

I want it to happen again.

I want you.

When I look back his jaw is clenched, and I don't know whether he's angry or trying to restrain himself.

I get my answer a moment later.

One step closes the distance between us. He grasps my waist in one hand, his fingers splaying over my butt, and his other traps the nape of my neck. He pulls me to him and his lips descend on mine. I'm shocked for a moment, but the shock quickly filters away and is replaced by pure lust. I yearn to get closer to him and he obliges, feeling the similar need and lifts me up so I can wrap my legs around his waist.

I'm aware of him walking and the door sliding open and the next thing I know my back is on the bed and Jace is between my legs.

He kisses me deeply and my back arches. My hands grasp the smooth skin of his face since he just shaved and I hope he doesn't notice the slight tremble in my fingers.

He presses me down into the bed, our bodies and mouths moving in a rhythm all their own.

I feel like I'm losing every ounce of control I have, and I don't even care.

His tongue tangles with mine, and I moan softly.

Holy fuck this is a million times better than last night.

My hands move to his hair, tugging on the strands, and he grabs them, pinning them above my head with one single growled word. "*No.*"

No has never sounded so hot before.

But I'm pretty sure he could say potato right now and I'd think that was hot too, so my opinion is a little cloudy.

Since my hands are restrained, I move my hips against his, needing to touch him in some way. I feel hot and achy all over and my clothes suddenly feel so tight I want to rip them off.

In between kisses, my breaths come out as heavy pants, and I hope like hell they sound sexy and not like a fat dog trying to go up the steps.

That'd be embarrassing.

"Confession," he begins, and I pull in a lungful of air while I wait. "I fucking love these shirts."

Then he lets go of my hand and jerks my shirt off, tossing it behind him, before lowering his mouth to mine again.

I have a collection of shirts with funny and sarcastic sayings. I figured he never even noticed them, he doesn't make comments about what I'm wearing, but with that one simple statement he's confessed so much more than *I fucking love these shirts*, he's telling me he notices, that he pays attention to me more than I ever thought, and that fills me with so much joy it's a bit ridiculous.

His lips move to the shell of my ear, and I shiver as he then traces a trail with his tongue down my neck and over the curves of my breasts.

"Jace," I plead.

I don't even know what I'm begging for—him to touch me, kiss me, or fuck me—it doesn't matter, I just need him.

"I'll take care of you," he whispers, looking up at me with hooded eyes.

Oh, God.

I never in a million years thought Jace would ever look at me like that, and now that he has I think I might be addicted.

He glides his fingers lightly down my stomach, and I shiver.

My chest heaves with each breath, and I still feel starved for air. It's like with our intensity we've sucked every molecule out of the room and we're slowly suffocating.

Honestly, it wouldn't be a bad way to go—looking at a lusty Jace.

His fingers stop at the button of my jeans, and I hold my breath.

His teeth dig slightly into his bottom lip, and he looks up at me, asking for permission.

I nod slowly, just once; I don't have the energy for more.

He flicks open the button on my jeans, and I shudder.

He looks up again. "Nova?" He sounds unsure.

I swallow thickly. "Keep going," I nearly beg. If he stops, I think I might die.

He hesitates for a second longer, but when he sees that I'm not going to stop him, he continues.

The sound of my zipper sliding down is so loud I swear everyone in the hotel must hear it.

I lift my hips so he can slide my jeans off. His eyes are on mine the whole time, and he removes them slowly, almost tenderly, and nothing like the madness when he took my shirt off.

He drops my jeans to the floor and then climbs up my body. He holds his weight above me in a push-up position and then lowers, kissing me again.

"You make me crazy," he whispers softly, his nose grazing the side of my face as he slides down my body.

The feeling is mutual. But I can't find the words to tell him that. My throat is dry, and I can't speak. My heart is beating out of control, and a part of my brain is sensible enough to be worried, because I don't think your heart should beat *this* fast.

He loops his fingers into the sides of my gray underwear and slides them down.

His eyes rake over me and he bites his lip again.

I'm dreaming. I must be dreaming. I have the sudden thought.

But no, this is one-hundred percent real.

I don't know how we went from talking about our kiss to *this*, but that's us. Zero to sixty in two seconds and no looking back.

I suddenly hate that he's still dressed and I'm basically

naked, but before I can give it another moment of thought, he spreads my legs and lowers his head.

My heart nearly falls out of my chest with the first swipe of his tongue.

Sweat dots my skin and my fingers dig into the bed covers.

My back arches, and I moan. I'm think I say his name, too but I can't be sure.

It might be shocking to some, but sexual history is rather bland.

I had a steady boyfriend back home and we had sex, but it was the basics. He never gave me oral and I didn't ask. We broke up two years ago. Last year, I was still recovering from everything that went down between us so I wasn't interested in going out with anyone. Not even for a one-night stand. All I wanted was to keep my head down and focus on school. The rest didn't matter like it does to other people.

One of his hands skims up my stomach and his fingers dig into my breast. It's not gentle, but it's not rough, either, and I love it. It's like he wants me to know that this is real, that he's here too, that he knows how crazy I feel. He pushes the cup of my bra aside so he can grasp me fully, and I wiggle my way out of the straps and sit up enough that I can remove it.

I'm completely naked now and he's still dressed, but I suddenly don't care like I did before. I'm going to blame it on the pure high I'm riding.

His fingers join his tongue and that's it.

"Jace," I pant. "Oh, God. Oh, God. *Oh, God.*"

My body shakes with my orgasm. I've never in all my life experienced an orgasm that powerful and he hasn't even fucked me yet.

His body leaves mine so suddenly that I feel like I've been showered with ice water.

My high quickly disappears. "Jace?" I question.

He tugs on his hair, his jaw tight.

"Jace?" I say again, damming back the tears.

Something's wrong.

"I shouldn't have done that." His words are no more than a broken whisper but they hit me like shrapnel. Each individual word cuts into my skin, lacerating the tender and frayed edges of my already worn heart.

Before I can protest, he turns sharply on his heel and storms out of the room, slamming the door behind him.

I lie there, completely naked and vulnerable, wondering what I did and if this is my fault.

seven
...

nova

"YOU SERIOUSLY DON'T KNOW where Jace is?" Thea asks incredulously as we're guided to a booth in the back.

"No," I say. "He left this morning and he didn't say where he was going."

"Huh," Cade mutters, and I can tell he's thinking. "That's weird. If he was going to leave I would've thought he would've gone last night." He waggles his brows up and down so we know for sure what he's implying.

He and Rae sit on one side of the booth, and I sit with Thea on the other.

Xander's mom chose to stay behind at the hotel since her husband and daughter are on their way in.

I pick up my menu and scan the items. Nothing stands

out to me. I'm not hungry at all after what transpired this morning.

It was great, magical even, all up until he ruined it.

I've never felt so humiliated in all my life, and *that's* saying something.

I feel like crying but I've refused to let a single tear fall because of his stupidity. This is what I spent the whole last year of my life avoiding, and this shows me that I was right to avoid it.

The waitress comes by, and I order a coffee and water.

I look at the menu some more and pick out something random so I don't hold everyone else up. Besides, it doesn't matter what I order—I won't be able to eat.

The waitress comes back with our drinks and we place our food order.

I'm quiet, subdued, but no one calls me on my melancholy attitude because I'm like this most of the time.

I'm the loner.

The shadow.

The person that simply exists.

After about ten minutes of sipping my coffee and gazing out the window, I decide it's time I injected something into the conversation.

"Did you decide how you're going to surprise Xander?"

Thea nods. "Scare tactic for sure. I hope he pees his pants."

Cade shakes his head. "You're nuts. Poor guy."

"Hey," Thea defends, "we're married. We have to keep things interesting. Can't have him getting bored."

Cade snorts. "You've only been married like three months. What could possibly be boring? Shouldn't it all be new and exciting?"

Thea shrugs. "I like to keep him on his toes and always guessing."

Cade shakes his head, completely mystified by his sister. Thea is a creature all her own. She's a total girly girl with the sweetest heart and the sassiest tongue.

"Here you go, guys," the waitress says with a smile, appearing with a tray of food. She passes out our food, and I eye my eggs and toast with disdain. My stomach feels like a block of lead is lodged there and I haven't even taken a bite. "Is there anything else I can get you?" she asks when all the dishes are on the table. We shake our heads. "All right, I'll be back in a bit."

I push my eggs around the plate with my fork and take a bite of toast. It tastes like cardboard in my mouth, and I try not to gag.

Everyone else eats and chats, oblivious to the fact that I'm barely hanging on to my sanity.

Two years. No one has touched me in *two* years and no one has ever touched me like *that* and he just fucking leaves. That's not okay. I'm a strong girl, I've had to be, but that hurt.

I know the connection between us isn't one sided but when he acts like that it makes me feel like it is.

I would've never left *him*.

Ugh.

Boys suck.

I sigh and force myself to eat three bites of egg so my plate looks a little empty.

Everyone finishes and we head over to the hotel Xander and his team are staying at since they should be heading out for practice soon, if they haven't already.

I keep checking my phone, expecting a text from Jace, but none comes.

I itch to ask Cade if he's heard from him, but Cade's not stupid. He'll pick up on something and start asking questions if I sound too worried or nosy.

We file into the hotel lobby and Rae, Cade, and I take a seat while Thea hides behind a potted plant near the elevators. I keep expecting her to pull out a pair of binoculars.

"She's insane," I say to Rae. She sits beside Cade with her legs draped over his. He rubs his hand over her thigh, and I don't think he even realizes he's doing it. It's just second nature for him to touch her in some way.

Rae shrugs, brushing her long brown hair over her shoulder. She flashes a smile. "There has to be at least one crazy in every group. She's ours."

"I guess that's true," I agree.

"So ... Joel?" she muses with a raised brow.

"What about him?" I ask at the same time Cade asks, "Who's that?"

"Just some guy in our classes," Rae supplies. "He has a thing for Nova."

Cade glances over at me, shaking his shaggy hair from his eyes. "Do you like him?"

"No," I scoff. "He's annoying."

"I thought Cade was annoying at first, and look at us now," Rae reasons, smiling at her boyfriend.

"That's different."

"How?" she probes.

Because I like Jace, but he left me naked and alone, shaking from the best orgasm of my life.

"It just is," I say instead.

She blows out a puff of air, clearly frustrated with me.

"Why don't you go out on one date with him?" she pesters. "One date won't hurt anything."

My face scrunches up in complete disgust. "I don't *want* to go on a date with him. I don't like him. Let it go."

Rae's eyes flash with hurt but she nods. "I'm sorry." I'm surprised she apologized but I nod in thanks. "I just love you, and I want you to be happy."

"What makes you think I'm not?"

She raises a brow like that's a stupid question. "You seem completely *un*happy most of the time. You're quiet, and sullen, and withdrawn. I worry about you. I've been in a bad place before, a *really* bad place, and sometimes I still go there, but I want you to know I'm here for you and it does get better."

"Thanks," I mumble.

I'm saved from her getting any deeper by some of the NFL guys coming into the lobby. It's obvious who they are by their sheer size and the way they carry themselves. They're dressed in suits and ties and look incredibly nice. Probably going for some sort of interview or something. I'll be honest, football isn't my thing. No sport is. So, my knowledge is limited.

I scan the guys, looking for Xander. Normally, it's easy to pick him out of a crowd—the guy is a giant—but these guys are all tall too. It's just a sea of giant men.

Thea must spot him, though, because she hops up from her hiding place and runs, jumping onto the back of who I *hope* is Xander.

We hear him cry out in surprise at being "attacked" and then his surprised exclamation of, "Thea?" can be heard.

The other guys head out of the hotel and one claps Xander on the shoulder before he leaves.

Rae, Cade, and I go to join Thea.

"Surprise!" Thea dances excitedly in front of her husband.

"Wow." Xander shakes his head. "You're all here. This is crazy. I didn't expect this."

We were all supposed to have dinner earlier in the week but Xander ended up having to leave early, so I haven't seen him since the wedding.

"We couldn't miss your first game man," Cade says, going to hug his best friend.

"Your parents and sister are here too," Thea tells him. "Xavier might make it but ... *Yale*," she says like that's explanation enough for his brother's absence. "Jace is here too," Thea continues. "But we lost him."

"Lost him?" Xander asks, placing his hands on Thea's waist and pulling her into him. She smiles up at him, completely in love.

My heart pangs with ... it's not jealousy, but a longing for that.

I thought I was over wanting to be in love, that I'd been through enough, but I was wrong.

Thea shrugs. "You know Jace. He disappears but he always returns like a loyal yard dog."

I press my lips together to hold in my laugh.

Only Thea.

"I'm really happy to see you guys," Xander says, smiling at each of us. "This is the best surprise. And you—" he bends his head to Thea "—I've missed you."

He whispers something else and then kisses her.

"Ew." Cade gags. "That's my cue to leave. I have no desire to watch my sister make out. Bye." He quickly turns on his heel and strides out the hotel doors.

Xander breaks from Thea with a grin. "I love you and this is amazing, but I have to go before I get in trouble."

"I understand." Thea stands on her tiptoes and kisses him one last time. "Can I see you later?"

"If I can get away I'll let you know. No promises, though. Thanks for coming, guys," he says to Rae and me. He hugs each of us before heading outside.

Thea watches him with a dreamy sigh. "I hope his ass always looks that good." When she notices us watching her with amused expressions she adds, "I mean, I'd still love him anyway, but it's a *very* nice bonus."

Rae shakes her head and loops her arm through Thea's while I take the other side.

I never thought I'd have friends like these—yes, they're

nosy, and all too curious about my love life, but they're also the kindest, most thoughtful people I've ever met, and I'm lucky to know them.

Sometimes life gives you what you think you don't need when you need it the most.

And me?

I needed friends.

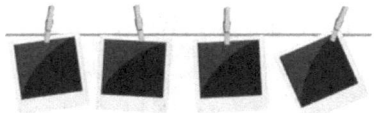

We arrive back at the hotel and file into the elevator.

Thea gets off first, then Rae and Cade, and then I'm left alone, riding up to the eleventh floor.

The doors slide open, and I look down at my feet as I walk.

It's a habit I developed because it means I don't have to talk to people as often. If you're not looking people tend to ignore you.

A pair of dark boots that are *not* mine enter my vision, and I freeze.

My gaze slowly travels up, and I find Jace sitting on the floor in front of our hotel room door. His head is bowed, his jaw firm. He must feel my stare because his head suddenly whips up and his green eyes connect with my brown ones.

"I didn't have my key," he says by way of explanation.

Anger surges in my veins, and I sling my room key at him so it lands in his lap. I turn promptly on my heel, heading back to the elevator and away from him, because I can't stand to fucking looking at him.

I feel so humiliated.

He left me.

He put his fingers in me, his mouth on me, and he fucking left me.

"Nova," he calls, and his hand grabs my arm a second later.

I swivel around and out of his hold. I've never been a violent person but I shove him as hard as I can and I'm pleased when he takes a step back. Granted, it's only one, but it's something.

"Nova," he pleads.

"Shut up," I snap. "You do *not* get to play Mr. Innocent here. Do not do that to me." I point a finger at him. I'm way shorter than him, and trying to appear menacing is difficult, but his throat bobs and I hope he's feeling remorseful, because he *should*. "I am not some fucking rag doll you can drag around and do whatever you want with. I am a person. I have feelings. And right now, I'm *humiliated*."

"Nova—"

"I said *shut up*." I glare at him. He raises his hands innocently. "*You* kissed me last night. *You* kissed me this morning. *You* carried me to bed. *You* put your hands and mouth on me—yes, I wanted you to, but my point is *you* started it, and it's completely unfair that *you* left. *You* hurt me," I pause, inhaling a deep breath. "You hurt me," I say again, because I want him to understand.

"I know I fucked up." He rakes a hand through his hair. "I'm sorry."

I shake my head back and forth. "You're sorry? That's all you have to say."

He groans. "I don't know what else to say."

I shake my head. "Unbelievable," I mutter. "Maybe you could explain what the fuck happened and why you left, because I keep going over what happened and trying to figure out what I did, and I've got nothing." I raise my hands and let them fall to my sides.

He rubs his hands over his mouth. "I don't know how to do *this*." He waves a hand at me.

I throw my hands in the air and shout, "What does that *mean*?"

He crosses his hands behind his head and inhales a deep breath before letting his hands fall to his sides. "I don't know how to do *this*." He waves a hand between the two of us. "I *care* about you, Nova. I've never had a girlfriend, let alone been with someone I care about. I purposely stay away from people I know to avoid ..."

"Feeling anything," I supply, defeated.

"Yeah," he sighs. "It's easier to not feel or get attached. You're the most important person in my life, and I don't want to lose you."

I bite my lip, fighting tears.

I will not cry. I will not cry. I will not cry.

"You're going to lose me if you keep doing this to me," I

tell him breathlessly. "You can't kiss me or touch me and then take it back. It doesn't work like that. I'm not some plaything you can use at your whim. I'm not asking you to promise me forever," I snap. "*You're* the one making it complicated."

He shakes his head. "You don't get it," he snaps, his anger palpable. "I can't just fuck you like any other girl. With you it would *mean* something. Don't you fucking get that? You're not someone I can just walk away from after it's done."

"That's exactly what you did!" I shove a finger into his chest.

He takes a step back. "I needed to clear my head before I did something stupid."

"And by stupid, you mean have sex with me?" I shake my head. "You're unbelievable."

"I'm not done talking to you," he says when I start to walk away.

I pause and glare at him over my shoulder. "Really? Because I am."

I press the button for the elevator and he stands behind me.

"You're not listening. I want to have sex with you so fucking bad, Nova. I've fantasized about it more times than I'd care to admit." I will the elevator to come faster. His body crowds behind me and he lowers his head to my ear. All the oxygen is sucked from the room, just like it is every time he's this close to me. "But if I fuck you, I'm going to want to do it again. You wouldn't be a one-time thing. You're like a drug to me and I can't walk away even though I should."

The elevator chimes as the doors open. I step inside and face him.

"I guess it's a good thing I'm strong enough to walk away for the both of us."

The doors slide closed on his stunned face and a sob finally breaks free from my throat.

I lean against the elevator wall, and I let myself cry, hating myself the entire time for feeling anything for him.

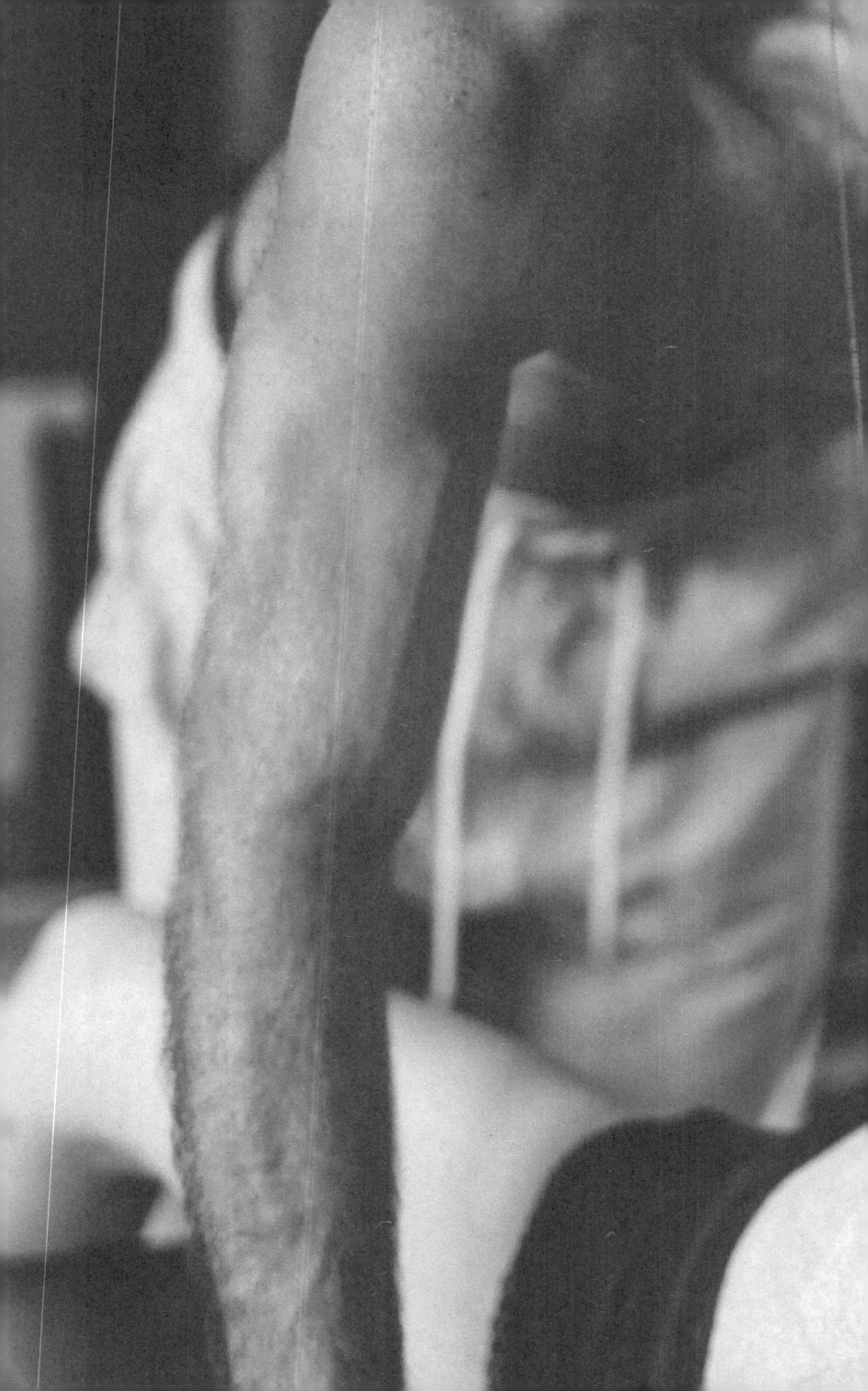

eight
...

jace

I STAND THERE, stunned, as the elevator doors close.

I guess it's a good thing I'm strong enough to walk away for the both of us.

Doesn't she get it? The last thing I want to do is walk away from her. I know I shouldn't have left. I get that it was a dick move. But what I felt in that moment eclipsed every single emotion I've felt in my whole life.

It *terrified* me.

So, I fucking ran.

I let out a groan that sounds anguished and despaired. I've never been this torn up over a girl before. Nova's important to me. She's my friend, and she's someone I love. I've grown close to her in the last year, she fucking lives with me, and I don't want to lose that. I don't want to lose *her*. And I know if I do this, I'll push her away, because I can't be her boyfriend. I'm just not the kind of guy that can be someone's boyfriend.

Am I?

I turn away from the elevators and head back down the hall. I pick up the room key and head inside.

The room is the same as I left it, except the bed is no longer ruffled and there's no Nova.

I sigh and sit on the edge of the bed. I lean my elbow on my knees and drop my head down, fisting my hair.

I've made a fucking mess of things, and knowing me I'll only make it messier, because I'm the destroyer, not the fixer.

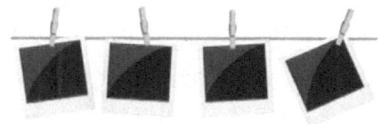

Cade texts me.

Rae texts me.

Cade texts me again.

But I hear nothing from the one person I'm desperate to hear from. It's been three hours since she stepped in that elevator. Three fucking of hours of madness. I sat in the room for a bit, then left and walked around, thinking I might bump into her, then when that proved futile I came back.

Now, I sit on the bed, waiting and hoping for her to come back.

I'm a fucking pathetic piece of shit.

I say I'll never pine for a woman, and that's exactly what I'm doing.

I've become the exact opposite of everything I thought I was.

Maybe I was never really that guy?

There's a soft, hesitant knock on the door, and I leap from the bed like it's on fire.

I stride over to the door and breathe a sigh of relief when I open it to find Nova.

"You're here," I breathe.

"I'm here for my bags," she snaps, looking at a spot on my chest instead of my eyes.

"What?" I say, flabbergasted as she storms past me.

She hastily begins gathering all her things.

"*Nova*," I snap, my tone urging her to explain.

She halts, her shoulders tense with her back to me as she leans over her bag that she's placed on her bed. She doesn't have much to put in it and could be out of here in under a minute if I let her.

"Talk to me," I plead.

She turns around, fire in her eyes, and fuck if mine don't burn with the same flame.

"Yes," she seethes, "because 'talking' has worked out so well for us before." She uses air quotes and damn if it isn't the sexiest thing I've ever seen. It's probably wrong how much I'm turned on by her anger.

"I don't want you to leave," I tell her. It's more than I should admit, but it's the truth.

She turns away and zips up her bag with a sigh. "I have to."

She slings the bag over her shoulder and starts back for the door. I grab her hand and stop her. I could pin her to the wall, cage her in and make her feel small, but I don't want that, not yet.

"You think I left because what happened on that bed meant nothing to me, but you're wrong." My words are a low, quiet growl. "I had to leave because it meant *everything*."

I release her arm, hoping my words have finally gotten to her but she merely presses her lips together, shakes her head, and leaves.

Again.

I dress for dinner, fuming the whole time.

The room is too quiet.

I fucking hate the silence.

I know I'm going to see Nova at dinner and it's going to be damn near impossible to keep our friends from figuring out that something has happened between the two of us.

Luckily, I'm a good actor.

I tuck my white button-down shirt into my dress pants

and try not to cringe. It's not that formal wear is anything new to me, it's just that I fucking hate it. My dad's a Senator and before that he was Governor, so formal functions were the norm growing up.

I stuff my room key in my wallet, put it in my pocket, and head out.

I meet everyone in the lobby and Nova stands by Rae, away from me.

Before I can go to her, Thea directs us outside to where two taxis wait. One is a car and the other is a minivan.

Nova climbs in behind Rae in the car and Cade joins them in the back, where I know it must be cramped quarters. I grab the front seat. Thea goes with Xander's family in the minivan.

I have no idea what restaurant we're meeting Xander at, but Thea must've told the driver of our car to follow the minivan because he does so without speaking to either of us.

We finally arrive at a modern looking, white, one-story building. *Ocean* is spelled out in a dark blue script lit up on the side the building.

I get out and pay the driver.

"Xander's already inside. He has our table," Thea tells us, looking at her phone.

The eight of us head into the building and up to the hostess table.

The girl working jumps when she looks up from the menus she's organizing and notices our large group.

"Oh, hi," she says, placing her hand over her heart like

she's been startled and it's racing. "Welcome to Ocean. Party of eight?"

"We already have a table," Thea speaks up. "Kincaid?"

"Ah, yes. Right this way."

The girl motions for us to follow. She's dressed in a deep-blue silky blouse and a tight black pencil skirt. Under normal circumstances I wouldn't be able to take my eyes off her, but now my eyes keep straying to Nova, trying to catch her eyes, hoping to see if I can gauge what she's feeling and read her mood.

I have no such luck.

The hostess leads us to a large table out on a deck that overlooks a canal.

Xander sits at the table with another guy that's tall and beefy enough that he must be another football player. I don't keep up with sports so I don't recognize any of the players. The only reason I know what I do about football is because I became friends with Cade and Xander in high school where they both played before we all moved on to the same college and they played again.

"Hey, guys." Xander stands, slapping hands and hugging as need be. "This is my friend Sullivan. He's a halfback."

I have no idea what a *halfback* is.

Everyone takes their seats, and I purposely am the last one left—and sure enough, they left an empty spot beside Nova for me. I'm not happy at *all* that she's also beside *Sullivan*. After all, what the fuck kind of name is Sullivan? I also don't appreciate the way he's looking at her—like she's gorgeous and interesting and amazing, because she *is* all those things but I don't want *him* noticing them about her. I'd rather he look at the fucking wall ... or ocean, because a wall isn't really applicable at the moment.

Nova slides her chair slightly closer to Sullivan, and I bristle.

I lower my head to her ear—no one will think anything of it, because they're used to us having our secrets—and whisper, "I don't bite."

Her breath catches and dark eyes dart up to mine. I catch the briefest flash of desire before she shudders her eyes and looks at me with disdain instead. But it was there, even for a second, and that's what matters.

She turns away from me and starts speaking to Sullivan.

"So, Sullivan, you're the halfback? That's interesting."

Before Sullivan can say anything, I snort and interject, "Halfback? What does that mean? All I can think about is a half-rack of ribs."

Nova gives me a disgusted look.

Sullivan laughs. "My primary responsibility as halfback is blocking. I protect the quarterback or whoever happens to have the ball. I'm also an eligible receiver so sometimes I get to run the ball."

I look away. I was hoping the halfback was more of a benched player, but of fucking course not.

Nova leans into him with interest, which pisses me off more because I know she has no real interest in him and is only trying to get a rise out of me, which is unfortunately working.

The waiter shows up to take our drink orders and for the moment Nova can no longer train her attention on Sullivan.

When the waiter leaves to get our drinks, conversation ceases while we all look at the menu. I keep darting furtive glances at Nova, which she studiously ignores.

I've never been this torn up and confused in my life.

I don't know what I want.

But I do.

But I *don't*.

Fuck.

My eyes scan the menu, but I don't see the words.

Nova's arm brushes mine and she jumps away. When I glance over I note the goosebumps dotting her arm.

She can pretend all she wants that I don't affect her, but it's a lie and we both know it. I'm as potent to her as she is to me.

The waiter appears with our drinks, and I lift my fancy-pants beer to my lips. I fucking hate this kind of beer, dark and rich tasting—and by *rich* I do mean in the money sense and not the actual taste. Any time I'm forced to go to some event or function for my dad, it's this kind of beer and wine as the drink options, which led me to hating it. But, of course, a nice restaurant like this only has this and not my usual go-to.

Figures.

Now I have to drink this disgusting stuff and listen to Nova prattle on and on to Sullivan.

It's like my own personal hell or something.

I flip the thick pages of the menu and finally settle on a steak, figuring I can't go wrong with that.

We place our orders and conversation buzzes around us.

"How's the bar?" Cade asks me after a few minutes.

I lift my eyes and look across the table at him with a shrug. "Same old, same old. I like it there."

"What about your music?" he asks. "How's that going?"

Again, I shrug. "Just writing and playing when I can."

All I've wanted since I was a junior in high school was to make a go of my music. My father was steadfastly against it, wanting me to follow in his footsteps. I haven't talked to him in years except for the rare occasions where he calls and forces me to attend some function because it makes him look good in the media and around other politicians if he appears to be a loving family man. But he's as far from a loving family man as it's possible to get. I wouldn't even attend those functions if I didn't know the consequences weren't worth the defiance.

But my defiance by not following in his footsteps was worth every hate-filled word he lobbed my way.

No fucking way was I going to wear a suit and tie every day and deal with other politicians. That life isn't for me.

"Are you okay?" Cade asks, and I realize I've grown morose with my thoughts about my dad.

"Yeah, fine."

I feel the weight of Nova's eyes on me, and when I glance over, I see the worry in them before she looks away hastily.

"I hear you finally settled on a major," I speak to Thea, hoping to steer the conversation away from myself.

Thea's smiling at Xander, and she glances down the table at me. "Yeah, I'm going to do something in social work. I want to help kids and women who have been affected by abuse."

I wrap my fingers around my beer bottle. "I think you'll be great at that."

I honestly do too. Thea has the kind of personality that you can't help but instantly like her. She's bubbly and excitable, but she's also warm and caring.

"Thanks." She flips her light-brown hair over her shoulder. "It feels good to finally know what I want to do and be sure of it. I've been in limbo too long." She smiles up Xander. "It's like everything has finally fallen into place."

I look at Nova again—at the vibrant blue hair, her pale skin and freckles, her upturned nose and full lips, and I think about how everyone else's life is *falling into place* and mine is *all over the place*. It's like there are a million puzzle pieces in front of me, and I can just make out the picture—it's fuzzy, but it's there, but there are also pieces missing and those gaps are where the problems lie.

The waiter comes back to take our orders, and with so many of us, I swear it takes an entire year before we're done.

Nova strikes up conversation with Sullivan again, and I groan. I don't mean to do it, but that doesn't stop it. Her eyes dart to mine along with Rae and Cade's.

"Stubbed my toe," I mutter to cover myself.

None of them are buying it, though, and I don't blame them.

I look across the table, over Cade's shoulder, at the water

in the canal. I hope the slow, hypnotic, lap of the water will calm me.

It doesn't.

I've never felt so miserable in my life and the fact that it's over a girl because I'm *jealous* makes it even worse.

Jealousy is a ridiculous emotion. It robs you of common sense.

I rub my sweaty palms on the knees of my pants.

I hate that I'm this torn up. I want to be unaffected and aloof, but I'm anything but.

This dinner can't end soon enough.

After a few more minutes, I stand with a mumbled excuse that I'm going to the bathroom.

Once there I stare at my reflection the mirror.

I look like I'm calm, cool, and collected, but my eyes betray the battle raging inside.

I'm a mess.

I wash my hands and splash my face. I place my hand on either side of the sink on the marble top and lean forward, breathing out.

Get it together, Jace. You've never acted like this before. Now doesn't have to be any different. She's just a girl.

The problem is she not *just* a girl. She's Nova.

I shake my head and dry my hands. I leave the bathroom, strolling slowly through the restaurant and back onto the deck.

I drop into my seat, bumping Nova in the process and she glares at me. I revel in her anger, though, because at least it's *mine*. I like knowing I make her feel something, because it means I'm not alone.

"So, you're in college with Thea?" Sullivan asks her, and I bristle.

This dude has no fucking right to try and get to know her. Why the fuck did Xander even bring him?

"Yes," Nova says, leaning into him like she's *so* interested. I resist the urge to roll my eyes.

"That's cool," he says lifting his wine glass to his mouth. *What kind of pansy ass drinks wine?* "What are you studying?"

"Photography and graphic design," she supplies. "How'd you get into football?"

This time I do roll my eyes. I know Nova has no desire to know about this guy's reasoning for liking a fucking sport.

He rests his elbows on the table, angling his body toward her. He's putting out all the signs that he's attracted to her, and I'm not having it.

"I started playing when I was really young, only eight, and I stuck with it. I love it. I can't imagine myself doing anything else."

"But shouldn't you?" I pipe in. "It's not like you can play football for your whole life."

He chuckles. "Of course. That's why I have my realtor's license. Maybe I can sell you a place if you ever need it."

"Mhmm, sure," I grumble, finishing off my beer. I lift the empty glass when I spot the waiter across the deck and he nods in acknowledgement.

When the waiter comes back with my beer he also carries

a tray filled with food. Another waitress is behind him carrying another tray.

He gives me my beer and sets about unloading the food.

It smells great and looks even better, but still, I have no appetite.

It doesn't help that Nova won't stop jabbering with jock boy—that's what I've dubbed him.

I cut into my steak with a force that rattles the table.

"Dude," Cade says, his tone a warning one.

"Sorry," I mumble, glaring at my plate like it's what I'm mad at.

The anger at myself is building. I shouldn't care if Nova flirts with some guy, even if she is doing it to bother me. It shouldn't matter to me. I've always been able to shut off my emotions when it comes to this kind of thing and to have it suddenly bother me so much is jarring.

Dinner ends and we thankfully say goodbye to Sullivan and Xander, but not before I see Sullivan ask Nova for her number.

She gives it to him gladly, smiling at him the whole time.

But her eyes? Those are on me.

Taxis take us back to the hotel and we split off. Nova tries to stick with the others and get away from me, but I'm not having it and slip into the elevator with all of them.

They get off first, leaving me alone with her.

Thank God.

"I still don't want to talk to you," she says when she sees my mouth open in the reflection of the elevator doors.

Before I can respond, they slide open to the next floor and she steps off.

I follow.

"Jace," she hisses when she notices I've followed her off the elevator. "Leave it be."

This time I *do* pin her to the wall. I brush my nose against hers, fisting one hand in her hair and forcefully yanking her hair back. It's not enough to hurt, but enough to show her I won't be ignored. Her hands are on my stomach and she digs her long nails in so that I can feel them even through the fabric of my shirt.

I don't even know what I intend to do, I just know I can't let her go.

"What do you want?" she asks through clenched teeth. Her words convey disinterest, but her body says otherwise.

The uneven rise and fall of her chest says I'm getting to her.

The flutter of her lashes against her cheeks says she's struggling to remain composed.

The slight dig of her teeth into her bottom lip tells me she's turned on.

I press one of my legs in-between hers and when she *moans* I fucking own that sound.

I lower my head to her neck and dig my teeth into the sensitive skin there. She jumps as I bear down. It doesn't hurt her, but it *will* leave a mark, and that's what I want.

"I like games." I graze the shell of her ear with my lips, then nibble on the lobe. "So, keep running—because I'm going to win. I *always* win."

I release her, reveling in her small gasp, and I walk back to the elevator.

When I step inside and turn around I find that she's watching.

I smirk and salute her with two fingers.

This isn't over.

Not by a long shot.

nine
. . .

nova

"RUN THE BALL! I said run the ball, dammit!" Thea yells, pointing her finger angrily at one of the guys on the field.

I'm surprised she still has a voice at this point.

Our seats are near the field and fairly close to where the guys sit.

"Xander!" Thea screams at her husband where he sits on the bench. "They're idiots!"

Xander either ignores her or doesn't hear her, but Thea is not deterred.

When our team loses the ball, she screams shrilly, "Are you fucking kidding *me*? Idiots! You're all idiots!"

"Excuse me," someone in front of us says. "But there are children around, so could you keep the vulgar language to yourself?"

Thea fumes. "Bite me."

Rae sighs and smiles politely at the woman. "I'm sorry. We'll try to keep her down."

"Keep me down," Thea repeats and snorts. "Good luck."

I adjust my baseball cap—with the team colors and logo on it—and wiggle in my seat. I even bought a jersey to wear—are football shirts called jerseys? *They are, aren't they?*

I turn, my mouth open, poised to ask Jace—who sits beside me, yippee—and then realize I'm not talking to him.

I hastily turn back in my seat to face the field, but not before I miss the flash of his smile.

"Something you wanna say?" he prompts.

I shake my head.

Ignoring him might be childish, but it's all I have. Every time I open my mouth my words go over his head.

The game continues below and Thea sits on the edge of her seat, jumping up every once in a while, before someone gripes and she sits back down.

Thea's standing with her hands on her hips, shaking her head back and forth. "Xander might be new to the team but he can play better than this. They need to put him in."

"Thea," Cade warns.

"Shut it," she snaps. "You know it too."

"What position does Xander play?" Rae asks. "I don't think you ever told me."

"Wide receiver," Thea answers, not taking her eyes off the field. Glancing sheepishly at Rae, she adds, "I probably didn't tell you because I didn't want you to think I liked him."

Rae rolls her eyes. "Yeah, because that *so* wasn't obvious already."

"Hey," Thea defends, tugging at her own jersey with KINCAID printed on the back and 26. "It totally wasn't."

"Keep telling yourself that."

Thea sits back down on the edge of her seat, and I swear she's biting at her perfectly-manicured nails.

"You know," Jace drawls beside me, "I have never been able to wrap my head around the joy so many people find in football. This is boring."

I press my lips together to keep any possible words from leaving me.

He leans closer to me, brushing his arm against mine where I have it on the armrest. I jolt away and he chuckles. "I know you find it boring too."

I'm sure all the color has been leached from my lips with as tightly as I have them clasped.

"At least it's a nice day," he continues, unbothered by my silence. "A few clouds, blue sky, *hot*." He pauses and his lips quirk. "Although, it's a fair bit chilly in this particular spot."

I roll my eyes.

"Are you never going to speak to me again? Is that how we're going to play this? You do realize we live together, right?" he whispers so the others can't hear. He continues on, "You're going to have to see me every day and you're seriously not going to say a word?"

"This is your fault," I finally snap. "If I don't want to talk to you, that's my prerogative. You made your bed now lie in it."

He leans impossibly closer. I'm convinced he likes getting in my personal space because he likes seeing what it does to me.

"Maybe I want to lie in it with you."

"Ugh, you're gross," I mutter under my breath and lean away from him and closer to Rae.

Jace moves with me, though. There's no escaping him.

"You weren't saying that when I was going down on you."

I gasp loudly, but the sound is thankfully drowned out by the crowd as they cry, "Ooh!" Then erupt into cheers with a touchdown.

"Did we score?" I ask stupidly.

"Yes, dummie!" Thea snaps, clapping her hands and whistling.

I clap, because it feels like the right thing to do.

Beside me, Jace has leaned back in his seat, and I hope this means he's done pestering me.

I hate how my whole body is so aware of him.

It's entirely unfair that one person can affect me so much.

The game continues and toward the end, Xander gets put in.

When Thea sees him jogging onto the field, she screams so shrilly that several people slap their hands over their ears.

She stands again, bouncing on the balls of her feet. "That's my husband! That's my husband! Xander, I love you!"

When Thea sits back down, Rae remarks, "You said husband without flinching. I'm proud of you."

Thea grins back. "I *know*. I've come so far."

Now that Xander is on the field, I pay a little more attention to what's happening. I still don't understand any of it, but that hardly matters. The time ticks down and we're tied. I find myself at the edge of my seat, hoping for a miracle. I might not like football, but I *do* have a team to root for now.

The ball is passed and a player is running, *running, running*.

"Touchdown!" Thea yells.

As a group, we jump up and down in excitement. Well, all of us except for Jace. He simply stands. He's not one for jumping.

The game comes to an end and we're all riding high from the win.

Thea and Xander's family separate from us and head off somewhere so they can see him.

The rest of us head out of the stadium and grab a taxi back to the hotel.

I end up next to Jace, but he's surprisingly well behaved.

The four of us end up in the elevator together. Rae and Cade chat excitedly, still on a high from the win, while Jace and I stand on the opposite side saying nothing.

Cade and Rae get off on their floor and I'm left alone with Jace. I sigh heavily, expecting him to start in on me again, but he's surprisingly quiet.

The doors slide open onto my floor and I step out.

Behind me, he says, "Confession, I *never* give up."

Before I can respond, the heavy metal doors have closed and he's gone.

I shake my head and head down the hall to my room.

My very quiet, very boring room.

I collapse dramatically on the bed, staring at the ceiling.

I wish I could change the way I feel about Jace as easily as I change the color of my hair.

But life isn't that simple. We can't snap our fingers and make something happen. The fact is, no matter how hurt and mad I am, it doesn't change my underlying feelings for him.

My heart still aches for his touch while my mind warns me away.

It's a complicated thing, being split into two by what you want and what you think is necessary.

ten
...

jace

OUR FLIGHT HOME is a quiet one—mostly because everyone's exhausted. We had to be up at the crack of dawn to get to the airport in time, and it's a good thing we got there early because the place was packed.

Nova sleeps with her head on my shoulder. I know when she wakes up and discovers this fact she's going to be pissed, but for now I revel in the small amount of contact.

At least in her sleep she can't pretend to hate me.

Because that's all it is—her pretending. She can't hate me any more than I could ever hate her.

It's just not possible.

I rest my head against hers and close my eyes.

I haven't slept in days.

The first night here I couldn't sleep because I was thinking about the kiss.

The next two nights I couldn't sleep because Nova wasn't there.

It was better dwelling on that than my mom, though. That's a sure way to put me in a foul mood.

Eventually, I drift off to sleep, and when I wake up, we're touching down.

Nova jerks away and lets out a scream, her sleep-rattled mind not realizing what's happening.

I wrap my arms around her and draw her close. "Nova," I plead. "*Nova*," I say again sternly when I worry she's about to burst into tears. Wild and frantic brown eyes meet mine. "We're landing," I tell her. "Everything is okay."

Her breaths are uneven but I can see her processing my words. After a moment, she nods and wiggles out of my hold.

I miss her already.

The plane taxis in and once it's docked we grab our bags and head out.

We say goodbye to our friends before splitting off from the group, where they head to the garage and we head out to the parking lot.

Nova is quiet and withdrawn. There's so much more I want to say. I want to push her and see how far I can bend her before she *really* snaps, because her anger is better than her silence.

But for now, I opt not to say anything.

I'm biding my time.

After all, don't they say good things come to those who wait?

For once in my life I'm going to fucking wait.

Or try, at least.

We reach my truck, and I unlock the ancient thing.

My dad with his fancy foreign sports cars is horrified by my truck, but I don't give a fuck.

It's yet another thing he can add to his endless list of things I've screwed up.

I toss my bag in the space behind the seats and Nova does the same. She buckles her seatbelt and looks steadfastly out the window.

I start the truck and turn the music off; I don't have any interest in listening to it right now.

Sunlight filters between the clouds and I marvel at the mountains in the distance. It doesn't matter that I've lived here my whole life, I'm still filled with awe every time I look at them.

We reach the apartment, and before Nova can hop out, I lock the doors.

"That's childish." She glares at me.

The lock on that side is broken, and it won't unlock until I push the button.

"Maybe so," I agree. "But I want to talk."

"We could've talked on the way here," she counters.

"I needed that time to think."

She sighs and looks out the window, her vivid blue hair flowing around her shoulders.

"Jace," she says softly. "Stop beating this into the ground."

I undo my seatbelt and turn in my seat to face her. "I hate

fighting with you—I don't even know if that's what we're doing but it feels like it. I don't want us to continue on with this ... this *coldness*," I settle on, for lack of a better word. "I miss you." My voice cracks with the honesty.

She's silent, staring at her lap and fiddling with a rip in her jeans. Finally, she says, "I miss you too." Hope soars in my chest. "But that doesn't take away the embarrassment I feel about what happened." *And there goes all my hope.*

I reach over, wrapping a piece of her hair around my finger. Her eyes lift to mine, and I see the turmoil there. The embarrassment she speaks of, worry, anger, maybe even regret. But I also see lust and desire, so I know me walking away that morning didn't ruin everything. This is salvageable. Whatever *this* is.

"I'm sorry I'm such an asshole," I tell her and her lips quirk ever so slightly.

She shrugs. "You're not an asshole *all* the time."

I laugh then. I can't help it. "But most of the time?" I prompt.

"Eh." She rocks one hand back and forth in the air. "Maybe only some of the time."

"Some," I repeat. "That's better than most."

The small smile she was sporting disappears, and I know I'm most likely not going to like what she has to say. "We can pretend that our kiss and that morning hasn't changed anything, but that's all it would be. *Pretending*. It did change things between us, and I don't think we can come back from it."

My body tenses. "What are you saying?"

"I think it's best if we avoid each other for a little while. I know that's hard with us living together, but I'm hoping if …" she pauses, her teeth digging into her lower lip. "I'm hoping if I don't have to see you every day then maybe my feelings will go away."

Before I can respond, she leans over my body, her breasts brushing my arm, as she pushes the button that unlocks her door. Her bag is already in her hand and she darts out of the truck.

I watch her leave and disappear into the apartment building, still stunned by her last words.

By the fact that she doesn't want to see me because then maybe her feelings will go away.

I hope like fuck that's not true, because I know there's no way distance is going to erase what I feel.

Something this all-consuming can't be so easily forgotten.

But there's a nagging voice in my head that says, *What if it can?*

eleven

...

nova

I GO TO SCHOOL.

I go to work.

I avoid Jace as much as possible.

Wash. Rinse. Repeat.

It sounds so much easier than it is.

Avoiding Jace is nearly impossible.

Not only is he always around, I can't help but crave being near him.

He's my best friend, and I love spending time with him. Be it watching a movie, or making a dinner, or just hanging out. To suddenly not have that time with him sucks.

I know it's for the best, though.

When I arrive home from class, Jace is already gone for work.

Hallelujah.

I drop my backpack on the floor and kick off my black Converse. I pad across the room to the kitchen and fix a bowl of cereal.

Silence echoes around me. It's been my friend and enemy for the last two weeks since we got back from Florida. My friend, because it means I don't have to be worried about being swayed by something Jace says. My enemy, because I miss talking to him.

I know I did this to myself and I'm to blame, but it doesn't make it any easier.

I hop up on the stainless-steel counter, letting my legs dangle as I eat my cereal.

I've been living off cereal and Pop-Tarts the last two weeks. Jace normally does all the cooking, and he still does, but since I've been avoiding him that means he hasn't been making enough for me to eat too.

I think he's trying to force me out of my dungeon—and by dungeon, I mean my bedroom.

It's where I spend the majority of my time.

Jace is working today, so I know he'll be gone until the wee hours of the morning.

It gives me a chance to hang out in the apartment and do my own thing.

Like dye my hair.

Normally, I stay with one color for a few months before moving on, but lately I've been restless and changing it every few weeks.

I bought a new color while I was at the drug store today.

Green.

I'm not sure how I'll like it, but the blue needs to go.

Every time I look in the mirror all I can hear is Jace telling me how much he loves it. It's driving me insane.

I finish my cereal and wash the bowl and spoon, leaving them on the towel on the counter to drip dry, then I pick my shoes and backpack up and carry them to my room.

Unzipping my backpack, I pull out the hair dye.

I figure there's no time like the present.

I head into the bathroom and begin the tedious process of changing my hair color. I would be better off going to a professional and getting it done, but part of the original rebellion the first time I did it was doing it myself, so I've kept up the tradition since then.

Hours later, I stare at my reflection and my green hair. It's a darker green, not a minty one, and I love it.

It's getting late, after ten, and I'm tired from classes and work. I had late classes today so I picked up an early shift, and now I'm regretting that, because I'm too exhausted to enjoy my evening to myself.

If you weren't ignoring Jace then you wouldn't be too tired to go to the bar and hang out with him.

I wince at my own thoughts because they're true.

I walk into my room and collapse onto my bed. "God, I'm pathetic," I mumble out loud.

I grab my notebook and pencil, figuring writing a letter to Owen will keep me sane.

Owen.

My dirty secret.

One I'll never share with anyone.

I push away my pain at that thought and begin to write.

Dear Owen,

I used to think I wasn't the screw up my parents made me out to be.

I get good grades.

I care about people.

I'm kind.

I work hard and I love fiercely.

But I'm discovering that they were right. I am a screw up. I continuously do things I shouldn't.

I shouldn't like Jace the way I do, but I also shouldn't have pushed him away, because now I'm miserable.

And when I'm sad I think of you even more.

Don't get me wrong, I think of you all the time, you're always in my heart, but it's different when I'm sad.

Sadness makes me think of the what ifs.

And life can't be spent dwelling on the what ifs. What ifs exist to haunt us—to tease us with possibilities of things we can never confirm.

I'm rambling now.

But this is my truth; I miss you, and I love you, and I think of you every day. I always will, until my very last breath.

Love,

Nova

. . .

I tear the piece of paper out of the notebook and fold it, laying it in the drawer with countless others.

Letters I have to write to cleanse my soul, but I'll never actually send.

I burrow beneath my bed covers and turn on the TV. I think some mindless reality TV is exactly what I need.

I eventually drift off to sleep and I'm awakened sometime later by the sound of voices. At first, I think it's the TV, but when I flick it off, I still hear the voices.

I quickly pick out Jace's voice, but there's another, and it's distinctly female.

My body tenses, and I freeze in place, all my sense on high alert.

I hear the girl giggle and he says something low.

I feel like my heart is about to fall out of my chest.

Betrayal coats my tongue like a sticky syrup. I have no right to feel that way, I know. Jace and I aren't together, and I've spent two weeks barely speaking to him, but he *knows* how I feel and that's what hurts the most.

How dare he know how I feel and bring a girl back here. I've lived with him since May, and not once, in all that time, has he brought a woman here. I figured he was going to their places. After all, his room is open to the whole apartment.

I close my eyes and count to ten.

Their voices are still there.

I can't stand it so I put the TV on and turn the volume up louder. No way in hell am I going to listen to the guy I like have sex with another girl.

I roll onto my side and squish my eyes closed, but I know sleep is never going to come now.

Not when I have a visual in my head playing out what I imagine is happening just outside my door.

It's going to be a long night.

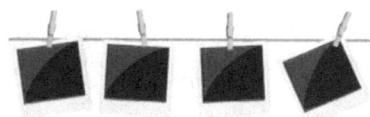

I peel my eyes open and find sunlight filtering into my room.

It's Saturday, which means no classes but I have to go into work at one.

At least I have most of the day to myself.

I sit up and last night's events come rearing to the surface of my mind.

I exhale a shaky breath, wishing the hurt I feel would leave as easily as the air in my lungs.

I tumble from my bed and putter around my room, busying myself as I avoid the inevitable.

I make my bed, I straighten the items on my desk, I rearrange my stack of school books.

When there's nothing left to do, I open my door into the apartment.

Jace is leaning against the counter, looking like a freaking Greek statue—ridiculously handsome and carved to perfection—a coffee cup dangles loosely from his fingertips and he wears a beanie. He looks adorably sleepy and put together all at the same time and I hate the fact that beneath my irritation I still feel attracted to him. My eyes roam over his bare chest —I can't fucking help it—drifting lower to where his sweatpants sit dangerously low, exposing the V of muscle that disappears into his pants.

"Where's the girl?" I ask, looking around.

He shrugs.

I roll my eyes and head into the bathroom when it becomes obvious that he's not going to answer. I can't blame him since I'm the one that's been giving him the silent treatment.

I use the bathroom and brush my teeth. When I come out, Jace is cooking breakfast.

I pour myself a cup of coffee and take a seat on one of the stools.

"I hope you had a nice night," I find myself saying. I don't know why I can't seem to shut up. I haven't really spoken to him in the last two weeks, just a muttered, "Hey" here and there.

Jace turns away from the stove and pads over to me, leaning across the stainless-steel counter. He's large and commanding, and I feel like all the oxygen has been sucked from the room.

"Two weeks," he begins. "Two weeks of nothing from you and then you think I fucked a girl and suddenly you'll speak to me again." He smirks that stupid fucking smirk that I hate to love. The one that quirks up on one corner and makes his green eyes shine. He bends down so he's closer to my height. "Confession ..." he pauses, licking his lips and he seems to be thinking over what he wants to say. "She didn't taste as good as you."

I feel a nail pierce my heart, hammered in by his words.

He winces. "Fuck," he breathes. "That didn't feel as good as I thought it would."

"What?" I snap, standing. "Hurting me hurts you? Newsflash, that's what happens when you care about someone." I storm around the counter toward him and he swivels to face me, towering above me. I can feel tears flooding my eyes and I dam them back. I've cried enough over him. We're not together, we never were, so it doesn't matter. It *shouldn't* matter.

"This is making me fucking crazy," he snaps suddenly, startling me. He rips off his beanie and tosses it away. "I don't know why I said that to you. It was a lie. I didn't go down on her and I didn't fuck her. I brought a girl back here to make you jealous. I wanted you to hear her, that's it. Nothing else happened."

My lower lip trembles. "I don't believe you."

He steps closer to me, lowering his head. "Yes, you do."

"Don't do that," I snap.

"Do what?" he asks with a knowing smile.

"Look at me with those *'I'm so cute you have to believe me'* eyes. It confuses me." I move a step back, trying to create enough space that I can think straight.

He moves another step forward, eating up the space I created only a moment before. There is no escaping him.

"The last two weeks have been hell," he says. "I don't like not talking to you. I don't like not being with you. I've barely even seen you." His hand finds my waist and my lips part with a breath at the touch. His lips find my neck. "I want you," he whispers.

My resolve is crumbling.

"You left," I protest weakly.

"I know," he murmurs. "Never again. Let me make it up to you. Let me make it right."

I feel like I'm at war with my own mind and body.

I want him, but the desire to protect my heart is strong.

But my heart is already hurting so is giving him a chance really such a bad thing?

"What does this mean?" I ask him. "What are we?" I don't mean to put a label on it, but I need to know if this is just sex or something more.

"I don't know," he confesses. "I've never been someone's boyfriend before. I don't know if I can do that. But I do know that I'm tired of trying to fight this. I'm tired of denying that I feel more for you than just friendship. I've never wanted anyone more than I want you."

I swallow thickly. Fear chokes me.

"Give me a chance," he pleads. "I know I screw up at every turn, but I also know that I care about you and you care about me, and that means something, right?"

I stare into his eyes, and there's no denying the complete honesty in his words. He's breaking down every wall I've built around my heart—not just in the last two weeks, but in the last two years as well.

When you've loved someone and it's ended in devastation, it makes you weary and less willing to take risks with your heart.

But some things are unavoidable.

Jace is like a car speeding down the road headed straight for me and I can't move out of the way fast enough. I don't know if I want to move. Maybe I just want to end it all—or maybe it's not the end, and the beginning instead.

"I don't know if I want to be your girlfriend," I tell him, because I feel like he needs to know that. "But if we do this we have to be exclusive."

He cups my cheeks in both hands, smoothing his thumbs over my freckles. "I'm yours," he whispers, his eyes flaring, and I believe him.

Before I can blink, his mouth is on mine and he's kissing me like his life depends on it.

I don't know how we went from the silent treatment to this, but I don't care to stop and figure it out.

He groans, and I revel in that sound, that I make him lose his mind the way he's been making me lose mine for months.

He picks me up easily and my legs wind around his waist. A moment later my butt rests on the counter and he stands in-between my legs.

He kisses me like his life depends on it.

Fire builds inside me, and he matches it in intensity. His fingers glide down my waist, over my butt, and down to my thighs. I shiver as he moves back up, his fingers sliding beneath my shirt, teasing at the skin of my stomach. My breaths are rapid as he moves his lips down my neck and over the curves of my breasts peeking beneath my sleep shirt. His eyes flick up to mine, and I wonder if he can feel how fast my heart is beating.

An ache builds inside me, only one he can sate.

If I'm honest with myself, we've been tiptoeing around this a lot longer than the last few weeks.

Our chemistry has been sparking since the first time we met, but I wasn't interested in sex, and Jace needed a friend more than he needed a bed buddy. So, we found a happy medium. But our spark never dulled, and instead, as our friendship grew, so did it.

"I can't decide if I want to take my time with you or fuck you senseless," he murmurs, lips against my throat.

"Both," I plead, and I'm surprised by how broken and wanton I sound.

"I fucking love the sound of that." His hand is on my throat and he tilts my head back. I gladly let him.

As I lean back, he glides his hand from the space between my breasts down to my shorts. My breaths come in quick, short pants. I can't even be embarrassed.

He leans over my body, and I feel swallowed whole. I've never paid attention to the size difference before, but Jace is *tall*—over six foot—and I'm barely five-two. I feel tiny with him hovering over me. But I don't dislike the feeling like I thought I would.

His body is warm against mine and I glide my hands over the hard planes of his abs. His skin is hot, like the fire that rages below the surface of my skin is also beneath his.

He kisses me and then pulls back.

"Bed first, counter later," he says brokenly.

Before I can blink, he's pulling away from me so he's no longer stretched over me on the counter. He grabs me and picks me up again, and like before, my legs wind around his waist. He carries me over to his bed, still unmade since he just got up.

He sits down with me straddling his lap.

I gasp, surprised when I feel his hardness pressing against me.

"Don't be so shocked." His lips tip up. "I'm in a perpetual state of *turned on* any time you're around."

"That so?" I ask, rubbing my fingers of his smooth jaw.

He tips his head and then moves in to my neck, nuzzling against me.

"Confession," he begins, "I jacked off in that club's bathroom in Florida." Shock courses through my system. He pulls back slightly. "Does that bother you?"

"Were you thinking of me?" I ask, my core clenching at the thought of him hunched over in that club bathroom touching himself as he thought of me.

He nods once.

"Does it bother you if I think that's hot?" I counter.

"Why are you so fucking perfect?" he growls, taking my lips in his. It's a searing kiss, one I feel all the way to my toes.

I always thought that was a myth—feeling a kiss everywhere, but with Jace, I realize it's the complete truth. It's like all my senses are on high alert the moment his lips touch mine.

I rock against him, my nails digging into his shoulders.

I feel content and needy all at once, and it's a strange combination.

I was ready for this in Florida, and I think he was too but he was scared, but there is no fear now. Not for either of us.

My hands are on both sides of his face and I kiss him back with everything I have. I want him to feel how much I want this, how much I crave *him*, just the way he is. He's intense and controlling and desperate and I don't want him to hold back. I want it all because I'm the same way and I want to *finally* unleash that part of myself that he awakens. I spent too much of my life pretending to be a *good* and *sweet* but that's not the real me.

"Don't go easy," I whisper against his lips.

His hand fists in the back of my hair, pulling my head back. "Never."

I close my eyes, my body shaking with desire and we haven't even done anything yet.

He awakens something in me that's always been there, lying dormant, waiting for me to meet my match.

I don't know where we'll go from here, we're two broken people trying to piece ourselves together, but maybe with each other's help we can make something beautiful out of our messes.

Jace kisses me with a ferocious vigor, his lips bruising against mine. His hands find their way under my shirt, and he doesn't stop until he finds the undersides of my breasts. He makes this desperate groaning sound and I fucking own that. I love knowing I undo him the same way he undoes me.

I arch into him, my body unconsciously begging for more.

He curves his head against my neck, and I feel his lips press against the spot where my pulse races.

My fingers grasp at his hair and his hands cup my breasts fully. Nothing has ever felt this good before, not even that morning in the hotel. Something tells me if we keep this up it's only going to get better and better.

I roll my hips against his and air hisses between his teeth. His eyes are at half-mast and he looks like he's fighting to maintain his composure.

He moves suddenly and pins me to the bed with his large body.

I shake with excitement as I watch him with wide eyes, body coiled with anticipation.

He edges up my shirt, removing it slowly, but when my breasts come into view it's like he loses all that control he was trying so hard to hold on to.

He tears at my shirt and I'm forced to sit up and help him get it off before he rips it. It's like he's lost to his desire, a maniac, and I fucking love it.

Seeing him unravel before me is the most beautiful thing I've ever witnessed.

He moves down my body, his lips leaving an icy trail in their wake. I shiver, my toes curling and back bowing.

He presses his lips to the inside of my thigh and his lust-darkened eyes meet mine. The green depths brew with a storm of emotion. He looks like he wants to devour me, and I'll gladly let him.

My breath quickens and his hands glide up my stomach, his fingers pressing into my skin with enough pressure to bruise.

I swallow past the lump in my throat—the lump that I'm sure is my heart as it frantically tries to escape the confines of my chest.

His eyes leave a searing trail on my body as he stares at me. It's like he sees right through me, straight to the bone.

I bite my lip as he grabs at my sleep shorts.

I shake my head and use my foot to shove against his chest.

He grins as he towers above me. My hair is splattered around my shoulders and I try not to think about the fact that my top half is completely naked. I want to be confident in my boldness.

"You first," I say, and I'm surprised by how clear and confident my voice sounds. The last time I was left completely naked and emotionally raw. No way am I going to be the first one to get naked this time.

Jace's lips tip up in a smirk and I wonder what I've gotten myself into.

He spreads his arms out at his sides. "Undress me, then."

"Wh-What?" I stutter, staring up at him.

"You heard me." He bends so he's now hover over me, bracing his weight on each of his hands pressed to the bed beside me. He ducks his head, bringing his lips to my ear. "Take what you want, Nova."

I shiver. He eases back and stands before me again.

I sit up slowly, my hair falling forward to hide my breasts.

Fear clogs my arteries and my whole body freezes.

Take what you want. His words echo through my skull like a ball in a pinball machine.

Taking what I want has never come easy for me, and it's always come with consequences. But I'm an adult now, and I don't see what consequence I could possibly have to worry about in this scenario, other than a broken heart, and seeing as mine's already been broken beyond repair I can strike that off my list.

Jace's lips part as he watches me, his eyes hooded.

He's incredibly sexy. I've always known it. It's more than his looks too—even though he's hardly lacking there with sculpted cheekbones and full lips and those *fuck-me* eyes—there's just something about him that draws you in even when he's pushing you away. He's enigmatic and entirely beautiful.

"You're staring." His deep voice breaks through my thoughts.

"I'm taking what I want," I throw his words back at him, "and right now, I want to look at you."

He fights a grin. "Like what you see?"

"Yes," I say breathlessly. My eyes run from the top of his sandy head, down his tattooed arm, over his muscular chest, and stop at the band of his sweatpants where the faintest hint of his black boxer-briefs peek out.

My breath catches.

There's no going back from this. I know I should stop this right here and right now, but I can't.

Take what you want.

I lick my lips and drop to my knees. A startled sound leaves his throat as I pull down his pants and underwear in one swoop.

I press my lips together, intimidated by the size of him.

I'm suddenly reminded of my extremely limited sexual encounters.

I've had sex plenty of times, but only with one guy, whereas Jace is known by everyone as having no shortage of women come to his bed. I begin to worry that I won't be good enough for him and the last thing I want is to be a sucky lay.

"What are you thinking?" he asks, his voice husky. His fingers curl into my hair and he tips my head back. My eyes flicker to his hard cock. "It won't bite," he says with a slight grin. "But I might." His teeth flash in the morning light pouring in from the window.

My tongue is lodged in my throat and speaking feels impossible. I don't even know what I'd say if I could speak.

I hear the ocean crashing against the sand, and I wonder where the sound is coming from since we don't live near the beach. I realize quickly that it's the blood rushing through my body. I've never been so scared or turned on in my life.

He grasps my chin. "You're scared," he comments. "Why?"

I shrug. "I don't know."

He stands in front of me, me still on my knees, and assesses the situation. "Do you want me to tell you what I want you do? Would that make you feel better?"

Would it? I don't know? I hate feeling so naïve. Normally,

I crave control, but in one of my most vulnerable moments all I want is to hand the reins over to him.

I nod.

He wets his lips with a swipe of his tongue and his Adam's apple bobs.

"Wrap your hand around the base of my cock," he instructs, and I do as he says. The muscles in his stomach jump at my touch and he breathes heavily. "Good," he praises. He reaches down and rubs his thumb over my bottom lip. "Now add your mouth, sweetheart."

I do as he says and wrap my mouth around the tip. It feels like it's been forever since I've given a blowjob. I was young and inexperienced then, and frankly, I didn't like it. I'm still inexperienced but I am a little older and I'm with someone else so I'm hoping that will make it better.

"Like that," he encourages when I take him deeper.

I shake with nerves, and I'm sure he notices but he doesn't comment on it, for which I'm thankful.

I take him as deep as I can and then I back away. I move up and down him, finding my rhythm and moving my hand as well. He moans, and I take that as a good sign. His fingers fist in my hair and he tugs lightly. Not enough for it to hurt but so that I know he's there.

Hearing the little sounds he makes spurns my own desire. My skin prickles with awareness, like my body is tuned into a new frequency and everything is so much sharper.

I swirl my tongue around the tip and he gasps, his hold on my hair tightening. I rake my nails down his thighs and he hisses between his teeth. Having Jace unravel in front of me might be the greatest thing I've ever witnessed.

He lets go of my hair suddenly and pushes me back.

I frown, worried I've done something wrong.

He pants, fighting to get enough air into his lungs. "Not you," he says, noticing my look. "I refuse to come in that pretty little mouth before I've had my fill of you."

Oh.

He lifts me easily onto the bed, and before he joins me, he removes my shorts and underwear.

"Condom," he mutters, reaching for the drawer.

I don't bother telling him I'm on birth control. I figure it's better to have all the bases covered than to be sorry later. He grabs the foil packet and tears the top off with his teeth.

I feel wild, like my blood is barely contained beneath the surface of my skin, just waiting to release.

He rolls the condom on and before I can blink he's over me. He grabs his cock and guides it inside me. He's not gentle about it, but he's not harsh, either. It's more like he's so impatient that he can't go slow. My body isn't used to the intrusion, though, and I flinch. It's been a while and Jace is large.

He stops and freezes. "You're not a virgin, are you?" He looks at me with horrified eyes. I don't know why guys are so fucking scared of virgins.

"No." I shake my head. "It's just been a while."

"Oh." He nods like this is answer enough for him.

He pushes in all the way, and I cry out. He covers my lips

with his in a bruising kiss. He pulls back, giving me a moment to breathe and adjust.

"Are you okay?" he asks.

I count to five, giving myself a moment to assess the situation. I nod.

He presses his hands to the insides of my thighs, spreading my legs, and he fucks me relentlessly. I've never truly been *fucked* before, and I realize now what I've been missing all this time. My body craves this. I need it as much as I need oxygen to breathe.

My nails dig into his back. I need something to hold onto before I float away into oblivion.

"You're so fucking beautiful," he growls, lips pressed to my collarbone. He kisses his way over my breasts, taking a nipple in his mouth.

A part of me can't believe this is happening while another is breathing a sigh of relief and saying, *finally*.

He raises and his hands glide down my sides to my hips where his fingers dig in with a bruising pressure. I gaze up at him in shock and awe.

"Let go," he tells me, and I know he's not talking about having an orgasm.

He's pleading with me to get out of my head and unleash myself.

"I'm scared."

He bends and kisses me. It's both soft and sweet and searing all at the same time.

"This is me," he whispers. "It's okay."

Heart beating wildly, I take his advice and let go. I push at his shoulder and he rolls to the bed so I'm straddling him.

"Sit up," I instruct. "I want to feel you everywhere."

He does as I say, his chest plastered to mine. I move my hips up and down, rolling them from side to side. My hair falls forward and he pushes it back, ducking his head so he can watch where we're joined. Watching him watch us turns me on unlike anything else.

My nails dig into his shoulders as I hold on, my hips continuing to rock. I can feel myself getting close and as much as I crave that high, I also never want this moment to end.

He takes my face in one hand, tilting my head back. He looks at the arch of my neck and then down to my breasts in front of him. "You're beautiful," he murmurs the words with so much emotion that I wonder if he actually meant to say them out loud.

I glance down, watching him fuck me, and then slowly raise my eyes up. I start low, at the base of his cock, over his belly button and abs, his chest, and finally my eyes connect with his once more.

And that's it.

I follow over the edge into oblivion.

Nothing else exists except him and me and pleasure.

I cry out, panting his name. My fingers rake down his back, and I know they're going to leave a mark. I'm selfishly pleased by that fact—that he'll have to bear a physical reminder of this moment. Even if he walks like the last time, I'll be carved into his skin.

Jace waits until my orgasm is over before flipping us again.

He fucks me into the bed like he's gone mad. My fingers grasp for something to hold onto and end up tangled in his hair, yanking on the short strands. I've never been so wild in bed and I know deep down that I haven't even hit the tip of the iceberg. I crave more and with Jace. He's my perfect match in every way.

"Fuck," he growls, his forehead damp with sweat. Mine is equally as damp. I didn't know sex could be such a work out. Apparently, I've been doing it wrong. He groans and bites his lip. His fingers dig into my hips and ass as he comes, and I find myself having another orgasm, riding on the waves of his.

We both breathe like we've run a marathon. Jace pulls out of me and steps away, disposing of the condom.

I feel like I'm floating on a cloud. I can barely keep my eyes open.

The bed dips and his warm body stretches beside mine.

I peel my eyes open to look at him. He brushes a strand of green hair from my eyes. He looks me over, as if he's making sure I'm not hurt. If I could find the words, I'd tell him I've never felt better.

"That was …" he pauses searching for the words. He settles on, "Wow."

I nod. I'm still lost, floating on that cloud. I don't want to come back down.

I gently stroke a finger over my stomach and shiver from the feather-light touch.

"Confession," he murmurs, his eyes dark with something I can't decipher. "That's the first time I've had sex since May."

May. I mouth the one word, doing the math in my head. That's four months ago when ...

"When I moved in?"

He nods, swallowing thickly. "I couldn't fuck someone else when the only person I wanted was you."

I close my eyes, fighting a wave of emotion I don't want him to see. "Jace ..."

"Don't say anything," he pleads, pressing a finger to my lips.

He gathers me in his arms and presses his lips to the top of my head.

I don't know what his confession actually means, and I'm scared to look to deep into it, but I think ... I think maybe this thing between is deeper than either of us wants to believe.

My only hope is that we don't drown in it.

twelve
...

jace

I DON'T KNOW what made me reveal that particular confession. I would've been better off keeping that tidbit of information to myself. It's too late to take the words back now, though.

I trail my finger down her bare arm and she shivers. Her lips are swollen from kisses and her brown eyes are wide with wonder.

Normally, I'd be out of here as fast as possible, or kicking her out. I'm not the kind of guy who snuggles and holds hands and talks about my feelings, but with Nova I simply want to hold her and be here.

She seems unsure, almost like she knows this isn't typical for me. But she's different. *We're* different. I might've left once, but I won't make the same mistake again. I don't know what this means for us, I don't know if it'll happen again, or even if she wants it to, but I do know I don't regret it and I wouldn't take it back for anything.

I trace my finger over her lips and she parts them. I slip my finger inside and she swirls her tongue around my finger. I find myself getting turned on again.

As much as I want to stay in bed all day and fuck her until she can't walk, real life awaits.

"We need to eat," I comment.

She laughs, her eyes dipping below my waist. "Really? Looks like you're ready for round two."

I groan. "Something tells me that with you I'm going to be hard until I die."

She laughs, her body shaking against me. She's always beautiful, but when she laughs it's like it turns a light on inside her and she's radiant.

"Food first," I tell her. Knowing Nova, she probably hasn't eaten properly in the last two weeks. The girl can't cook. I quickly learned that there would be no sharing of the food responsibilities between us. She made spaghetti one of the first nights after she moved in and it was like eating rubber. After that, I took over all the cooking duties. I don't mind. Cooking is one of the few things I'm good at and enjoy.

I kiss her one last time, because I can't help myself, and disentangle from her limbs.

I grab my sweatpants off the floor and pull them on sans underwear. I glance behind me and find Nova watching me. I wink and she blushes all the way from her chest to her cheeks.

I step down from the raised platform my bed rests on and head into the kitchen.

Half-cooked eggs sit congealed in the skillet.

I throw them away.

"Do you want any bacon?" I call to her. I look over and find her dressing. What a shame. I feel like there should be a rule where Nova's naked all the time. That'd be fantastic ... but I'd also never get anything done.

"Yeah," she says back, pulling her shirt over her head. "Black and crispy like my soul."

I laugh as I pull the bacon out of the refrigerator. "In other words, you want me to ruin it."

She heads over to me and hops up on the stainless-steel island. "We agree on most things, but the way we like our bacon is where we diverge. I can't eat it raw like you."

"Yeah, but you like it practically charred and burned."

She laughs, her legs swinging back and forth. "It's delicious like that. You're missing out."

I pretend to gag. While the bacon is frying, I pour us each a cup of coffee. She takes hers and uses the cup to hide her smile.

We've had breakfast together every morning since she moved in, except the last two weeks.

It was hell not talking to her, but I didn't know what else I could say to change her mind, and I decided giving her space was probably for the best.

Granted, space probably turned me into an even bigger idiot, which is why I brought that girl back here last night.

I *wanted* to make Nova jealous. I wanted her blood to

boil and for her to go off. I wanted any reaction, even a bad one, because after so much silence I couldn't take it any longer. But the moment that chick kissed me—fuck, I don't even remember her name—I knew I couldn't go through with it. I wasn't planning to anyway. I just wanted to make Nova jealous, but the chick didn't know that and she thought she was there to get laid. I'm surprised she didn't slap me when I kicked her out.

"Confession—" I'm full of them this morning, apparently "—I've never wanted to make anyone jealous before. Not like I wanted to make you jealous last night."

She sips her coffee and sets the cup on the counter by her side. I step into the space between her legs.

"Confession, I like that you wanted to make me jealous even if I wanted to pull that girl's hair last night. It took all my willpower to stay in my room."

I can't help it, I laugh—a laugh that comes deep from my stomach. When I sober, I say, "Picturing you yanking on a girl's hair is the funniest thing ever."

She shrugs. "That's what I wanted to do. She was probably some blond bimbo with fake extensions. Wasn't she?"

My lips quirk. "Maybe."

"So, you like blonds, huh?"

I shake my head. "I like *you*."

Surprise fills her eyes, like even after I fucked her senseless and confessed I haven't had sex since she moved in, she can't wrap her head around the fact that I like her. That I *want* her.

Do I love Nova? I don't fucking know. I've never been in

love before and my parents' relationship was rocky at the best of times so it's not like I have that to base something off of. All I know is this girl consumes me and makes me feel alive in a way I haven't in a long time.

Something begins to smoke, and I curse. "Fucking bacon." I totally forgot it was cooking.

I quickly grab the skillet and pull it off the stove.

Nova giggles and eyes the burnt pieces. "It's perfect."

I shake my head, smiling. "Yeah, I guess it is."

I dump the ruined bacon onto a plate—well, ruined by my opinion—and slide it across to Nova. I start some more for myself.

While it's cooking, I start on the scrambled eggs.

When the eggs are done, I slide some onto Nova's plate and the rest onto mine. I add my bacon and then carry our plates over to the small table. I know it's probably impractical to have both the island with barstools and a table, but I prefer the table.

Nova grabs our coffee cups and follows me over.

She sits across from me with a small smile gracing her lips like she finds this whole thing entirely amusing.

We've sat across from each other eating breakfast, lunch, or dinner numerous times, but suddenly it feels different.

Different isn't bad, though. I think different is actually pretty good.

We eat in silence, lost in our thoughts. Lyrics flit through my mind, and I itch to grab my notebook and write.

Music is a huge part of my life, but I don't have time for it like I used to. I naively thought I'd be discovered and become the next big thing, but that thought process has only led to heaps of disappointment. I don't know what I'll do with my music degree. Maybe I'll become a teacher or maybe I'll tend bars for the rest of my life. Either option pisses off my father, because his dream was for me to get into politics like him. Over the years, I've asked him about *my dreams* so many times that the words have become meaningless.

"I'm really hating the fact that I have to work today," Nova says, breaking into my thoughts.

I grin. "Because you want to stay here with me all day, right?"

She looks away and then back with a small nod. "Yeah."

"There will be time for that later," I tell her, a promising tone to my voice.

She bites her lip, wiggling in her seat, and I want nothing more than to fuck her on the table. I'm trying to be responsible, though. Take it slow. Well, slow for me.

"Are you working tonight?" she asks. What she's really asking is, *Are you going to be home late?*

I shake my head. "This is my off weekend, but I'm going by in the evening to play." I nod at my guitar even though she'll know what I mean anyway.

"What time?"

"Seven," I answer, picking up a piece of bacon.

"I get off at six. Do you mind if I go with you?"

"Of course not." She nods, tucking a piece of hair behind her ear. "The green is interesting," I tell her.

She wrinkles her nose. "Does that mean you hate it?"

"No, I like it," I assure her. "I just wasn't expecting it. What color are you going to do next?"

She shrugs. "I haven't decided yet."

"You should do rainbow."

She laughs and finishes her eggs. "I haven't done that one yet."

"What color has been your favorite?" I ask her.

"Passion purple," she responds, and I chuckle. We always have a laugh at the ridiculously colored names. Some are downright stupid. "What's your favorite?"

"The blue ... what was the name for that one?"

"Well, I called it Smurf blue but the bottle said Razzleberry."

"What's this one called?"

She plucks at a piece of her green colored hair. "Enchanted Forest."

"I think we could come up with better names," I comment, finishing my coffee.

"Probably. What would you call this one?" She points at her head.

I press my lips together, thinking. "Green Goblin."

She snorts. "Good one. Although, that's probably copyrighted."

"Fuck, well, I tried."

She smiles, and it makes me ridiculously happy to see her smile. There aren't a lot of people in the world that I care about their happiness, but she's probably number one. She doesn't smile or laugh enough. Sometimes a darkness creeps into her eyes, and I'll do anything to make it go away.

She finishes her breakfast and stands with her dirty dishes. "I'm going to go shower," she says.

Nova. Shower. Naked. Wet.

I'm so fucked.

"Mhmm, yeah," I mumble, trying to cover up the fact that an intense fantasy is playing out in my mind.

She heads into her room and grabs some clothes before she goes into the bathroom.

I force myself to finish my food and coffee, although I can taste neither at this point.

When I finish, I clean my plate and cup. My eyes stray over to my messy bed and I itch to bust into the bathroom, grab Nova, and have that second round.

A knock on the door disrupts my thoughts.

"What the fuck?" I mumble to myself. Nobody ever comes here unless it's food delivery, and we rarely do that—plus, we also just ate breakfast.

I cross the few feet to the door and look through the peephole.

Dammit.

"What are you doing here?" I ask as I open the door.

"Well, hello to you too, *Jacen*," Thea slurs, coming inside.

"Sorry," I mumble. "Hello."

"That's better." She smiles.

"Why are you here?" I ask. "You never come over."

She heads straight for the black leather couch and sits down, making herself at home. "As you know, Halloween is in a few weeks."

"Four," I answer. "It's in four weeks. That's a month, Thea."

She waves away my words. "We're having a Halloween party."

"We're?"

"Me and Xander—and by extension Rae and Cade since it's also their house. And I guess my mom's now too," she rambles. "Although she'll probably hang out in her room the whole time so—"

"Get to the point," I plead.

Thea inhales a lungful of air. "Halloween is my favorite holiday, thus making this party very important to me."

"Did you just use the word *thus* in a sentence?"

"Yes, yes, I did," she says. "Anyway, it's very important that you dress up—"

"Thea—"

"This is important to me," she interrupts. "I do not want you bowing out or half-assing it. Didn't you ever want to be a superhero growing up?"

"No," I answer honestly. "I always wanted to be the villain."

"Perfect. Be the Joker then. Nova can be Harley Quinn."

"Everyone is going to be the Joker and Harley Quinn."

She sighs. "Then come up with something on your own, but make it good."

"What are you and Xander going as?" I ask, thinking that might give me some idea for my own costume.

"No idea yet. It has to be amazing, though." She gets a faraway look in her eyes, no doubt imagining all the things she could be. "I want to make this a yearly tradition." I groan. "Don't be so whiny. It's going to be fun. You'll see." She rummages in her purse for a piece of gum and pops it in her mouth. "Is Nova here?"

"In the shower," I answer.

"Oh, well tell her I said hi."

She stands and her eyes drift over the messy bed and back to me.

"I haven't made my bed yet," I say in response to her look.

She looks me up and down and I realize how little clothes I'm wearing and that it's blatantly obvious I'm not wearing underwear.

"Mhmm, sure," she responds.

I know she doesn't believe but I'm thankful she doesn't delve further.

I walk her to the front door. "Bye," she calls.

"Bye, Thea."

I close the door behind her and breathe a sigh of relief. I think I've been holding that breath ever since she walked in.

A minute later the bathroom door opens and Nova pokes her head out, her body wrapped in a towel. "Was someone here?"

I scratch the back of my head. "Thea stopped by. Apparently, she's having a Halloween party and we have to go."

"Sounds fun," she says sarcastically before easing the door closed.

I grab my guitar and notebook and sit down on the couch, the lyrics from earlier resurfacing. I haven't felt like writing or playing since the trip to Florida, so the sudden urge feels nice. Any time I have a dry spell, I have the irrational fear that I'm never going to write a song again.

Nova comes out of the bathroom dressed in a pair of black skinny jeans with tears in the knees and a loose gray top over a lacy bra thing.

I close my eyes, trying to center myself and maintain control.

She makes it impossible to keep my cool.

"I'm going to work on homework," she says, and disappears into her room.

It's almost as if she too senses that we need space right now. If I'm too close to her then we might combust again and there's no chance I'd let her leave until we've fucked on every available surface.

There will be plenty of time for that tomorrow when neither of us have to work.

I grin, thinking of all the things I want to do to her tonight and tomorrow.

It's going to be fun.

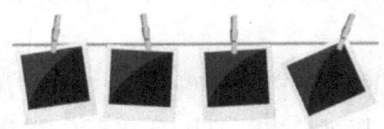

nova

I organize the stack of records while my mind is on repeat of this morning's actions.

I had sex with Jace.

I'm in a state of disbelief that it actually happened. A part of me is convinced that it was a very vivid dream.

Twenty-four hours ago, I was still mad and ignoring him, and now?

Now I don't know how I feel.

The anger is gone, but in its place is lust and confusion. I'm not naïve enough to believe that because we had sex it means we're going to ride off into the sunset and everything is going to be smooth sailing. I know that, realistically, it's only going to get more complicated. I can't bring myself to care about that, though. I'm too happy, and I refuse to dampen my good mood by dwelling on it. I figure we'll take it day by day and see where it goes from there. Does that make us friends with benefits? I don't know. Maybe. But I'd rather not put a label on it.

"You've been going through that stack for thirty minutes. Is everything okay?" my boss, Brenda, asks as she breezes into the main room from the back.

Brenda is an older lady, in her sixties, with wild curly gray hair and kind brown eyes. She's always dressed in a long skirt and breezy top with boots. A row of bracelets clang on every wrist, jingling every time she moves. She and her husband, Paul, own the record store. He's currently giving music lessons in the building they own next door.

"I'm sorry. Just lost in thought," I explain.

She gives me a perplexed look. "You're not normally spacey. Is something happening?"

I shake my head. "Strange morning."

She assesses me and then nods. "After you finish with that I need your help in the back. I'm old and not strong enough to lift these heavy boxes onto the shelves."

I laugh. "You're not old, Brenda."

She snorts. "You won't be saying that when you're my age."

She breezes away, leaving a waft of flowery smelling perfume in her wake.

I finish organizing and head in the back to help her. It doesn't take me long to stack the boxes on shelves and then I'm back out front.

A few customers come in, but it's a relatively quiet day, which turns out to be a good thing since I'm having trouble functioning.

The place is small so there isn't much to do except tend to customers and keep it tidy.

Sometimes teenagers from the local high school a few blocks over come over after school on the week days, and while some of them are nice, most of them are little assholes and only like to wreak havoc.

"Why don't you go on home?" Brenda suggests. "It's dead today and Paul and I want to close early."

"Are you sure? I'm happy to stay."

"Positive." She smiles, patting me on the arm.

I head to the back and grab my bag and coat. On my way back out, I wave at Brenda.

Outside, it's grown chilly in the early October air.

The chill reminds me of Thea stopping by and the impending Halloween party. I like Halloween, but parties aren't my thing, however I know I need to make more of an effort to do things with my friends. Ever since I moved in with Jace, it's become even easier to ignore them and that's not good. I'm lucky to have them in my life when otherwise I'd have no one.

It doesn't take me long to make the walk back to the apartment. Once inside the building I'm thankful for the heat and I know that colder weather is on the way. I guess this is what I get for being a Texas girl in Colorado. Even though I still haven't quite adjusted to the difference in weather, I've still decided Colorado is my favorite place in the world. It's beautiful here. Lush green trees, and snowcapped mountains, it's amazing. Sometimes I feel like I'm on an alien planet compared to the drabness of Texas. I suppose Texas isn't that bad to other people, but that place will forever be tainted by sour memories.

I take the elevator up to our floor and head down the hall.

It's quiet inside, and I wonder if Jace is even here. I saw his truck outside, but there are plenty of places he can walk.

I close the door behind me and look around. Jace's guitar leans against the couch and his notebook rests on the table.

Before I can start toward it, I hear a noise and look up.

I smile as I spot him through the open window, sitting

on the fire escape smoking a cigarette. His hair is a mess, like he's run his fingers through it a million times.

"Hey," I call and his head swivels to me.

"You're home early," he remarks, inhaling a drag of his cigarette.

I make my way to him and climb through the open window, sitting beside him on the metal grate. Below us traffic is stopped at the stoplight in front of our building.

"Yeah, Brenda told me I'd come home since it wasn't busy. How'd the song writing go?" I nod to inside the apartment at his abandoned guitar.

"Good." He grins and for a moment he looks almost boyish. "I finished one."

"Are you playing it tonight? I want to hear it."

His eyes grow clouded and he looks away. "I don't know, maybe. It's still so new. I like to work out the kinks first, but I like it, so who knows."

I lean my back against the brick and stretch my legs out, wiggling my black-combat-boot-covered feet.

The sky is cloudy, with the barest hint of the sun peeking through.

Jace extinguishes his cigarette and we sit in silence for a bit.

"It's cold," he says a few minutes later. "We should go inside."

I nod in agreement. The last thing I need is to get sick.

I climb through the window first and he follows, closing it behind us.

"Have you thought about your costume?" I ask him.

He makes a face. "No."

"You better figure it out," I tell him as I take off my coat. "All the good costumes will be gone."

"What do you think I should be?" he asks, taking a seat on the couch. I sit beside him, tucking my feet under me.

"I don't know." I think for a moment. "What about Batman?"

He rolls his eyes, stifling a groan. "No. Everybody is Batman, or Superman, or something with *man* in it."

I laugh, shaking my head. "Okay, so no to all of those."

"Have you decided what you're going as?" he asks.

"I have a few ideas."

"Tell me," he pleads.

"No." I shake my head. "I want it to be a surprise."

"Is it sexy? Please tell me it's sexy." He gives me puppy dog eyes, his bottom lip curling under.

"I'm not saying a word." I mime zipping my lips and throwing away the key.

He pounces on me, and I end up with my back flat against the couch with him over top of me. "I have ways of making you talk."

"Oh, you do, huh?"

He nods and brushes his nose against mine before pressing his lips to mine. A little moan escapes my throat, and I curse myself for being so affected by him. It's ridiculous, really, that one person can turn me to mush.

He parts my lips with his tongue, and I moan again, my fingers grasping at the fabric of his shirt.

I'm suddenly reminded of the feel of his body moving

against mine this morning, and I tear desperately at his shirt, trying to get it up and over his head. He pulls away with a laugh, grabbing my hands and pinning them at my sides.

"Nice try. Now tell me."

My brows furrow in confusion. "Tell you what?"

He laughs deep from his belly. "Am I that good of a kisser?" When I still look confused, he adds, "Apparently, I am." He lowers his head once more. "Tell me your costume ideas."

Oh. That. "No," I say, my voice embarrassingly breathless.

He kisses my neck. "Please?"

"No."

He sticks his finger in the neck of my shirt and pulls it down, kissing the tops of my breasts.

"Please?"

I close my eyes, centering myself. "No."

He moves down my body and pushes my shirt up my stomach. His soft lips press tenderly to my stomach just above the band of my jeans. "Please?"

"Jace." I squirm, trying to get away as he unfastens the button of my jeans and eases the zipper down. I can't even remember what game we're playing, but I do know I'm about to lose.

He slides my jeans down my legs and presses a kiss to the inside of each of my thighs. I whimper, trying to get away.

"Please."

"Would you believe me if I said I can't remember?"

He chuckles. "I *might* give you a pass."

"I'll tell you later, when I can form a coherent thought," I pant as his hand skates past the band of my underwear. I gasp as he presses a finger inside me. "Oh, God." My whole body clenches. "Jace," I breathe his name, struggling to keep my eyes open.

He pulls his hand away and rids me of the rest of my jeans, tossing them on the floor, and then slides my underwear down and off too.

He spreads my legs and looks at me like I'm a feast laid out before him.

He kisses his way down my thigh before he heads to where I want him the most.

"Oh, Jace," I cry out, one hand grabbing at the couch to hold on and the other tugging on his hair.

Pleasure zings through my body, and I can barely maintain reality.

His tongue swirls against my clit and I cry out, my back bowing above the couch. He presses his hand to my stomach, forcing me back down.

He blows his hot breath against me and I whimper.

He slips a finger inside me, then two, and curls them up.

"Oh, my God," I moan, biting my lip so hard that I taste blood.

"I love your pussy," he murmurs before licking me again.

Color explodes behind my closed eyelids.

"Give it to me," he pleads.

"Jace," I pant. "Fuck. I'm ... I'm ..." I cry out as the orgasm hits me, powerful enough that my legs shake and tears prick my eyes. I don't think I've ever come so fast in my life. I'm convinced Jace's fingers and tongue are magic.

He pulls his fingers from my body and kisses my stomach again where my shirt is still raised.

Then he kisses my collarbone and finally my lips. I moan, tasting myself on his tongue. I thought I'd be grossed out by something like that, but instead I find that I'm incredibly turned on.

I move to straddle him, and he pushes me back down on the couch, shaking his head.

"We have to go."

I glance at the clock on the table beside the couch and curse. We have thirty minutes to get to the bar and I need to clean up and change.

I nod and he releases me. He gets off the couch and heads to the bathroom.

I take a moment to catch my breath before I stand and head to my room.

I don't even bother fixing my jeans since I'm going to change.

I close my bedroom door, but I guess that's pointless now. Jace has seen me naked plenty of times.

I rifle through my dresser for a pair of shiny black skinny jeans. I pair it with a lacy black bralette and loose tank top. Then on top of that I wear an asymmetrical leather jacket to protect against the cold night air.

I brush my hair and braid it all on one side so it drapes over my shoulder.

"Shoes," I mutter to myself, crouching down to rifle through the bottom of my closet.

I settle on a pair of black flats, figuring that's nicer than my usual boots.

When I open my door, I find Jace stepping down from his room. He wears his usual ripped jeans, and a black t-shirt, paired with his heavy boots. His sandy hair is brushed away from his face and it makes him look older.

"Ready?" he asks, tucking his shirt into his jeans and adjusting his belt.

I nod and he grabs his black pea coat off the back of one of the kitchen chairs.

He holds the door open for me and lets me step out into the hall first. We walk down the hall silently together, and I push the button for the elevator. I startle when I feel Jace's hand pressed to the small of my back. Maybe I shouldn't be surprised he's touching me, but I am. Jace doesn't show much affection for anyone. I know he cares about his friends, me included, but his *care* is usually in his words, not his actions.

The elevator opens and we step on.

I expect his hand to fall away, and when it doesn't, I smile and move a little closer to him. The smell of his cologne wafts over me which nearly makes me moan. It's a mix of mahogany, bourbon, amber, and something else that's entirely Jace.

I itch to hold his hand, but I remind myself that he's not my boyfriend and that whatever this is with us is so completely new and it's best not to rock the boat.

The doors open and he guides me into the lobby and onto the street.

"Do you want to take the truck?" he asks.

I breathe out and smile when my breath fogs the air. "No." I shake my head. "Let's walk. It's not that far and the night is beautiful."

Even though it's not that late it's already been dark for a few hours. The stars shimmer above us with a few clouds floating along. If I squint I can just make out the shape of the mountains in the distance in between the tall buildings.

Jace nods, shoving his hands in his coat pockets.

"What's your favorite time of year?" I ask him. "Favorite season, I mean."

He shrugs and a wrinkle creases his brow as if it's a question he really has to think about his answer to. "Now—fall. I like the colors of the leaves and the cold air. What about you?"

"Same," I tell him honestly. "There's something magical about fall. The leaves are dying, but they're beautiful in their demise. I want to be like that."

"Beautiful when you die?" He chuckles.

I shake my head with a wistful smile. "No, I want to be graceful even when everything is falling apart. I want to be strong enough to not crumble when things get rough."

I startle when I feel his pinky loop through mine. I glance down at our joined fingers and then to his eyes. It's not hand holding, but it's something.

"Why do I have a feeling that's already true about you?"

I look away, emotion clogging my chest. There's so much about myself I haven't shared with Jace—or any of my friends. I've tried so hard to bury that girl I was, but the fact is she's *right here*. She's me. No matter how many times I deny that, pretend I'm a whole new person now, it's not true.

"You have no idea how truly extraordinary you are," he murmurs.

When I lift my gaze to his, I find him looking at me tenderly. That look makes my stomach dip with happiness.

We stop at a crosswalk, waiting for our turn to go, and he gently brushes his fingers over my cheek. I shiver and he smiles.

He continues with, "I see you. I always have."

I think I stop breathing. In fact, I know I do because little spots begin to dance behind my eyes.

Before I can respond it's our turn to walk and we cross the street.

I see you. I always have.

I know he's telling the truth, because I can say the same for him.

There are some people who you just *click* with. It's almost like déjà vu. You feel like you know them even if you've never met them before.

We finally reach W.T.F. and he opens the door, letting me in first.

The place is packed and we push our way through to the bar.

I spot an empty barstool and snag it while Jace heads over to the stage area and says something to the person in charge, letting them know he wants to sing.

The person nods and writes something on their clipboard before Jace makes his way over to me. There's not a free stool anywhere, so he stands behind me.

"Matilda isn't working," he whispers in my ear, as if he's worried that *I'm* worried about her. I hadn't thought about her once, but I do know she has a pissy attitude when it comes to Jace. I used to think it was because they had sex, but I asked him once and he was insistent that they never slept together but she's mad because she wants to and he turned her down. "Do you want a drink?" he asks.

"Yeah." I nod.

He leans around me, onto the bar, and motions for the bartender.

"Hey, Lance," he greets the bartender. "The usual for us."

"Sure." Lance smiles and goes to mix our drinks. A chair opens up beside me, and Jace snags it. We're so close together that his knee brushes mine.

Lance slides our drinks in front of us and Jace tips his chin at him. "Thanks, man." He walks off and Jace lifts his drink to his lips. Setting it down, he asks, "Do you want something to eat? Are you hungry?"

"I'll order something in a bit." I need to eat dinner, but I'm not quite hungry.

He nods and swivels in the barstool so he's facing the stage. I do the same. A girl is currently playing the piano and singing a slowed down version of a song I've been hearing a lot on the radio.

"Did you tell Cade, Rae, and Thea you were playing tonight? You know they'd love to come."

He shrugs. "Didn't think about it."

He drums his hands against his seat like it's no big deal.

"We're so bad at including them in things," I mutter.

He chuckles and removes his coat, draping it over the back of his chair. "Yeah, we are," he agrees. "Sometimes they get to be a bit much. Don't get me wrong, I love them, but …"

"But what?" I prompt when he trails off.

He shrugs. "It's easier with you."

It should probably worry me with how much my heart soars at his words.

Clipboard guy motions for Jace and he stands.

"Wish me luck." He flashes me a smile and then he's gone.

He makes his way through the diners and to the stage. There's a guitar and he grabs it before sitting on the stool in the middle of the stage.

He looks at home up there, like there's no other place he belongs.

He closes his eyes and takes a deep breath, like he needs a moment to center himself, and then he pulls a pick from his pocket and begins strumming.

He wets his tongue and opens his mouth. Like always, I'm immediately taken aback by the sound of his voice. It's soft, and husky sounding, utterly and completely perfect. His voice cracks on some words, like he's barely keeping a tap on his emotions.

The words of the song pour of over me, and I realize with a startling clarity that this song is about me.

My lips part in surprise, and I pay careful attention to each and every word, trying to decipher his meaning.

"She thinks she's got it all figured out, but she's putting on that damn mask again. Oh, she's a Supernova, Supernova, she's a Supernova, Supernova. It's what she is."

My heart beats faster.

"And I watch as she changes her hair, trying to hide from herself. Oh, little does she know, I'm running from myself too."

And faster.

"And I can see her hiding from the world. And I know she's got some pain, that I can't take way, take away."

My throat closes up and tears pool in my eyes. I don't know whether they're tears of sadness, or happiness, or a mix of both.

He sings the song softly, giving it a melancholy edge, and my lower lip trembles because it's beautiful, heartbreaking, and absolutely amazing.

I feel touched, but also scared, because he's noticed so much more about me than I give him credit for. He sees straight through me, to the parts I hide from everyone.

Like the hair.

He noticed that I dye my hair, because I'm trying to hide from who I really am.

Most people look at Jace and see your stereotypical, tattooed, bad boy. But he's more. So much more.

He finishes the song, and as the last note hangs in the air, his eyes meet mine.

I burst into tears while the patrons clap.

The restaurant suddenly feels too small, too stifling, and I abandon my drink and chair, rushing through the building and outside.

I burst through the heavy wooden doors onto the street.

I inhale big breaths of the cold air, hoping it'll soothe me, but I'm far too worked up. I bend, pressing my hands to my knees while his words swirl through my mind.

The streetlight flickers above me, and I move away from it, walking down the street.

The door to the restaurant flies open and I look back. Jace stands there, his coat hanging on his arm, and his hair now falling into his eyes.

"Nova," he calls to me, but I keep walking. "Nova!" His feet thud after me and a moment later his large hand wraps around my arm and he turns me around. "Nova," he says my name again, softly this time, almost tender sounding. "You're crying?" He frames it as a question even though it's very obvious that I am, indeed, crying.

I nod anyway, wiping at the stupid wetness clinging to my cheeks. "That song ..." My voice is thick, clogged with tears. "You wrote it about me."

"That's one." I raise a brow at this and he adds, "I've written a lot of songs about you."

"You have?" My voice squeaks with surprise.

He smiles, just a slight tilt of his lips like he feels shy over this fact. "I find that you're very inspiring."

My brows furrow. "Like your muse?"

He nods and slips his arms into his coat. He shivers, and I realize it's grown even colder as the evening progressed. I didn't even notice the temperature at first, my skin was so heated from being in the restaurant.

"Yeah, exactly like that," he adds. Softly, he says, "I didn't think it would make you cry."

I count, breathe out, and force a smile. "It was beautiful but it ..."

"It what?" he prompts when I flounder for words.

I shake my head. "I've never had someone see so much of me before. Things that I don't even voice. You notice it all."

He shrugs and clears his throat. "It's easy to notice something when it's like looking in a mirror."

I swallow thickly. "We're really fucked up, aren't we?"

He chuckles, and for some reason, that makes me laugh too. "Yeah, I guess we are. At least we have each other."

I inhale a deep breath and blow it out. "I still feel a bit freaked out," I admit with a sheepish smile.

He smiles sadly. "I probably shouldn't have sprung that on you like that. I'm sorry."

I press my lips together and rock back on my heels. "Will you play it for me when we go home?"

"Are you sure?" He raises a brow.

I nod. "I want to hear it all. I ran out before you finished."

He glances back in the direction of the restaurant and then to me. "Should we head home, then?"

I nod, shivering in the cold despite my coat. We start back toward the apartment and Jace pulls his cigarette pack from his pocket. He taps one out and cups his hands around the tip as he lights it. He inhales a long drag and blows it out, watching the smoke swirl through the air before it disappears.

"Confession, I don't even like these things."

"What?" I ask, my voice spiking with confusion.

"These." He holds out the cigarette and flicks the ash from the end.

My brows furrow. "If you don't like them then why do you smoke?"

He smiles sardonically. "To piss off my dad."

"Seems like a legit reason," I say dryly.

He shrugs and takes another drag of the cigarette. The tips flares brighter for a moment.

"My life is pretty much one big fuck you to my old man," Jace continues. I struggle to keep up with his long-legged stride as we cross the street, nearing the apartment.

"How so?" I question.

We don't talk about our home lives, though I've gotten the impression his isn't any better than mine, so the fact that he's being so open surprises me. I'm dying to know more about him and that part of his life, so while he's speaking, I want to get all the information I can.

He wets his lips, tilting his head toward the sky like the twinkling stars above hold all his answers. "He wanted me to follow in his footsteps and I refused." It's a vague answer, but it's more than he usually gives me, so I'll take it. "What about your parents?" he asks. "Did you stray from their grand plan?"

I snort. "I strayed *a lot*." I shove my hands in the pockets of my coat, wishing I'd worn gloves or something. It might be early October, but it's *cold*. "My parents are very ..." I pause, searching for the right word. "Structured," I finish. "They like things a certain way. The normal way. The right way," I ramble. "Right in their eyes," I add.

"I take it they wouldn't approve of green hair?" He fights a smile.

I shake my head. "They'd definitely not approve of that. If my mom saw me with hair this color she'd march me back into the bathroom and rip out every individual strand of hair until I was bald."

Jace looks at me sadly. "She sounds delightful."

I sigh. "My parents aren't good people, but they aren't bad, either, if that makes sense. I don't feel much love when it comes to them, too much has happened, but I know they've always done what they *think* is right. I tend to disagree and think it's the wrong thing."

"I think it's only natural to disagree with your parents, but it's especially easy to do when they're an asshole about everything."

"So, if your dad wanted you to follow in his footsteps, what was that exactly?" I ask, hoping to learn more.

He shakes his head. "I'm done talking about my dad."

And shot down.

I nod. "Fair enough."

We reach the building and he holds the door open for me.

The warmth floods over me and I rub my hands together. If it's this cold already I don't know how I'll survive the winter.

Jace and I head to the elevator and then up to the apartment.

Once inside, we take our coats off and Jace heads straight for his guitar.

"Do you want some hot chocolate?" I ask while he sits on the couch, the guitar resting in his lap.

He nods. "That sounds great."

I'm happy to have something to do so I get busy making the hot chocolate and pulling the marshmallows from the cabinet. Jace tunes his guitar while I do that, sitting on the couch looking way too hot for his own good.

"How many songs have you written about me?" I ask.

He presses his lips together, a telltale sign that he's thinking. "Five."

My jaw drops. "Five?"

"Yeah, there would be more but I haven't finished them."

I think I might pass out. "Do you write a lot of songs about girls?"

He smirks. "Jealous?"

"No." I snort. "Just curious."

He shakes his head. "No, you're the only one."

And there goes my heart pitter-pattering.

I pour our hot chocolate into mugs, add whipped cream, and sprinkle the mini marshmallows on top. I carry the mugs over to the couch and sit down beside him, tucking my legs under me.

He takes his mug and sets it on the table beside the couch. He strums the guitar once and the note hangs in the air.

"The song I played tonight is called 'Supernova'."

"'Supernova'," I repeat. "I love that."

"Good." He grins back. "Now be quiet and listen."

I laugh and wiggle around, getting comfortable.

He closes his eyes and begins to play.

Again, just like in the restaurant, time seems to stand still. All the air is sucked from the room, and I feel the emotion of the song so deeply it hits me straight in my soul.

"I can see her sadness in the dark, and I can hear her demons calling my name.

I can hear her cries from miles away, and I can see her frown when no one is watching." He opens his eyes and his gaze lights a fire inside me. I feel like I'm burning from the inside out. *"She thinks she's got it all figured out, but she's putting on that damn mask again. Oh, she's a Supernova, Supernova, she's a Supernova, Supernova. It's what she is."*

He tilts his head back, strumming the guitar strings and feeling the song.

"And I watch as she changes her hair, trying to hide from herself. Oh, little does she know, I'm running from myself too."

That line hits me like a ton of bricks. It doesn't seem real that he's noticed that about me. For a long time, I didn't even understand my desire to change my hair color.

"And I can see her hiding from the world. And I know she's got some pain, that I can't take way, take away. She's trying to tell me she's got it all figured out. But I know, oh I know, that no Supernova does. And I watch as she changes her hair. And I watch as she slips a word, that says she's not okay. Beautiful, she's a Supernova, Supernova, Supernova. It's what she is."

He leans his guitar against the coffee table and reaches for me, swiping his large thumbs over my cheeks. "Don't cry," he pleads. "I don't want to make you sad."

"I don't know if sad is exactly what I'm feeling at the moment," I admit, wishing I wasn't crying. I feel pathetic and stupid with my cheeks drenched in wetness. "It was beautiful. Amazing. I think I'm most blown away by how much of me you see. Things I don't mean for you to know."

He shrugs like it's no big deal.

I move closer to him and he reaches for me, pulling me against him. We end up lying on the couch, with me on top of his chest.

I lay with my ear against his heart and the steady *thump-thump-thumping* soothes my frazzled nerves. My tears seep into his shirt but he doesn't say anything. He rubs a hand soothingly against my back, his fingers creeping under my shirt.

I close my eyes, exhaling a shaky breath.

It's in this moment that I realize I'm dangerously close to falling in love with Jace and that terrifies me. Love has only ended in disaster and heartbreak of the worst kind for me. It's a pain I'm not sure I can survive again.

But I'm helpless to stop this feeling, and I must hope that if I fall, I learn to fly.

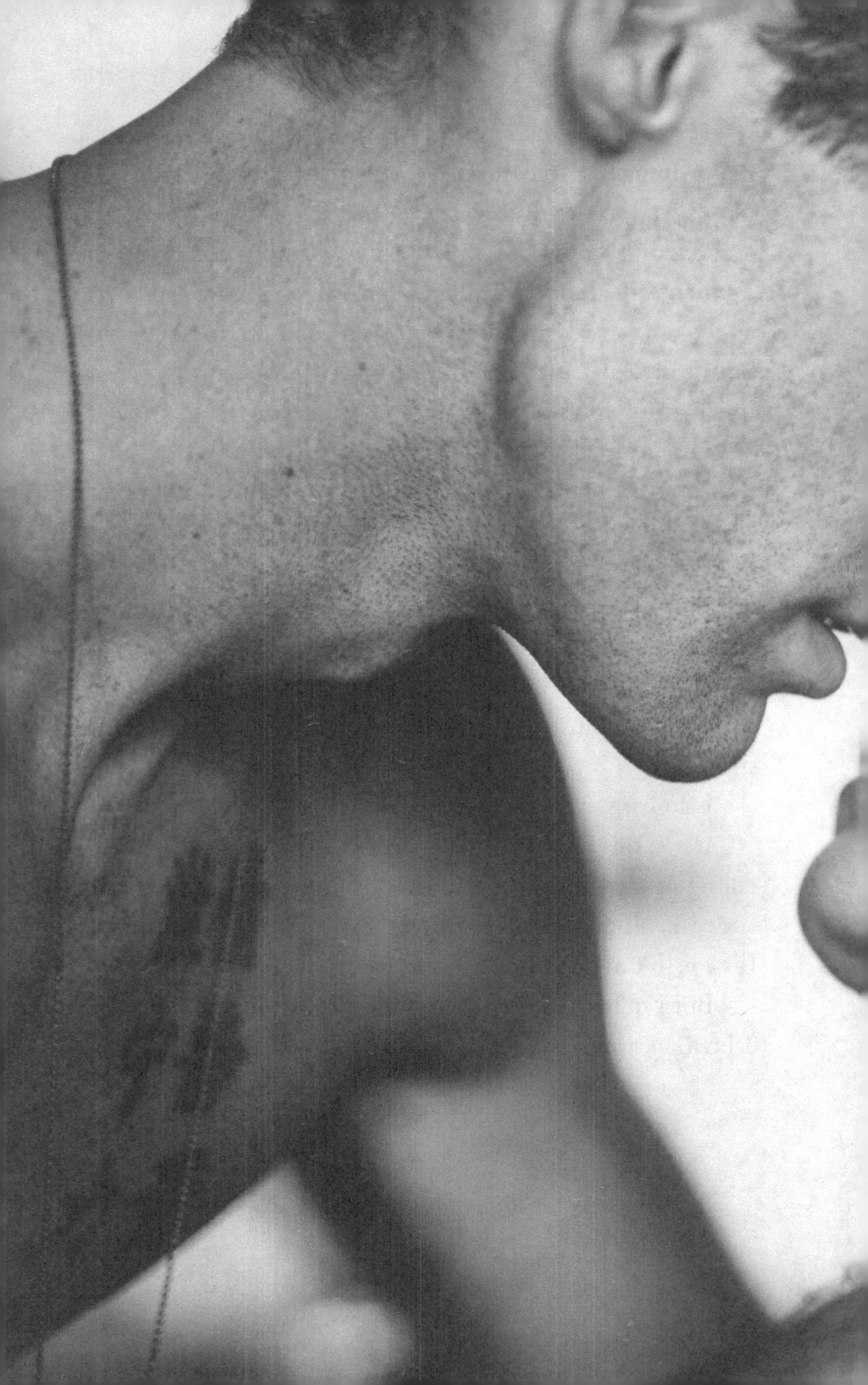

thirteen
. . .

nova

"YOU SEEM HAPPIER THAN NORMAL."

I glance over at Joel beside me. We're supposed to be working on an assignment focused on macro photography. The item I'm supposed to be photographing is droplets of water on a flower. Beside me, Joel is focused on a bug in a neighboring flower. The group projects our professor warned us about have already descended upon us. So far, working with him hasn't been too bad. After all, it was his suggestion to come here—to an indoor garden—to work on the macro photography project. It was a great idea. There are a ton of bugs and other little things to take pictures of.

"I wouldn't say I'm happier than normal," I hedge, though he's exactly right.

It's been over a week since Jace and I had sex, and it's safe to say it's been one of the best weeks of my life. It makes me sound lovesick, and maybe I am, but it's more than that. I've never felt so content in my whole life, like I'm finally doing and being who I'm meant to be.

Last year I was simply going through the motions, now I'm living my life and it feels amazing.

He chuckles and snaps a photo, the shutter of his camera clicking. "You're lying. Who's the guy?"

I snort, taken aback. "Why does there have to be a guy?"

"A girl then?" He raises a brow, waiting for my response.

"God no." I shake my head. "Not that there's anything wrong with that, but I'm not—"

He laughs, putting me out of my misery. "It's okay, Nova." He lines up his camera and takes another picture. "I understand why you shot me down so vehemently, though. There was someone else. It makes me feel better. I was thinking I was losing my touch." He lowers his camera, flashing me a boyish grin.

"There's no one else," I mutter.

"And I'm Jack Dawson."

"Who's that?" I ask, confused.

He stares at me like I've grown another head. "Have you never seen *Titanic*? I thought it was like rite of passage for teenage girls or something? Don't you all have a hard-on for Leonardo DiCaprio in that movie? That's who he plays—Jack Dawson," Joel rambles as he explains.

"My parents never let me watch that movie, and I haven't bothered since I've been away from them to try."

Joel blinks at me, his mouth openly agape. "That's it,

when we finish here, we're going back to my dorm and watching *Titanic*."

"I'm not going to your dorm to watch *Titanic*," I scoff.

"Fine, your dorm then," he concedes.

"I live in an apartment off campus," I snap.

"Even better." He grins, completely oblivious to my disdain for this idea.

"You're insane," I grumble.

"Come on," he starts. "You have to watch it."

"What do you get out of this?" I ask.

"Well ..." He smiles slowly, and I notice for the first time that he has a small dimple by the corner of his mouth on the right side. "You say there's no guy in the picture so this gives me an excuse to spend time with you in a no-date, no-pressure way."

"Has anyone ever told you that you're super persistent?"

"Once or twice." He shrugs and starts walking away from me, looking for something else to photograph.

I nervously fiddle with the sleeve of my sweater. Letting Joel come to the apartment is probably a terrible idea, but it *is* only a movie. Jace and I aren't together officially—besides, *nothing* is going to happen with Joel. I'm not interested in him, at all, although I hate to admit I'm starting to like him as a friend. Being forced to work with him in more than one class has shown me he's a nice guy.

Besides, I now can't admit to him that there is a guy, even if I don't understand what that guy's role in my life is.

Joel and I spend another hour at the garden before heading out.

He follows me to the apartment and parks behind me in the space Jace would normally use.

I feel weird leading him into the building and up to the apartment. Even though I'm doing nothing scandalous it feels that way.

I let him in and he whistles. "Damn, this place is nice."

I shrug. It is nice, much nicer than the housing on campus, at least.

I drop my backpack on the ground and then gently place my camera bag on top. *That* is precious, my school bag not so much.

"Do you want a drink?" I ask. It seems like the polite thing to do.

"Sure. Anything is fine."

I scurry over to the refrigerator, happy to have something to do while Joel picks up the remote and turns the TV on.

I grab two bottles of water and then rummage around for popcorn and other snacks. I find a box of popcorn and it's empty.

"Who keeps an empty box of popcorn?" I mutter to myself. Jace. That's who.

Since popcorn's out I end up dumping different kinds of chips in a bowl and calling it a day.

I carry the bowl and two bottles of water over to the couch as Joel switches the TV over to Netflix and brings up this movie.

"How long is this movie?" I ask.

"Four hours, I think."

I nearly choke on my tongue. *Four hours? Jace will prob-*

ably be home in four hours! Tell this clown to get out of your house! I know it's too late for that. It'd be beyond rude to force him out. I'm stuck now.

Joel clicks the movie on and gets comfortable on the couch.

Meanwhile, I feel like I'm about to throw up and I'm cursing my very existence. *Seriously, what the fuck was I thinking?*

I sit down on the couch, on the opposite end from Joel, and set the bowl of chips on the space between us. I hand him the bottle of water and he smiles in thanks.

I unscrew the cap and take a long sip. I suddenly feel like I'm stuck in the Sahara and dying of thirst.

The movie opens with haunting music, and I begin to regret my decision even more.

"You're shaking the whole couch," he comments, never looking away from the TV. "I'm not going to hurt you, if that's what you think." He sounds sad now and I wince.

"I know that, this is just weird. I've never brought a guy here," I admit, "and while you're not here for *that*, it doesn't erase the awkwardness."

He finally looks at me, this time with a small smile. "It's just a movie. *Breathe*. Sit back and enjoy it. Something tells me you're always wound too tight."

He's right about that. My upbringing made me highly distrustful of people and caused me to constantly walk around with a tight feeling in my chest. I lived my childhood feeling on pins and needles and that's carried over into adulthood. It's not something I seem to be able to shake overnight.

I force myself to focus on the movie, and I'm surprised by how quickly I get sucked into it. Everything about it is beautiful. I don't understand what my parents found so horrible about it that it was banned from our house—other than the nudity, but seriously I know what a girl looks like naked, that's what happens when mirrors are in bathrooms. You kind of can't avoid seeing yourself naked.

As the movie progresses and the ship hits the iceberg the intensity magnifies.

It's dark in the apartment, save for the glow coming from the TV, and I itch to turn on a light but I can't seem to make myself move from the couch to do it. I'm riveted, waiting to see what's going to happen next.

When they end up in the water I cover my eyes, because there's no way this can end well.

"Stop that." Joel pries my hands from my eyes. "You've made it this far, you can't quit now."

"Nope." I shake my head. "Someone I love is about to die. I know it."

Sure enough, Rose starts begging Jack to wake up, that someone's there to rescue them, but my sweet little Jack Dawson has turned into a frozen popsicle.

She pries his hands off the door she's floating on, kisses them, and watches him sink beneath the surface of the ocean.

"No," I sob. "That's not fair."

Sobbing for a fictional character might be pathetic, but in that moment, I can't bring myself to care. Jack Dawson was compassionate, daring, thrilling, and hot, and I have to mourn his fictional passing.

The door to the apartment opens and Jace startles. "Nova?" I try to get control of myself but Jack Dawson *just died* and these things take time. "Who the hell are you?" he snaps, flicking on a light. "Did you hurt her? Answer me!"

"Whoa! Whoa!" Joel raises his hands innocently with Jace towering above him. I still sit on the opposite end of the couch, hardly within touching distance of Joel, but I'm secretly pleased that Jace would come to my defense so easily. "We're just watching a movie." Joel points to the TV screen. Jace looks over his shoulder at the TV then to me. "You're crying because the pretty boy died?"

"Jack was amazing," I defend. "I haven't seen this movie before," I add. "I wasn't expecting it."

Jace laughs. "It's *Titanic*. You know, based on the actual Titanic catastrophe where a whole lot of people died. I think it's natural to expect people to die in the movie version."

"Don't be an ass." I toss a throw pillow at his head but he dodges it easily.

Jace's attention quickly zeroes back onto Joel. "Again, who the fuck are you and why are you in my apartment watching a movie with Nova?"

"I'm Joel—we have class together. We were working on a project and Nova mentioned she'd never seen *Titanic* so—"

"So, you thought you'd rectify that." Jace nods to himself and then points at the door. "Get out."

To me, Joel says with a smirk, "I thought you said there wasn't a guy?"

Jace growls. "*Out.*"

Joel grabs his stuff and leaves while the movie continues to play in the background. Jace locks the door behind him and then turns to glower at me.

"No guy, huh?"

"Uh …" I stare at him in confusion as he slowly stalks forward.

He doesn't stop until he's right in front of me and then he bends so we're eyelevel. I hold my breath as he leans in close so he can whisper in my ear. "I assure you, there's very much a guy."

I shiver as he pulls away. In a flash, he has my hair wrapped in his fist and he tilts my head back. I moan and his eyes dilate at the sound. "I'm not a jealous kind of guy, Nova. You make me crazy."

I close my eyes and my tongue slips out to wet my lips.

I feel his lips graze my cheek, the slight stubble on his chin scratching my skin, and my eyes pop open again.

"What will it take for you to see that?"

His hold on my hair loosens and he moves his hand to my neck. I squeak when he jerks me forward so we're nose to nose.

He stares at me for a moment before his lips crash against mine. I moan again and he presses his lips more firmly against mine.

"Mine," he growls between kisses. "Remember that," he whispers. "You're mine," he says huskily. His hands roam every available surface of my body.

I twine my arms around his neck and he lifts me up. My

legs circle his waist as he carries me. I'm expecting the bed to hit my back, but I startle when I feel the hard press of the wall. Unexpected heat shoots through my body when I realize this fact. There's something undeniably hot about the thought of him taking me against the wall. Like he's too frantic to make it the few feet to the bed.

He fumbles with the button of my jeans and when he finds it and slides down the zipper he makes this happy little sound in the back of his throat. He loosens his grip on me so he can slide my jeans and underwear down my hips. I lean my head against the wall, my face tilted to the ceiling as I struggle for air. I hear the jingling of his belt and the sound of his zipper sliding down and I break out in a sweat all over.

"Condom," he mutters. "Need a condom."

"I'm on birth control," I tell him, my voice barely above a zipper.

Shocked green eyes meet mine, and I expect him to say something about how you can't be too sure or something like that, but instead he wraps his hand around the base of his cock and guides it inside me in one hard, sure, thrust.

"Oh, my God," I cry out as my back hits the wall. It might be painful if my body wasn't so flooded with adrenaline right now.

He presses his mouth to my collarbone and bites.

My skin begins to feel too tight and I itch to crawl right out of my own body. It's the strangest sensation but not an entirely unpleasant one.

His lips move from my collarbone, up my neck, to my

ear. He tugs gently on the lobe and I gasp, my inner muscles clenching around him.

"Holy fuck," he rasps. I roll my hips against his and he hisses. "Fuck, Nova." He rests his head in the crook of my neck, his breath tickling my skin. He stands up straight and holds my hips in his hands. His thrusts are fast and hard and utterly perfect. I cry out a moment later as I come and then he's right behind me. I shake and he holds my body weight so I don't collapse.

I hold onto him tightly, afraid if I don't I might melt into a puddle of goo. I feel the hard surface of the wall disappear from my back and a moment later I'm lying across his soft bed and he pulls from my body carefully. Warmth seeps onto my legs, and despite the heat, I shiver.

I'm sure I look a mess, with my jeans and panties around my ankles, hair mused and lips swollen, but I can't bring myself to care. I don't think I've ever felt better.

Jace comes back with a damp washcloth and wipes between my legs. The sudden tenderness jolts me. I'm amazed by how he can be raging one minute as he fucks me against the wall and the next he's gently wiping me clean.

When I'm clean, he tosses the cloth away and then proceeds to help me out of my clothes.

"Why are you getting me naked?" I ask him.

His brow is furrowed in concentration as he lifts my sweater over my head.

"Because I can and because I want to," he says huskily.

"I think I like that answer," I admit. Probably a bit too much.

His teeth flash white in the darkness.

Once I'm completely naked he places a soft kiss to my neck. "Never do that again."

"What?" I ask, confused. "Jace!" I cry out when he bites my shoulder.

"Never bring a guy back here—especially one that says, *'So there is a guy?'* This is me reminding you that there's *definitely* a guy." His tongue swirls around my nipple. "He can't do to you what I can." He slips to fingers into me easily and I moan. "He can't make you feel what I feel," he breathes, his lips brushing mine as he speaks, purposely teasing me because he knows I want him to kiss me. I roll my hips, rubbing against his fingers. His fingers leave me and I whimper. A moment later he touches them to my lips with a one-word declaration. "Suck."

I wrap my mouth around his fingers and do as I'm told, swirling my tongue around. I watch with delight as his eyes dilate and his teeth dig in the slightest bit to his full bottom lip.

"Shit," he murmurs as I release his fingers.

I look up at him with owlish eyes, silently saying, "What next?"

He answers the question by cupping my cheek in one hand and angling his lips over mine. I wrap one leg around his waist and pull him close. He still wears his jeans and boxers and he'd pulled them back on after he left me, though he did remove his shirt.

It's not long before his jeans and boxers are on the floor with the rest of our clothes and he's inside me. He moves slower this time, savoring it, and that makes me even hotter. I gasp when he hits a certain spot and when he does it again, and again in succession I fall over the edge. My vision blurs around the edges and for some reason I feel like crying. He presses a kiss to my temple and that makes the urge even stronger so I squish my eyes closed. His lips trail down the side of my cheek, my neck, top of chest, and over the swells of my breasts.

Jace gently rubs his fingers over my clit and my eyes shoot open, connecting with his. A moment later another orgasm hits me and he follows suit.

I close my eyes again as he lies beside me, both of us breathing heavily, and I know for certain that there *is a guy* whether I like it or not. Jace has ruined me.

fourteen

. . .

jace

I WATCH the cigarette smoke curl through the air. Images of Nova lying naked in my bed play through my mind. Leaving her this morning was the worst kind of torture but with Xander back in town for a game the guys and I agreed to meet up for lunch. I'd much rather be with her, but they can't know that—which means I need to be paying some sort of attention to the conversation.

"I'm going to ask Rae to marry me."

That sentence serves as a dose of ice-cold water poured over me.

"W-What did you say?" I stutter. I rub at my ears like something might be lodged there and nearly burn myself on the stupid cigarette in the process.

"I'm going to ask Rae to marry me," Cade repeats, rubbing his hands on his jeans.

I raise my beer, signaling to the waitress to bring me another. I wish there was a way to tell her I need about ten of them.

"Wow, congrats, man." Xander claps Cade on the shoulder, grinning.

"Don't congratulate me yet," Cade says, with a shrug. "She could say no."

Xander chuckles and shakes his head. "She's not going to say no."

"You don't think it's too soon, do you?" Cade rambles. "I mean, we've been together officially for almost a year and just because we're engaged it doesn't mean we're getting married the next week."

"If you're already freaking out about a wedding maybe you shouldn't ask," I suggest. The idea of *both* of my best friends being married is frightening. I can't imagine being the only unmarried one. How fucking weird would that be?

"No, not me," he snaps, his tone implying that I'm stupid. "Rae can be very flighty about commitment. I don't want to scare her off."

"She loves you," Xander tells him. "She's not going anywhere."

"I really love her," Cade says softly. "I can't lose her because of this."

"You're overthinking it," Xander says, leaning back in his chair.

"I don't know, Rae is ... well, Rae," I input. I know I'm being an asshole but I seriously can't comprehend a world where both Xander and Cade have a *wife*. What kind of nonsense is that? Last time I checked we were three high school kids trying pot for the first time. Now they're both going to be married? What the fuck is next? Babies and retirement?

Xander sends me a scathing look, and I raise my hands innocently.

"Rae loves you," Xander says with a serious look. "She's going to say yes."

"It's a big deal," Cade continues. "I don't want to fuck this up, and I can't even ask you for advice on a proposal because my sister got drunk and proposed to *you*. You got off easy."

Xander chuckles. "I'd hardly say our way was easy."

"Fuck," Cade curses. "My palms are sweating and I haven't even proposed to her yet."

"When are you planning to do it?" I ask. I need time to mentally prepare for this.

"Christmas or New Year's. I haven't decided exactly when or how. I just want it to be memorable."

Xander reaches for his water and takes a drink before saying, "Whatever you do will be memorable."

"Yeah," I pipe in. "If you propose to her in the bread aisle of the grocery store she's going to always remember that and think that spot's special." The waitress finally returns with my beer and sets it down. I grab it and chug half of it in one swallow.

Cade glares at me. "And this is why you don't have a girlfriend."

"I don't have a girlfriend because I don't want one. If I

wanted one, I'd have one," I tell him, fishing for another cigarette. I can't even remember what happened to my last one. I spare a glance under the table and find it lying there with a hole now burned in the carpet. *Shit*.

Cade shakes his head. "You have no idea what you're missing out on."

"I think I'll live." I light my second cigarette and inhale a drag, letting the smoke fill my lungs for a moment before blowing out.

"Why exactly are you so anti-girlfriend?" Xander asks.

"I'm not anti-girlfriend. I just don't need a ball and chain."

Cade chuckles and taps his fingers against the table. "You're so clueless, dude."

"About what?" I snap.

"Everything."

I glare at him and Xander. "So, you guys suddenly know everything because you're married and you practically are?" I wave my fingers through the air. "Fucking ridiculous."

Cade sighs and picks up his beer. "One day you're going to fall in love and you'll see."

"See what?" I seethe. I'm about five seconds from bolting.

"You'll see," he says again, and I realize that's all the answer I'm going to get.

I pull out my wallet and lay down some bills. "I'm thrilled this lunch turned into a Dr. Phil session, but I'm out."

"Jace," Xander calls after me. "Come back. We haven't even eaten yet."

I lift my hand behind me in a wave.

I push open the door and step outside into a blast of cold air. I head down the street to my truck and once in the cab I pull out my phone and call Nova.

"Are you hungry?"

"Starved."

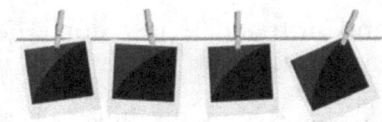

"I thought you were eating lunch with the guys?" Nova says before taking a bite of her club sandwich.

We ended up at some little café within walking distance from our place. Neither of us has eaten here before, and the food is surprisingly good.

I shrug.

"Oh, no," she says, picking up on the fact that there's more. "What happened?"

"Can you keep a secret?" I ask her.

She looks at me like I'm stupid. "Have I ever told anyone one of your confessions? Do you really think so little of me?"

"I'm sorry," I defend, raising my hands. "This is big."

"What is it?" She pleads.

"Cade is planning to propose to Rae and somehow the conversation turned to me and not having a girlfriend." I shrug like it's no big deal.

"Ah, I see." She smiles.

"What?" I snap.

"The conversation turned serious so you left. It's kind of your thing."

"It's not my thing," I mumble. She eyes me. "Okay, so maybe it is."

"You can't run anytime things get serious. You'll end up alone." I wince and she adds, "I'm sorry, but it's true."

"Running is all I know," I admit.

She wipes her mouth with a napkin. "I hate to admit it, but I'm kind of glad that this time you ran *to* me and not *away* from me."

"You're kind of my safe place."

Her face lights up and something inside me clenches. It's an unfamiliar feeling, one I can't quite discern, but I best compare it to the dip in your stomach when a rollercoaster goes plummeting back to Earth. It feels both terrifying and exhilarating all at the same time.

"Besides," I begin, "they can make fun of me all they want, but I mean, I basically have a girlfriend."

"Oh, you do." She smiles, her green hair falling over her shoulder.

"Yeah." I reach over, brushing the strand of hair away. "This really hot girl with freckles lives with me, and we have the most incredible sex, and spend pretty much every moment together so it's basically like having a girlfriend."

"Mhmm," she hums. "Only I'm not."

I lean into her, skimming my lips over her jaw. "You're something."

"But I'm not your girlfriend," she repeats. "So, you won't mind that I invited Joel to Xander's game?" I nearly come out of my seat and she smiles with triumph.

"That asswipe isn't coming," I mumble, reaching for my water glass. My throat suddenly feels very dry.

She smiles back. "I was talking to him the other day in class about my plans and it came up and he mentioned he loved football, so yes, I invited him."

"Why were you talking to him?" My fists clench against the table. Jealousy rears its ugly head inside me.

She laughs. "Because we have classes together and we're kind of friends now."

"Friends?" I repeat. "Since when?"

"Since *Titanic*."

"Ah," I breathe. "Wall night. That was a great night." I repeat those events over in my mind.

She shakes her head. "Anyway, Joel is coming to the game and you *will* be nice to him. After all, you're not my boyfriend but he is my friend." I bristle. She takes a sip of her water and sets the glass back down. "He's a good guy."

"He wants to fuck you," I mumble.

She snorts. "So do you."

"I *do* fuck you. There's a difference."

She laughs and shakes her head. "Well, I don't want to fuck him."

"That makes me feel better." I eye my half-eaten sandwich.

"You don't *sound* like you feel better," she comments. I look up from my food and find her watching me with a coy smile.

"That's because *he* still wants to fuck you."

She laughs. "We could talk in circles about this all afternoon."

"You really don't like him?" I ask. I know I sound pathetic asking it, but I can't help it. I know that she spends a lot of time with him in class.

"Only as a friend."

I groan. "I'd prefer that answer to be, 'No, Jace. I hate his guts'."

She laughs. "You're insane. And I did hate him in the beginning but he's really not that bad, but *only* as a friend."

"I want to punch him," I grumble.

"*Jace*," she scolds.

"What?" I ask innocently. "I said I *want* to punch him, not that I will. I should be commended for not punching him the night I walked in on you two."

She laughs like I've said the funniest thing she's ever heard. "You make it sound like you found us going at it like a couple of teenagers in our parents' bed."

"Might as well have." I cross my arms over my chest. My appetite long ago disappeared.

Her lips quirk with amusement. "You're jealous."

"Am not," I scoff, which, of course, only reaffirms the fact that I am jealous.

"Whatever you say," she sing-songs.

I'm clearly not very good at controlling my emotions. The game is tomorrow, so I doubt I can learn enough self-control by then to not act like a complete dick to *Joel*. What kind of name is Joel anyway?

Nova curses, her gaze on her phone.

"What is it?" I ask, instantly on edge since something seems to have upset her.

"It's nothing bad," she rushes to assure me. "Thea wants us all to go out tonight or to come over to their house for a movie night."

"Let's go out," I say.

If we go out there's a chance Nova and I can sneak away for a bit, but if we're shut up in their house watching a movie then we'll have to be on our best behavior.

"I agree." She types back a response. A minute later her phone vibrates. "She wants to know if I have any suggestions on where to go?"

"Depends—do you want to dance, hear good music, or get drunk?"

She sighs and presumably relays that question to Thea.

"She says a bit of all of that."

I think for a moment and say, "2.0. It's a club downtown—fairly new, nice but not stuffy, with live music and DJs, and a big ass bar."

She shakes her head, laughing under her breath. "You know everything." She texts the information to Thea and then sets her phone aside. "Maybe I should ask Joel if he wants to go to the club?" she taunts.

I lean across the table and slam my lips to hers, showing her exactly what I think of that suggestion. I kiss her roughly, but she loves it. I can tell from the soft little purring sound she makes.

I release her, and she breathes, "I'm definitely asking Joel now."

"Over my dead body," I growl.

She smirks and picks up her phone, quickly typing out another text. She gets a response a moment later. "He said he'll be there."

I bristle. "*Great.*"

Something tells me tonight is going to be interesting.

My jaw drops when Nova walks out of her bedroom that evening.

"Are you *trying* to kill me? You are, aren't you?" I say, looking her up and down.

She wears a form-fitting black dress with an open back that has some kind of crisscross design with thin pieces of fabric, and because this is Nova, she pairs it with a pair of black combat boots and a choker necklace thing. She grabs her leather jacket from the hanger by the door and slips it on.

"It's just a dress," she says, adjusting the jacket so it sits right on her shoulders.

"A fucking tight one," I grumble. It makes her ass and tits look amazing—but the problem is I won't be the only guy that notices that fact. I'm sure Joel will *love* it. Fuck, Joel.

She tries not to smile and fails miserably.

I glance at the time and grumble, "We better go."

"You know, if we arrive together they're going to think something is up."

I narrow my eyes on her. "We're riding together."

"Sure. Suit yourself," she says with a little smirk, and I wish more than anything I could see inside her thoughts.

I shrug into my jacket and grab my keys off the table. I pass Nova and glance back at the table with a smirk. "We're going to fuck on the table." I drop that little bomb and smile in satisfaction as her jaw unhinges. "Let's go." I nod toward the door and she squeaks into action. I hope she spends the entire evening imagining what I'm going to do to her on that table. Whatever she comes up with won't be nearly as good as the real thing, but I like playing with her.

A few minutes later, we slide into the cab of my truck.

I could drive a fancy sports car if I wanted—my dad would *love* that—but my ancient truck suits me. It feels right. With the holidays approaching I find myself thinking about him randomly more and more. We're due for our annual call soon, and I'm dreading it. Every year I hope he'll forget about me and he never does.

I dismiss thoughts of my dad from my mind. I'm good at

that—ignoring things. It's easier to pretend the bad doesn't exist.

The drive is short, and I park around the block from the club. Nova hops out and I meet her at the front of the truck.

I tap out a cigarette and smoke as we walk.

"Why do you keep smoking if you don't even like it?" she asks, her breath fogging the chilly hair.

I shrug. "Bad habit more than anything, I guess."

"You should quit." She kicks at an errant pebble on the sidewalk.

"But don't you think it adds to my cool factor?" I joke, wiggling my brows.

She shakes her head. "I think the tattoos do a pretty good job at that."

I chuckle. "You like my tattoos, don't you?"

It's dark but I swear her cheeks flush. "Maybe," she mumbles.

The club comes into sight and I say, "Do you know if the others are here yet?" She fishes her phone out of her— "Did you just pull your phone out of your bra?"

"I had to put it somewhere," she mumbles. She types out a text and it chimes a moment later. "They're inside and Joel says he'll be here soon."

"Yippee." I flick my cigarette onto the ground.

"Be nice." She smacks my stomach. "He's not even here yet and you're already grumbling."

"He better not ask you to dance."

She laughs. "You *do* realize our friends don't know we're ... whatever we are. It's going to look suspicious."

I give her a steely look as we cross the street and get in line for the club. "Do I look like I care?"

She shrugs. "I'm just saying. We have nosy friends, and they're going to put two and two together if you're glued to my side."

I lean into her and she moves closer to the building. "So, are you saying you'll have no problem with me asking some other girl to dance? Buy them a drink? Maybe lean in and kiss them," I whisper the last part, my lips grazing her ear and she shivers.

"I get your point," she says, her back ram-rod straight. "We'll make do as best we can."

I chuckle. "That's what I thought."

The lines moves a bit but it still feels a mile long. Nova shivers, and I wrap an arm around her, drawing her small body close to mine.

"Oh, hey, guys," Joel runs up to us, slightly out of breath.

"Hey, Joel." Nova smiles at him.

"Hey, Joel," I mimic, my tone less than friendly unlike hers.

Joel flashes a panicked smile my way and falls into line beside us.

"I think our project is coming together," Joel says to Nova.

"What project?" I growl.

Nova looks up at me. "The one we were working on the day he came over to watch *Titanic*. It's on macrophotography."

"What the fuck is that?"

"Basically, it's photographing really small things and making them look large," she explains.

"Why do you have to do that together?"

She laughs. "Because our professor hates us."

"Nah," Joel pipes in. "I think she's trying to help us. Every photographer is stronger at something and has a distinct style—so we can all help each other."

"True," she agrees.

We finally reach the front of the line, pay, and get stamps on our hands to get in.

The music is loud and the lights flash in different colors.

I follow Nova through the club and to a table our friends have commandeered. It's a huge U-shaped booth. Nova slides in beside Cade, and I snag the space beside her, which forces Joel to the opposite side beside Thea.

"Everyone, I'd like you to meet Joel. Joel, this is Thea, Xander, Cade, and of course you know Rae already."

"Hey." Joel waves awkwardly, his shoulders hunched. He's clearly uncomfortable which makes me smile.

"What about Jace?" asks Thea, pointing at me.

"We met outside," I tell her.

"Oh, right, of course."

"Can we order some drinks?" I ask. There's no way I can make it through this night sober.

"Already ahead of you," Cade says.

About that time a waitress brings a whole tray full of different drinks.

I grab my beer and take large gulp, nearly choking in the process.

Nova gives me a look that says, "Are you okay?" Which I answer with a nod.

"I feel so boring," Cade comments, sipping his beer, "because I'd much rather be at home sitting on the couch."

"You've officially become an old man," Thea tells him. "Congratulations."

Cade drapes his arm over the booth behind Rae. "If being old means I don't have to go out, then I welcome it."

"I'm just glad we're all out together. We don't go out as a group enough," Rae adds.

"Speaking of group things," Thea pipes in. "The Halloween party is next weekend. Please tell me you have costumes figured out." Her eyes latch onto me and then Nova.

"I have mine," Nova says. She looks up at me, waiting.

"I'm going as myself," I mumble. "Real scary costume there."

"Jacen," Thea scolds, and I cringe at the use of my full name. Only my dad calls me Jacen, and I hate it for that reason alone. "You need to pick one or I'll pick it for you." The look she gives me says that I definitely *don't* want her to pick it. She smiles at Joel beside her. "Do you like costume parties? You're welcome to come if you'd like."

Joel shrugs. "I'm working that night but if I wasn't I'd love to."

"Aw, too bad, what a bummer," I say in a tone that shows I don't think it's a bummer.

Nova smacks my knee with the palm of her hand beneath the table.

Nobody seems to notice my comment, or if they do, they ignore it.

"Let's dance," Thea says to Xander.

"Sure." He sets his drink down and Joel steps out of the booth so they can leave.

"Wanna dance?" Cade asks Rae.

Rae makes a face, like the thought of dancing is disgusting to her, but she nods. "Yeah, sure."

"Do you mind, guys?" Cade asks, motioning to Nova and me.

"Not at all," I say, glad to be rid of everyone. Well, except Joel.

I stand and Nova slides out of the booth so that they can go dance.

Nova takes her seat again and I do the same. We stare across the table at Joel who grins at us.

"Your friends don't know, do they?"

"Know what?" Nova asks, playing innocent. When in doubt it's best to act innocent.

"That you're together. Or fucking. Or whatever it is you guys are doing."

I bristle.

"You can't say anything," Nova pleads.

"Why don't you want them to know?" Joel asks, clearly confused why we'd keep this a secret.

"Because our friends are nosy fucks," I mumble and Nova jabs an elbow into my side.

"It's just easier this way," she tells him. "The less complication the better. It's hard to explain something to someone that you don't quite understand yourself." She looks up at me through thick dark lashes.

Joel raises his hands in surrender. "I'm not going to say anything to them."

"Thank you," she says, sagging in relief.

Joel stands. "I'm going to go get another drink. You guys want anything?"

We shake our heads.

I breathe a sigh of relief once he's gone.

"Come on." I stand. "Let's dance." I hold out my hand to her and she looks at it like it's a snake that might bite her.

"What if they see?" she whispers.

"It's just a dance. We've danced together before."

She sighs and slips her hand into mine, knowing I'm right.

I lead her out onto the dance floor and we bleed into the crowd, becoming one among many.

Her eyes dart around nervously, searching for our friends.

I take her face between my hands, forcing her to look at me. "Forget about them," I plead. "All that exists right now is me and you. That's all that matters."

"Why aren't you more nervous?" she asks. "You're Mr. Non-Commitment."

I shrug, moving my hands down to her waist and drawing her flush to me. "This is different."

We move to the beat of the song, but I don't think either of us is actually listening.

"How?" She blinks up at me, the lights flashing different

colors over her face. First blue, then red, purple. "How is this different? What are we doing?"

I dip my head to her ear. "I don't know," I answered honestly. "I've never done this before, but if for one minute you think that you're just another girl to me, you're wrong. Erase that thought from your mind right now. This is *more*." She squeaks as I pull her impossibly closer. "I don't know what tomorrow will bring for me, for us, but I'm willing to try. Just give me time. I'm sure I'll fuck this up, but don't give up on me. *Please*."

Her hands squeeze against my shoulders. "For this to work, we're going to have to be honest about things, okay?"

"I can do that," I tell her.

"That also means we have to tell them. Not tonight, but soon. We can't hide this from our friends forever. But for now, while this is still so new, we'll stay quiet."

I bend my head and press my lips softly to hers. She's stiff at first, but after a moment she relaxes beneath me.

I know Nova and I haven't put a definition on our relationship, but I think, maybe, she's my girlfriend.

That thought once would've sent me running in terror, but as I press my lips to hers, her body flush to mine, I feel no fear, instead I only feel content. But worry is still lodged in the back of my mind, because nothing good in my life has ever been easy, and I'm sure this will be no different. But I want to try, and that counts for something, right?

fifteen

. . .

nova

I PICK up the camera lens and look at it before placing it back on the shelf in the classroom.

Joel spreads out copies of prints from photos we took when we went out to practice our macro-photography. Now we've been tasked with making some sort of collage out of them. I don't understand the purpose of it, but it's for our grade, so we have to do it.

Our professor was kind enough to lend us her classroom for the afternoon. We're not the only students who have utilized it to our advantage, and there are several other groups working as well, including Rae and her partner.

Joel's phone buzzes, and he glares at it before sighing, picking it up, and reading the text. He types back an angry response.

"Girl trouble?" I ask.

"Something like that," he grumbles, his hair falling forward into his eyes. He shoves it angrily away.

I take some of the prints and line them up so we can look at all of them.

There are ten photos total—five for each of us—and we have to find some way to blend them together.

Thankfully, we don't have to use all the photos if we don't want to, but we have to use at least three.

It's easier said than done, seeing as each photo is so zoomed in—the point of macro-photography—and a collage is more than just cutting and pasting images together.

It's supposed to be a collection or combination of things but it should make *sense,* and there lies the problem.

"I don't know how we're going to do this," I mutter, starting at a photo of a flower petal and then one of tree bark.

"We'll figure it out," Joel replies, his phone buzzing again. He eyes the phone, and his lip curls with irritation.

"Someone's really up your butt about something," I tell him. "You must've done something bad."

He shakes his head and doesn't respond, shoving his phone in his pocket when he's done typing out a text.

"Let's do this," he says, rubbing his hands together.

We get to work, and after about an hour of going over things, I stand and stretch.

"I'm going to grab a coffee and come right back. Do you want anything?"

He flicks a piece of hair out of his eye. "Uh ... a coffee sounds good and food. I'm starving."

"You got it." I grab my wallet from my backpack and head out.

Only two other groups are still working, whereas when we started there were five, and we only have the classroom for another hour. Hopefully, we'll be done by then. If this drags on longer than that I think I might die.

I walk across campus, inhaling the crisp autumn air. I hear a couple of people talking about an upcoming school football game. I went to a few last year but that was only because Cade and Xander were playing. Since they're no longer here, I haven't bothered—besides, with Xander in the NFL I'd rather go to one of their games if I'm going to sit through one.

I pull my phone from my pocket and type out a text to Jace—letting him know that we're still working on the project. I told him this morning that I'd be working after class with Joel, but I figured I'd be done by now, and I don't want him to worry.

He responds back almost immediately.

Jace: Hurry back. I miss you.

Me: I'll make my lateness worthwhile. I promise. ;)

I smile to myself. Never in a million years did I imagine I'd *ever* be with Jace, or that I'd be sending him suggestive text messages.

I finally reach the small on-campus café, and I'm forced to put my phone away before I can see his response.

I order coffee for Joel and me, as well as a muffin for myself and a personal pizza for Joel. I don't know if the pizza will be any good, but I figure if he's starving then it's better than a muffin. I grab two waters while I'm there, figuring we'll want that next.

Once our coffee and the food is ready, I take the bag they put the food in, add the water bottles, and head back to the classroom.

"And then there was one," he says when I enter the room, and I notice that all the groups have now left.

I sigh. "Lucky us."

I hand him his coffee and bag with the food.

"Mmm, pizza," he hums, pulling out the small cardboard box that holds it. "For you, I assume?" He finds the muffin and holds it up.

"Yep, thanks."

"You got waters too." He grins, pulling them from the bag. "You thought of everything."

"Except napkins," I grumble. "I think I have some tissues in my backpack, though."

"Oh, yeah, didn't think about that," he agrees. "Greasy fingers and prints do not mix."

"No, they don't," I agree.

I take a sip of coffee and look at how he's arranged the photos. We've been rearranging them non-stop for the last hour, trying to figure out the best way to group them.

"Hey, I like this." I point to the way he currently has them arranged.

He tips back the chair he's sitting on so the front two legs come off the ground.

"You do? This is my favorite so far too." He takes a bite of pizza and fights a smile.

"I think it's perfect."

While Joel eats, I cut and glue the photos the way he'd arranged them.

After about five minutes of working in silence, I look up at him.

"I wish you could come to the party," I say, referring to the Halloween party Thea's throwing.

He swallows a bite of pizza. "I might be able to make it. My boss said he might not need me this weekend, so if he doesn't, then I'll go."

"You have a costume?" I ask. "Because Thea will kill you if you show up without one."

He chuckles and drops a piece of crust in the box. "Yeah, I have one."

"What is it?" I ask.

"I'll tell you mine if you tell me yours."

I shake my head. "Never mind. Surprise me."

I haven't even told Jace what I decided to do for my costume so I'm definitely not telling Joel before him.

Joel's phone buzzes, and he curses, swiping it off the table before I can see the name on the screen.

"I think you need to dump whoever that is. She sounds like a clinger."

"*She's* something all right."

I furrow my brows. The way he says *she's* makes me wonder if he's actually talking to a girl at all. I'd just assumed …

"Let's finish this," he says, typing out a text and putting

his phone away. "I have other homework I have to finish tonight."

"Uh ... yeah, okay."

It doesn't take us long to finish and then we head our separate ways.

I can't seem to shake my confusion about all his text messages and his odd behavior.

My gut tells me something more is going on than he's telling me—and I figure I'll learn what it is eventually, because the truth never stays buried for long.

It always comes out when you least expect it.

sixteen

...

nova

THE AIR CRACKLES with intensity and silence reigns.

It feels like the calm before the storm, the moment where the whole world goes still but electricity sizzles through the air.

I can feel him watching me, but I try to ignore his searing gaze.

I take a bite of my eggs, my eyes glued firmly to my plate.

I finish and stand to carry my plate to the sink.

"Fuck this."

I jump as his plate goes clamoring to the ground and food rains all over the floor by my feet.

Before I can blink, he's in front of me, his presence commanding. He takes my plate from me and slings it in the direction of the sink. It misses, hits the cabinet, and breaks into a million pieces.

"Jace," I gasp.

He grabs my face, pressing his lips firmly to mine and stealing all my breath.

He lifts me up and carries me back to the table. My butt touches the hard surface and he releases me, using his body to press me down onto it.

"What are you doing?" I ask on a gasp when he releases my lips.

He kisses his way down my neck. "I told you I was going to fuck you on this table. I couldn't stand waiting any longer when you look more appetizing than my breakfast."

His words make my heart race.

"I have to get ready for class," I protest weakly.

"And I have to find a stupid costume for this party tomorrow, but fucking you is much more appealing."

He has a point there.

"Lay back," he coaxes. "I'll take care of you."

Our eyes meet and he urges me to trust him. I nod once and do as he says. I lie back so I'm completely flat on the table.

"Take your shirt off," he commands.

"You first," I parry.

He shakes his head, his lips tipping up in his trademark smirk. "I make the rules, not you."

I lick my lips, turned on more than I can ever comprehend by his bossy attitude.

I reach down and slowly lift my shirt. His gaze follows my fingers as they curl around the fabric of my shirt, and I lift it up, exposing my stomach and then my breasts. When it's off I drop it to the floor and lean back on my elbows. The gesture lifts my breasts and he looks at them with heat in his eyes.

When we first started sleeping together I felt completely out of my league and inexperienced. Jace has helped me to become a lot more comfortable with myself in the last few weeks. I still have my moments where I feel silly and unsure, but thankfully they're not as often as they were.

"Are you going to just stand there and look at me?"

He presses his finger to my lips. "Shh."

My eyes follow his finger as he trails it between my breasts. I shiver, craving the warmth of his body on mine.

He runs his hands down my thighs and then steps away.

"The rest." His voice has taken on a husky edge and he presses a shaking hand to his lips.

I oblige, and remove my sleep pants and underwear. He watches as the clothes drop to the floor and then he devours me slowly with his eyes.

Fire.

I am fire and he fans my flames. He makes me burn brighter, he doesn't try to dull my spark.

"Beautiful," he murmurs, the words barely a sound but I can read his lips. "Lay down and spread your legs."

I oblige. A bit of that old fear creeps around the edges of my mind, but as he lowers and presses his lips to my sensitive flesh all my thoughts melt away.

The table is cool beneath my back, and surprisingly not that uncomfortable.

Jace swirls his tongue around my clit and I gasp, my hips arching up to meet his mouth.

He grabs my hips and forces them back down, pulling his mouth away long enough to growl out one simple command. "*No.*"

My chest rises and falls as I struggle to get enough air. I cup my breasts, my eyes flicking down to his sandy head between my legs. His fingers dig roughly into my thighs, so much so that it hurts, but I still don't want him to lessen his grip. If he does I'm afraid I might float away.

The stubble on his cheeks grazes my sensitive skin, and I shiver.

He plunges two fingers into me while still sucking on my clit, and I cry out immediately as I orgasm. My whole body shakes, and when I finish, I feel loose and languid. I can barely keep my eyes open but I manage to do it and watch as he reaches behind him, hooking his thumbs into the back of his shirt and pulling it off. He tosses it behind him and makes quick work of his jeans.

He steps back up to the table and loops his arms around my legs, pulling me to the edge of the table so I'm half hanging off and he's supporting my weight.

He plunges inside me in one hard thrust.

"Oh, my God," I cry out, reaching up so my fingers scratch his abs.

He bends and captures my lips with his. He sucks on my bottom lip and lets it go with a pop. It feels slightly puffy and I'm sure it'll stay that way most of the day—a constant reminder of this moment.

A moment that will now play out in my mind every time I look at this table.

He peppers kisses all along my neck and chest, paying special attention to my breasts.

My fingers delve into his hair, tugging on the short strands. He hisses between his teeth and I smile in satisfaction.

It causes him to retaliate by biting my shoulder. I yelp and he chuckles, soothing the bite with a lick of his tongue and then a tender kiss.

He glances down, watching where we're joined and I plead, "Fuck me harder."

His eyes jolt to mine, the green all but completely leeched from them. Instead, they're twin, dark orbs, like he's become some other creature all together.

He holds my hips steady and obeys my command—which is a miracle, because normally he does the opposite of my pleas, but he must need this as much as I do.

He fucks me desperately, like he's about to lose me.

I cry out as I come a second time and then he's coming too, groaning as he finds his release. The desperate, almost pained sounds he makes are enough to make me orgasm again. Something about watching and hearing him lose control always turns me on.

Our bodies are pressed together, damp with sweat. He rests his head on my chest, his ear pressed to the spot where my heart beats.

"That was fucking amazing," he says, his voice hoarse.

"Yeah," I say, lazily running my fingers through the longer strands of hair by his forehead. I can barely think, let alone form a sentence.

Minutes pass and once we've both caught our breath he pulls away and helps me off the table.

His eyes roam over me from head to toe, and I squeal when he sweeps me into his arms.

"Jace," I cry out, trying to wiggle out of his arms.

"Shower," he commands, so I stop fighting.

"Just shower?" I raise a brow.

He grins down at me, suddenly looking very boyish and much younger. "I'll be a good boy."

"Mhmm," I hum. "I've heard that one before."

He sets me down when we reach the bathroom and closes the door before turning on the shower.

"In," he commands.

"You're so bossy," I grumble.

"You fucking love it when I'm bossy," he reasons. He has a point there.

I step into the shower and he follows behind me.

"I really do have to get to class," I tell him.

His arms wrap around me from the back, and I lean my head behind me onto his chest so I can look up at him. He bends and presses a tender kiss to my shoulder. I shiver, his tenderness surprising.

"I know," he murmurs against my skin.

He washes me then, from head to toe, his touch light and almost sweet.

When he finishes, he dries me, staring into my eyes the whole time.

Have you ever felt like someone sees you? Really sees you? Not the you that the world sees, but the stripped version? The *real* you? The chaos of your thoughts and the impurities of your heart? I think Jace can see right through me, to the darkness beneath that saturates my heart. That fact both terrifies and exhilarates me. It awakens something in me I long ago thought dormant. It reminds me that I'm alive and that the world keeps spinning even if we stand still.

"Go get dressed," he commands, kissing me tenderly, completely unaware of the storm of thoughts rolling through my mind.

I nod once and scatter out of the bathroom, the tension popping like a pin into a balloon. I wonder if he noticed. I hope he was unaware but I see no way he didn't feel it too.

In the safety of my room, I close the door and lock it—better safe than sorry; I can't trust myself when it comes to Jace.

I dress quickly and look at the time. I do need to get to class, but I have some time to spare, so I grab my notebook and sit on the edge of my bed, writing furiously. I can't get the words out of me fast enough.

Dear Owen,

It's been too long since I wrote to you and for that I'm sorry. I promise it's not because I forgot about you—nothing could ever make that a true statement because you're always on my mind.

I think about you every day. Mostly when I'm about to fall asleep.

I think about the color of your eyes and the softness of your hair beneath my fingers.

It breaks my heart that you can't think of me in the same way.

I'm a ghost to you.
I don't exist.
That's what hurts the most.
Love,
Nova

I finish the letter, rip it out of my notebook, and fold it up, sticking it with the others where it will remain forever.

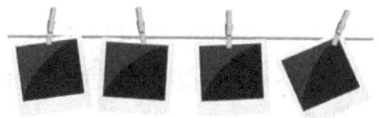

I appraise my costume in the bathroom mirror.
I turn side to side, checking every angle.
I think I did a damn good job.
My green hair is curled and fluffed so it's a wild mess, while my face is covered in white makeup, with tattoos drawn onto my face and down my neck. My lips are a vibrant red

and I've purposely smeared it around. My eyes are surrounded with a smoky gray color and I've slathered the mascara on. My outfit consist of purple pants, a white button down shirt with a green vest over top, and a long purple jacket.

The Joker is hardly an original costume, but since I had the green hair already it seemed a natural fit.

"Nova." Jace bangs a fist against the door. "I need your help."

I reluctantly open the door and he gapes at me. "What do you need?" I ask.

"Holy shit," he mutters, "you look fucking amazing."

I look him up and down. "You're not wearing a costume."

He makes a face of disgust. "I went to the costume store yesterday to get something but everything was stupid so I got the brilliant idea to paint my face to look like a skull—only I forgot that I can't paint." He points to his face and I can see evidence of paint left behind where he's scrubbed it off. "Help me," he pleads, holding the face-painting set out to me. "Have mercy on me, I beg of you." He throws in pouty lips for good measure.

I sigh and take the kit from him. "Come here." I point to the closed toilet lid for him to sit down.

He does as I say and I flip open the palette.

"Thea is going to kill you for not wearing a *real* costume," I warn him.

"This is a real costume," he argues.

"I'm sure she won't see it that way." I laugh. "Now be quiet."

He mimes zipping his lips and throwing away the key.

I take my time mapping out how I want the skull to look and then I work on adding the colors more heavily to his skin, and then being sure to blend them so there's no harsh lines.

It takes me a good thirty minutes before I'm happy with the final product.

I step back and assess him.

He blinks up at me. "What's the verdict?"

"You make a hot skeleton. Though, when you're as hot as you are I'm pretty sure you can pull off anything."

He laughs, placing his hands on my hips and tugging me close to him. He rests his hands on my ass and looks up at me. "You think I'm hot?"

"You know you're hot."

He grins. "That's not what I said. You think I'm hot?" he repeats.

I look away and mumble, "Yes."

He slides his hands up my waist. "I think you're hot, so I guess we're even."

He stands and the small bathroom now feels even smaller. I'm convinced the walls have moved closer together.

"Confession," he lowers his head so his lips graze my ear, "it's going to be impossible for me to keep my hands off you tonight."

"Confession," I say breathlessly, "I don't want you to."

He grins at that. "Tonight?" he asks.

I know what he's asking. "Tonight," I echo.

Fear fills me at the thought of telling our friends, but I feel excited too. Our relationship is complicated and maybe a little weird, but it's still real and shouldn't be treated like a dirty little secret.

Jace smiles and it fills me with happiness that *he's* so okay with this. He was so hesitant in the beginning, but I think he senses it too, the rightness that him and I are together. We just ... *click*.

My phone buzzes on the bathroom counter and I grab it.

Joel: Hey, I ended up not having to work. Think I'm still invited to the party?

Me: Of course. You better have a costume though or Thea might hurt you.

Joel: I have a costume.

Me: What it is it?

Joel: Tsk, tsk, Clarke. A man has to have some secrets.

Me: That's mean.

Joel: That's life.

I type out the address and tell him I'll see him there.

I head into the apartment and find Jace changing into a black t-shirt. He's decked out now in head to toe black and coupled with the face paint it's an intimidating sight.

"Joel's coming to the party," I inform him.

He growls. "No."

"Will you stop with that?" I snap, slightly irritated. "He's my friend."

"Yeah, your friend that has a dick. Do you know what guys with dicks do?" I raise a brow, knowing he's going to tell me regardless of whether or not I want to know. "They fuck hot chicks."

"And I'm a hot chick?"

He snaps his fingers together. "Exactly."

I shake my head. "You're insane."

"I'm right," he reasons. "Trust me, the guy has thought at least once about what you look like naked, but since I'm also a guy I'm going to say it's safe to assume that it's much more than once and more like a couple hundred times."

"Can we go?" I say, edging toward the door. "This conversation is giving me a migraine."

"Just stating the facts." He grabs his leather jacket and shrugs into it.

We take his truck to our friends' house, and I'm shocked by the number of cars on the street. I mean, I know Thea said it was a party but I kind of expected it to only be us. Guess I was wrong.

Jace has to park on the street about a block away and we walk from there.

We reach the door and I hesitate, wondering if I should knock or just go in, but the problem is solved for me when the door swings open, revealing Thea.

"Oh, thank God," she breathes in relief. "People I know. Get in here."

Thea's decked out in skin tight leather-looking black pants, a black off-the-shoulder fitted top, big poufy hair, with her lips colored a bright red.

"Sandy from *Grease*?" I surmise, stepping into the house with Jace following me.

She smiles and nods. "My Danny is around here somewhere. He wasn't too thrilled about the couple's costume thing but he has since warmed up to the idea and even sang his own rendition of "Greased Lightning". It was glorious."

"I'm sorry we missed that." Truly, I am. Xander singing a song from *Grease?* That had to be hilarious. "I hope you do a duet later."

She snorts. "Not likely but if I drink enough, it's a possibility." Her eyes flit over Jace. "*Jacen Kensington*," she hisses his name over the music pumping through speakers in the family room to our right. "That is *not* a costume."

"I'm a skeleton." He points at his face.

"Unless that's painted *all* over your body, then it's not a fucking costume." She glares at him. "You're in regular clothes. This is blasphemy. The King of Halloween is rolling over in his grave."

"There's no King of Halloween," Jace retorts.

Thea sticks her chin up haughtily. "If there was a King he'd be rolling over in his grave. You're an insult to all Halloween loving people."

Jace shrugs. "I just never got into it."

Thea gapes at him. "Have you ever even seen *Hocus Pocus*?" He shakes his head. She clutches at her chest like an old lady would clutch her pearls. "Are you kidding me? I can't believe I'm hearing this. This breaks my heart. You're coming over and watching *Hocus Pocus* tomorrow, got it?"

"Halloween is over tomorrow," he grumbles.

"Every day is Halloween where *Hocus Pocus* is concerned."

"I have to work," he mumbles weakly.

"You aren't working all day, I'm not stupid."

He sighs. "Fine. Nova's coming too, then."

"Hey," I defend. "I *have* seen *Hocus Pocus* before."

"Yeah, but—" He wraps an arm around me. "Since you're kind of my girlfriend now you owe it to me to be there for moral support."

Thea's jaw drops. "What did you say?"

I glare at Jace, semi-pissed that he let that bomb drop but also surprised that he went through with telling them. I thought we'd get here and he'd change his mind and decide tonight wasn't the best time to say something. Suddenly, I wonder if *I'm* now the one holding back in the relationship more.

"Nova and I are together," he says.

"Oh, my God," she squeals, clapping her hands together. "This is amazing. I always thought you two had amazing chemistry. It's about damn time. Come on." She reaches for my hand. "We have to tell the others."

Jace's arm drops from around me and he grabs my other hand as Thea pulls us through the house and to the kitchen. Xander's sitting on one of the bar stools, dressed in black jeans, with a black t-shirt tucked into them, boots, and his black hair slicked back. He's even shaved for the occasion. I can't even recall a time where I've not seen Xander with some sort of scruff on his cheeks.

Cade stands beside him dressed in jeans, with a white

button down shirt with a vest over that sports a gold and maroon crest and tie, with a long black cloak completing the ensemble. I realize belatedly that he's dressed as a Harry Potter character—the wand in his hand helps.

Across the island, pouring a drink, is Rae dressed as a cute scarecrow with jeans, a plaid shirt, a straw hat, and her face painted to complete the look.

"None of them are in real costumes," Jace defends.

"Yeah, but I like them more than I like you," Thea jests, releasing her hold on me. "Guess what I just learned," she says to our group. There are a few other people milling about in the kitchen, someone dressed as Batman, another as Wonder Woman, and I even spot someone dressed as Marty McFly from *Back to the Future* so props to them for being creative. "Guess," she says again when they all just look at her.

Xander wraps his arm around her waist and pulls her close to him. "That nobody loves Halloween as much as you?"

She smiles at him. "That might be true—but no."

"Just tell us," Rae says, leaning against the counter with a bottle of water clutched in her hand. "I hate guessing games. Nobody ever gets it right."

Thea pouts slightly. "You guys ruin all my fun." She shakes her head. "Anyway, I learned that our very own, self-proclaimed, single-for-life friends are dating. Each other—in case you didn't get my implication."

Cade chokes on his drink and wipes his mouth with the back of his hand. "Dude, I ... I'm shocked."

"When did this happen?" Rae asks, her lips downturned. I can tell from her posture that she's slightly hurt by this news. I don't think she's upset that Jace and I are together, but more that I didn't tell her. I've never been all that good at talking to people, that's why it's always surprised me that it's so effortless with Jace.

"Not long," I mumble. I figure an ambiguous answer is the best route.

"So, yeah," Jace says, looking at me with a smile. "That's that." Pointing at each of our friends he adds, "Don't make this a big fucking deal, okay?"

"There goes my plans for a party," Thea jokes. "Whatever will I do?"

"Come on." Jace takes my hand and tugs me from the kitchen. "Let's get away from these freaks."

"We love you too," Xander chortles, lifting his beer in the air as we leave.

Once out of earshot of our friends, Jace leans down to my ear. "That went better than I thought but I wanted to get out of there before they asked us to all hold hands and sing Kumbaya."

I laugh. "That still might happen, you know."

"I hope you're ready to run then."

We enter the living room, which seems to be the main gathering place. Several people sit on the couch while others stand and chat. A few people even use the clear middle space for dancing.

Jace guides me to a corner area and positions me so my back is to his front. I smile even though he can't see—but this, this is nice. I never thought I'd feel content in a relationship again, but with the Jace the fear of heartbreak barely even registers, because this feels so right.

"Hey, Nova!" a male voice calls over to me.

I look around and my eyes land on a guy dressed as Green Arrow. "Joel! Hey!"

"*Joel*," Jace growls, and I elbow him in the gut.

"Be nice," I hiss.

Joel makes his way over to us from the foyer.

"I thought you were working," Jace says, and I elbow him again. "*Hey*, quit that," he whispers in my ear.

"Then *be nice*," I reiterate.

"It was a question," he mumbles innocently.

"I ended up being off," Joel explains. "So, I wanted to swing by if I could. I love costume parties."

"Hmm, interesting," Jace comments.

"Cut it out," I hiss, ready to elbow him again.

"Anyway," Joel clears his throat, "I just wanted to say hi. I'm going to go get a drink. I ... um ... take it you two let your friends know you're together?" He points to us where we stand cozily together.

I smile up at Jace. "Yeah, they know now," I tell him.

Joel nods. "Good. That's good."

He turns and leaves, and I swear I hear Jace growl.

"What?" I look up at him and find that his lip is curled in a snarl.

"He still wants to fuck you, and it's pissing me off."

I laugh and step out of his embrace so I can face him. "He does not," I argue.

"He does." Jace nods. "I can tell. He needs to stop."

I place my palm on his hard chest, feeling the planes of his muscle through the thin cotton. I lean up and brush my lips softly over his before I murmur, "I guess it's a good thing you're the only guy I want to see me naked."

"Better be." He places his hands on my waist, his fingers grazing my butt.

I stretch up on my tiptoes and kiss him. He kisses me back with fervor and I know he's purposely trying to take it to X-rated levels so I quickly pull away and shake my head.

"Nice try," I say.

He grins like a little kid who's gotten caught with their hand stuck in the cookie jar.

The music changes and I tug on his hand. "Dance with me."

"How is it we always end up dancing?" He chuckles.

"I think we just like to move together, even if we have to do it with our clothes on."

He laughs and my stomach flutters with happiness at the sound. He used to rarely smile or laugh, and now he does it often. It makes me feel slightly victorious.

Xander and Thea have come into the living room and dance a few feet away where Thea steals glances in our direction. I do my best to not let her stare get to me.

Jace skims his hands up my sides, grazing his fingers beneath the curve of my breasts, and I shiver. He knows how to get to me faster than anyone else ever has. It's like he has a direct line to my vagina.

The song playing is hot and sultry. The kind of song that

makes you want to strip off your clothes and have sweaty, mind-blowing sex. It doesn't help that the guy I'm dancing with is sex on a stick.

He rubs his hands down my body and squeezes my butt. Lowering his head, he murmurs, "If you keep looking at me like that I'm going to have to fuck you."

"Is that a promise?" I breathe, looking at him through hooded eyes.

His eyes flash a stormy green and he takes my hand, guiding me from the room.

He leads me through the house and to the back laundry room. He shuts and locks the door behind us.

I move a few steps back and he stalks forward, closing the distance like a predator cornering its prey. I'm sure the prey doesn't normally want to get caught, but I can't help but love getting tangled in his web.

My heart thunders in my chest, and in the back of my mind I worry about what I'm thinking about doing in my friends' house, but when it comes to Jace there's no such thing as common sense.

His fingers tangle in my hair and I gasp as he draws my head back. He closes his mouth over mine, his tongue plunging inside. I claw at his shirt, wild with need and desire. His hands roam from my back down to my butt, where he pulls me against him so I can feel his hardness.

He releases my hair, and I stumble back from the sudden release of pressure.

His face paint is now streaked with red from my lips, and

I love seeing it—love seeing the chaos that is us represented so fully.

I pull in a ragged breath, watching him. His shoulders are hunched and he stares at me.

Waiting.

I move.

He moves.

We crash together, a tangle of limbs and teeth. We tear at each other's clothes, not able to undress the other fast enough. This wildness feels so natural that it's hard to believe that I've only ever experienced it with Jace. I feel like he's shown me my true colors. Passion bleeds red behind my eyes as he picks me up and pushes my back into the wall.

I cry out as he pushes into me. I should probably care about someone hearing, but I don't. All that exists is him and me and this.

I breathe out heavily, unable to catch my breath.

He takes my hands and pins them above my head, fucking me with a reckless abandon.

He kisses me deeply, stealing my breath and maybe a little bit of my soul in the process.

He bites my bottom lip, and I moan. He chuckles at the sound and releases my lip with a pop. Holding my hands in one of his he uses his free one to grip my chin, angling my head so I'm looking right at him.

"You love this, don't you?" he growls. "You love it when I fuck you."

"Yes," I pant, clinging to his shoulders.

"Say it," he commands. "I want to hear you say it."

"I love it," I breathe, fighting to look away.

He seals his lips over mine and then murmurs, "Good girl." He releases me and my chin stings as blood flows back to the places where his fingers marked me. He leans his forehead against mine and looks down. "Watch us," he whispers, and my eyes flow down to where we're joined. The sight of his hard cock moving in and out of me sends another flood of desire through my body. "Nobody can fuck you like I can." He brushes his lips against my ear. "Remember that."

He lets go of my hands, and I sag against him. His fingers dig into my ass as he holds my weight. He fucks me desperately, like he's afraid I'm about to disappear.

It feels too soon, but I'm coming. The peak hits and I cry out. He slams his lips to mine, our teeth crashing painfully together as he silences my cries. His tongue tangles with mine and I tug on his hair.

He comes a moment later, groaning into my neck with his fingers gripping my hips.

His body sags against mine as my legs fall to the ground.

Before Jace I'd never been fucked against a wall.

Now it's happened twice. I'm convinced it's my favorite place to have sex now.

We each struggle to gain control of our breathing, for the moment content to cling to each other as we come down from our high.

Several minutes pass before we find the energy to right our clothes. His makeup is ruined, a combination of sweat and frantic kisses, and I'm sure mine hasn't fared better. There's nothing I can do to try to salvage it.

Jace opens the door and we sneak out, back into the party.

More people have arrived and the hallway is thick with guests. We can barely push our way through. We pass Joel, making out with a girl dressed as Princess Peach. I smack Jace's arm and force him to look.

He chuckles and slings his arm around my shoulders.

"Good, maybe the prick will get a girlfriend so he'll stop staring at you."

I shake my head, not about to argue with him again about Joel liking me. We round the corner into the family room and find that chaos has erupted.

Thea dances on the coffee table singing "You're the One That I Want" to Xander, who stands with his arms crossed over his chest and a horrified expression on his face. She crooks a finger, urging him forward to sing with her. He shakes his head, trying not to laugh. Unfazed, Thea shrugs her shoulders and continues to sing and dance. Several other people sing along with her.

"She's crazy," Jace says in my ear. "But I kinda like her. Don't tell her I said that, though."

I laugh. "Don't want anyone to know you have feelings?"

He grins, his eyes lighting. "I gotta keep my street cred."

"I'm going to go get a drink," I tell him, heading for the kitchen.

"I want one too," he says, following.

I grab a beer out of the cooler on the counter and hand it to Jace, then grab another one for myself.

Jace clinks his bottle to mine.

"What are we cheersing to?" I ask.

He tugs his bottom lip between his teeth, thinking. "Possibilities," he finally answers.

I nod, smiling. I like that answer. "To possibilities," I echo.

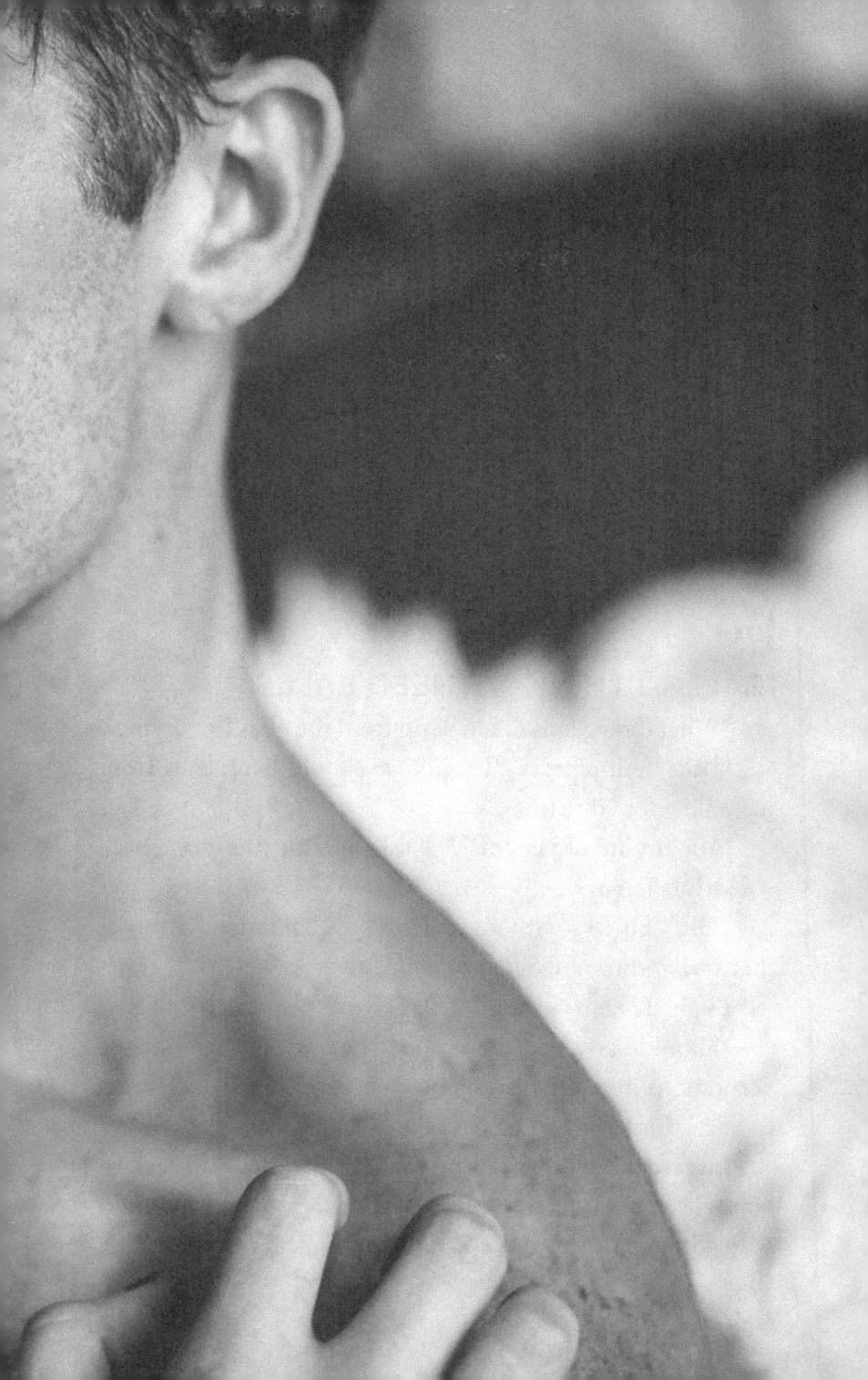

seventeen

...

jace

"BALLS. I THINK WE NEED BALLS."

"What did you say?" I look up from the glass I'm drying.

"Balls," Eli repeats. "I think we should hang balls from the ceiling for Christmas."

"You mean ornaments?" I ask, placing the glass back where it belongs.

"Oh," Eli says with a small gasp. "That's right. I forgot that's what those are called."

I sigh. There's never a dull day when you work for Eli.

"Shouldn't we be more concerned with Thanksgiving decorations if you're planning to decorate?" I ask, beginning to mix a drink for a customer.

Eli rests his elbows on the bar. His dark hair is speckled with glitter. I don't think I'll ever understand his obsession with glitter. The shit gets everywhere and won't go away.

Eli waves a hand dismissively at my words. "Nobody cares about Thanksgiving. It's Halloween and Christmas and that's it. Nothing else matters."

I laugh. "Speak for yourself. I think a lot of people like other holidays."

"Then they're stupid."

I shake my head. Eli has no filter. It's one reason I like him as a boss.

"Move, *Jacen*," Matilda snaps, bumping me as she passes.

If she was a guy, I swear I would've hit her by now.

"Matilda," Eli scolds, but that's as far as it goes.

I give the customer their drink and return to Eli. "So, who's going to hang these ornaments from the ceiling?" I ask.

"You, of course."

I sigh. I should've known.

"Hey," Nova greets breathlessly, dropping onto one of the stools.

"Hey," Eli says.

"She was talking to me," I tease, and wink at her.

"Why?" Eli wrinkles his nose. "I'm cuter."

"I need your help," Nova says to me, ignoring Eli's comment.

"With what?" I lean my elbows on the bar.

"I need to take your picture."

I groan. "No."

"Please?" she pouts. "It's for school. I have a project and I have the perfect idea, but I need your help for it."

I tug on my hair. "I'm not getting out of this, am I?"

She shakes her head. "Nope."

"Out of the way, *Jacen*." Matilda bumps me again as she passes.

Nova snorts. "I know you hate your full name, but adding the *en* to your name still isn't that great of an insult."

"Don't say that where she can hear or she might have to get creative."

She laughs. "She doesn't have the brains to be creative."

"Be nice, kids," Eli warns.

"Sorry, Dad," I joke.

"I am far too young and fabulous to be your dad." Eli flips his head to the side with a flourish.

"Are you hungry?" I ask Nova.

"Um, yeah. I want a burger."

"Coming right up," I tell her, and spin around to enter her order into the system.

Eli hops off his bar stool. "I'm going to be in my office. Try not to kill Matilda while I'm gone."

"No promises," I call after him.

I get Nova a glass of water without her asking.

I tend to the other people at the bar. The place is packed, and it's not even our busy time.

I'm curious as to what Nova needs me to do to help with her project.

Something tells me I don't want to know.

Nova's burger is ready about fifteen minutes later and I bring the plate to her.

"I have to eat and run," she says. "I have to get over to the record store."

My brows furrow. "I thought they were closed by this time."

She nods. "Normally, yes. They're doing some kind of special promotion thing—trying to get people to buy records and sign up for guitar lessons. It's like a party of sorts. Food. Drinks. You get the idea. I said I'd come in and help keep the place organized."

I nod. "Ah, I see."

She bites into her burger. "Oh, man, that's good. I was starving. I skipped lunch."

I look at the time. "It's six-o-clock. You have to eat," I scold.

"Didn't have time." She shrugs.

I shake my head. I don't have time to stand and chat but I let her know with my eyes that I'm going to make sure she eats every bit of food on her plate.

She salutes me mockingly, and I try not to laugh.

She was starving because it isn't long until her plate is clean.

"Thank you," she says, laying some cash on the bar. I growl. I hate it when she pays. I always take care of her bill. "I'll see you later." She dashes away before I can give the money back. I take it and shove it in my pocket. I'll figure out a way to get it back to her later.

I know she knows that I never cash her checks for rent. She never asks why, and I never comment on it. She keeps writing them, and I keep taking them only to rip them up and throw them in the trash.

I hate my dad, but I don't hate the money he gives me.

Every month like clockwork he deposits ten-thousand dollars into my account. I never spend that much, so I have a ton saved up. I know Nova doesn't have a lot so taking rent money from her isn't necessary. I'd rather her have money for other things.

Sometimes I get pissed at myself for accepting the money from my dad, but then I remember all the shit he put me through as a kid, and I think I fucking *deserve* that money.

He's used me my whole life, I might as well use him too, right?

The apartment is dark when I get home, and I half-expect to find Nova asleep, but instead she sits in the middle of my bed with her legs crossed in the tiniest pair of black underwear and a loose white top that falls over one shoulder. I can see her nipples through the thin cotton, and I'm instantly hard.

In her hands is a camera and she holds it up, clicking the button.

A polaroid prints out.

"What are you doing?" I ask huskily, toeing off my boots.

She rests on her knees and leans, aiming the camera at the floor—toward my feet.

"My project," she answers, slipping off the bed and stalking forward. "*Moments.*"

"You're taking my picture for your project?" I raise a brow, waiting for her answer.

She lifts the camera toward my face and snaps another photo. It prints out and she grabs it, placing it on the table.

"Yes," she answers. "You know how you said I inspire you to write music?" I nod. "I think you inspire me with photography." She wets her lips with a swipe of her tongue. "Portrait photography isn't normally my thing, but I've wanted to take your picture for a long time, and for our project we had to do something with meaning. I thought of you first and the whole idea for the project sort of fell into place."

"Tell me more. Why did you say moments?"

Her lips quirk up into a smile. "Moments. I'm calling it *Moments*. The focus is on the little details and how they piece together to make a bigger picture."

"You're a genius," I tell her.

She beams at my words. "I thought it was a good idea."

She takes a picture of my lips.

"Take your shirt off," she commands.

I smile slowly. "You don't tell me what to do."

She shakes her head. "Not tonight. Tonight, I'm in charge."

I fight a smile and she takes another picture.

"Shirt. Off."

"You're a bossy little thing, aren't you?" I laugh.

I hook my fingers into the back of my shirt, and she says,

"Wait." She moves behind me to take a picture of my fingers in my shirt. Once she has it, she says, "You can continue."

I grin, but she can't see it.

I remove the shirt slowly. Revealing a little of my skin at a time, letting her take as many photos as she wants.

There's something intensely erotic about letting her take pictures of me like this. It feels like I'm exposing a part of myself that isn't normally seen.

She stands in front of me once more and snaps another photo.

"Drape the shirt over your shoulder," she commands.

"So bossy," I say again, and she glares which I'd hoped she would. She's cute when she's angry. She crinkles her nose, which makes her freckles stand out more, and purses her pouty lips. When she's mad, it makes me want to grab her, and kiss her, and fuck her, and show her how to channel that anger into something else. She takes a photo of the shirt dangling over my arm. "Where to next?" I ask her.

"Sit on the couch."

Normally, I hate someone telling me what to do. I blame it on my father, who controlled every aspect of my life growing up, but I don't find myself feeling that way now that Nova has turned the tables on me.

I do as she says and sit down.

She takes a photo that shows all of me, then she moves in, getting one of just my hand where I have it clutching the back of my head. Then she gets a close-up of my lips, my eyes, and my chest.

My heart beats like a steady drum in my chest.

I watch her carefully, my skin prickling with awareness at her proximity.

I feel so exposed as she takes my picture.

Stripped bare and splayed raw.

But I don't stop her. I don't want to.

She sinks down onto my lap, straddling me, and murmurs, "Touch me."

I wrap my finger around her choker necklace.

"Take a picture," she says breathlessly and hands me the camera.

I take it from her and snap a photo of my fingers tangled in the black cord.

I release it and grab her neck.

Click.

Her eyes flare with desire.

Click.

She bites her lip.

Click.

I grab her hair.

Click.

I snake my fingers under her shirt.

Click.

I lift her shirt off.

Click.

I aim the camera at her bare collarbone.

Click.

Then her stomach.

Click.

She takes the camera back.

"My turn," she says, her voice thick with desire.

She takes a picture of my belt buckle.

"Aren't these getting a bit X-rated for school?" I comment.

She grins like the cat that ate the canary and leans forward, pushing her breasts into my chest so she can whisper in my ear, "Some are for me."

I growl and push her down onto the couch, shielding her with my body.

"Then you won't mind if I take some for me?"

I don't wait for her to answer.

I seal my lips over hers. I kiss her desperately, like I didn't just kiss her this morning. I feel like I haven't touched in her years, when in reality, I just had her this morning in the shower before she had to leave for class.

I cup her breasts as I kiss her, loving the fullness of her in my hands.

She moves her arms, getting the camera out from in-between us. I growl in satisfaction because now I can feel her more fully against me.

Her skin is soft and smooth like butter. I could touch her forever.

The camera clicks and because my eyes are closed I don't know what she's taken a photo of, or if she even meant to do it. It could've been a complete accident.

I gather my arms around her back and she wraps her legs around my waist as I grind against her.

I pick her up and stand from the couch with her in my arms.

I carry her to the bed with her arms wrapped around me.

She still holds the camera and when I release her so she lies back on the bed she snaps a photo of me standing above her.

She places her foot on my chest.

Click.

I grab her leg, gliding my hand down her thigh.

Click.

I grab her thighs and pull her to the edge of the bed to meet me.

Click.

I take the camera from her.

"That's mine."

I shake my head. "*Ours.*"

Her hair is splayed around her and she looks beautiful.

Click.

She sits up, and I rub my thumb over her lip.

Click.

Her dark lashes flutter against her cheeks.

Click.

She takes the camera, and I smirk as she undoes my belt.

Click.

The button comes undone next.

Click.

Zipper.

Click.

My jeans slide down to the floor.

I feel like I might explode from the need to touch her, but there's something infinitely more powerful about *not* touching her, about relinquishing control to her, if only for the moment.

She rakes her nails down my chest, and I shiver.

Click.

She pulls down my boxer-briefs just slightly, so the barest hint of un-tanned skin shows.

Click.

She removes them entirely, and I step out of them, snatching the camera from her again.

I grab her underwear forcefully.

Click.

I slide them down her hips, and when they reach her knees, I stop to take another photo.

Click.

I remove them completely and take a picture of her bare hips.

She snatches the camera from me and drops it on the bed.

"Touch me," she begs. "Please."

I don't have to be told twice.

I spread her legs, kissing my way down her thigh. I revel at her little gasp when my tongue touches her pussy.

"Oh, Jace," she moans, her hips bucking and her fingers tugging on my hair.

I swirl my tongue around her smooth skin, sucking at times.

She writes against the bed and it fills me with satisfaction to feel her fall apart beneath me—to know that *I* do that to her.

Sex has always been just about sex to me—the act itself. But with Nova it's so much more.

It's an art form.

I move up her body, swirling my tongue around her right nipple and gripping her left breast in my hand. She moans, her hips rising to meet mine. With my free hand, I push her hips back down to the bed and hold them there. She whimpers and I smile, kissing her.

"Jace," she breathes between our lips. "Need. You," she pants brokenly.

I move my hand in-between us, finding her slick and wet already. I easily slip a finger inside and she gasps at the intrusion, her wide dark eyes flashing up to mine. She looks at me with an inexplicable trust. She knows I won't hurt her and that I'm about to show her the greatest kind of pleasure.

I skim my lips down her neck, and she shivers, her nipples tightening.

I add another finger and her eyes close.

I grab her chin. "Eyes open, Nova."

Her eyes reluctantly flutter open, the warm brown all but swallowed by black and thick with lust. Her lips are pink and pouted, already swollen from my kiss and the night's only just beginning.

The tiredness I felt upon getting off work has completely disappeared. I feel alive in a way I didn't know was possible.

"You're beautiful," I tell her, my teeth biting into her shoulder.

Marking her.

Claiming her.

She glides her hands from my waist, up my chest, circling around my shoulders where she locks her fingers together at the base of my neck. She takes one hand and traces a shaking finger over my lips.

"So are you."

I grab her hand in my own, kissing her fingers before locking our fingers together and placing our joined hands over my heart.

This moment feels profound.

I don't know if she quite understands my meaning—that I'm showing her, since I can't say it, that my heart is hers. I never thought I'd give it to anyone—to love is to give someone the power to destroy you—but these few short weeks with Nova have been some of the best of my life, and I've never felt stronger, or happier.

Nova's fingers tremble in mine, and I think, I hope, at least, that she does understand.

I release her and grab her hips, sliding her up on the bed.

I follow, and she spreads her legs to accommodate my body.

My eyes find hers, and I grab the base of my cock, guiding it inside her.

She gasps, her hips fighting to move but I hold her steady. Her teeth dig into her bottom lip and her nails rake down my back.

"Jace. Oh, God," she whimpers, her legs shaking.

I ease back out and in.

"J-Jace. Please. Fuck me hard."

I shake my head. "No."

She trembles beneath me.

"I need—"

I silence her with a kiss and pull back. "I know what you need. Trust me. You trust me, right?"

She swallows thickly and nods, her eyes vibrant.

"I need to hear you say it."

"I trust you."

I've never made love to anyone before. It's always been hard, and fast, and your stereotypical *fuck*. I never thought I'd want this—slow love-making with *feelings*. But fuck, I think this is the hottest thing I've ever experienced in my life. Every moment, every second, feels infinitely slow down.

My hair falls in my eyes, and I flick my head to the side, ridding myself of the annoyance, because I don't want to miss a moment of this. I want to watch her.

I slide in and out of her slowly and her lips part as little pants escape her. Her eyes roam my body, from my head down to where we're joined. When her eyes find the spot where my cock moves in and out of her, she moans and clenches around me. My little Nova likes to watch, and I fucking love that it turns her on as much as it does me.

I cup the back of her neck and draw her to me, kissing her until we both have to stop and catch our breath.

I lower my head to the crook of her neck, pressing my lips to the spot where her pulse races.

Her pussy clenches around me, and I know she's close.

I wrap my hand around her neck, applying a little pressure, and she clenches again.

So close.

I sit up and grab her legs, lifting her to meet me.

"Oh, my God." Her head falls to the side and her lips part as she comes. Every little sound, every little gasp, I fucking *own* that.

I've never seen anything more beautiful than Nova coming apart beneath me, ripped at the seams by what I, and I alone, do to her.

A shiver runs down my spine as I try to fight my need to come, but it's impossible. It hits me, and I'm unable to stop it. I come, shouting her name, with black spots dancing behind my eyes. I fall onto her, careful to hold my weight so I don't crush her. It's the strongest orgasm I've ever had in my life. Nothing has ever felt that powerful before.

I roll off her, my chest rising and falling rapidly as I struggle to get enough air into my lungs.

Nova turns onto her side and loops her leg through mine and drapes her arm over my body with her head pillowed on my chest.

Exhaustion so sudden that I don't see it coming overtakes me, and I fall right to sleep.

eighteen
...

nova

I STEP out of the bathroom, drying my damp hair with a towel.

Jace looks up from his guitar and the notebook in his lap, scribbled with notes.

His mouth drops when he sees me.

"Y-Your hair," he stutters, swirling his finger around his own head. "W-What color do you call that?"

I smile and sit down on the coffee table across from him, tilting my head to the side. "Me," I answer.

He shakes his head. "You're a brunette?" I nod. "I've never seen you with normal colored hair before. I mean, I always assumed you were a brunette, but it's different seeing you this way. What made you decide to go back to your natural hair color?"

"You," I answer.

"Me?" He sets his guitar down so it's leaning propped against the couch.

I nod. "Yeah ... your song you wrote ... I kept thinking about it, how true it is. I dye my hair to hide who I am, who I really am. I don't want to hide anymore." I shrug, like it's as simple as that.

He leans forward and reaches out, ghosting his fingers over my cheek. I lean into his touch with a sigh.

The decision to dye my hair brown again wasn't an easy one.

After I moved to Colorado and was on my own, I knew I wanted to do something *big*—something my parents would've been horrified of. So, I dyed my hair purple. Then the colors kept changing, but while the color might've changed, *I* never did. I've still been the same old Nova underneath, and Jace helped me to realize that. I shouldn't be ashamed of who I was or who I am.

It was time for me to go back to brunette—to embrace who I am.

"Do you hate it?" I ask nervously.

He grins. "You look beautiful. You're always beautiful."

I sigh in relief. "Thanks. It ... It feels good. It feels right to be brunette again. I know that probably seems silly, it's just a hair color, but—"

He presses a finger to my lips, silencing me. "It's not silly. I understand."

"You do?"

He nods. "You've finally realized that you're strong

enough to protect yourself on your own, that you don't need a shield."

"You know too much," I tell him.

He chuckles. "I'm quiet. We see and know everything." He winks.

I shiver. How is it possible that talking about something like *this* he manages to turn me on?

I move to sit beside him on the couch.

And then his phone rings. He swipes it off the coffee table and looks at the name flashing on the screen.

He curses.

"Who is it?" I ask, wondering who's caused him to tense up and for lines to form between his brows.

"My father."

He stands and answers the phone. "Hello?" His voice is tight, clipped, as he speaks through clenched teeth. "I'm fine, sir, and you?"

Sir?

He paces the length of the room and the tension radiating off him is enough to set me on edge.

They exchange a few more clipped words before Jace opens the large window and slips out onto the balcony.

Shirtless and in bare feet.

In the middle of November.

I shake my head and grab a jacket and socks and take them out to him but he doesn't even notice me when I place the items on the metal grate beside him where he crouches. He looks like he's seconds away from launching himself off the balcony and onto the ground below him. I know a thing or two about parents driving you to madness.

I make my way back into the apartment and sit on the couch, waiting for him to finish his conversation.

Fifteen or so minutes later he gets off the phone and comes back inside, shivering since he neglected to put the jacket and socks on.

Men.

He looks pale and sick, and I think it has little to do with being cold and everything to do with his father.

He stands in front of me, hands on his hips, and holds up a finger, begging me to give him a moment.

Which I do.

Sometimes we all need a minute to steady ourselves for the impending storm.

He presses his lips together and finally speaks.

"My dad wants me to attend some fucking family holiday dinner thing next week. It's some sort of fancy Thanksgiving gala thing for a bunch of uppity fucktards he works with and he needs me there playing the part of the dutiful son." Jace snorts and rolls his eyes. "I don't know why he can't just leave me alone." He mutters the last part under his breath. He groans and presses the heels of his hands to his eyes. Letting them drop, he says, "Come with me."

"What?" I gasp.

"To the party-gala-ball-thing," he rambles. "Please," he begs. "It might be bearable if you're there."

"Jace," I hedge. "I don't know."

"Please." He sinks to his knees in front of me. Vulnerable. Open. Begging. "Please," he says again. "I know it's not your kind of thing. It's not mine, either. But I have to go. Please, be my date."

How can I so no to that?

I nod. "I'll go."

"Thank you." He hugs me to him.

Something tells me that me going to this thing is a bigger deal for him than he's letting on, but I don't say anything. He wants me there, so I'll be there.

He releases me. "You're going to have to get a dress."

"I'm sure I have something—"

He shakes his head. "Not even the dress you wore to Xander and Thea's wedding would be fancy enough for this. Trust me."

My mouth pops open. Maybe agreeing to this wasn't such a good idea.

"Well," I say, hoping my apprehension doesn't show on my face, "I guess I better ask Thea and Rae to go shopping."

He nods. "Good idea."

Oh, good Lord—if he's agreeing I need to go shopping with Thea *then this must be a super fancy thing.*

"I'll talk to the girls," I say.

He kisses me quickly before pulling away. "Thank you. This means more than you know." He stands and rubs his hands on his jeans. "Now I *really* need a cigarette."

I shake my head as he disappears back through the window to smoke.

I text Thea and Rae in a group chat and they both readily agree to go shopping tomorrow.

I hope I can find something because if I have to go shopping again I just may die.

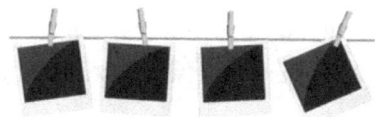

"What about this one?" Thea asks, holding up a shimmery, pink, mermaid gown.

I point a warning finger at her. "If you show me one more pink dress I'm barricading you in a dressing room and leaving you here."

Thea pouts. "*No* would've sufficed."

I sigh. "Pink isn't my thing. If I have to where a stuffy ball gown I need to at least feel like *me*."

"And who are you again?" Rae jokes, ruffling my dark brown locks of hair. "I can't get over the brown. It seems so much weirder than the green or blue."

"It's just because you've never seen me with normal hair," I reason, looking through dresses on a rack.

"What kind of event are we dealing with?" Thea asks. "That'll help me decide what dress style is best."

I sigh and shrug. "All Jace said was, *"It's fancy. Like really fucking fancy. Think celebrities on the red carpet kind of fancy."*"

"Oh, that helps," Thea says, rifling through some dresses.

She's the one that brought us to this boutique on the

opposite side of town. It's two stories in a high-rise building with dresses *everywhere*. If I can't find one here, then there's something wrong with me.

"What kind of color would you like?" Thea asks, her tongue sticking out between her lips as she concentrates on the dresses.

"Preferably black," I answer. "But I'm open to other options, as long as it's dark or jewel tone. Do *not* give me anything pastel or I might strangle you with it," I warn.

"No pastel. Noted."

I flip through dress after dress, each more hideous than the last.

"What about this one?" Thea holds up a navy dress encrusted with silver beaded detailing.

I gag. "No."

She groans. "Nova," she scolds. "You hate everything."

"There has to be something here," I whine.

"What about this?" Rae points to a deep purple dress on one of the store mannequins. It has a sweetheart neckline and a ball gown skirt.

"I like the color but it's too poufy."

Rae and Thea exchange a look. I know they're getting put out with me, but if I have to wear a fancy dress I need to at least feel like myself.

I move to another rack.

"How about this?"

I turn around and bust out laughing at the pale blue confection Rae holds.

"I didn't pick it." Thea raises her hands innocently.

Minutes pass as we search quietly to ourselves.

"Oh, my God," Thea gasps. "I think I found it. I'm serious."

We both hurry over to her side to see what she found.

I gasp. "It's perfect."

I reach out to touch the silky black fabric.

"Try it on." Thea shoves the dress into my chest. "Hurry, hurry. I want to see it on."

She shoves me into a dressing room and swishes the curtain closed with a flourish.

I change as quickly as I can, but apparently not quickly enough.

"Are you not done yet?"

I scream when I look down and see Thea poking her head beneath the curtain.

"Thea!" I scold.

"What?" She looks up at me innocently. "You have a cute butt," she notes.

"Get out." I shoo her away.

"I know what a girl looks like naked," she grumbles. "It's not a big deal." But thankfully she shimmies out from underneath the dressing room.

I can hear Rae laughing through the curtain. "I hate you both," I grumble.

"Impossible," Thea says. "We're both far too lovable."

I finish putting the dress on and appraise myself in the mirror. I run my hands down the front of the dress and smile.

It's perfect.

I open the curtain and they both gasp.

"That's amazing on you," Rae tells me.

"You look like a real girl now," Thea jokes. "This is perfect."

I move to the mirror and look at the dress from every angle.

The bodice of the dress hugs my chest, all the way down to my hips, where it flows out and cascades down to the floor. What makes it so eye-catching is the detailing on the chest. There's see-through mesh fabric and lace detailing that extends to the back. It's simple but incredibly sexy. I know Jace will lose his mind when he sees it.

"You have to get it," Thea says. "You're not going to find anything better than this." I nod in agreement. "Oh!" she cries. "Shoes. You need shoes. And jewelry. I'll be right back."

Before either Rae or I can say anything, she takes off for the opposite end of the boutique.

When she returns, she holds out a pair of black stilettos and silver chandelier earrings. I wave away the earrings but take the shoes. I slip them on, instantly six inches taller, and wobble.

"Think I can get away with wearing boots under my dress?" I ask.

"Not a chance," Thea says.

I sigh. I know she's right.

"Guess I better practice," I mumble.

I teeter back into the dressing room and change back into my clothes before heading to buy the dress and shoes.

I balk at the price since it's nearly two-months' worth of

rent, but since Jace never cashes my checks it's not that big of a deal. He even tried to get me to take his credit card with me today to buy my dress, insisting I wouldn't need to buy one if it wasn't for him, but I refused.

Once I'm armed with my garment and shopping bag, the girls and I head around the corner to get a bite to eat.

Shopping makes you hungry, apparently.

I find myself smiling, and laughing, and enjoying myself.

Normally, when I hang out with just the girls I'm counting down the minutes until I can leave and do my own thing. It's not that I don't like my friends, it's just hard to sometimes feel like I belong.

I think maybe I've finally found my place in the world.

nineteen
...

jace

I TUG on my solid black tie.

My all-black tux feels suffocating, and I haven't even stepped foot out of the apartment.

It's going to be a long night.

I appraise my appearance in the bathroom mirror, looking for any flaw my dad might find.

I shaved—so he can't call me a hoodlum for not shaving.

My hair is slicked back and gelled, so there's no chance it's going to fall in my eyes—something else he hates.

The only thing I can find that he might find fault in is the scowl on my face I can't seem to erase.

I turn off the bathroom light and sit at the kitchen table, waiting for Nova to finish getting ready.

Nothing prepares for the sight that meets me when she walks out of her room.

"Nova," I squeak.

She ducks her head bashfully. "What do you think?"

"You ... You look ... Wow."

I'm at a loss for words. She looks amazing in a floor-length black dress. It's sheer and lacy in the front and ... it's just fucking mind-blowing.

I stand and cross the room to her.

I place my hands on her hips and draw her to me. I lower my head and kiss her quickly so I don't mess up the dark lipstick she wears.

"You don't look so bad yourself," she comments with a smile. I step back with a smirk and let her check me out. "Does your dad know you're bringing me?" she asks.

I shake my head. "It's better the less he knows," I mutter.

She makes a face. She's about to learn all too soon what an asshole my dad is. It's something I hoped I could spare her from, but I'd much rather have her at my side than suffer alone tonight.

Or worse, get groped by a bunch of old socialites because that's happened before.

"Are we taking your truck?" she asks, picking up a clutch from the kitchen table.

I snort. "My dad would kill me if I showed up in my truck. He sent a car."

"Oh ... should we go then?"

I sigh. "Yeah. There's no point in delaying the inevitable."

I lock up behind us and we're silent through the elevator ride.

I guide her outside and the driver of a parked black Escalade hops out.

"Mr. Kensington?"

"Yep, that's me," I say.

He gets the door, and I help Nova into the car before climbing in behind her.

The door closes and he climbs back in the driver's seat.

Nova and I don't talk during the drive. I think her silence is from nerves while mine is purposeful. I don't know this driver, so I don't trust him, and I don't want to risk the chance of anything I say getting back to my dad.

An hour later we pull up outside a mansion that's located away from the city.

The driver waits for our turn before letting us out at the steps. Somebody waits there to open the door, and I slide out, turning to hold a hand out to Nova.

She wobbles, unsteady in her heels, and I hold tightly to her so she doesn't fall.

"Are you okay?" I whisper against her hair.

She nods, looking around with wide eyes. She swallows thickly. "It's just now occurred to me that I've never asked you what your dad does."

I wrinkle my nose in distaste as we start up the stairs slowly. "He's a Senator."

Nova nearly falls over and I don't know whether it's my words that have bowed her, or she's just clumsy in the death traps she calls shoes.

"A-A Senator?"

Definitely the Senator thing then.

"Yeah," I say, my brows furrowing in confusion. "Is everything okay?"

"It's nothing," she mutters.

I watch her carefully, noting the panic written plainly on her face, making it obvious that there is something wrong. Unfortunately, I don't have time to press the matter.

We enter the mansion and are ushered through to a ballroom.

There are tables set up for people to eat at with white table cloths. The rest of the room seems to be reserved for dancing and mingling.

I place my hand against the small of Nova's back and search the tables for my father.

It's better to get this introduction over now rather than later.

I finally spot my father speaking to another man by the bar, a scotch in his hand.

He looks exactly the same as the last time I saw him nearly a year ago.

We have the same angular cheekbones, sharp nose, and full lips. Even our hair is the same color, though his is turning gray. The only thing I have from my mother is my green eyes. My dad has pale-blue eyes. It's like they're leached of color and happiness.

Nova shuffles awkwardly at my side, her head swiveling from left to right as she tries to take in everyone and everything.

I lean down to whisper in her ear, "That's my dad." I don't point. Pointing is frowned upon, but I look in his direction and I know that we favor enough that she won't be able to mistake who I'm speaking of.

When the man my dad's speaking to finally leaves, I guide Nova over to him.

My father sees us coming and he looks us both over carefully.

"Jacen," he says in greeting when we stop in front of him.

"Father," I reply. "This is Novalee."

"Novalee *what*?" he hisses. "I taught you how to properly introduce someone, I expect you to do it."

I need a drink and the night's only just begun.

"Novalee Clarke," I say, the words grating through my teeth.

He smiles in satisfaction. "Do you speak?" he asks Nova.

"Y-Yes, sir," she stutters, her eyes still flitting around nervously.

I give her a peculiar look. It's not like Nova to lose her cool like this. Something more is going on, and I don't understand what it is.

"Dad," I hiss. "Be nice. She's my date."

"Whom you didn't inform me that was coming. That wasn't very thoughtful of you, Jacen."

Suddenly, I feel like I've been transported back to the past. I no longer stand in the ballroom, instead I'm a scared six-year-old boy, standing in the kitchen as his father scolds him for making a mess while he was trying to make a sandwich.

"He's just a boy," my mom told him.

"A boy must learn to be a man from the start."

I shake my head back and forth, returning to the present. "Nova, this is my father, Heath. Dad, we're going to find a table."

I grab Nova's hand and start to pull her away.

"We weren't finished," my dad calls after us.

I turn around. "What do you want to say? Huh?"

A dark cloud passes over his face. "Not here. I mean it."

I laugh humorlessly. "I'm a pawn. That's all I am to you."

"Do not make a scene, Jacen," he warns.

"Don't worry." I smile. "I'm good at pretending."

I drag Nova over to a table as far away from my dad as I can get.

I pull out a chair for her before dropping down into the one beside her.

"Your dad is ... intense," she comments.

"He's something else, that's for sure." A glass of water already sits at each seat and I grab the one to my right and drink it greedily. I'd prefer something alcoholic but I'm so parched that this is perfect. I tug at my too-tight collar. "I shouldn't have brought you here," I groan. "He's ... he's ..."

She places a reassuring hand on my knee. "I know a thing or two about controlling parents. I can handle it."

"But you froze back there."

She shakes her head. "It had nothing to do with your dad."

"Then what is it?" I ask, tilting my head to the side as I appraise her.

She swallows thickly, her eyes doing another scan of the room. "I'll tell you later."

I press my lips together. Something tells me later might turn out to be never.

She changes the topic. "So, your dad's a Senator, huh?"

"Yeah," I sigh and lean back in my chair—if my dad sees he'll scold me for that, but fuck it. "Hard to believe I grew up as a politician's son, isn't it?"

"Kind of." She smiles. "You're the complete opposite. The music, the tattoos, the *bad boy* vibe ... I definitely wouldn't have pegged you as a Senator's son."

"I think my dad's career and his overall assholish personality is what steered me toward music and everything. I wanted to do something that would piss him off and it turned out I loved it. He hates me working at the bar, which was why I took the job to begin with."

"I'm surprised he hasn't figured out a way to get you fired," she comments.

"You know," I breathe, "that surprises me too. He has more important things to focus on now than where I work." I shrug and tug at my collar. I swear it's getting tighter by the second.

Music plays and people dance, chatter filling the area. Everyone goes on with their lives, oblivious to how bad some other people's lives are. That's something that's always bothered me—how inherently selfish most people are that they don't notice another person suffering. I swear, I could be drowning right in front of them and they wouldn't even notice.

Nova glides her hand up my thigh and squeezes lightly. I look over at her. Soft curls frame her face where they've escaped from her up-do. I've only ever seen her with her hair down or in a messy bun, so it's weird to see her looking so ... *elegant*.

I cup her cheek and she sighs at my touch.

"Let's dance," I say.

Dancing is better than sitting at this table being miserable. Besides, I'd rather be occupied than have to talk to one of my dad's friends, and it's only a matter of time until one of them finds me.

Nova nods and takes my hand. I lead her out onto the dance floor. I feel my father's shrewd eyes searing a hole into the back of my head. There are plenty of people dancing so Nova and I bleed easily into the crowed and the weight of his eyes falls from my body.

I place one hand on Nova's waist and hold her other in mine. I guide her easily around the dance floor with a little smile on my face. Dancing with Nova just might make this night bearable.

"I know now why you had to have dance lessons."

I laugh. "Have to make Daddy Dearest look good. It'd be unfit if his kid didn't know how to dance or properly hold a fork." I snort.

Nova's fingers tighten around my shoulder. "I'm sorry things were bad for you. I know you haven't told me much, but I understand."

"It wasn't all bad," I admit. "At least, when my mom was alive."

"I wish I could've met her," she breathes, her brown eyes wide and doe like.

I sigh. "I do too. She would've loved you."

My mom would've welcomed Nova into her life with open arms. She would've been the daughter she never had. It makes me sad to think about what could've been if she hadn't died, but she's gone, and I can't change that.

I twirl Nova around the dance floor and we grow quiet, lost in our thoughts.

The ballroom is decorated in blacks and whites with large chandeliers hanging from the ceiling. The floor is shiny black and white marble and it's so clean that I can see my reflection in it when I look down.

"Confession—I dream in black and white."

I look down at Nova at her words. The irony of them, when I was just thinking about the black and white room, isn't lost on me.

"Color is overrated," I whisper in her ear.

She shivers and her body moves closer to mine.

I breathe in the scent of her shampoo—lavender and something else that's entirely Nova.

"Your turn," she says, as I spin her around.

I think for a moment. "Confession," I begin, "I used to think happy endings were overrated."

"And now?"

"I'm looking at mine."

Her cheeks warm at my words and she pillows her face on my chest, over my heart.

This girl has singlehandedly turned my whole world upside down. It'll never be the same again, and neither will I, but it's all for the better.

We dance to another song before everyone's called to the tables to eat.

I groan as I find our place at my father's table.

I wish I could avoid him all evening, but it's an impossibility.

Thankfully, he's tied up beside some politician buddies of his so Nova and I end up a few seats away from him.

When we're seated, Nova's nervousness returns. She seems jumpy and almost like she's looking for someone. It makes no sense.

Our meal is served, and with my father across the table it makes it difficult to talk to her about it, but I *know* something is going on.

The meal seems to drag on forever, and by the time we're finally served dessert I'm ready to make a dash for the door.

My dad tries to drag me into the conversation any chance he gets, because apparently looking like a family man makes him more desirable or something. I don't fucking know.

"This is my son, Jacen," my father introduces me.

"Nice to meet you," the man holds his hand out to me. He's tall with black hair, speckled with gray at the roots. "I'm Harry Mitchell."

"No," Nova gasps beside me.

"*Novalee?*" the guy beside Harry, who's closer to my age, and probably this guy's son, speaks.

My head swivels from the guy to Nova. I've never seen Nova look so utterly terrified before. She's pale and sweaty, like she's just seen a ghost.

"Novalee," he says again, "is that you?"

She forces her head up to look at him and she looks like she's about to burst into tears. "Hi, Owen."

"You two know each other?" I ask.

Harry clears his throat and fiddles with his tie. "They were friends growing up."

"We dated, Dad." Owen rolls his eyes. "How are you?" he asks Nova.

"Fine," Nova replies, her eyes darting down to her lap.

"Can we talk?" Owen asks her.

"I don't think that's the best idea—" his father interrupts and Owen glares at him.

"Please," Owen says to Nova.

She nods and stands from the table.

"Nova?" I question, my hand grazing hers.

She shakes her head, pleading with her eyes for me to let her explain later. I nod and watch her go, even though it kills me.

Once they're gone, Harry clears his throat. "I'll see you later, Heath. Take care."

He melts away from our table and I'm left alone with my father. His eyes flash as he appraises me.

"I take it you didn't know about Novalee and Owen?"

"And you did?" I counter—because if he did ...

He shakes his head and smiles slowly. "No, just ... fate, perhaps?" He smiles and leans forward, crossing his fingers together. "If you didn't know about this, what else do you think you might not know about this girl?"

I clench my teeth, anger eating away at me, because for once, he's right.

twenty
. . .

nova

THE DOOR to the apartment closes and Jace throws his tux jacket on the kitchen chair.

Three, two, one ...

"I didn't want to talk about this in the car, but I need to know about that guy."

I shrug and kick off my heels, audibly sighing in relief. "You know I dated once before."

He wets his lips, his hands on his hips. I can tell he's fighting not to get angry, and I can't blame him.

"Do you still love him?"

I snort. "Owen? Of course not."

"I saw the way he looked at you," Jace whispers. "He ... he looked at you like you'd been ripped away from him and he'd been starving ever since."

I bite my tongue, fighting tears. "My history with Owen is ... complicated."

"I just, I want to know if ... if there's any part of you that longs for him."

I step forward and close the space between us. "Absolutely not," I answer. "What I had with Owen is long over. He's a part of my past, a huge part, but that's it. Nothing more. I *promise*."

He nods, and gently caresses my cheek. "I'm beginning to realize that you're incredibly important to me. Maybe too important." He rubs his finger over my bottom lip, tracing the contour. "I love you."

Cold.

I am cold all over.

Frozen.

I can't move.

"What?" I gasp, the tiniest little sound.

"I love you," he says again with such surety.

Three words I thought I would never hear from Jace. Three words I never counted on. Three words that I longed for desperately.

The tears that had pooled in my eyes, spill over. "Really?"

He nods, his hand gliding down to rest at the back of my neck. "I love you," he says again.

I laugh through my tears. "I love you too," I breathe.

I'm not just saying the words because he did, I do mean them. Jace has meant the world to me for far longer than the time we've been together, and this time has only served to show me how perfect we are for each other.

He crashes his lips to mine and I gasp into his mouth. His tongue slides against mine as he backs me up until I hit the wall. He picks me up, sliding my dress up my legs so he can caress my bare thighs.

He carries me to the bed and sets me down beside it.

I turn around and look at him coyly.

He gets the messages and finds the zipper of my dress, sliding it down.

When it's undone, I let the dress fall down and pool at my feet.

I turn around to face him in my black lacy lingerie. I never wear anything so fancy, but Thea told me a fancy dress called for matching lingerie, so we ended up shopping some more after lunch that day.

Jace's eyes heat with desire and my nipples tighten.

The expensive lingerie was worth every penny for that look in his eyes.

He makes quick work of the buttons on his black vest, then his dress shirt, and finally his pants.

When he stands in only his boxer-briefs, we stare at each other for a moment.

I'm sure he must be able to hear my heart because it's beating far too fast and loud.

Love.

Jace loves me.

And I love him.

I never in a million years imagined this scenario, but we make perfect sense.

"Are you going to touch me?" I ask.

He smirks. "You really shouldn't have said that."

He moves lightning fast, and I scream as my feet go out from under me.

My back lands on the bed, and I bounce a few times.

"That was mean." I laugh.

He drops down on top of me, holding his larger body above me in a push-up position.

"You like it." He grins and kisses me.

My whole body sings at his touch.

He kisses down my neck and between my breasts and over my stomach. He stops with his lips poised above my panties.

My chest rises and falls with each heavy breath I take as I wait.

It feels like forever before he loops his fingers into each side of my underwear and pulls them down my hips. He drops them onto the floor and his eyes shine as he appraises my body, stopping on my covered breasts.

"That needs to go too."

I sit up and he finds the clasp easily. It pops and the straps slide down my arms, falling to the bed.

He covers my breasts with his hands, testing the fullness. My back arches into his touch.

I've never craved someone before.

Their touch.

Their scent.

Their everything.

But Jace awakens some slumbering beast inside me that I never knew existed.

I push at his shoulders and he falls to the bed with a smirk.

"Why do you always get to have all the fun?" I ask.

"What do you want to do?" he asks.

I lean over him, my hair making a curtain around us, and whisper in his ear, "Anything I want."

He lies back on the pillows, crossing his arms behind his head.

"I'm yours."

I lick my lips as I remove his boxer-briefs and my heart thunders in anticipation.

I take him in my hand, making a fist around him.

He hisses between his teeth and my head jerks up. "Did I hurt you?"

He shakes his head. "No. Definitely not."

I lower my head and wrap my lips around him.

"Oh, fuck." His hips buck off the bed.

I'm used to being the powerless one, so having him come undone beneath me fills me with feeling I've never experienced before.

I lower my mouth down, bit by bit.

I release him and then swirl my tongue around his tip.

"Fuck!" His hand fists in the back of my hair, and I moan.

I lower my head again, taking as much of him as I can until I gag before pulling back.

Again and again I take him until he snaps and pushes me away.

"No more," he pants.

He pushes me onto the bed and covers my body with his.

I watch as he fists his cock and guides it inside me.

My fingernails dig into his arms as he slides all the way in.

"Oh, God," I moan at the fullness.

He moves slowly, rocking in and out of me with a gentleness that threatens to make me cry. He rolls so that I end up on top.

I grab the camera off the nightstand and take a picture of my hand on his chest.

Then another of his face that gets blurred by my hair falling forward.

"Give it to me."

I hand him the camera and he takes a photo of his hand on my back.

Then another with him digging his fingers more forcefully into my shoulder.

There's a reason I chose the title *Moments* for my project.

It's moments like this, ones where we're so close to losing our minds, that time slows down the most.

Where his finger on my lip and my nails in his back adds up to a much larger picture.

Each moment is precious in its own right, but you put them together and it's magic.

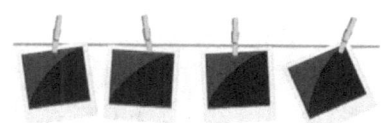

Jace lifts his coffee cup to his mouth, his eyes glued to the book he's reading. Every little bit he looks up at me and I know there's something on his mind that he wants to talk about, but I wait for him to speak.

He looks adorable this morning. His normally harsh edges are softened by his sex-rumpled hair and the dorky glasses he wears in the mornings.

I eat my cereal quietly, waiting.

Finally, he closes the book with a sigh.

"Are you sure this Owen thing is over?" he asks.

I laugh. "I told you I loved you and then spent the night showing you how much—so yeah, I'm over him." He doesn't look appeased. I sigh. "Will you feel better if I tell you about him?"

"I don't know?" he answers honestly. "Maybe."

"We broke up two years ago—and I'll be honest, it wasn't our choice to break up. My parents are very strict and his parents wanted to avoid scandal."

"Scandal?" he repeats, his brow furrowing in confusion.

"His dad was our Mayor but he was running for Governor."

"Oh, I see. I know how that is." Jace nods. I'm sure he does know. If his dad is a Senator he's probably been in politics for a long time. "But how was you dating Owen such a big scandal?"

"My dad's a minister and he didn't feel like I should be involved with a politician's son, and Owen's dad felt like my background might harm in the election," I explain. It's not the whole truth, not by a long shot, but I can't get into it.

Jace grins. "Bet you never thought you'd end up involved with another politician's son."

I sigh. "The irony isn't lost on me. I fled my hometown, moved hundreds of miles away, and ended up back at square one. Life's funny like that." I push my cereal bowl away and cross my fingers together. "I promise you, Owen and are done. If he feels anything for me still that's on him. I'll admit, I'll always feel a sense of fondness for him, but that's it. It's certainly nothing like what I feel for you."

"Thank you," he says, and I know he means it. "This whole relationship thing is new to me. I'm not used to feeling so jealous and protective all the time."

I reach across the table and wrap my hand around his. "Trust me, you don't need to worry about Owen, but if you need to ask me something about him you can. Any time. Okay?"

He nods. "Thanks. I will ... if I need to."

He goes back to reading, and I finish cleaning the dishes.

Even though things should feel better I still feel like Owen hangs over us like a dark cloud marring a clear blue sky.

Something tells me a storm is coming.

twenty-one
...

jace

THANKSGIVING PASSES, and Nova and I spend the day with our friends. It ends up being a surprisingly nice day. Probably one of, if not the best, Thanksgivings I've had since my mom died.

Now, with a little over week until Christmas, I'm overcome by how different my life is now than from a year ago.

"I'm playing tomorrow night at W.T.F.—I think I'm going to invite everyone," I tell Nova.

She looks up from the Polaroids splayed out on the kitchen table. Her project is due tomorrow and she's been slaving away over it for the better part of two weeks, piecing together the photos to make ... something.

I don't know what yet because I'm not allowed to look. Any time I try to sneak a peek she yells at me.

I tune my guitar and wait for her response.

"What?" she says after a moment, having registered that I've spoken. "What'd you say?"

I sigh. This project has killed some of her brain cells, I swear.

"Tomorrow's Friday night, and I'm playing at the bar. I was thinking about inviting everyone. I know Xander's back in town."

"Oh." She thinks for a moment. "Yeah, that'd be awesome." She bites her lip.

"Spit it out, Clarke," I urge, knowing she wants to say something.

"Can I invite Joel?" I groan. "Please," she begs. "He's been dating this one girl, so he'll probably want to bring her. But I haven't hung out with him in a while, and this is perfect because everyone will be there."

I pinch the bridge of my nose. "Yeah, sure, why not."

"Thanks." She smiles.

I sigh. I think I'd do anything to make that girl happy, to see her smile. I've become everything I used to make fun of. I'm a lovesick sap, and you know what? I'm *glad*. Loving Nova has been the bravest, and greatest, thing I've ever done.

I work on my newest song while Nova finishes her project.

Sometime later, she says, "I'm done. You can look now."

I set my guitar aside and hop off the couch like my ass is on fire, but I've been dying to see this thing forever.

I jolt when I see it.

"Is that ... that's me?"

She grins. "You can tell?"

I nod, my mouth slack, completely blown away by the complexity of what she's done. I see now why it's taken her weeks to complete. Pictures of me, and her, are laid out together in a way that forms my profile. It's remarkable.

"You're amazing," I tell her, and bend to kiss her.

She wraps her arms around my neck. "You think it's good?"

"I think it's fucking incredible. I'm framing it and hanging it above my bed when you get it back."

She laughs, positively giddy. "Really?"

I nod. "It's incredible. So are you."

She kisses me again and releases me. I look down at all the photos on the table.

Pictures of my hand on her hair, her hand on my chest, our legs tangled together. So many intimate photos placed together.

"What's your professor going to think of this?" I ask, worried that she might get marked down for the sexiness of it.

"She's cool with it. I told her my idea early on and she thought it was unique and couldn't wait to see it."

I smile and kiss her again. I can't seem to stop kissing her. Or touching her. I'm like a moth drawn to a flame.

"Nobody else is going to see this, right?" I ask. "It's not like you have to present it to the class."

She laughs and shakes her head, her messy bun bobbing. "No. Just the professor."

"Good," I breathe. "One stranger seeing me in my underwear is enough."

She frowns, thinking maybe I'm not okay with this. "None of the photos show your full face and if it does it's shadowed."

"I'm messing with you," I tell her. I look down at the photos again. It's truly amazing and I understand why she chose to title it *Moments*. It's perfect. I kiss her again quickly and back away. "I'm going to call Cade and tell him about tomorrow."

"Tomorrow?" she asks, puzzled.

"W.T.F.?"

"Oh, right. Sorry. You've said that like three times. I'm just distracted."

"Mhmm," I hum, watching her carefully as she straightens the pile of unused polaroid's. Something tells me her distraction is more than her project, and I worry that I might not like what is.

nova

I gather up the Polaroids I didn't use and carry them to my room, putting them in my drawer where I keep my letters.

My letters.

My heart pangs.

I haven't written to Owen in over a month. There were times I used to write to him every day.

I pull out my notebook and sit on my bed, figuring it's time I wrote him another letter.

Dear Owen,

I'm sorry I haven't written to you in so long. I promise you, I still think of you every day. If you could only know how much you're on my mind. Especially in the last month. I think that's why I haven't written to you in so long. I've been picturing your face in my mind and it hurts, so I've avoided you.

Avoidance isn't always good, though.

In fact, it's never good, because then something builds up inside you until it bubbles over.

I'm afraid the secret I keep about you is going to ruin everything. It's my own fault for not being honest about you.

I don't know how to speak the truth anymore though. I've buried this secret for so long that sometimes it feels like it was all a dream.

Know this truth, though.

I love you. I always will. Always.

Nova.

I rip out the piece of paper and fold it up, placing it with the others and now the polaroid's. Tears cling to my lashes.

Owen.

Owen is such a huge part of my life, one I never acknowledge out loud, and last month, it brought back so many memories, some good, but most of them not.

I wipe at the tears that spill over and take a deep breath, burying the feelings the same way I've buried my memories for years.

If you bury something deep enough, it'll eventually disappear, right?

"I forgot how much I loved this place," Thea says, taking a drink of her water.

Xander sits beside her, his hand on the back of her chair. Beside him is Cade, and then Rae, and finally, me. Jace isn't with us since he's performing next.

"The food's great for a place called W.T.F.." Cade dips a cheese fry in ranch.

I pick at my own meal, a cheeseburger and fries, and wait anxiously for Jace to take the stage. He said he was performing a new song tonight. One he wrote about us.

"It's nice to hang out like this," Rae chimes in, stealing one of his fries. He smiles at her and leans over to kiss her nose. "We don't see you and Jace enough."

I snort. "You see me practically every day."

She glares at me. "At *school*. That doesn't count."

"Okay, you got me there," I concede.

Between work, school, and spending every waking minute I can with Jace it's been hard to make time for our friends. While I'm in this blissful honeymoon stage with Jace it's hard to want to do anything else.

"Sorry I'm late," Joel says, shrugging off his scarf and coat. A pretty blond stands at his side. "This is Sarah."

"Hi, Sarah." I wave.

"Hi," everyone else chimes in.

"Hey." She waves back, her cheeks either flushed from nerves or cold.

Joel takes the empty seat beside me, leaving the last one for Sarah.

"Has he gone on yet?" Joel asks.

I shake my head. "No, not yet."

"You know, I don't think I've ever told you, but I love the brown hair." Joel flicks a piece of my hair.

Sarah watches the exchange, clearly confused.

"I used to dye my hair crazy colors," I explain. "Finally went back to my natural."

"And shocked the socks off all of us," Thea pipes in.

When she and Rae picked me up for dress shopping they both gaped at me like a fish and then proceeded to ask me a million different questions. Well, Thea asked the questions, Rae just stared.

"Oh, that's cool," Sarah says, clearly not that interested. Joel leans down and whispers something in her ear and she blushes.

The person performing finishes and Jace takes their place.

He sits on the stool, the spotlight shining right on him.

He's dressed simply in his usual jeans and a t-shirt but the way he holds himself he could be dressed in the most expensive suit known to man.

He clears his throat and adjusts the microphone.

"This is a song I wrote. I call it "Dark Hearts"."

He strums his guitar and begins to sing.

"They say they don't know us. They say they've never met someone quite like us. They say that we're crazy. They say that we're running, from our demons, from our demons." His eyes close as he sings, and you can tell that the whole room has disappeared for him. That all that exists is him, the music, and the words. *"And I remember looking in her eyes, holding back tears from that night. I find it hard to find the sun in the rain. I'm finding it hard to find myself when all I do is change."* His eyes open then and find me in the bar. *"They said they don't know us. But they don't understand. No one understands. But I've figured it out. We've got dark hearts, dark hearts, and our demons won't let us go. Just tell me how I get out of this suffering. Just tell me how I forget this pain* and be happy. *And the pain is pulling me under,*

maybe I should give them names. Tell me, can my dark heart ever go away?"

The song ends and I jump to my feet clapping.

He's amazing. More amazing than he ever gives himself credit for.

Several other people join me and Jace smiles, a little grin that tilts his lips on one corner. He bows his head slightly and exits the stage.

He comes over to our table and I wrap my arms around his neck.

"I love you," I whisper in his ear. "You're amazing."

"That was great, Jace," Joel says.

"Thanks." Jace smiles but he's looking at me. "I love you too," he murmurs in reply to what I said. He kisses me and wrap an arm around my waist. He sits down in my seat and pulls me down onto his lap. His guitar rests against the table.

"The people love you!" Eli breezes over to our table.

I laugh when I take in his ensemble. He's dressed in a pair of black slacks, with a black button down shirt, and a purple sequined vest with a matching purple top hat.

"I think I need to give you a whole show on Saturday nights," Eli continues. "Oh, and thanks for hanging the balls." He points at the ceiling where hundreds of ornaments dangle.

Jace mock-salutes him. "That's me—Jace the Ball Handler."

I laugh and take a bite of a fry as Eli moves to another table to ask them if they're enjoying their evening.

"When are you playing again?" Thea asks, leaning into Xander as he glides his hand up her neck.

Jace shrugs. "Maybe next week. Depends on what I feel like doing."

"Well, if you do, you need to invite us. This was fun." She steals a cheese fry from Cade's plate.

"Hey," Cade scolds. "That's mine."

Thea bites into the fry with a smirk. "Mine now."

Xander shakes his head.

"How long have you been writing songs?" Rae asks Jace.

Jace shrugs, rubbing his fingers up my thigh. "Since high school. It became a sort of escape."

She nods. "I see. You're really good. I mean, I've seen you play before but I don't think I ever realized you write songs too."

"I might've played a cover when you saw me," Jace explains. "Sometimes I do if I'm not feeling a recent song I've written and I've gotten sick of playing old ones."

"Maybe." Rae shrugs. "It was last year."

"Are you going to eat that?" he asks me, pointing to my burger.

I shake my head. "No, I'm done."

He picks up my burger and finishes it in three bites—which is quite a feat considering how much was left.

"How do you feel about your final?" Joel asks.

"Pretty good."

"Pretty good?" Jace repeats. "Your project was fucking amazing."

"What'd you do?" Rae asks. I blush, leaning into Jace.

"Took pictures of me naked," Jace tells her.

"Oh, ew. Didn't need to do that." She covers her eyes like I've stuck one of the photos in front of her.

I smack Jace's shoulder. "You can't see anything like *that* in the photos. It's mostly close-ups or shadows. Kinda abstract in a way." I shrug. It's hard to explain without showing them and I didn't show them in class because it feels private. It was hard enough to hand it over to my teacher.

"What'd you guys do?" I ask them, hoping to steer the conversation away from me, Jace, and our pictures.

Rae launches into an explanation of her project and then Joel explains his.

While they speak, Jace polishes off the last of the fries on my plate.

We stay for a good two hours chatting before we all decide to part ways. It's after eleven, and I'm exhausted from many late nights working on my project and falling into bed with Jace.

Jace and I wave goodbye to our friends and start to walk back to the apartment.

"Oh, my God," I breathe. "Look!" I point to the sky. "It's snowing!"

Jace laughs as I twirl around trying to catch a snowflake with my tongue.

I finally catch one, and dizzy, I bump into him. He wraps a hand around my arm to steady me.

"Careful," he warns. "You might fall."

He's right. The ground is quickly growing slick with snow. I twine our gloved hands together and hold onto him as we finish the walk back to the apartment. By the time we get there there's nearly an inch of snow already on the ground, with more falling by the second. We've already had several snows the last few weeks, but nothing major. This looks promising, and it's just in time for Christmas.

Jace and I burst into the warmth of the apartment lobby and laugh as we pull our gloves off, heading for the elevator.

We hold hands as we ride up in the elevator. Sometimes it boggles my mind, how easily we touch now, when in the beginning even holding hands in public felt like such a milestone.

I yawn as we step out of the elevator and Jace pulls the keys from his jeans pocket. He unlocks the door and waits for me to step inside first.

The apartment looks cozy and ready for Christmas.

A Christmas tree sits in the corner by the TV and there are little lights strung around the stainless-steel island. I asked him if we could decorate for Christmas and I was shocked when he agreed. He seemed happy to help and I even caught him sneaking some presents under the tree.

I shrug out of my coat, scarf, and gloves as he locks the door.

I kick off my boots and scurry into my room to change. When I come out, Jace sits on the island in a pair of low hanging sweatpants and his beanie.

I open the refrigerator and grab a bottle of water, feeling his eyes on my ass the whole time.

"What'd you do with the extra Polaroids?" he asks.

I turn around and wipe my mouth with the back of my hand. "They're in the drawer of my desk. Why?"

He grins. "I have an idea."

He hops off the counter and hurries into my room.

I drink another sip of water and put the bottle back in the refrigerator. I yawn, eyeing his bed desperately. I need sleep. I've gotten too little the last few weeks.

"What's taking so long?" I call with a laugh, and step into

the doorway of my room, or what used to be my room since I sleep in Jace's bed now. "Jace?" I say, puzzled.

He turns around and my blood runs cold. Clutched in his hand is a piece of paper. One of my letters.

My eyes close. "Jace, it's not what you think." I bite my tongue at my pathetic excuse. It sounds silly, but it's true.

"Not what I think?" he says through clenched teeth. "It's fucking obvious, Nova!" he yells, spit flying. I wince.

"It's really not." I press my lips together, fighting tears.

He storms forward, the piece of paper shaking in his fist.

"*I still think of you every day. If you could only know how much you're on my mind. Especially in the last month.*" He throws my words back at me. "It's exactly what I think it is. I asked you if you were still in love with him and you said *no*. You said *no*, Nova." He clenches his teeth, a muscle in his jaw clenching. He looks close to tears. He pushes past me and out into the kitchen.

"Jace," I cry, following after him. "Let me explain. That letter isn't what you think it is."

"It's not a love letter to your ex? You're not pining for him?"

"No!" I cry. "I'm over him, I promise you."

He flips the page to another letter gathered in his hand. "*It's been too long since I wrote to you and for that I'm sorry. I promise it's not because I forgot about you—nothing could ever make that a true statement because you're always on my mind. I think about you every day. Mostly when I'm about to fall asleep. I think about the color of your eyes and the softness of your hair beneath my fingers. It breaks my heart that you can't think of me in the same way. I'm a ghost to you. I don't exist. That's what hurts the most."*

"Shut up!" I scream at him. "Stop it! This isn't fair!"

"You know what isn't fair?" he seethes. "Me, finally giving someone my heart and having it ripped apart in front of me. I love you, Nova. *I. Love. You.* I've never loved anyone before and this whole time it was a lie because you're still in love with your ex." He paces back and forth in the kitchen like it pains him to stand still.

I shake my head, my face wet with tears. "He's *not* my ex," my voice cracks.

Jace snorts and rolls his eyes. "I'm not stupid, Nova."

"He's my son."

Jace stands still. He's frozen. Lips parted. "What? What did you say?"

I wipe my tears away, my chin quivering. "He's my son."

Jace looks up at the ceiling, like it holds all the answers in the world. "I don't believe you," he finally says.

"It's the truth," I croak. "He's my son," I say again, because it feels so good to finally say the words out loud.

Jace looks at me like he's never seen me before, like he doesn't know me, which hurts like nothing else could because he knows me better than anyone.

I turn and head back to my room, gathering the rest of my letters.

"Take them," I say, shoving them at him. "Read them. You'll see."

He takes them reluctantly. "I need to go," he mumbles.

I fight more tears. "Please, don't go," I beg.

He looks at me, his heart breaking and mine too. "I have to. I can't look at you right now." I wince. I deserve that. I deserve worse, but it still hurts.

He grabs his coat and heads for the door. He looks back at me, and I feel like he wants to say something but he shakes his head and leaves, closing the door quietly behind him, which is a hundred times worse than if he slammed it, because it means he's in control.

I drop to the floor and cradle my knees to my chest. I let myself cry for Jace, for Owen, and most importantly, I cry for me.

twenty-two

. . .

nova

TICK TOCK.

Hours pass, and I sit stationary on the couch, watching the door.

Tick tock.

Every minute, every second, seems to stretch infinitely as I wait.

Tick tock.

I keep hoping he's going to come back. That he's going to open the door and fall at my feet and tell me he's sorry, that he understands why I had to keep this a secret. But I also know Jace, and he's incredibly stubborn, so I know the chance of that fantasy becoming reality is slim to none.

It's after four in the morning when I finally drag my exhausted body to bed.

I feel numb.

I didn't want Jace to find out about Owen like this. I *wanted* to tell him, but I couldn't. How do you possibly find the words to tell the man you love that you got pregnant at fifteen? It's not exactly an easy conversation, especially when you add in all my family drama.

It turns out getting knocked up when you're fifteen and a minister's daughter is a bad idea. Throw in the baby daddy's father being the town mayor and it's a recipe for drama.

I wrap my arms around my pillow, hugging it like it's Jace.

I miss him and he's only been gone hours.

I know he had every right to leave, I don't blame him, but it still hurts. I would've loved to have the chance to explain myself. I hope he reads my letters to Owen and understands —that he sees the truth.

But for all I know he might stomp all over them or light them on fire.

Realistically, I know he'd never do that. Jace is a lot of things but he's not vindictive, at least not to the people he loves.

Eventually, I drift off to sleep. It's fitful and full of nightmares and I wake more exhausted than I was when I fell asleep.

I get up and Jace still hasn't returned.

I wonder where he went.

The bar maybe? It would've still been open and I'm sure Eli would've let him crash at his place.

Or maybe he went to Cade's? No, because if he had Thea or Rae would've surely texted or called.

I know he wouldn't have gone to his dad's so I have no idea where else he could've ended up.

I brush my teeth and hair and clean my face. It makes me feel slightly better but dark circles still cloud the skin beneath my eyes. I gather my hair up in a messy bun and change into a pair of sweatpants and a loose shirt that says *Bed Hair Don't Care*. Something tells me I'm going to spend the day moping and that calls for comfy clothes.

I'm not hungry, but I want something to do so I make breakfast.

I toast some bread and start a pan with scrambled eggs.

I'm shoveling the eggs out onto a plate when the door opens.

My body instantly stiffens and I put the pan into a sink full of water.

The door clicks shut and Jace walks quietly across the room to me.

We stare at each other, the island separating us. I want to run to him, to crash into his arms, but I know more than likely he wouldn't want that. He can probably barely stand to look at me.

Jace eyes the food I've laid out, which is honestly enough for five people. I may have gone overboard with the amounts.

The silence is unbearable so I decide to break it.

"Confession, I can cook."

"I can see that." He continues to stare at the food and not me.

"Confession," I say again, "I like it better when you cook. Your food's better and you're hot when you cook. Plus, I think it's cute when you try to teach me." I'm rambling at this point, diarrhea of the mouth, but I need to fill the silence with *something* even if I make myself look like a bigger idiot in the process.

He sighs and scrubs his hands over his face. He looks as exhausted as I do.

"You have a son," he states.

My chest pangs and I nod. "I do."

"Where?" he asks, looking around like I've hidden a kid behind the couch.

I laugh but there's no humor in the sound. "Adopted," I say, wrapping my arms around my chest. It still kills me to say that word.

Adopted.

My son is adopted.

He pulls out a stool at the island and drops onto it. "Tell me everything. I ... I need to know."

"Did you read my letters?" I ask.

He nods. "I did. They're in my truck. Safe and sound, I promise. I wouldn't destroy them if that's what you're worried about."

I shake my head. "I didn't think you would. Here, eat something."

I split the food up and give him half. I'm not sure how much either of us can eat, but it helps to have something else to do.

A minute passes and his soft green eyes meet mine. "Tell me. Please."

I sigh, leaning against the island. "I don't know where to begin. Give me a minute," I beg.

When I moved to Colorado a year and a half ago, I blocked out everything that happened back home. It was easier to cope that way.

"I met Owen when I was twelve and he was thirteen. We didn't start dating until I was thirteen, almost fourteen. Our families were fairly close, his family attended my father's church so we grew up together, and I was friends with Owen's sister, who was a year younger than me. My parents weren't thrilled when Owen and I started dating because I was so young and my dad was worried about the trouble I might get into, but Owen was a good kid, and he became like family." I inhale a deep breath. "When I was fifteen I got pregnant. We were stupid, careless," I mutter. "We'd had sex plenty of times and we got cocky, I guess, thought there was no way I'd end up pregnant. And then I did. When I saw that little plus sign it was like a death sentence. I knew my parents were going to kill me. Owen was just as freaked out. I mean, we were fifteen and sixteen. We were *kids*. What did we know about being parents?" I take a moment to gather myself. I've never told anyone this. Ever. "My parents were livid when we told them. I've seen my dad raging mad before, once when I was playing with neighbor and we broke a window, but I'd never experienced him being *this* mad. He was scary silent, like the calm before a storm, and my mom was beside herself, mumbling about the *shame* I'd brought upon our family.

Owen, oh, God ... Owen tried to remain so positive, telling them that he was going to take care of me and the baby, and my dad *laughed* at him. He told him he was crazy if he thought he could take care of a family at his age. At the time, I was outraged, because I believed Owen, but now that I'm older I know my dad was right. We were children ourselves." I push the eggs around my plate with the fork. I know I should try to eat something, but I can't. Telling Jace all of this makes me feel like throwing up. "We figured telling his parents couldn't be worse than telling mine. We were wrong. His parents were far angrier than mine, especially his dad. He was in the early stages of campaigning for Governor and thought the scandal of his son's teen pregnancy would cost him the election."

I startle when Jace takes my hand. My eyes meet his and he rubs his thumb across my knuckles. His touch makes me feel the tiniest bit stronger.

"My parents were against me getting an abortion, which is what Owen's dad wanted me to do. I didn't want that, either. So, it was decided that we'd give the baby up for adoption." I shake my head. "I didn't want that, *either*. I wanted to keep the baby but my parents refused to help me financially and Owen's family wanted the whole thing to disappear, and Owen himself ... Well, I think his parents got to him and made him see how much a baby would change his life. How it would keep him from college and following in his father's footsteps and so I was the only one who wanted my baby but I wasn't strong enough to fight for him. I was young, and pregnant, and no one wanted to hire me, so I couldn't make money on my own. It became obvious that the only option was to follow through with the adoption. Owen and I at least got to pick the adoptive parents, but our parents forced us to do a closed adoption, meaning once we gave him up we got no pictures or updates on him. He was just ... gone. Some days it's hard to believe he ever existed. I got to hold him for a solid five minutes after he came out of me before they took him away. I screamed. Oh, God, Jace, I screamed so loud. I begged with them to give me more time, but they said it would be easier this way. That the more time I spent with him the harder it would be to give him up. He was so cute and small." I wipe at my tears. I don't know when they started but my face is completely damp. "He had a brown hair like me and Owen's thin lips and button nose. He was perfect."

"Is that why you call him Owen?"

I sigh. "Yeah, I suppose so. He was Owen's mini-me except for having my hair color. I think I started calling him Owen because it was easier than naming him something I would've picked. If I'd done that it would've been too easy to dwell on what could've been. By calling him Owen a lot of times I just pictured, well, Owen, in my head."

Jace squeezes my hand. "I'm sorry."

My lower lip quivers. "I miss him. I love him so much and he doesn't even know who I am. It was a closed adoption, so he might not even know he's adopted. He's old enough to be calling his adoptive parents Mommy and Daddy and that breaks my heart. I'm his mommy and I don't exist. I'm nothing to him."

I pull my hand from his and cover my face, sobbing for everything I've lost.

Every moment and memory with my son that should've been mine.

The first time he smiled.

The first time he laughed.

When he got his first tooth.

When he walked.

His first words.

I've missed all of it.

"Fuck, Nova. I'm so sorry." I startle when his arms wrap around me. I wasn't even aware of him getting up from the chair. I hiccup and hug him back, my tears dampening his jacket that he still hasn't taken off.

I cling to him like he's a buoy in the ocean and the only thing holding me up.

"I'm sorry too," I croak. "I'm sorry I didn't tell you. I didn't know how. I'm sorry. I'm sorry. I'm sorry," I ramble.

His arms tighten around me, and I feel his lips brush against the top of my head.

"I'm not mad, Nova," he says. "Not anymore. But I am hurt. I'm hurt that you felt like you couldn't tell me this."

I pull back slightly so I can look at him as I speak. "If there's *anyone* I could tell, it's you. I haven't ever told anyone this. I had him and everyone returned to their normal lives like he never even existed. My parents never spoke about him and Owen and I broke up so my only tether to him became my letters. It was the only way I could remind myself that he was real and not a figment of my imagination."

Jace rubs my shoulders. "You were so young. You shouldn't have had to go through that virtually alone."

"It is what is. I've learned that life is rarely fair and you have to roll with the punches."

"I wish you would've had someone on your side."

I sigh and step out of his embrace, drying my eyes. "I do too, but I'm old enough now to realize that adoption was the best thing for him. I couldn't provide for him at that age, and the family that adopted him were good, decent, people who wanted a kid. I know they've taken good care of him. I just wish I'd been a part of his life. An open adoption would've made this a lot easier on me, but Owen's parents insisted that it was closed. They wanted to ship the baby off and tie the whole thing up in a neat bow." I shrug. "I finished high school and applied to as many out of state schools as I could. So, I ended up here."

He hugs me again, pillowing his head on top of mine. "I'm thankful for whatever Divine intervention led you to here. To me."

I close my eyes, breathing in his musky scent. "I love you," I murmur.

"I love you, too."

My fingers tighten in the fabric of his jacket and I breathe out.

Maybe, just maybe, everything will be okay.

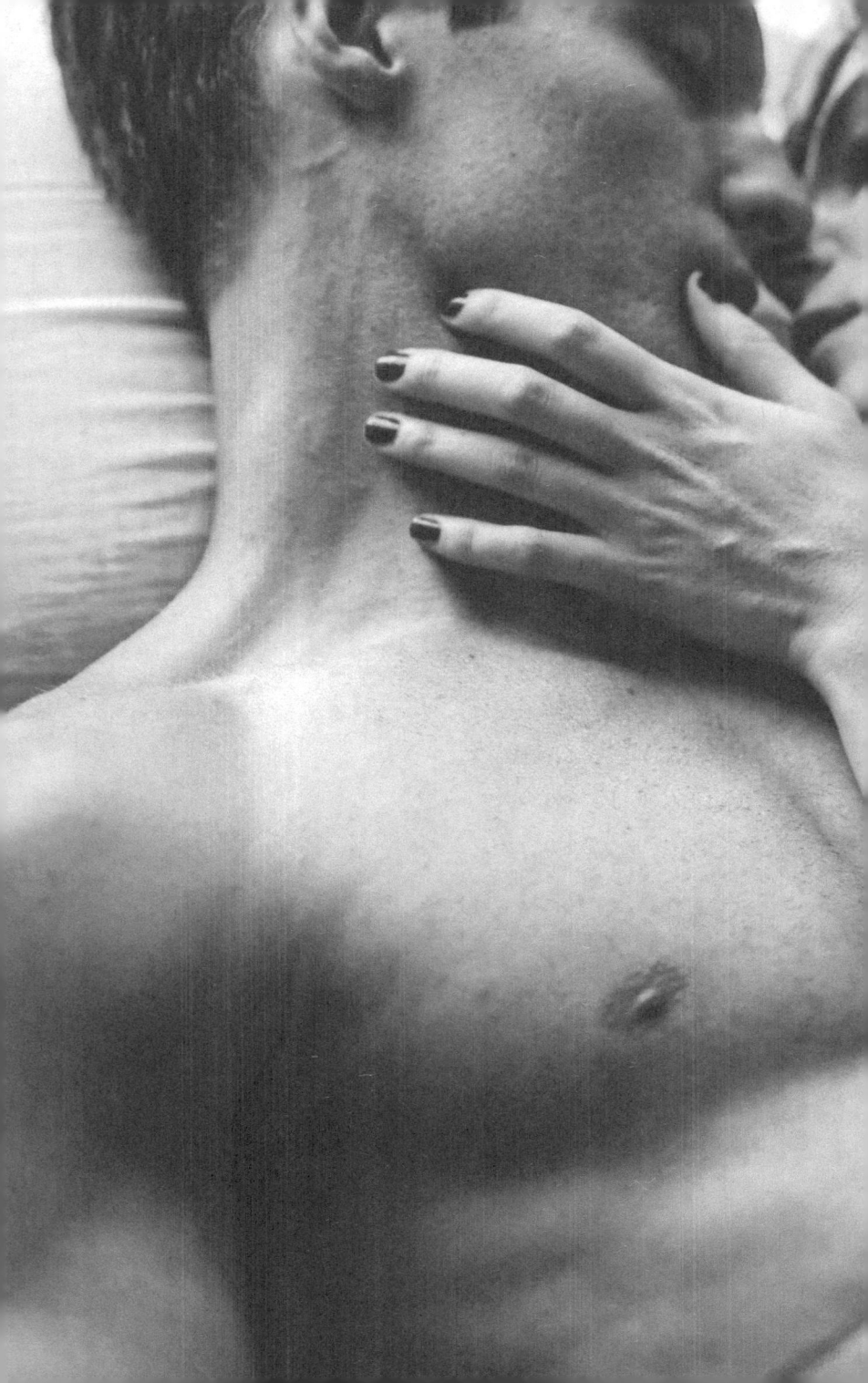

twenty-three
...

jace

NOVA'S STORY is heartbreakingly tragic. When I left last night, I was livid. First, because I thought she was writing love letters to her ex, then because I thought she was lying about having a son to cover herself. But the truth shone in her eyes.

"He's my son."

That confession rocked me more than any other one she's ever told me and she didn't even preface it with *confession*. But that's exactly what it was.

Nova releases me and steps back, her face splotchy from crying and making her freckles more vivid than normal.

I clear my throat. "At the Thanksgiving party I took you to, you kept acting funny, and then you spoke with Owen ... What did you guys talk about?"

She grabs a paper towel and uses it to dry her face. "I was

acting funny because I thought I might run into his father. He'd become Governor, and I knew he had plans to try to move up politically." She makes a face. "I didn't think Owen would be there." She pulls in a lungful of air. "I hadn't seen him since he graduated and went to college. We didn't stay in touch, not even through social media."

"But you had a kid together." I shake my head in disbelief. I can't imagine having a kid with someone and never speaking to them again, even if the relationship is over I'd think a bond like that would last a lifetime and I'm a guy.

She shrugs. "To be honest, I felt angry with him for not sticking up for me and our son. He was so unattached to it all, but he didn't carry the baby inside him so I suppose that makes a difference."

"Still," I mumble.

"Anyway—" she waves a hand through the air "—that was the first time we'd seen each other in years. He wanted to tell me he was sorry, that what happened was and will always be his biggest regret." She smirks slightly. "Then he asked me how serious it was with you."

"What'd you tell him?" I ask, curious of her answer.

"I told him I was madly in love and I'd found the person that I was going to spend forever with."

"Not marry?" I joke.

She shakes her head. "Marriage is overrated."

I place my hands on her hips and pull her body to me. "I wish I could make all of this right for you."

She sighs and wraps her arms around me, laying her head on my chest. "I do too. I want to see him more than anything." She pulls back and looks up at me. "Where'd you go last night? I know you didn't go to Rae and Cade's because someone would've told me."

I laugh. "Joel's."

Her eyes widen in shock. "You stayed in Joel's dorm room?" I nod. "How'd you pull that off? How'd you even get his number?"

I chuckle. "I got his number a while back. I wasn't going to let you hang out with some douche that wanted to fuck you and not have his phone number so I can pester him every time you're together."

Her mouth drops open. "That's why he's always glued to his phone when we hang out." She smacks my arm but it barely hurts.

"Yeah, so, I just texted him and asked if I could crash on his floor and he let me. End of story. It's not that exciting."

She shakes her head and backs away, hopping up on the island. "I can't believe this. You spent the night with Joel. Whoa."

"It sounds fucking dirty when you say it that way," I mutter, picking up an orange and tossing it from hand to hand to have something to do.

"Wow. I'm blow away right now. I need a moment to process this."

"Stop it." I pinch her side and she giggles. "Oh." I grin. "Ticklish, are we?"

She holds up a warning finger. "Don't you dare."

"Too late."

I tickle her mercilessly, her laughter filling the air.

It's a stark difference compared to what happened in here last night.

My anger.

Her tears.

It was fucking awful. I've never had to deal with heartbreak before, and last night was only a taste of what it might feel like if I lost Nova. A life without Nova is unimaginable to me now.

"Stop. Stop. Please stop," she begs. I finally do, and I kiss her, because it's been too long since I've felt her lips on mine. I know it hasn't even been a day but it feels like forever.

She moans, her body leaning into mine like she can't help but get closer.

I release her and press my forehead to hers.

"Are we okay?" she asks.

"We're okay," I say. "But you need to tell everyone. This isn't the kind of secret you should keep from any of us. They need to know."

She sighs and nods. "Yeah, I'll tell them. You're right. They deserve to know." She presses her lips together and kicks her feet back and forth nervously. "Are you sure you're okay with this whole thing? When you left you were so angry."

I take her face in my hands, forcing her to look at me. "I was caught off guard. I found those letters with *our* pictures, and I just went off. I was pissed, I'll be honest. I thought you were writing to your ex and still in love with him and then I was hurt that you'd put our photos with letters to him." I take a breath. "Then when you said he was your son. I didn't know how to process that. It wasn't at all what I was expecting."

She nods. "Understandable."

"There is one thing that's bothering me." I pause, gathering my thoughts, and finally ask, "Would you have ever told me if I hadn't found those letters?"

"Honestly?" She shrugs, looking down at her lap. "I don't know. I'm not sure I would have. I haven't talked about him out loud since he was born. When you go that long without saying anything it becomes kind of easy to brush it away. But I'd like to think I would've."

I nod. That's answer enough for me.

I hug her to me, breathing in her scent.

It's crazy that there's a little boy out there somewhere in the world that's half of the girl I love. If he's anything like her then he has to be pretty amazing.

And I'm going to do whatever it takes to find him.

twenty-four

...

nova

"I THINK THEY'RE BROKEN," I hiss at Jace.

He bumps my shoulder. "I think you're right."

Cade, Rae, Thea, Xander, and even Joel, stare at Jace and me.

We called a family meeting—because we didn't know what else to call it—at the house Cade and Rae share with Xander and Thea. I insisted that Joel come too because he's become a really good friend and if I was telling the others then I figured I should tell Joel too.

"Y-You have a kid?" Thea stutters, the first to speak. She absentmindedly pets her dog, Prue, who sits between her and Xander.

I nod. "Yes. I have a son."

Now that I've finally admitted the truth I find myself saying it more and more—even out loud to myself, simply because it feels so fucking good to finally admit it, like peeling your bra off after a long day.

Probably a bad analogy.

"How old is he?" Joel asks.

"He's four."

"Wow." Joel shakes his head. "This is fucking insane."

Cade and Xander both sit with twin expressions of confusion like they can't quite process what I've said.

Rae is silent, and I think she's still processing this news. Honestly, she's probably hurt that she filled me in on her biggest secret while I didn't confide in her about this.

"Let me get this straight," Cade starts, holding up two fingers. "One, you guys are dating—like you're boyfriend and girlfriend?"

"When you say it like that it makes it sound like we're in kindergarten," Jace grumbles under his breath to me.

"Two," Cade continues, ignoring Jace. "*You* have a kid." He points at me.

"That'd be a yes to both." I nod, clasping my hands together. It feels awkward standing in front of the five of them while they sit on the couch and Jace is at my side. I feel sort of like Jace and I are about to perform or something. Maybe if we did some impromptu magic it would snap them out of their stupor. Then again it would probably make things weirder.

"Pinch me," Cade says to Rae.

"What?" She looks at him like he's crazy.

"I'm having trouble believing this is real," he tells her.

"I'm not pinching you." She shakes her head.

"Fine," he grumbles. "I'll do it myself."

He pinches his arm, hard, and yelps. "Ouch that hurt. Yeah, this is real."

I shake my head. My friends are nuts but I love them.

"I think I've been transported to an alternate universe," Cade rambles, shoving his shaggy light-brown hair from his eyes. "One where Jace has a girlfriend and said girlfriend has a kid."

"Not an alternate universe," I interject. "It's very much real life."

"Where's Ashton Kutcher?" Cade asks, looking around for cameras. "We're being Punk'd, right?"

"Stop it," Rae scolds him.

"This is very much real," I say. "If you have any questions feel free to ask them. Now that you all know, I'm an open book." Thea raises her hand like we're in class. "Yes?" I prompt when she doesn't speak immediately.

"You were fifteen?"

"Yes." I nod. "Only fifteen."

"Wow," Thea mouths. "That's crazy. I can't imagine having a kid at my age, let alone fifteen. Were you scared?"

"Terrified," I answer honestly.

"Your parents ..." Rae starts. "This is why when you talk about them it's obvious that you kind of ... hate them."

I nod slowly. "Yeah. I wouldn't say I hate them, exactly, but I definitely don't love them. It's just easier if I stay away. I feel too much anger and resentment when it comes to them."

Rae frowns. She has a good relationship with her parents so I'm sure a tale like mine is hard to connect with. If she'd been in my situation her parents would've been supportive, probably not thrilled, sure, but they would've been there for her. I had no one.

"Can you find him?" Thea asks. "Can you find your son?"

Jace's hand flexes against the small of my back.

"It was a closed adoption," I explain with a shrug. "I met the parents, spoke with them while I was pregnant, and once I chose them, that was it."

Thea frowns, tears pooling in her eyes. Xander wraps a comforting arm around her shoulders.

"That's so sad," she says, dabbing at her eyes. "I can't imagine."

"It sucks," I say.

Those two words hardly sum up the gist of what I feel, but it works.

"If you picked the couple don't you know their name?" Rae asks.

I shake my head, my lips thinning. "No names are exchanged. They didn't know mine and I didn't know theirs. I picked them based on what was in their bio and since I liked them the adoption agency arranged for us to meet. They were from out of state, but I didn't even know what state they were from. They keep it all very private to protect both parties."

Rae nods sadly. "I understand."

"There's nothing you can do?" Thea presses. "Can't you reverse it and say you changed your mind and want an open adoption? That's your son."

I shrug helplessly. I feel like all I'm doing is shrugging and shaking my head but it's the only thing applicable.

"I'm sure you can, but it'd cost a lot in legal fees. I don't have money for that."

"But he's with a good family, right?" Xander asks.

"Yeah," Thea pipes in. "Tell us about them."

I sigh. I practically have their bio memorized. I used to read it every night before I went to bed, my hand lovingly grazing my round belly. "The wife is a former professional ballet dancer, now working as an elementary teacher. At the time, she was still teaching ballet once a week. The husband was a mechanic and they met when his wife came into the shop one day. She taught him how to dance, and he used to think he had no rhythm but he found he just needed the right partner. They'd been married for five years and together for eight. It said they'd started trying to have kids two years into their marriage but found out after a year of trying that she couldn't have kids. So, they decided to adopt. They'd already been on the waiting list for two years, and had one adoption fall through. I figured if I couldn't take care of my baby, then they'd be a good fit. They were normal, sweet people, who wanted a baby more than anything. I gave them that." I wipe my tears away, cursing myself for crying yet again.

It's practically Christmas, I shouldn't be bawling every minute.

I'm surprised to find both the girls crying too, and Xander and Cade both have a slightly glazed look to their eyes.

Jace rubs soothing circles on my back and lowers his head, his lips grazing my ear. "I love you. You're the strongest person I know."

I warm at his words and smile up at him. "I love you too."

"Am I the only one that finds that weird?" Cade asks.

"Yes," Thea replies, and throws a pillow at him. He catches it easily. "Ignore Cade," Thea tells us. "He thinks only he's allowed to be in love."

"Ha, ha, ha," he fake laughs. "You're so funny."

"It's true." She sticks her tongue out at him.

Sometimes watching Cade and Thea bicker made me long for a sibling of my own, but realistically I know it's probably good my parents started and stopped with me. They weren't very good at parenting me, strict and controlling. It was more than parents dealing with an unruly kid, because I was never *bad*, but they made me feel that way.

Yeah, yeah, I got pregnant, but it wasn't like I was drinking or doing drugs or at parties every night like some kids.

My parents were the kind of strict where I couldn't have a cellphone, had to be home by eight, and where the dumbest things set them off.

My mom used to get mad if I left clothes on the floor in the morning—and when I say mad, I mean the kind of mad where she'd yell and scream and throw things.

My dad was even worse.

He was always watching every little thing I did, looking

for fault in it. From the way I held a fork to how loud I closed a door.

It was like I couldn't breathe in my own house.

"Are you okay?" Jace asks, rubbing the back of my neck.

He's so incredibly in tune with me that it's strange at times.

I lean into his touch. "Yeah, I'm okay."

"Any dark thoughts in that pretty little head of yours that you want to share?" he prompts.

I shake my head. "No, I'm good."

"Good." He nods.

It feels good now that everyone knows. I didn't realize before how Owen's existence was like a hundred-pound weight dragging from my ankle, weighing me down.

Now, for the first time in four years, I feel free.

twenty-five

...

jace

"THAT FEELS NICE," I murmur sleepily to the feel of Nova's lips trailing down my chest, her silky hair tickling along the way.

It's been an adjustment to seeing her with silky brown locks, but I've decided it's my favorite look on her because it's one-hundred percent her.

She laughs softly, her fingers hooking into my boxer-briefs. I lift my hips and she pulls them down.

She's hasn't even touched me and I'm already half-hard as she wraps her fingers around me.

"Merry-fucking-Christmas to me," I murmur with a sleepy grin, my fingers tangling in her soft hair as she takes me in her mouth.

Sex with Nova never gets old. It's always new and exciting and better than the last time. Monogamy never used to be my thing, but being with Nova has shown me a whole new world. With her, everything is so much better and right feeling.

She plays with me, her mouth a wicked and tempting thing. I've never come in her mouth before. Fuck, I've thought about it, but I always end up wanting to finish inside her pussy, and this day is no different. I urge her off me and she crawls up my body with a satisfied little smirk, wiping her mouth.

I hold her hips and she positions herself above me.

She sinks down slowly and we both moan.

She collapses onto my chest, her hair all around me, and rocks her hips.

I capture her lips in mine, nibbling on her bottom lip.

"I love you," I tell her.

I never thought love was for me. I thought it made you weak, and pathetic, and that it would ruin my life. I was wrong. Loving Nova has made me stronger and happier than I've ever been, like I can take on the world, and the best part is I still feel like I'm *me* when I'm with her, but a better version.

I think maybe that's how you know you've found the one—when they don't change you but simply make you a better you.

"I love you too," she breathes, sitting up and raking her nails down my chest. I hiss from the sting.

She looks like a fucking goddess above me. Dark hair, wide doe eyes, pouty lips, and those freckles.

I have a major love for Nova's freckles.

I cup her round perky breasts in my hands and squeeze slightly. She moans, arching her back.

I sit up, holding her body to mine and angle my head into her neck as I rock my hips up to meet hers.

Her nails rake down my back and she tilts her head back as she gasps.

I press my lips to the skin of her neck and feel her shiver.

She lowers her head, her brown eyes dark with intensity. She looks at me like I'm all that exists, like I'm her whole fucking world.

She comes apart above me, her whole body shuddering, and then I can't hold back any longer.

I wrap my arms around her, holding her against me as we both come down from our high.

A few minutes pass and we stay wrapped in each other's arms.

Finally, she says, "Merry Christmas, Jace."

I kiss her. "Merry Christmas. Come on, let's see if Santa left us anything," I joke, disentangling my body from hers.

She flops onto the bed, and I smack her ass.

I pull on a clean pair of boxer-briefs and a pair of sweatpants.

"I don't wanna move." She hugs a pillow to her chest.

"There are presents," I coax.

She rolls over onto her back, and I can't help but eye her breasts. They're perky and just the right fullness.

"You know, Christmas just isn't as exciting as it is when you're a kid."

"I don't know," I say, bending down to kiss her because

she looks just too fucking delectable lying in my bed, which let's face it, it's our bed now. "This morning was pretty fucking exciting."

She sighs, fighting a smile. "That it was. Ugh, okay." She groans and rolls out of the bed. I watch as she pulls on a tiny pair of gray underwear, a tank top, and loose gray jogging pants. She claps her hands together and says, "Gimme my presents."

Last year there was no Christmas tree in my apartment, and definitely no presents, but this year the tree is so big it takes up practically a whole corner of the apartment and there are probably too many presents. I don't normally buy presents for anyone, but this year I went out and got stuff for Nova and our friends too. For the first time since I lost my mom, I felt happy to celebrate the holidays.

"Hang on, we need music," Nova chimes, jumping off the step from the bedroom into the living space.

She sprints over to the counter in the kitchen and turns on the Bluetooth speaker, fiddling with her phone.

A moment later, Christmas music filters through the air.

She turns around and starts dancing as she comes toward me. She shakes her hips and her tongue sticks out slightly between her lips. With her hair piled messily on her head, I don't think she can get more perfect.

"One more thing," she says, and grabs something off the table.

"No." I shake my head and hold my hands out in front of my body, waving them back and forth to stave her off. "Don't even think about it."

"Come on. Don't spoil the fun." She catapults herself at my body and tries, and fails, to get the Santa Claus hat on my head. She falls to the ground, and I hold out a hand to help her up. "You're too tall." She pouts.

"Will it really make you happy if I wear the stupid hat?"

She grins. "More than you can believe."

I sigh and take the hat from her, putting it on. The things we do for the people we love.

"You look hot."

"Old fat guys with white beards is what does it for you?" I ask with a raised brow.

She laughs. "No, you half-naked is what does it for me."

I grow serious. "Why do you love me?"

She tilts her head to the side, appraising me. "There are a lot of reasons. I love how much you care about people, even if you try to act like you *don't* care. I know you'd drop anything to help one of the guys or girls if they needed you. I love that you took me in when you didn't have to. I love that you play and write music. I love that you work so hard. I love your smile and laugh—and most importantly, I love that you do both so much now. When I first got to know you, you never did either. God, Jace, I love everything about you. Even things I might hate, I love instead. Like how you *always* leave your toothbrush on the counter, and how you never make the bed. Things like that. I find myself smiling because I love *you* and every little thing that makes you *you*."

"Fuck." I fight a smile. "You could've stopped with the caring about people."

She laughs, the kind of laugh that comes deep from her

belly. "Hey, you asked. Now come on, we have presents to open."

A few minutes before she didn't want to get out of bed, and now she's the one dragging me to the presents.

We sit on the floor by the tree and she eagerly looks at the presents, handing me one of mine and taking one with her name.

"On the count of three," she says. "One, two, three." She counts down each number on a finger and then we rip into our packages like lunatics.

I chuckle. "A kindle?"

She smiles bashfully. "You read a lot. I thought you might want to try this."

"It's perfect." I lean over and kiss her—frankly, I'll use anything as an excuse to kiss her anymore.

She looks down at the item in her lap, fighting laughter. "Really?"

"It was made for you."

She shakes her head and holds up the shirt. "Make Me Coffee. Yeah, it's appropriate."

"I figured you wear your funny saying shirts all the time, so one can finally be from me."

She folds it and lays it aside. "Another?" She nods at the packages.

I hold out my hands for a present and she hands me one.

We both rip into the packages, then the next, and another, until finally we're done and surrounded by the carnage of wrapping paper.

"I'll clean up," Nova says, standing up and already gathering up the paper.

I help her so it doesn't take too long and then grab a trash bag and hold it open while she stuffs the paper inside.

"I guess we should get ready and head over to Cade's?" she asks.

"You can start getting ready," I tell her. "I'm going to make us something to eat first."

"Okay, thank you." She stands on her tiptoes and kisses my jaw before hurrying into the bathroom before I can pinch her butt.

While she showers, I make the batter for homemade waffles. It's not as complicated as people make it out to be, I just usually don't make them because I hate the mess it makes in the waffle iron. But I figure it's Christmas and this calls for a special occasion.

While I stir the batter, I munch on one of the cookies Nova and I made last night.

Nova insisted that making cookies on Christmas Eve was tradition and we had to do it.

I think maybe we started a whole new kind of tradition when I ended up fucking her on the counter, but since we did finish making the cookies, I count it as a double win.

I wonder if Nova didn't come up with the idea to make cookies because she was craving normalcy. I know the last few days had to have been draining for her—admitting she has a son, and telling not only me but all of our friends. The girl deserves a round of applause for her strength. She's amazing.

I pour the batter onto the hot waffle iron and close it, listening to the batter sizzle.

It doesn't take long for me to make all the waffles and Nova comes out of the bathroom, freshly showered with her damp hair hanging like a dark curtain, and the white towel wrapped around her body.

She once told me she found me *lickable* when I came out of the shower wet with a towel around my waist. I didn't understand what she meant, and I might've even laughed, but I totally understand it now.

"Mmm," she hums. "That smells amazing." She pads over and inspects the plate of waffles. "Save some for me," she jokes, before heading into her room to change.

Honestly, her room is mine now. It's where she sleeps and primarily lives. I need to just move her stuff into my dresser and turn her room into an office or something.

I fix two plates and coffee and set everything on the table.

Nova comes out of her room dressed in a pair of ripped jeans, a sweater, and her damp hair piled on her head.

Fucking perfection.

"God, this smells amazing." She closes her eyes and inhales the scent with a dreamy smile.

She takes a seat, and I sit across from her.

She grabs the butter and slathers it on her waffle and then dumps a butt load of syrup on top of that.

"What?" she says when she notices me eyeing her.

I grin. "Nothing."

She narrows her eyes, crinkling her nose. "That look does not say *nothing*."

I nod at her plate. "You want some actual waffles with your syrup?"

She juts her chin in the air. "The syrup is what makes it good."

I shake my head and add a *little* syrup to my waffles.

"Well, you're just a fun sucker, aren't you?" she jokes, eyeing my plate.

I lift my coffee cup, trying to hide my smile. "Maybe I don't want to be a sticky mess."

She rolls her eyes. "I'm going to use a fork, not eat with my bare hands, so I doubt I'll get sticky."

"You'd be surprised." I take a drink of coffee and set my mug down.

One of my favorite things to do with Nova—besides the obvious—is eat breakfast. Our morning chats have become like a lifeline to me. I can't imagine not starting my day eating breakfast and drinking coffee with her. Those two weeks when she was pissed at me and wouldn't talk were some of the worst times of my life in recent years.

"What are you thinking about?" she asks, eyeing me with a bite halfway to her mouth.

"You," I answer honestly.

"What about me?" She balks.

I shrug. "Just thinking about us. This." I wag a finger between us. "I like our routine."

"Oh." She straightens in her seat and wiggles a bit. "I like it too," she admits.

"We're good together, aren't we?" I ask her. "Like ... we just click."

Her eyes twinkle like I'm so fucking amusing. "Yeah, we do."

We finish breakfast and she insists on washing the dishes while I get ready.

It doesn't take me long to shower and get dressed, and then we gather up the presents for our friends and head out.

"Confession, I love the rain," Nova comments when we reach the lobby and look through the doors to the outside world. She smiles as she says it.

I chuckle. "Confession, I love the snow, which that rain is going to be soon when the temperature drops just a little more."

She laughs. "Or it could be ice—a mix of our favorites together."

I shake my head. "Ice fucking sucks. It's clear and slippery. How's that fun?"

She giggles, the sound of her laughter lighting up my whole world. "That sounds like the start of a bad dirty joke.

I roll my eyes. "You're worse than me."

We head outside into the rain. It's more of a mist than actual rain and *cold*. It's definitely going to start snowing.

Nova clutches the bag with the presents and I open the passenger door of my truck for her. Once she's in I close the door and jog around to the driver's side.

"Can you let them know we're on our way?" I ask her. "Thea's already texted me like fifteen times, asking when we're going to get there."

She snorts. "Why does she always text you and not me?"

I check my mirrors and pull out onto the road. "Because she loves to irritate me, that's why. I think she gets some kind of sick enjoyment out of making me snap."

"Yeah, that sounds like Thea. Don't worry, I'll let her know."

The rain slicks against the windshield and I turn the wipers on so I can see.

"You know," Nova begins after a few minutes of silence, "I think this is the best Christmas I've ever had, and it's not because of any of the presents, but because I get to spend it with people I love."

"Like me?" I wag my brows.

She laughs. "Yes, you, and our friends too. Back home, Christmas wasn't a happy affair and more of an obligation." She shrugs. "This ... This was everything I'd already dreamed and hoped it could be."

My chest pangs. Nova's childhood was as bleak and depressing as mine, and now that I know her whole story, I think it's safe to say it was even worse. I'd take my controlling father over her nasty parents any day. What her parents, and Owen's, did to her is inexcusable and unforgivable. She should be angry at the entire world, but she's not. I think she used to be a little lost, but now she's finally found her way.

I reach for her hand and finally reply with a choked response, "I'm glad."

We're about ten minutes from Cade's house when she exclaims, "You were right! It's snowing!"

Sure enough, the rain is turning to snow, and little white tufts float down onto the truck.

"There's something kind of magical about snow," she beams, looking out the window.

"Yeah, there is," I agree. "It's so pure. Not a lot is

anymore."

The rest of the drive Nova watches the snow with a wide-eyed expression. We finally arrive at Cade's and I park in their driveway.

"Thea said to come in through the garage. I have the code," Nova tells me.

"All right, I'll get the presents then."

I hop out and go around to her side, taking the bag from her. I lock my truck and follow her to the keypad. She puts in the four-digit code and the door whirs up.

We head inside and find everyone in the family room.

"We brought presents!" Nova says unnecessarily, pointing to the bag I carry. Her excitement is adorable, though. Nova used to try to fade into the background, but now she glows with happiness. My chest puffs with pride, because I know I had some fucking part in that.

"Presents!" Thea squeals like a cracked out five-year-old.

Xander wraps his arm around her waist and pulls her down onto the couch when she runs by him, headed for Nova. She falls into his lap and glares.

Their dog, Prue, lifts her head from the cushion in the corner and observes the scene. She must dub everything as okay because she promptly lies back down.

"Haven't you had enough presents?" he jokes.

"You can never get too many presents."

He sighs and shrugs, looking at me with an expression that says, *I don't know what to do with her.*

I set the bag down and let Nova pass out the gifts.

"Your stuff is still under the tree." Rae points. I grab the gifts that are for me and Nova and find a spot on the floor to sit. Nova finishes handing out the gifts and sits beside me.

We all tear into our gifts.

Thea busts out laughing. "Oh, my God. *Unicorn Meat.*" She holds up a can that looks like a can of Spam but does in fact say *Unicorn Meat.*

Nova laughs with her. "You're constantly saying you're a unicorn, *so.*"

"This is hilarious." Thea sets the can down. "But I could never eat myself."

"I don't know," Xander jokes. "You taste good." He bites at her shoulder.

"Ew, fuck! No! That's my sister! Don't talk like that in front of me! La, la, la!" Cade covers his ears with his hands.

Rae rolls her eyes and smacks Cade's arm. "You're being ridiculous. They're married. You can't freak out over everything one of them says."

He lowers his hands. "Yes. Yes, I can, because that's my sister, and *you*—" he points at Xander "—are gross."

"Oh, please." Thea rolls her eyes. "Do not act like you haven't put your mouth on Rae's vagina, because seriously." She holds up a hand, daring him to speak.

Rae flushes and Cade glares at his sister. "Not everyone is as comfortable talking about sex as you are."

Thea sighs. "You're such a prude. Grow up."

"Grow up?" he repeats. "I'm older than you."

"Then act like it," Thea spars.

"I love them," Nova leans over and whispers in my ear. "They make me wish I had a sibling."

"Eh, I think we're pretty lucky that we don't. That doesn't look like fun to me."

"I disagree," she says, watching them in awe.

I finally look down at the gift in my lap and jolt. It's a journal, inscribed with my name and the year. I flip it open to the first page and find written on it;

For songs.

Love Rae and Cade

I swallow thickly. I didn't even know that they paid attention to my song writing. I know a journal probably seems like a simple thing to most people, but to me this feels like the world, because it means my friends pay attention to me more than I give them credit for.

"What is it?" Nova asks, like she senses the shift in me.

So fucking in tune with me it's ridiculous.

I hand her the journal and her lips part. "Oh," she murmurs. "Wow." She runs her fingers over the black leather cover. "This is perfect for you."

"Yeah, it is."

"Glad you like it," Rae says, noticing our conversation.

"I love it," I say honestly. "Thank you." I take it back when Nova hands it to me.

I set it aside and open my gift from Xander and Thea.

"Holy shit," I curse when I see the contents of the box. "Are you fucking serious right now?" I ask, holding up the tickets.

Xander chuckles. "Told you he'd love them," he tells Thea.

"This is ... Whoa."

I stare down at the tickets for Twenty-One Pilots in awe. I've mentioned maybe once or twice that I like them, months ago, and again, the fact that either of them noticed is what touches me the most.

Plus, it's fucking Twenty-One Pilots and that's amazing anyway.

Nova looks at the tickets in my hand and her jaw drops. "Seriously?" She knows how much I love them since I play their music in the apartment all the time. I think maybe I've got her slightly addicted.

"Wow, guys, I don't even know what to say." I'm not a crier, and I've never been one to get emotional easy, but *this* has gotten to me.

"We love you," Thea says. "We might not tell you often enough, but we do. You're more than a friend, you're family. Both of you."

I look at Nova and then them. "I think of you all as family too. You're more of a real family than my father is."

They've been there for me more than he ever has. And these gifts prove that they pay attention, that they *know* me. They didn't give me a generic gift card to a store. This took thought and that's what means the most.

I look down at Nova's gifts in her lap and notice a framed picture of her, Thea, and Rae. It makes me smile.

Nova and I both thought we were outcasts.

Loners.

That we just didn't belong.

But all along we already did, we just didn't see it.

This is where we fit, one piece of a beautiful puzzle.

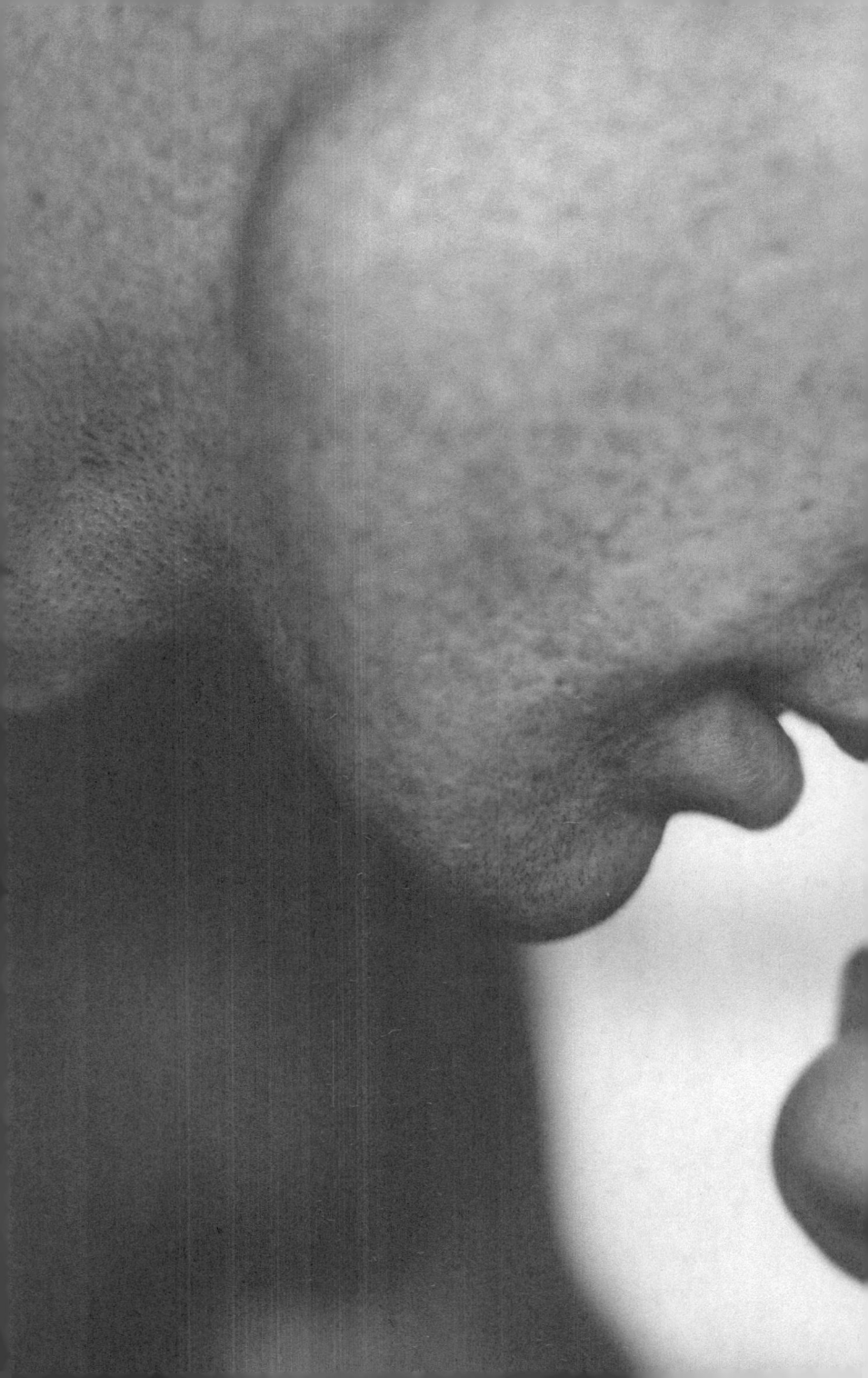

twenty-six
...

nova

"UM ... JACE?"

"Yeah?" he asks from the couch, scribbling in his new journal.

"Look." I point out the window of Cade and Rae's house.

"Well, fuck." He closes his journal and comes to stand beside me to look out.

The street is blanketed in white. At least a foot, and it's still coming down.

"Guys," I call into the kitchen, where the four of them cook. They insisted on making dinner and didn't want Jace and me to help.

"Yeah?" Rae says back.

"Please tell me you don't mind if we crash here."

"No, of course not. But why?" She appears in the

doorway to the kitchen. "Oh," she says, finding her answer when she sees what we see. "We have a blow-up mattress. It'll be fine."

Jace looks at me out of the corner of his eye, his lips twitching.

We both know a whole evening with our friends is bound to get interesting.

Dinner is ready soon after that and we all sit down to eat.

Cade and Thea's mom, who's been living there since her divorce, comes down and joins us all for dinner.

"How are you guys?" she asks, hugging Jace and then me.

"We're good. How're you?" I ask her, taking the seat beside Jace. "I thought you weren't here since you didn't come down before."

"Oh," she says as she waves a hand through the air and takes a seat beside Thea, "I wanted to give you all time to do Christmas without me."

"You didn't need to do that," I tell her. "We don't mind."

"It's okay, really," she assures me. "Now that I'm away from Malcolm I find that having time to myself is something I enjoy. It was hard to come by before." She forces a smile.

All the drama that went on with Thea and Cade's family a few months ago was something out of a soap opera. None of us really talk about it anymore, not wanting to stir up bad memories. I think we all are especially wary of Cade's feelings on the matter. When everything blew up he kind of become the center of attention for his former football fame and the fact that even a big, muscled, football player can be the victim of physical and verbal abuse. He dealt with a lot of people calling him a pussy for never fighting back, but what they don't realize is that when someone starts beating you down as a child, by the time you're an adult you still feel powerless.

"This looks delicious," Jace says, changing the subject.

He's right, the meal looks amazing. They made grilled chicken in some sort of marinade with a rice and vegetable mix.

"It smells good too," I add with a smile.

As we eat we talk about school, and work, and life.

It's nice to catch up with all of them.

When we finish with dinner, Jace and I insist on doing the dishes.

"Stay on your side." I bump his hip with mine.

"Stay on *your* side." He bumps me back, the water sloshing in the sink.

"You're the one that's crowding me," I defend.

He snorts. "Are you kidding me? You're always trying to get closer to me."

"Am not," I argue, fighting laughter.

"Face it, you can't resist my body."

I gasp. "I so can."

He grins devilishly and lowers his voice so the others in the next room have no chance of hearing him. "You couldn't go one day without my cock."

"Jace!" I shriek and splash him with water.

He looks down at his soaking wet shirt and then at me. "Did you just *splash* me?"

I swallow thickly at the dangerous glint in his eye. "No," I squeak.

"Liar." He grabs a handful of the suds on top and throws them at me.

I scream and jump back, batting at the bubbles in my hair like they're a fluffy monster.

He laughs at my reaction.

"Oh, you think this is funny?"

"Fucking hysterical."

I grab a handful of bubbles and launch them at the side of his face. Now it's my turn to laugh because he looks like a lopsided Santa Claus.

"Oh, that does it." He scoops two handfuls of bubbles and water and goes to throw it at me.

I scream and take off running but feel it pelt me in the back.

Then his arm comes around my middle and he hauls me against him. My feet come off the ground, and I kick, trying to get away. I can't stop laughing, though.

We collapse onto the floor, a tangle of limbs, both laughing our asses off.

We look up to find our friends watching us with amused expressions, which only makes us laugh harder.

"I'm so glad you two finally saw what was right in front of you. You're perfect for each other," Thea says.

Jace picks himself up off the ground and holds out two hands to help me up.

"Sorry about the mess," he tells them. "We'll clean it up."

"We set up the air mattress in the family room," Rae says. "It's not the most comfortable, but I figure it's better than the couch."

"I think we should watch a movie tonight. Maybe *Jaws*," Thea suggests.

Xander chuckles and kisses the side of her forehead. "You and *Jaws*."

"Hey, you like it too," she defends.

He grins back. "That I do."

"Anybody else feel like we're missing something?" Jace asks.

Thea and Xander chuckle, but give no explanation.

"We can watch something else," Thea concedes, even though nobody fought against it. "We should probably do something Christmas-y."

"Ooh, I know," Rae chimes with more enthusiasm than usual. "We could watch all the *Santa Claus* movies. The ones with Tim Allen. I love those." She blushes slightly when she realizes her exuberance.

"That's a good idea," I agree. "I've only seen the first one and that was forever ago."

Thea and Rae exchange a look. "You've only seen the first one?" Rae asks.

"Yeah." I nod. "That's what I said."

"It's settled then. We're watching all of them. I'll get the first one on. Xander, you make the popcorn, and *please* do not drench it in butter."

"Maybe I'll just make you your own not butter drenched bowl."

"That'd be perfect." She flips her long hair over her shoulder and heads into the other room. Cade and Rae follow.

Jace and I clean up the water while Xander makes the popcorn and gathers other snacks. By the time we clean up our mess he has a tray full of drinks so Jace carries that into the family room. I wait with Xander and help him put all the popcorn into individual bowls so we don't have to all fight over it.

"Make an extra bowl for my mom," Thea calls into the kitchen. "She said she'd come down after she takes a bath."

Xander I finish doling out the popcorn into seven individual bowls. I fit four onto a tray and Xander handles the rest.

All the lights are off in the family room, only the glow of the Christmas tree and the TV illuminating the space.

Thea has piled blankets and pillows onto the couch and air mattress so everything feels like one over-flowing space.

I set the tray down on the center of the mattress and grab a bowl for Jace and me. I flop onto the couch beside him and he takes the extra bowl from me.

Everyone finds a seat and Thea starts the movie.

A few months ago, I wouldn't have enjoyed something like this, now there's no place I'd rather be.

The house is silent and everyone else is asleep, but I find myself having trouble falling asleep. Jace must be having similar trouble because he keeps playing with my hair. Normally, that would lull me to sleep, but nothing seems to quiet my mind tonight.

"Jace?" My voice cracks as I break the silence.

"Hmm?" He hums in response.

I roll over onto my stomach and prop myself on my elbow so I can see him. He crosses his arms behind his head and squints at me since he doesn't have his glasses.

"Do you think he had a good Christmas?" I ask softly. "My son, I mean."

Jace gets a sad look and nods. "I'm sure he did."

"I hope he believes in Santa."

"He's four, right?" I nod. "He still believes." He grabs a piece of my hair and wraps it around his finger.

"I wish I could tell him Merry Christmas and give him a hug. God, Jace, that's all I want. I just want to hold him. I need to remind myself that he's real."

"Fuck," he groans. "I wish you could hold him too."

"I don't even know his real name."

Now that Jace and everyone knows about my past, I find myself thinking about him even more. I've always wondered about him, things that other people probably wouldn't think about, but as his mother, I crave. Like his smell—it's silly, but I wonder what he smells like. His sound of his voice. The feel of him in my arms. So many questions I'll never have answers to.

"I'm sorry," he whispers softly, gathering me into his arms.

I burrow into his body, wishing he had the power to make everything right but knowing in my heart that nothing can ever change this.

twenty-seven
...

jace

SLEEP EVADES ME.

I spend the whole night holding Nova and wishing I could make things different for her. I never even thought about the fact that she doesn't know her son's real name. I can't imagine living like that.

I've looked into the adoption as much as I can on my own, but like she said, it was closed so there's not a lot of information.

There's not even a record of Nova going into the hospital to have the baby. I have a feeling Owen's father erased that tidbit of information. I can't imagine being so fucking power hungry that I'd do anything to hide the existence of my grandchild. I guess I should believe it, though, because it's exactly the kind of thing my father would do. Men like that are all the same.

I kiss Nova's head as she sleeps and she wiggles against me, murmuring something in her sleep that I can't understand.

I want to find her son for her so she can have that peace of mind. I think maybe if she sees him, even if it's only a picture, she might finally have the closure she needs. I know I'm going to have to hire an investigator, and a lawyer, to hopefully get this thing straightened out.

I brush my fingers through her hair and her fingers flex against my chest as she sleeps.

"I'm going to find him," I whisper in her ear. "I promise."

Even if it takes me years, I'll find him.

I know I will.

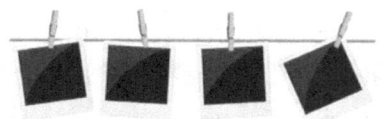

"I smell coffee."

I turn around and smile at Nova as she enters the kitchen. We didn't have pajamas to wear last night so she stole my shirt and I wore my boxer-briefs. I slipped my jeans back on when I got up, just in case someone else came down. Nova must not have had the same worry because she's only in my shirt, which comes down to the tops of her thighs.

"Hey, beautiful."

She smiles sleepily and comes to wrap her arms around me from behind.

"Mmm," she hums, rubbing her face against my back. "I love you."

"Do you?" I chuckle. "Or do you just want coffee?"

"Both." She lets me go and pulls out a chair, sitting down at the breakfast table.

The coffee finishes and I pour us each a mug, carrying them to the table and sitting down.

Outside the world is covered in a thick blanket of snow. At some point in the night the plows came through and cleared the streets. Now piles of snow block most of the driveways.

Nova sniffs her coffee and takes a sip. "You always make it perfect."

"I think you tell me that so I'll make it every morning and you don't have to."

She smiles, curling her fingers around the mug. "Maybe."

The stairs creak, and it isn't long before Rae creeps in.

"I didn't want to wake you guys, but—"

"We were already awake," Nova finishes for her.

Rae nods and pours some of the coffee I made into a mug. She takes a sip and moans. "That's good."

"See, I told you," Nova chirps.

"Do you think you guys will be able to get out today?"

"Ready to be rid of us already, Rae?" I place my hand over my heart. "I'm hurt. I'm really hurt."

Rae flushes and leans her hip against the counter. "That's

not what I meant. I figure you guys don't exactly like being trapped here."

My phone rings and I groan. "Hold that thought."

I hop up and jog into the family room, searching for my phone.

I finally find it wadded up in the blanket we used to cover up with.

I'm not surprised when I see that it's my dad calling. It's the day after Christmas, and he didn't call yesterday so he's probably finally remembered his flub. I've always found it funny how he spends the whole year ignoring me and then around the holidays I'll receive two or three phone calls from him, usually requesting me to show up somewhere, like the stupid Thanksgiving ball thing.

"'Sup?" I answer, just to spite him.

"Honestly, Jacen, use more than one syllable to greet someone. '*Sup* isn't even a word."

I try not to laugh. Hearing my dad say '*sup* makes his anger totally fucking worth it.

"What can I help you with?" I ask, sitting down on the couch.

"*What can I help you with?*" he mimes. "We're not in a department store. I'm your father."

I roll my eyes to the ceiling. Nothing I do or say is good enough, I know this and I've long ago accepted that fact.

"Merry Christmas to you too, Dad," I mumble.

"Christmas was yesterday," he supplies.

"I know," I grind out. "You didn't call."

"Neither did you," he counters.

I sigh. I fucking hate conversations with my dad. "Get to the point. Why'd you call?"

"New Year's Eve I want us to have dinner together. Bring your little girl toy too."

"She's my girlfriend, dad," I grumble.

"Bring her," he hisses. "We have something to discuss."

I groan. The last thing I want to do is spend New Year's Eve with my dad, but I always know I have no choice. He tells me what to do and I do it.

"We'll be there."

"Perfect. See you then."

The line clicks off and I lay my phone down, pinching the bridge of my nose. A five-minute conversation with my dad and I already have a migraine.

Nova tiptoes into the family room and when she sees I'm no longer on the phone asks, "Your dad? What'd he want?"

I pull her down onto my lap and bury my face in the crook of her neck.

I already feel better.

"We've been summoned."

It's all the answer she needs.

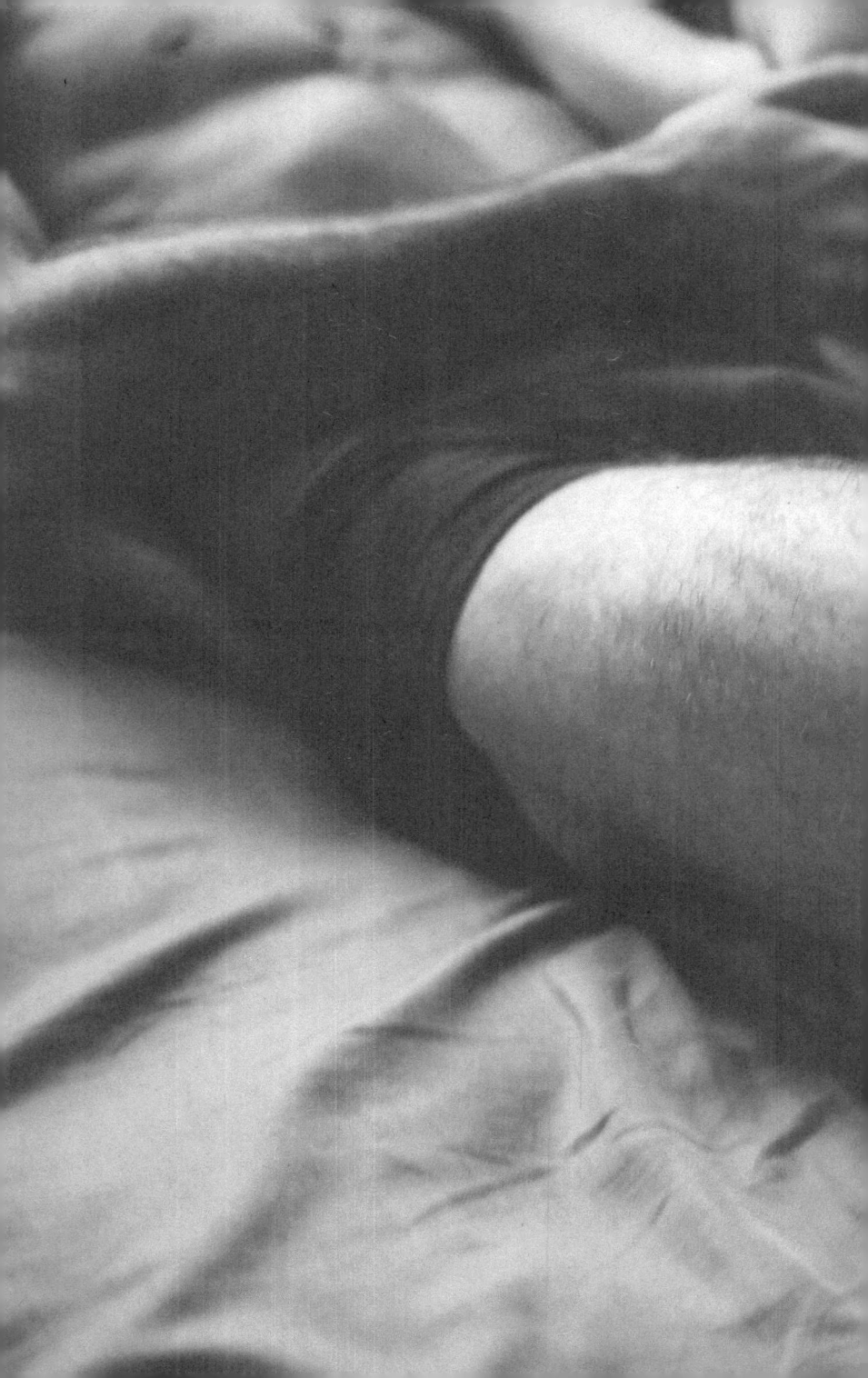

twenty-eight

. . .

nova

"I DON'T HAVE to get dressed up, do I?" I lean my head out the bathroom door.

"Jace?" I prompt when he's silent for too long.

"I mean, not like you were for the one thing, but you'll need to dress nice."

I sigh and grumble under my breath about what an asshole his dad is.

Jace appears in the doorway dressed in a pair of black dress pants and a black button-down shirt. He looks sleek and sophisticated, like sex on a stick.

"So, I should wear a dress?" I surmise, turning back to the mirror to finish applying mascara.

"Um, yes," he hedges, watching applying my makeup.

"What kind of dinner is this?" I ask. "Is there a chance Owen or his dad might be there?"

"I honestly don't know." He frowns.

"Jace," I groan. "You need to ask questions so I have answers."

I finish with my makeup and then move past him into my room. I scan the items in my closet, looking for something that might be acceptable for the night.

I end up having to ransack my whole closet to put together my look, but in the end, I'm happy with the black tights, sequined short black skirt, and black top look. I pair it with black boot heels and my black leather jacket.

"How do I look?" I ask Jace.

He sets his guitar aside and smiles crookedly. "Fucking hot."

"Fucking hot—does that translate to hot enough to fuck?" I joke.

"You're always fuckable." He stands and walks over to me, his presence captivating. He wraps his hands around my waist and I stretch up on my toes to be able to reach his neck. He starts to bend to kiss me and I cover his mouth with my hand.

"Nuh-uh. Nice try. You can't mess up *this*." I point at my face. "It took too long to get perfect."

"It was already perfect," he grumbles.

"I'm sure your father wouldn't appreciate me showing up with my lipstick smeared. Save it for later."

"Fine," he relinquishes.

I grab my clutch off the coffee table. "We should go. Is he sending a car again?"

He shakes his head. "No, I'm driving. There must not be

anyone at this dinner he's worried about impressing if he's letting me drive my truck."

Jace looks away and out the window. I feel like there's very much a part of him that craves his father's acceptance, while also realizing that nothing he ever does is going to be good enough for that man. With his mom gone, I think he's been very much alone in the world.

But not anymore.

"All right," he says as he takes my hand, "let's go."

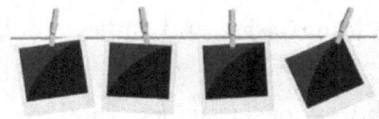

"It's smaller than I expected," I say when we pull up outside the colonial-style two-story home. "I mean, it's still *large*, but I was expecting ... gargantuan."

He chuckles. "Yeah, I can see how you'd get that impression, but no, this is where I grew up. I've always been surprised he kept the place."

"It's beautiful."

It really is. A brick pathway leads to the front of the house, and the snow we've had covers the ground in a soft white embrace. The driveway is long and winds around the back of the house. Jace follows it and parks outside the garage.

He cuts the engine and breathes out, like he needs a moment to collect himself.

"Ready?" I ask, when he makes no move to leave the cozy warmth of the truck.

He finally nods.

Instead of going in through the garage, we head for the front door. The pathway is neatly shoveled and covered in salt to melt the ice.

At the door, Jace takes another deep breath before ringing the doorbell.

When it swings open we're met with a woman in a work uniform. "Mr. Kensington is in his office working. He'll be done in time for dinner," she tells us, and steps aside so we can come in.

She collects our coats and leaves us in the hallway.

"What now?" I ask, looking around. The foyer is hardwood and the walls are painted a deep blue color. Above us a chandelier hangs from the second-story ceiling.

"Want to see my room?" Jace asks.

"You still have a room here?" I ask.

"If he hasn't gotten rid of it." He shrugs. "Last time I was here it was exactly as I left it."

"I'd love to see it." I hope he doesn't notice the eagerness in my eyes, but I've always been curious to know what Jace was like when he was younger. This is like a key.

Jace nods toward the stairway that curves through the foyer in an L-shape.

"This way."

I follow him upstairs and down the hall, passed several

closed doors. He finally stops at the last one and his shoulders tense as he inhales a breath. When he lets it out he swings open the door.

He steps inside and I follow. The room is large, with lots of windows, which gives it an airiness. The walls are painted a light gray color with abstract white stripes overlapping to make different shapes. Some of the shapes are painted randomly with a darker gray color.

His bed is a simple mattress that's pushed to a far corner. The comforter is black and tossed haphazardly over the mattress like he still lives here and got up and couldn't be bothered to make the bed, which makes sense since Jace *never* makes the bed.

The floor is a thick plush beige carpet, but I couldn't tell at first because it was so covered in random crap like clothes, shoes, magazines, books, music sheets, you name it and it's probably on the floor.

The walls have posters of bands and models and an old guitar rests against the wall.

"That was my first guitar," he says, when he sees where I'm looking.

"You didn't take it with you?" I ask, wondering why he'd leave something like that behind.

"My dad bought it, so I didn't want to keep it."

"Is that why there's so much ... stuff here?" I ask, peering into an open dresser drawer full of shirts.

"I wanted to start new," he explains.

I nod, and smile at him. "I can understand that all too well."

I pick up a little league trophy. "You played baseball?"

He chuckles and shoves his hands in his pockets. "For like a month. I think I only got that for participation. I wasn't exactly a sports kind of guy."

"Nothing wrong with that." I put the trophy back and pick up a picture frame. "Is this your mom?"

He comes to stand behind me, his body a wall of heat behind me. I feel him nod before he speaks. "Yes."

"She was beautiful. You have her eyes." She has a kind face, and his green eyes, with flowing red hair. "What was her name?"

"Melissa," he says softly.

"Tell me a memory, one good memory you have here."

He picks up the picture frame, looks at it closely, and then replaces it.

"I remember being maybe four or five and my mom was pushing me on the swing out back. She was singing ... something from Mary Poppins, I think, and I remember feeling so loved. She was truly radiant."

"I hate that I'll never get to meet her."

"I do too."

He reaches down and twines our finger together. I lean my head on his shoulder, hoping through touch alone that I can make him feel the smallest bit better.

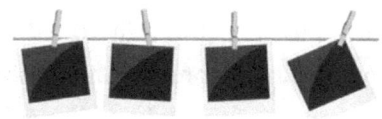

jace

Nobody's come to collect us for dinner yet, which I find strange.

"I'm going to go look for my dad." I let go of her hand. "You wait here." I point to my bed.

"Are you sure? I can come with you."

I shake my head. "Nah, I'll spare you the drama I'm sure is about to unfold."

She nods once. "Okay, I'll be here then."

I leave her alone in my childhood room and head downstairs to my dad's office.

It's funny how this house is exactly the same as it was when I was growing up, but it hardly feels like home. It's further proof that it's not the place that's home, but the people.

The hardwood floors creak beneath my feet as I head down the hall to my father's office. It's silent inside and I push the door open.

"Dad?" It's empty, the room dark.

But I thought ...

I start to leave the room, but something draws me forward, to his desk. Papers are scattered there like he left in a hurry.

I flick his desk light on and my eyes scan the papers.

Confusion rattles my brain, but as understanding sinks in my heart begins to race at the reality of what faces me.

Nova's name flashes before my eyes, intermingled with

Owen's and his father's. The papers are laden with dates and information about her. Fuck, I even see a report card.

But that's not what makes my blood run cold.

I pick up the piece of paper, my hand shaking.

Adoption papers.

"What are you doing in here?" His voice booms.

My head whips up, the papers clutched in my fist.

"What did you do?" I glare at him.

He steps into his office, dressed in a suit and his hair slicked back. The man always looks impeccable, like nothing can touch him.

"You're my son. After I spoke with Harry and he informed me of his son's past with your ... escort, I thought it was best to dig into her past myself, see what I was dealing with if my son's associating with someone like her."

"Someone like her?" I scoff. "You mean someone who's beautiful, and smart, and artistic, and fucking amazing? I'm *lucky* she wants someone like *me*."

He shakes his head. "She's not on your level, son."

I spread my arms wide. "Who is, Dad? Tell me, who the fuck do you think is a match for me? You think you're so much better than everyone else, and that by extension I am too, but you're wrong. You're the worst kind of person there is."

He shakes his head, still calm. "Everything I do, I do because I love you."

"Love," I repeat with a laugh. "You think you *love* me. You don't know the first fucking thing about love!"

"Stop using that kind of language in my house, and *do*

not raise your voice to me. You are a child." He points an accusing finger at me.

"I stopped being a child the minute Mom died," I tell him, anger shining in my eyes. "You weren't here and I had to raise myself and last time I checked, I am twenty-fucking-three, which is hardly a child."

"I did what I had to do."

"You mean *work*? You worked all the fucking time and you made my life miserable. And Mom? She died and you weren't fucking there! Where were you? Probably working or fucking some whore, because let's face it, you never really loved Mom, did you? Fuck!" I cry out when he grabs me by the neck and shoves my face into the wall. I'm jolted, not having expected that at all. He's never laid a hand on me, not once. He preferred to use words, not fists, but it seems something I've said has sent him over the edge.

"Do not—" he shakes me "—*ever*, accuse me of cheating on your mother. I would *never* do that. If there's one good thing I had in this world, it's her." He squeezes my neck slightly, a warning, and lets go.

Air whooshes back into my lungs and I grab my neck. It's going to be bruised, that's for sure.

Tears shine in his eyes, something I've certainly never seen.

"Get out of my house, Jacen."

I don't move. I think I'm stunned.

"*Out*," he yells.

I force my feet to move and flee his office just as Nova starts down the stairs.

"I heard yelling and banging. Is everything okay?" she asks, hurrying toward me.

I shake my head. "We're leaving."

"W-What?"

"Come on." I urge her to the door.

"My jacket," she mumbles, looking around blindly for it.

"I'll buy you a new one." I push her toward the door. I need out of this house. *Now.*

She watches me, wide-eyed, and seems to pick up on there being something of urgency.

We burst outside into the blistery cold, both of us instantly shivering.

I place my hand on her lower back, guiding her to my truck.

We get inside and I start the truck, pulling out of the driveway as fast as I can.

"What happened?" she asks. "Jace?" she prompts, placing her hand tenderly on my knee. "Talk to me, please. Don't shut down."

"He shouldn't have done that." I shake my head, anger still coursing through my veins.

"Done what?"

I shake my head, searching for the words. "Shouldn't have looked into you. It was wrong and invasive. You're important to me and he pried into your fucking life. He *spied* on you. Shit, Nova." I slam on the brakes and look down at the papers in my lap, elation replacing fury. "Holy shit," I exclaim.

"What?" Her lips part in confusion. "What's going on?"

I hold up the papers. "We're going to find your son."

"What?" She's still confused.

I pull off the road so we don't get hit and put the truck in park. "My dad must've hired an investigator or something to look into your past, after he spoke with Harry Mitchell—Owen's dad."

"Why would he do that?" she asks, her nose crinkling.

"Because he's my dad, and that's what he does. He had a background check done on my prom date back in high school, so I honestly shouldn't be that fucking surprised that he did this."

"Okay, but what does this have to do with my son." Nova shakes her head, not following my gist.

"Because—" I wave the papers in her face "—we have the adoption papers. We know the adoptive parents' names now."

Her mouth parts into a perfect O and then she bursts into tears. "Are you serious?"

"Yeah, I am."

"Oh, my God." She unbuckles her seatbelt and crawls across the console to get in my lap.

I hug her to me.

All I've wanted for the last month is to reunite Nova with her son, even if only through a picture, and now thanks to my dad, I just might be able to do that and more.

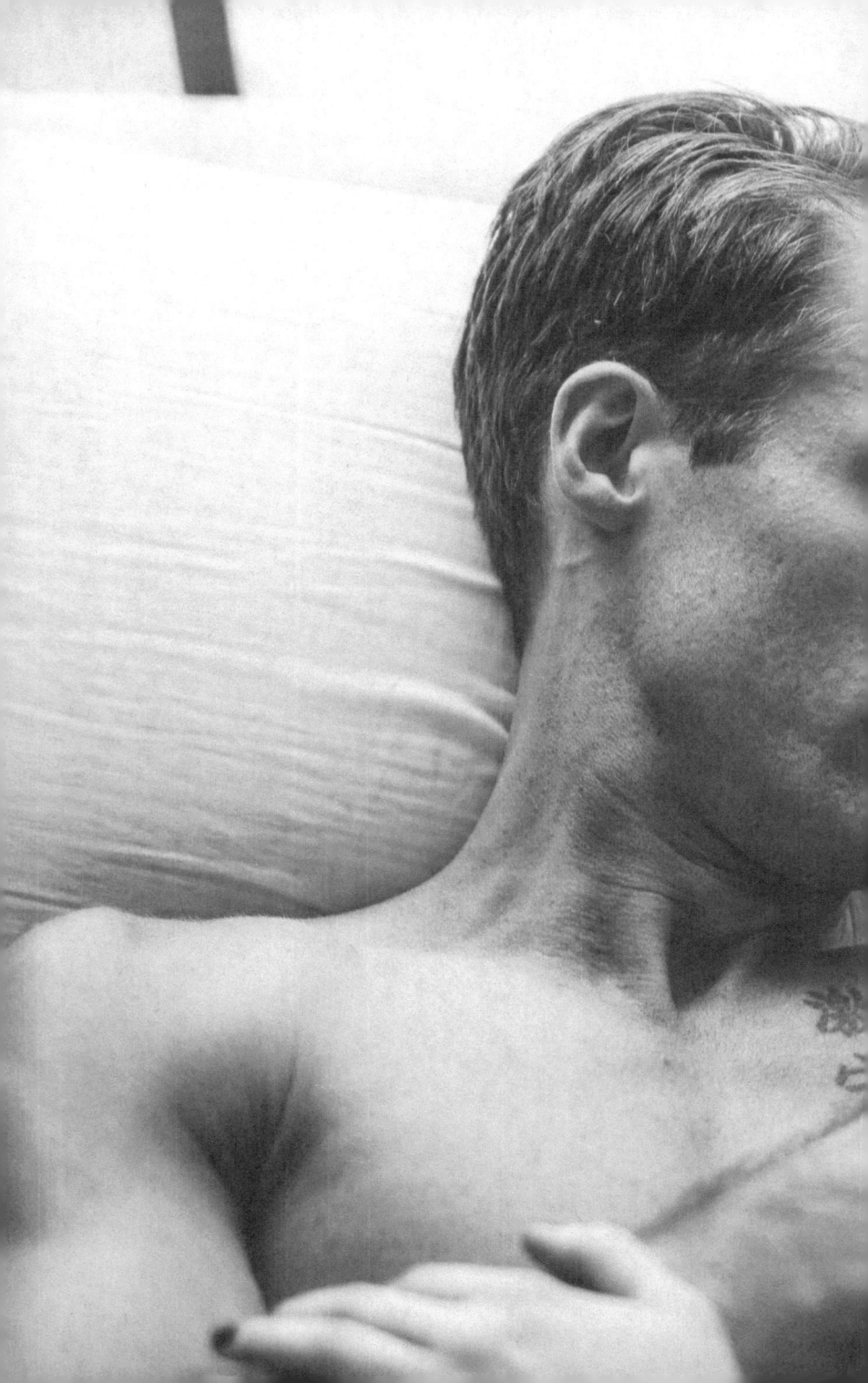

twenty-nine

nova

"WE'RE GOING *to find your son.*"

Jace's words have echoed in my head non-stop for the last couple of days.

A constant loop as I go to work and the bar.

"We're going to find your son."

For four years, I resolved myself to the fact that I'd never know him. Never see him. Never hear his voice.

Never, never, never.

Never has now become maybe.

I think *maybe* is the dirtiest temptress to ever exist.

Maybe just hangs there, waiting.

Something could happen, or it could not.

I don't know what the future holds.

Maybe has given me a hope I didn't have before.

I lock up the record store and bundle my coat around my

body. It's late and snow flurries begin to fall from the cloudy sky.

I head over to W.T.F. and find Jace manning the bar. The place is packed but I manage to find a stool.

"Hungry?" he asks in passing, setting a drink down.

"Starving. I skipped lunch."

He gives me a look that tells me exactly what he thinks about me skipping lunch.

"What do you want?" he asks.

"Um ... cheese fries and a B.L.T.."

"Coming right up." He spins around to enter my order into the computer.

He's busy bartending so we don't have much time to talk. It isn't long until my meal is ready and he brings me my food.

"Have you talked to your dad?" I ask.

He shakes his head. "He keeps calling, wanting to meet up and apologize, but ... I mean, so much damage is done and him looking into your past ..." Jace shakes his head. "Unforgivable."

"If he hadn't done that we wouldn't have the birth parents' name."

Jace raises a finger. "Don't defend him."

I raise my hands innocently. "I'm not. You know how I feel about my parents. I'm just saying. Maybe ... maybe you owe it to *yourself* to speak with him one last time. There might be a missing piece. You never know."

Jace looks doubtful. "I don't know."

"Just think about it."

I know from what Jace has told me that his dad wasn't a good man while he was growing up, but the way I see it, people aren't born evil, they're made, and there has to be more to his father than meets the eye. Don't get me wrong, I don't like the guy, and probably never will. He was rude at that stupid Thanksgiving gala thing, and snooping into my past was the final peg. But I feel like it's important for Jace to have ... closure, some sort of understanding, I guess. He doesn't have a mom. All he has left is his dad, no matter how awful he is.

I eat while Jace works and then I hang out at the bar.

I wait until he gets off and we head out together.

When it's nice out, Jace walks to work, but since it feels like Antarctica he's been driving so we pile into his truck.

I yawn, exhaustion taking over as he pulls out onto the street.

It doesn't take us long to arrive at the apartment and we head straight inside.

I shower and change into my pajamas and climb into Jace's bed. My eyes are heavy and I struggle to keep them open.

"Come to bed," I plead, patting the empty space beside me.

"In a little bit. I want to look for a little while." Jace picks up his laptop and sits on the couch.

I sigh. Every night since the fateful dinner Jace has been scouring the internet, searching for more information on the birth parents. They must be perfectly normal people because so far, his search hasn't turned up much.

"Are you sure?"

He nods, already zeroed in on the screen.

I'm too tired to fight him and fall right to sleep.

"I found them!"

I jolt awake at the sound of Jace's exclamation.

"Huh?" I blink the sleep from my eyes.

"Nova." His eyes shine. "I know his name."

That gets my attention. I hurry out of bed and to the couch.

"You know his name?" I repeat.

Jace nods. "Greyson. His name is Greyson."

I start sobbing. I can't help it. All these years of not having a face or a real name for him has been hell. But now I finally know.

"How'd you find him?" I ask.

"His adopted mom has a Facebook. It took me a while to find it because it's connected to her maiden name—Sarah Evans, instead of Sarah Hollis. But I found them, and, Nova, you're never going to believe this."

"What?" I ask around my tears, not sure I can handle any more news.

"They live in Boulder."

I stare at him, dumbfounded. "No," I say in disbelief.

"Yes." He nods. "He lives forty minutes from here."

"I can't believe this," I cry, my hands shaking. I feel like I'm coming down from an adrenaline high.

"Believe it. Do you want to see a picture of him?" Jace asks, fighting back his own emotions thanks to the onslaught of mine. "He looks like you."

I clutch my chest. "I-I d-don't know," I stutter. "I'm scared."

He grabs my hand. "I'm right here. I've got you."

I close my eyes. Jace has me. He always has.

I nod. He turns the computer around to face me and another sob breaks free of my chest.

"He has freckles," I blurt, shocked. I didn't expect the freckles. "Oh, my God." I struggle to get enough air into my lungs. I peer at the image on the screen of the little boy, of my *son*.

Four years of dreaming about what he looks like and I finally know.

He's more perfect than I ever imagined.

"He has my nose too." I point to his slightly upturned nose. There are pieces of Owen in him too, from his mop of dark hair to the shape of his face. "He even has my eyes." I move my finger to point to his round, chocolate colored eyes. "He's ... Wow."

"I know." Jace squeezes my hand.

"He's the most perfect little boy I've ever seen."

"You know what I can't believe?" Jace starts and waits for

me to nod for him to continue. "The fact that you gave up your baby for adoption, to a family that you didn't even know where they lived, and a couple of years later you moved from Texas for college, and ended up forty minutes from where your son ended up. That's just ... insane. It's like you were drawn to him."

"Yeah, it's like I was ... That's crazy." I shake my head. The screen starts to darken and my fingers dart out, swiping over the mouse pad to light it up again. "Do you think they'll ever let me see him?"

"I don't know," he answers honestly. "Do you want to message her?"

I bite my lip. "I'm scared."

"I'm right here."

"What do I say?" Now that the opportunity is here I feel clueless. I don't want to do this wrong.

"Speak from the heart," he tells me.

I take the computer from him switch to my account before messaging Sarah.

Dear Sarah,

You have every right to exit out of this message and pretend it doesn't exist. In fact, I wouldn't blame you if you do that.

I'm Novalee Clarke and four years ago, I was a scared fifteen-year-old kid, and I gave you your son—he's a beautiful little boy, by the way.

It was the hardest thing I've ever had to do, and if I'm honest with you a closed adoption wasn't what I wanted. I wanted to be able to be a part of his life, even if I couldn't be his mom, but there were other people in my life who didn't think that was the best thing for them.

I know you don't owe me anything.

I know you can block me, and pretend I don't exist.

I expect that.

I understand that YOU are his mother now. I understand that he might not even know he's adopted. That's okay. I just want to see him. Even if you don't let me meet him, if I could just see him, it would mean the world to me. You have no idea.

Nova

I click send on the message, squeaking as I do.

I close his laptop and Jace wraps his arms around me. "You did it," he murmurs, rubbing his thumb against my arm to soothe me.

"I did it."

"I'm so proud of you." He presses his lips to my forehead.

"Why? It was just a message." I sniffle, rubbing my face into his shirt.

"I know, but it took a lot of guts for you to do that."

I burrow closer to him, seeking shelter in his embrace.

"Confession," I start, clearing my throat. I look up at him with wide eyes. "Sometimes I'm shocked that we got *here*. That we're together. We both had every reason in the world to avoid relationships."

He kisses me. "It surprises me too, sometimes, that I can

be this happy and content. I used to think a relationship was a burden, but it's not. Being with you has made me a better man."

I straddle his lap and wrap my fingers around his neck. "You're amazing," I tell him. It's true, though. He has no idea how remarkable he is. His dad has spent his whole life tearing him down, and now I want to build him back up—show him that he's none of the things he always thought he was.

"Am I?" He smiles crookedly, his hands skimming up my back, under my shirt. I nod. He presses his face into the crook of my neck. "You're amazing too, you know." His hands move around to my front, gliding up my stomach. He lightly grazes his fingers under the curves of my breasts.

"W-What were we talking about?" I stutter, my eyes falling closed.

He chuckles. "Nothing important." He nips at my chin and I moan.

"Jace." I clutch at the back of his head. "I need—"

"I know what you need."

He lifts my shirt over my head and his eyes rake over my body. I have the urge to cover myself, but I know that will only make him mad, so I let him look.

"You're beautiful," he murmurs, before capturing my lips in his. The kiss is bruising and rough, but I expect nothing less from him anymore. His fingers delve into my hair at the nape of my neck, tugging my head back.

My hips roll against his, and I claw at his shirt.

The last few days we've barely touched each other,

because we've been so busy with school, work, and looking for my son.

Jace breaks the kiss and I sit back so he can pull his shirt off. His hair is a mess and his eyes are wild.

I trace my finger down the center of his chest and around his abdominal muscles. His hips jerk, and I grin, biting down on my lip.

"That was mean," he says, his voice choked.

I skim my finger back up his chest and he captures my hand, pressing the palm flat against his heart. I feel it thumping madly beneath his heated skin.

Before I can blink he grabs me and flips me onto the couch. He hooks his fingers into my pajama pants and underwear and yanks them down forcefully.

"Now who's the mean one?" I joke.

He doesn't answer me. He lowers his mouth, swirling his tongue around each of my nipples. My back bows off the couch, my hips seeking his.

I reach blindly for his jeans and manage to find the belt. I make quick work of undoing it.

He chuckles. "Eager, are we?"

"Yes," I pant, my lips seeking his.

There's no point in lying. I'm desperate to touch him. It's been days, and I need him. My body craves him like a drug.

He sucks on the spot where my neck meets my shoulders and then his lips glide down between my breasts, over my stomach, before he sits back on his knees and gazes down at me. I know I'm flushed, and my hair's probably a mess, but I don't care, because the way he looks at me always makes me feel beautiful.

He pops the button on his jeans and slides the zipper down.

My pulse jumps in my throat and his eyes trace the movement, his lips tipped in the slightest little smirk.

He stands and steps out his jeans before returning to his previous position, knelt between my legs on the couch.

I stare at him as he grips his cock, stroking his hand slowly up and down his length.

"You like that?" he asks. "You like watching me touch myself?" I swallow thickly and nod. He grins. "God, you're fucking perfect."

He guides himself to my entrance and pushes in.

"Oh, my God," I cry out, my hips lifting off the couch. He presses a hand to my stomach, pushing me back down. I whimper.

"Shh." He presses a finger to my lips. "Relax."

I close my eyes for a moment, and he slips out the slightest bit before slamming back in.

"Jace," I moan, my eyes popping back open.

He flicks his hair from his eyes, which flame a vibrant green.

The muscles in his stomach flex as he moves his hips and mine rise to meet his.

He kisses me, stealing what's left of my breath.

He murmurs something into my hair that I can't quite decipher, but it sounds a lot like, *"Made for me."*

I rake my nails down his back, urging him closer to me.

His chest presses into my breasts, and his arms rest on the narrow space of couch beside my head.

He grasps my chin and tilts my head back, pressing his lips to my throat.

My hips jolt when his fingers find my clit, and an orgasm hits me so powerful that my legs shake and my eyes rolls back into my head.

He pumps into me a couple more times before his own orgasm hits. He collapses on top of me, careful to hold his weight, and we both struggle to regain our breath.

After a minute, he pulls out and goes to clean up. I can barely move so I just lie there.

He comes back and stands over me with a chuckle. "Can't move?"

"No," I answer, blinking up at him.

He scoops me up into his arms and I laugh as he carries me to bed. He drops me down onto the soft mattress and climbs in behind me, pulling the blankets over us.

I burrow close to his warmth and fall to sleep with a smile on my face.

thirty

. . .

nova

THE LAPTOP TAUNTS me where it rests on the coffee table. I itch to check it for a message from Sarah, but I'm terrified that there's nothing, *or* that she's telling me to stay far away from her son and that I can never see him. Honestly, it's the answer I'm expecting. She's his mom now, so she has every right to be leery of me stepping back into his life. I'd never expect to replace her, but it's a tricky situation all around.

"Hey, you're up." Jace smiles from the kitchen, making scrambled eggs.

He wears his glasses, which makes him look like a hot nerd.

I smile back and slide into the barstool. Just being near him makes me feel a little more at ease.

"That smells delicious," I comment.

He pushes the eggs around the pan and grabs a mug, already filled with coffee, and hands it to me.

"You're a saint," I tell him. I inhale the heavenly scent of the coffee and take a sip. Before I know it, I've downed half the cup.

He finishes with the eggs and scoops them out onto two plates, along with buttered toast. He places one of the plates in front of me and refills my coffee before sitting down beside me.

I scoop some eggs onto a piece of toast and take a bite.

"Are you working tonight?" I ask him.

He sighs. "Yeah, unfortunately."

"We're supposed to meet everyone for lunch today, right? That is today?" I glance at the dry erase calendar on the wall, trying to remember what day it is. Since I've been out of school for the holidays it's been hard to keep track of the days. Not to mention my focus has been primarily on searching for my son.

Greyson.

I can't believe I finally know his name.

It feels strange and amazing all at once.

"Yeah, it's today." He attacks his plate of food like someone's going to steal it from him. *Someone* clearly worked up an appetite.

"I'm seriously the worst friend ever. I can't keep up with things."

Jace cracks a smile. "You've had a lot on your mind. It's understandable. Everything will die down soon."

I take another bite of toast. "Have you …"

"Looked at the computer?" He finishes for me, and I nod. "No," he answers.

I sigh. "I want to look, but I'm scared to know."

He nods, giving me a sad but understanding look. "Makes sense. How about this—I'll hide the computer, and no looking at it until we get back from lunch. That gives her more time to respond."

"That sounds good," I agree. It's going to suck waiting and not knowing, but I know there's probably little chance she's responded. The longer I wait to check, the better.

And there's always the chance that she *never* responds.

Jace and I finish breakfast and clean up before getting ready for the day. I spend much longer than usual styling my hair and applying makeup. Most days I let my hair do its own thing and makeup is something I usually only wear for special occasions. I dress in a ripped pair of jeans and sweater with a pair of sneakers.

Jace sits on the couch, playing his guitar and humming softly under his breath.

"Working on something new?" I ask, grabbing a water bottle from the refrigerator.

He looks up from his journal where he was scribbling furiously. "Yeah." He smiles crookedly. "Inspiration struck, and I wanted to see where it led."

I pick up my camera and sit across from him in the chair. "Can I take your picture while you write?"

He shrugs. "Sure."

"Confession—I normally hate portrait photography, but I love taking your picture."

He waggles his brows. "I'm very photogenic, huh?"

"Something like that." I snap a picture of him.

"Confession—I love that you love taking my picture."

I crouch down in front of him and take another photo.

He grows quiet and returns to working on his song, ignoring my presence.

He sticks his tongue out slightly between his teeth as he thinks. I zoom in on his mouth and take another photo. He flicks his hair out of his eyes, and I get a close-up shot of his forehead and the pesky strand of hair. I've always been more fascinated by the little things than the bigger picture.

After a while he sets his guitar aside and picks up the book he's been reading lately.

He leans back into the couch and starts to read, continuing to ignore my presence. I take a couple more pictures before settling beside him on the couch. I lean my head on his shoulder as he reads.

I've never been a big reader, and that was something that shocked me about Jace—that he always has a book to read.

"We better go," I warn him, when I realize that time's ticking away and we should've left ten minutes ago. We'll be late to the restaurant—we're usually the late ones of the group, so it's probably not much of a shocker to everyone else.

Jace looks at the clock and reluctantly sets his book down. He grabs his coat and I do the same.

Outside it's windy enough that long-fallen snow swirls through the air.

Jace and I head to his truck. My poor car only gets taken

out when I go to class and to work if the weather is bad enough that I can't walk.

The restaurant where we're meeting is a nicer Italian restaurant on the other side of town, closer to where they live.

I turn the radio up and sing along as we ride. My singing voice is nowhere near as good as Jace's but he doesn't complain.

When we arrive at the restaurant the place is packed and it takes us a moment to find an empty space. It ends up being kind of far from the restaurant so I'll probably turn into a popsicle before we get inside.

"Ready?" Jace asks me, shutting off the truck.

I nod, gathering my coat around me.

We make a dash for the building, hurrying to get out of the blistering cold wind.

Jace takes my hand and says to the hostesses, "Hey, we're meeting the Montgomery party."

She smiles. "Right this way—they're all already here."

"Of course they are," I grumble.

Jace chuckles and squeezes my hand.

She leads us to a table that's in its own separate room. I'm surprised to find that not only are all our friends there, but so is Cade and Thea's mom, and Rae's parents."

Jace and I take the two empty seats across from each other—so I end up beside Thea and he's beside Xander.

"What's going on?" I ask Thea under my breath. "Why are the parents here?"

"I don't know." Thea dances in her seat. "I *think* I know, but I don't know."

I roll my eyes. "Because that's not vague or anything."

I pick up the menu and scan the items. I wasn't feeling hungry, but suddenly I feel like I'm starving.

"What are you getting?" Jace asks.

"I don't know." I flip the pages of the menu. "Maybe lasagna, that's always good."

He nods. "Lasagna sounds good."

The waiter comes and we all place our drink order. It's a large group, so it feels like it takes forever for him to get that information.

I look at the menu for a few more minutes before deciding to just go with the lasagna since it's the safest choice.

I set the menu aside and glance at Thea.

She looks dreamily at Xander while he peruses the menu so I bump her with my elbow.

"What?" She blinks at me. "What'd I do?"

"You're making me sick," I joke.

"Oh." She blushes. "Sorry."

"Nah, I think it's cute that you love him so much."

She smiles and tucks a piece of hair behind her ear. "Sometimes it feels sort of surreal that we're together."

"I'm glad you guys finally saw what was right in front of you."

She laughs. "I don't know if getting married in Vegas was the right way to do it, but I don't regret it."

The waiter comes back with all our drinks and then takes our order.

"How have you been?" I ask Xander.

"Good," he responds with a smile. "Glad to finally be home for a while."

"Are you done for the season?" Jace asks.

"Yeah, our team is done for the year. I would've liked to make it farther, but we did good so I can't complain. We're going to do even better next year."

"Hell yeah you are," Cade chimes in, overhearing. "And we're all going to be at every home game next year. Right, guys?" Cade eyes Jace and me.

I laugh. "We'll do our best."

Cade clears his throat and a hushed silence falls over the room. "Rae," he prompts. "I've been wanting to ask you this for a while, but no time was ever right—I want you to know I love you more than I ever thought it was possible to love someone."

"Oh, my God," Thea whispers under her breath. "I knew it."

"Cade ..." Rae starts.

He gets out of his seat and drops down on one knee in front of her, pulling out a small black box from his pocket. He pops it open, revealing the diamond engagement ring inside.

"We've been through more than two people should ever have to go through, but I'd go through it all again if I knew you'd always be waiting for me on the other side. Will you marry me?"

Rae stares at him, dumbfounded, but she manages to whisper, "Yes." Then with more power she says, "Yes," again.

She catapults out of the chair and into his arm and he laughs as the force rocks him.

"I love you," she sobs. "Yes. A thousand times yes." She kisses him and then he finally manages to get the ring on her finger. "Wow." She gazes down at it. "That's amazing."

We all clap and congratulations are exchanged. Rae beams, but I can tell she's still in shock. I know she wasn't expecting it at all, because she would've told me if she suspected something.

Rae speaks to her mom, showing her the ring, and Cade stands back with the happiest smile on his face.

All of us are growing up and getting older and life is changing as we do. Last year at this time, Rae, Thea, and I had only known each other for a few months, and I'd only just been introduced to the others. It's funny how short a year can seem, but how much can change.

It makes me wonder what life might look like a year from now.

Something tells me it's only going to be filled with more love.

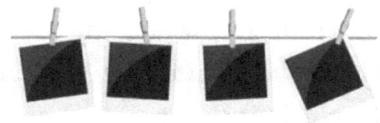

Lunch takes two hours and afterward, Jace drives around for another hour. I know it's nothing more than him stalling time but I don't call him on it.

By the time we arrive back home I'm a jittery and shaking mess.

"I think I'm going to throw up," I tell him honestly when he parks the truck. "I feel sick to my stomach."

He takes my hand in his. "It's going to be fine." His eyes are earnest, urging me to trust him. I'm terrified of rejection. After four years of not knowing anything about my son, I finally have a name, a photo, and his adoptive parents' names. It's a lot to process, especially when I realize it could all be yanked out from under me in a minute. "I'm here," Jace whispers, letting go of my hand to skim his fingers over my cheek. "I'm going to help you through this, okay?"

I nod, placing my hand on the truck door.

We head into the building and to the elevators.

The whole way up I feel like a clock is counting down.

Tick tock, tick tock, tick tock.

You might never see your son—it chants, taunting me.

The elevator doors open and Jace places his hand on my waist, guiding me to the apartment door. While he looks for his key I take a deep breath, wiping my sweaty palms on my jeans. My heart hasn't beat this fast, ever. It can't be healthy.

"What's taking so long?" I hiss.

"It's been like three seconds, chill." He slides the key into the lock.

"Feels like forever," I mumble, wrapping my arms around myself.

He opens the door and I follow him inside, drawn like a beacon to the laptop.

"Do you want me to look first?" he asks.

I wipe my hands on my jeans again. *How is it possible for your hands to sweat so much?*

"I don't know," I answer honestly. "I'm scared."

He grabs his computer and sits down on the couch with it in his lap. I sit beside him, my hands now shaking with nerves.

He lifts the lid and types in his password.

The Facebook browser is the first thing to pop up, still logged into my account, and I immediately see the red message flag.

My eyes flash to his and my heart beats impossibly faster. Dark spots begin to dance behind my eyes.

"Breathe," Jace tells me. "You have to breathe." He rubs his hand over my back.

"Confession—I'm scared."

"It's okay to be scared." He kisses the side of my forehead. "But you can be brave too."

I nod, open the message, and begin to read.

Wow. I can't say I ever expected to hear from you, but I must say I'm glad you reached out. My husband and I were willing to do an open adoption but your parents made it clear that wasn't an option. I'm sorry to hear that it wasn't your choice. It's made an already difficult thing, impossible for you, I'm sure.

I'm not sure how you found us, but I've always believed in fate, and something led you to us, of that I'm sure.

Greyson—our son, your son—knows he was adopted. We call you his Angel Mommy and Daddy who gifted us with their beautiful baby boy because they thought we could love and provide for him in a way they couldn't.

I won't lie, this won't be easy for us, just as I'm sure it won't be easy for you, but I think we can make it work.

We'd be happy to arrange for you to meet him.

You can message me back here and we can arrange a time and place to meet. I noticed you don't live far from us, so it should be easy enough to meet up.

Sarah

A sob breaks free of my chest. "Oh, my God." I tackle Jace and he moves the laptop out of the way so I don't knock it to the floor. I wrap my arms around his neck and hug him. "I'm going to get to meet my son."

He presses kisses to my hair. "I'm so happy for you."

"This is all thanks to you," I tell him, kissing him on the lips.

He shakes his head and laughs. "It's sort of thanks to my Dad."

I smile, tears pooling in my eyes. "Yeah, I guess it is." I sag against Jace, exhaustion overtaking my body now that I can relax. "I can't believe this. I feel like I'm dreaming."

"No dream," he murmurs. "This is one-hundred percent real."

"Wow," I breathe. "I think I'm in shock."

He chuckles. "That's understandable."

I rest my head on his shoulder.

For years, I hid from my past and Jace ran from his, and somehow, we ended up in the same place.

Life works in funny and mysterious ways.

At the time, you might not know why something is happening, but it all happens for a reason.

I climb off his lap and grab the laptop, typing back a response with a smile on my face the whole time.

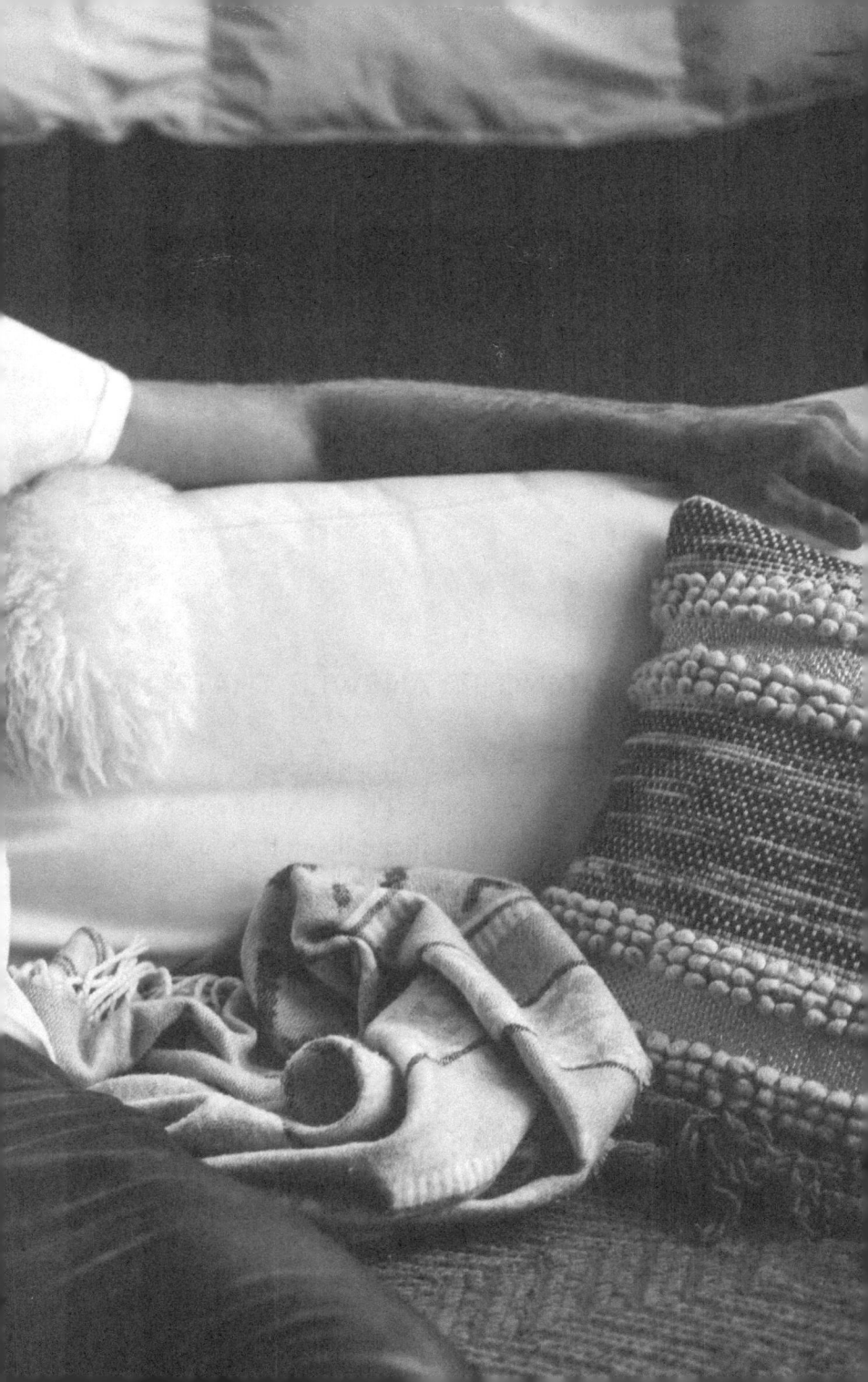

thirty-one
...

jace

"ARE YOU GOING TO ANSWER THAT?" Nova calls from the bathroom.

I eye my phone on the couch beside me. The Imperial March theme song blares from it. I'm not one to assign songs to people's numbers for when they call, but the song was too fitting for my father so I went with it.

"It's my Dad, so no."

She sighs and pokes her head out of the bathroom, her hair hanging down in a wet sheet.

"He's called every day since New Year's Eve," she reminds me.

"I have nothing to say to him." I turn the page on my kindle book, then realize I hadn't finished reading the page I'd just flipped.

I can feel Nova glaring at me. "I don't have the warm and

fuzzies for the man, believe me, but don't you think you should just talk to him? It must be something important if he keeps calling."

"Trust me—all he wants is to continue our conversation from before, maybe wring me over the coals some more, that's it. But if it'll make you feel better I'll call him back," I finally relent.

"It would."

I sigh and close the book.

My dad isn't one to call and keep calling, so I know Nova's right and something more must be up, but it's one of those things I just don't want to deal with. The man is constantly making my life unpleasant, so I've learned to avoid him.

I pick up the phone and call him back.

"Jacen?" he answers immediately.

"What do you want, Dad?" I figure it's best to cut straight to the point. I lean forward, resting my elbows on my legs and pinch the bridge of my nose.

"Things got ... heated on New Year's Eve before we could have dinner, and there's something I wanted to talk to you about."

"Then talk to me now," I grumble.

"No—we're going to meet for lunch, tomorrow."

I sigh. That's always the way it is with my dad, him telling me to do something and me doing it, no questions asked.

"Okay," I sigh. "Where?"

"How about that place you work?"

"W.T.F.?" I ask, surprised he'd suggest that.

"Yes—twelve o' clock."

"Okay," I agree. "See you then."

I hang up and Nova comes out of the bathroom. "How'd it go?" she asks.

"I have to have lunch with him," I grumble, scrubbing my hands over my face.

"It won't be so bad." She frowns.

"I hope not," I sigh. I rub my hands together and say, "I think I'm going to tell him that I'm done. I want him out of my life. He's fucking toxic. I'm going to tell him I don't want his money and he needs to leave me alone."

She nods. "If that's what you want to do—he gives you money?"

I nod. "Sort of. It's a trust fund account."

"Oh." She nods. "I see."

"Yeah," I sigh. I'm sure things are starting to make a little more sense to her. "Have you heard back from Sarah yet?" I ask.

"Not yet." She eyes my computer. "It's only been a day," she pauses, and I can see the uncertainty in her eyes. I know she's terrified Sarah will change her mind.

"Have you thought about contacting Owen?" I ask her. "Seeing if he wants to meet Greyson?"

She flinches. "I probably should, but ... is it selfish for me to want to meet him first and then contact him?"

"I don't know." I shrug. "I think it's understandable. Do *you* feel selfish for doing it?"

"I feel like it's what I *need* to do. After I get to see him I'll reach out to Owen then—after all, she might bail on me."

"She's not going to bail." I lay the book I was reading aside and tug on Nova's arm, pulling her down onto the couch with me. She lies down, stretching out with her head in my lap. I run my fingers through her damp hair. "We'll take everything one step at a time."

"It's scary," she admits. "Before, it was almost like he was a figment of my imagination. Now he's real, and I'm so close to finally meeting him, but I'm terrified that someone is about to pull the rug out from under me and be like, ha-ha think again!"

"You have to trust that everything will be okay." I wrap a strand of her hair around my finger.

She sighs. "I'm trying to."

I grow quiet, I don't know what else to say to her. I know the last month since she told me about her son has been hard on her emotionally. It's understandable. She kept his existence a secret for years. That had to weigh heavily on her. And now, in a matter of weeks she's gone from telling me, our friends, and now finding him. It's a lot to process.

I hope for her sake that she gets to see him, and maybe even be a part of his life in some way.

She deserves that.

But for now, we'll take it one step at a time.

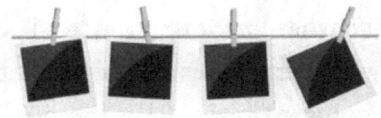

Nova's gone to work when I start getting ready to go meet my dad.

I wish she were here, because she'd talk to me and keep my mind off this lunch. My dad and I rarely spend time alone anymore—typically when he summons me it's because I need to attend something and put on the show of being his son—I can't even recall the last time we had lunch or dinner just the two of us.

I shower and shave, then dress in pair of slacks and a button-down shirt. I fucking hate getting dressed up, but I know if I show up in a t-shirt and jeans he'll spend ten minutes berating me on my clothes. I'd rather skip that conversation and jump straight into it.

I find it strange that of all the places we could meet for lunch he had to choose where I work, but I guess it could be worse. At least I know the place so I'll feel more comfortable, maybe that was his plan, but I can't imagine him thinking about my feelings when it comes to anything.

I shrug into my coat and grab my keys, heading out the door.

The moment I step outside a heavy weight settles on my chest. It happens every time I have to see him.

I choose to walk, even though it's freezing. I grab a

cigarette and tap one out, lighting it. I haven't smoked in a couple of weeks, I think, but suddenly, I *need* a cigarette more than anything.

I inhale the smoke and let it fill my lungs before breathing out.

By the time the cigarette is a small nub, I've reached the restaurant.

I drop the cigarette on the ground and extinguish it then head across the street and in the W.T.F.

I can't help but smile, wondering what my father thought of the name and logo with the whacky looking fork. He probably wasn't as amused as I am.

"You're not supposed to work until tonight," Eli says when I come in.

"I'm meeting someone," I tell him.

"Oh. My bad." He turns his attention back to the pile of papers at the table he occupies.

I head through the restaurant, scanning the tables. I'm early, but my Dad has probably been here for thirty minutes.

Sure enough, I find him at a table in the back, off to himself.

I'm sure he asked to be seated away from everyone.

"Hello, father," I say formally, removing my coat and draping it over the back of my chair.

He watches my movements, probably looking for anything I do wrong.

I slide into the chair across from him.

"Where's your girlfriend? I assumed you'd bring her, since I requested her presence at our dinner we never had."

"Leave Nova out of this," I hiss. "I don't know why the fuck you want me here, but leave me out of it. You lost the right to speak with her when you pried into her personal business."

He huffs and unbuttons his suit jacket, lacing his fingers on the table. "I make it a point to check into anyone you're involved with."

"I've never dated anyone before," I remind him.

"Yes—" his lips twitch "—but you have gone on dates, and you do have friends."

"Are you fucking kidding me?" I snap. "You've checked into my friends too?"

He smiles like the cat that ate the canary. "I make it a point to know about anything that might come back on me. I'm sure I knew about your friends' Vegas wedding before you did."

I stare at him in disbelief.

"Don't look at me like that," he snaps. "Surely even you can understand why I have to do it."

"You're unbelievable," I respond, half-tempted to leave. The only thing that keeps me from leaving is the fact that I know if I do I'm probably going to have to deal with more of his relentless calls.

"I'm sorry to interrupt—can I get you guys a drink? If you're ready to order I'll get that too while I'm here," the waitress points to our closed menus.

"Hi, Kelly." I smile at the waitress. She's not one I work with often since I usually work nights, but she's always been nice in passing. "I'll just have a water and a cheeseburger."

"Of course." She takes my menu. "And for you, sir?" She turns to my father.

"I'll have a water as well and the sirloin."

"I'll bring your drinks right out and put your order in." She smiles pleasantly and heads for the kitchen.

I sigh and look across the table at my dad. My leg bounces restlessly with nervousness.

We stare at each other—father and son by blood, strangers in reality.

A minute ticks by, and when he doesn't say anything, I brush an invisible crumb off the table.

"Tell me why we're here. I figured after the way things ended on New Year's Eve that it'd be a whole year before I heard from you. If that." I level him with a glare. "And yet you've called every fucking day—so get to the point."

"I have cancer." My blood runs cold. It hasn't been that long since I heard those words pertaining to my mom. "It's terminal."

I blink at him, at a loss for words. "I ... What?"

He wets his lips. "It's pancreatic cancer. They say there's nothing they can do."

I don't feel a lot of love when it comes to my father, but he's still my dad, and he's always been there. Even if I fucking hated that fact I knew if I really needed something I could go to him—albeit with my tail tucked between my legs.

"But you look fine," I say, still stunned.

He gives me a sad look. "Do I? Look closely, Jacen."

I never noticed it before but his cheeks have become sallow and his eyes have dark circles beneath them. His shoulders are hunched, which wouldn't be such a big deal for some people but he's always been a stickler on posture, now it's almost like he's grown too weak told his body up.

"H-How long?" I stutter out and force a weak smile when Kelly brings out waters. "How long do you have left?"

"That's why I wanted to see you ..." He pauses, touching his fingers to his lips. "It's a funny thing, coming to terms with your own lack of invincibility when you've spent your whole life projecting that you're untouchable."

"How long?" I ask again.

"Two weeks," he answers with a sad smile. "A month tops, but the doctors aren't optimistic."

I feel stunned.

Gutted.

This wasn't what I was expecting.

"I know I haven't always been the best father, or husband to your mother, and you might not believe me, but that's something I regret. You won't remember much about your grandfather—the one you're named after—but he wasn't a very good man, either. Workaholic and violent. He spent the majority of his time drunk. I guess growing up in that rubbed off on me. I didn't know any other way to be a man. I know it's not an excuse, but I want to help you understand." He crosses his fingers together and lays them on the table, leaning forward. "Everything I own is being left to you. You'll be well taken care of—won't have to work, if you don't want to."

My mouth opens and closes like a fish. I feel lost. Nothing makes sense.

"I'm sorry," he continues. "I know I just sprung this on you. I guess there's no good way to say I'm dying."

"No, there's not," I agree.

I can't wrap my head around how calm he is. I guess he's had time to accept his inevitable death while I've only had moments. If I was him I'd be angry, and throwing shit, and probably yelling at the top of my lungs about how unfair it was. But I guess when you have something worth living for that's your reaction.

My dad?

He has nothing.

Our food is brought out, but I can't even look at it.

"I don't expect you to miss me," he says, cutting into his steak. "I don't have that right after the way I've treated you. All I ask is ..." he pauses, gathering a breath. "Just please come to my funeral."

I nod, swallowing past the lump in my throat. I feel like crying for some strange reason. I think the little boy in me is mourning what *could* have been if my dad had been different.

"I'll be there," I finally say when I can find my voice.

This lunch didn't go at all how I'd planned. I'd honestly thought we'd get into a fight and I was going to tell him I was done, that I couldn't fucking do this anymore.

Little did I know that fate had already decided that fact for me.

In a couple of weeks, my dad will be dead.

He'll simply cease to exist.

Nothing more than a memory.

That's all that's ever truly left of any of us—a memory—so, I guess you better make sure they're all good ones.

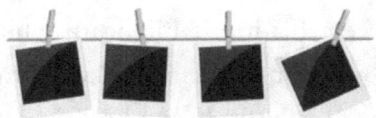

"How'd it go?" Nova asks before she even takes her coat off.

I set my book down and stretch my arm over the back of the couch. "It was ... unexpected."

"Elaborate." She unties her scarf and hangs it up with her coat. She looks cute with her chilled red nose and a floppy gray beanie and mittens. She takes those off and drops them in the basket by the door.

"He has cancer."

Her mouth pops open—my reaction exactly. "What?"

"He only has a couple more weeks to live."

"Oh, my God. Are you okay?" She rushes to me and jumps onto the couch beside me.

I nod. "Yeah, I am. We talked for a while ... It was the longest I think we've ever talked without fighting. Is it strange to say it was nice?"

"Not at all—he is your dad. Even though he's an asshole I think it's understandable for you to crave some sort of bond and acceptance from him. I can't believe he's dying."

"Yeah, and soon too." I laugh but there's no humor in the tone. "He says he has two weeks, a month tops, to live."

"Wow." Nova looks at me with wide, worried eyes. She touches her hand to mine, and I wrap my fingers around hers. My hand swallows hers whole. "I hate to say this, but do you think maybe he's lying?"

I shake my head. "'Fraid not. It's definitely the truth."

"I'm sorry." She wraps her arms around me and I let her hug me.

"Thanks."

"If you need to talk about it, I'm here, you know that, right?"

"I do." I tuck a piece of hair behind her ear, purposely skimming my fingers over her cheek. "Have you heard from Sarah?" I ask, desperate to change the subject. The last couple of hours my mind has only been occupied with thoughts of my father's impending death. I need something else to focus on.

"I have, actually," she beams, so I know it must be good news. "We're meeting next weekend at a local ice-skating rink. You'll come with me, right?"

"If you want me to."

"I definitely want you to." She nods. "I need you there to keep me from freaking out."

"Then I'll be there." I lean over and kiss her, my lips lingering a little longer than necessary.

All afternoon while I sat with my dad, I wished she was there, because her presence alone gives me strength.

It's funny, because I used to think love makes you weak. Now I realize it's the complete opposite.

Because of her, I'm stronger than ever before.

Because of her, I'm happy.

Because of her, I'm a better man.

So, life can throw whatever it wants at me—the good, bad, and the fucking ugly—because I'm ready.

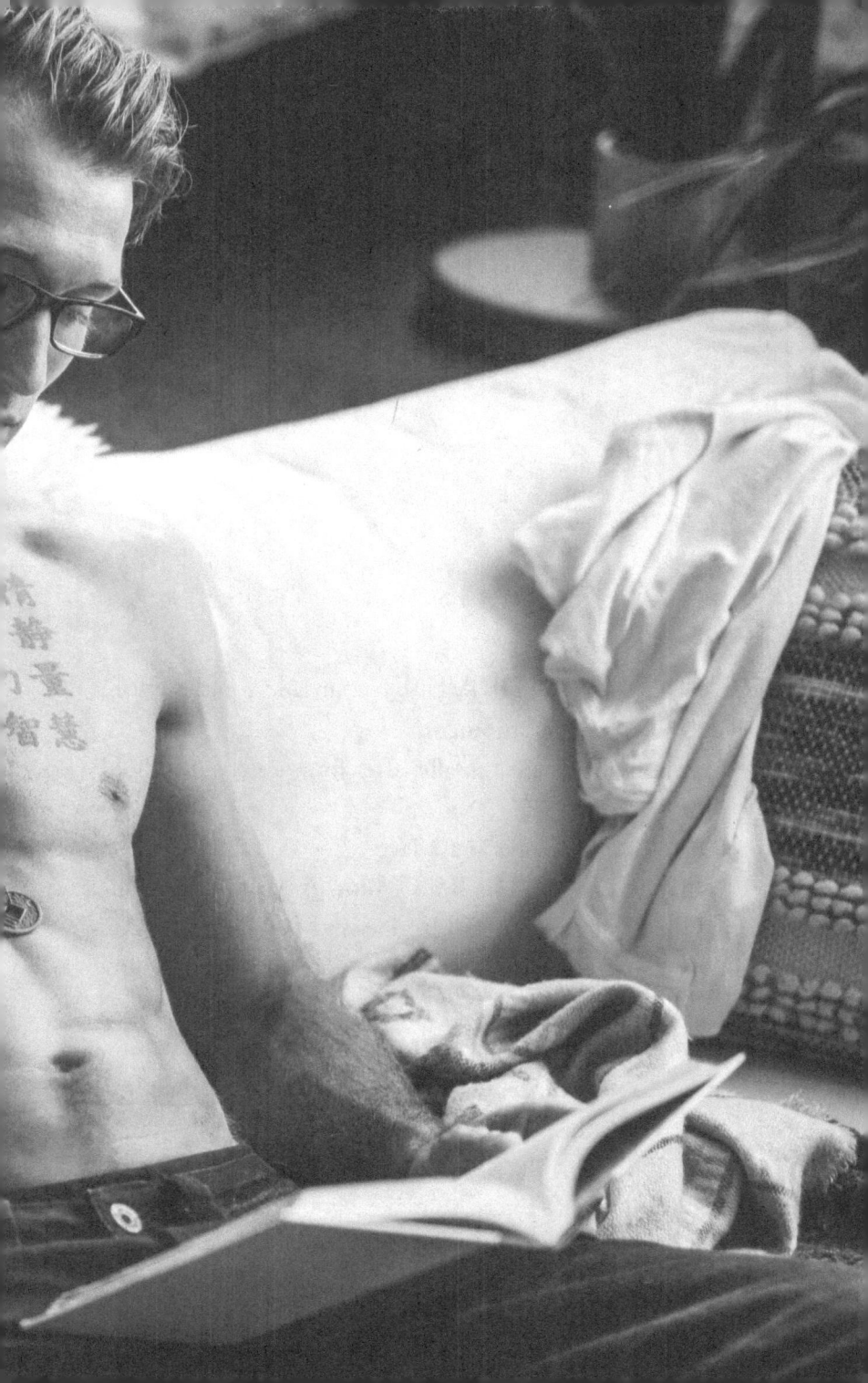

thirty-two
...

nova

I'VE PROBABLY DRIVEN Jace insane for the entire week leading up to this moment.

The moment where I finally, after four years, get to hold my son.

"Does this look okay?" I ask Jace.

"What the fuck?" His head whips up so fast from his journal that I'll be surprised if he doesn't have whiplash. "Are you wearing *pink*? I didn't even know you owned something pink."

"I borrowed it from Thea," I mumble, ducking my head. "I wanted to look nice and I asked her if she could help me and she gave me this."

"You don't look like you."

"Jace," I whine. "I need to make a good impression with them so they'll let me see him again."

His brows draw together. "You might as well wear a fucking dress then."

I huff. "You can't say *fuck* every other word with them, either."

He raises his hands innocently. "I'll be good, promise."

"Does it really look bad?" I ask, now doubting the flowing pink top.

He shrugs, his shirt stretching taut over his muscles. "No, it doesn't look *bad*. You just don't look like *you*. Don't you think that's important?"

"So, I should put my hair in a messy bun and wear my shirt that says *Adios Bitchachos*? I'm sure that'll go over real well."

"Well, maybe not that particular shirt." He snaps his fingers together. "What about the one that says, *All I care about is pizza (and like two people)*. That one is great."

"I can't wear one of those." I sigh from the doorway. "They'll think I'm insane. I'll find something else. I'm sure I have something that will work."

I take off the shirt from Thea and begin rummaging through my closet again.

I can't remember a time when I've cared so much about what I look like.

After thirty minutes of rummaging through my closet I finally settle on a gray sweater and jeans. It's not the nicest thing, sure, but it's simple and it's me. I think Jace is right, I have to stay true to myself. I can't portray myself as someone I'm not.

"Are you ready?" Jace calls as I'm putting my boots on.

"We needed to go like five minutes ago."

I bust out of the room. "I'm ready."

He grins when he sees me. "That's my Nova."

"I feel like I might be sick," I tell him, my stomach suddenly clenching.

He shakes his head. "You'll be fine. You're stressing too much."

I take a deep breath. "This is scary."

He crosses the room to me and takes my face between his hands. "I'm going to be there the whole time. If it starts to be too much, just look at me and find your center."

I smile up at him. "I love you."

He chuckles. "I don't know what I did to deserve you, but I'm fucking grateful for it. I love you too." He kisses me quickly and then grabs the keys from the counter. "We have to go, like *now*."

I know he's right. We're already running late, and I wanted to be there early so I could have a moment to prepare myself.

I grab my coat and put it on.

He already has his on so he waits by the door.

I rush past him once I have my coat on and he locks up behind us.

As we ride in the elevator, I type the address of the ice rink into my phone.

"It's twenty-five minutes from here. Think you can make it twenty?"

He smiles crookedly. "I can do anything."

Jace parks outside the ice rink—managing to make it there in nineteen minutes.

"Ready?" he asks, shutting the truck off.

I shake my head, panic seizing my chest. "I can't do this. I can't face him. I ... I abandoned him. I just gave him up."

"Shh," he hushes me. "No. Don't say that. Don't do that to yourself. You were fifteen. You did what you had to do. You giving up that baby might've been the hardest thing you've ever done, but I promise you it was the best thing for him. That right there proves to me that you're a good mom—because you cared more about his wellbeing than your own happiness."

My chin quivers. "You're going to make me cry."

"Fuck," he chokes. "I didn't mean to do that."

I take a couple of deep breaths and nod. "Okay, let's go in. I can do this."

He gets out of the truck, and I follow a moment later. He comes around to me and takes my hand. I instantly feel better.

We head inside together and rent some skates.

Sarah says Greyson loves to ice-skate and he says he's going to be a professional hockey player one day. I love that he's only four and already dreaming so big.

Jace and I head into the rink and sit down to put our skates on.

"Do you see them?" I ask, scanning the people there.

He shakes his head. "No. I don't think they're here yet."

I breathe out, the breath shaky. I've never felt this nervous in my whole life, not even when I was waiting for the pregnancy test to turn positive.

Jace rubs his hand over my back, trying his best to calm me.

"What if they don't come?" I glance sideways at him.

That's when I see him.

"Oh, my God," I gasp, tears springing to my eyes.

"Hello—Novalee, right?" Sarah and her husband appear with a little boy between them.

My little boy.

"Just Nova," I say, standing up. "Hi."

"Can I hug you?" she asks.

I stare at her, dumbfounded. "Um, yeah," I say, opening my arms.

She hugs me tight, like a mother squeezing her child. "Thank you," she whispers in my ear. "Thank you for giving me the best gift you could ever give me."

She lets me go and I find that there are tears in her eyes too.

"This is my husband Jimmy. And *this* is Greyson." She squeezes the little boy's shoulder lightly. He clutches a Ziploc baggie full of goldfish to his chest.

My heart ... My heart feels full, like after four years it's finally found the piece it's been missing.

The picture I saw on the computer doesn't do him justice.

He's the cutest kid I've ever seen.

His dark hair flops over his forehead and he looks up at me with wide doe-like brown eyes. His lips are full and the smattering of freckles across his nose only makes him more adorable. I couldn't see it in the picture, but in person he even has a tiny mole on his top lip like Owen has.

"You're perfect," I whisper.

"Greyson—" Sarah smiles down at him "—this is your Angel Mommy that we're always telling you about. She's the one that carried you inside her, and then she gave you to Mommy and Daddy to take care of because she knew you were a very special little boy and she thought we could help her with you. Isn't that amazing? You're so special you get *two* sets of parents."

I feel Jace stand behind me, his presence filling me with warmth.

I drop down to my knees so I'm at Greyson's height. "Hi," I say. I realize it lacks originality but I can't seem to think beyond that.

"Hi," he says back, bashfully cowering closer to his mom.

While it breaks my heart, at the same time I understand, because I'm a stranger to him.

"How old are you?" I ask him.

"Four." He holds up four fingers.

"Really?" I gasp. "That's cool."

"How old are you?" He asks me, leaning a little closer to me.

"Twenty. So many fingers they don't even fit on my hand."

He laughs at that and my God even his laugh his perfect. Everything about him is more than I ever imagined.

"I heard you like to skate."

"I do." He nods at this with a little grin, his hair bouncing. "I'm gonna play hockey one day."

"Wow, that's awesome. Do you want to go skate with me?"

He looks up at his mom and waits for her to okay it. When she nods, he says, "Yeah, that'd be fun. How do you say your name? I forgot."

"Nova," I tell him.

"Nova," he says. "Like a star?"

I break out in the biggest smile. "Yeah, exactly like a star."

"I love the stars," he tells me, taking my hand.

I gasp, pressing my lips together as I fight tears, because *holy shit I'm holding my son's hand*. It's small and warm in mine. We waddle out onto the ice and start skating together.

"You're really good," I tell him.

"Of course I am. I'm good at everything."

And he's definitely Owen's kid, because that's so something he'd say.

"So, I was in your tummy?" he asks.

"You were." I smile down at him as we glide on the ice.

He looks back at his mom and dad who are just now getting on the ice with Jace. I feel bad that I didn't introduce him, but I was so shocked I couldn't think straight.

"That's cool. Mommy and Daddy tell me that I'm

adopted, but I don't know what that means exactly. I'm only four, after all." He shrugs his slender shoulders.

"All it means is that you're very special and surrounded by a lot of love."

"Being adopted is a good thing, then?"

"A very good thing." I smile down at him, fighting tears.

The emotion clogging my chest feels like it's going to choke me. I can't believe this is happening right now. That my son is *here* and that I'm holding his hand.

It feels too good to be true.

We skate around and he holds my hand the entire time.

The others hang back, giving me time alone with him, for which I'm grateful.

The amount of love I feel for this little boy eclipses everything else in the world. It's a different kind of love too. It's a bond that transcends.

It makes me wonder about Jace's dad—how he could have treated his son so horribly. Our children are precious gifts, something meant to be cherished. I was forced to give my child up, but I can't imagine willingly ignoring one. It's heartbreaking.

I look behind me at Jace.

Despite it all, despite the darkness in both our hearts, we both still turned out pretty well. I guess it goes to show you that you can choose to be better, that you don't have to let life break you. *You* have the power to make things better.

We finish skating, and my heart begins to break all over again, knowing I'm going to have to say goodbye.

Hellos are the easy part. It's the goodbyes that rip you to shreds.

I look at Sarah and Jimmy with panic in my eyes. "Can I see you again? Can I see *him* again?"

Sarah takes my hand, looking at me with pity in her eyes. "Absolutely, sweetie. Jimmy and I were talking about it, and if you want, maybe we can speak to a lawyer about the adoption and change the terms so you can see him. We won't keep him front you." She squeezes my hand.

"Thank you." I burst into tears. "Thank you so much."

"No." She shakes her head. "Thank *you*, because of your selfless act we finally got the child we've wanted all our lives. Without you, we wouldn't have that. The way I see it, we're family. Bonded for life." She hugs me.

I hug her back, mumbling, "Thank you," repeatedly.

When she releases me, I hug Jimmy and then I bend down, opening my arms to Greyson.

"Can I have a hug?" I ask him.

He dives into my arms without a second of thought, which only makes me cry harder. I bury my face into his hair, inhaling the scent of his shampoo. It smells like watermelons which makes me smile.

I realize that this is my first time hugging him, but it won't be the last, which only makes me cry harder.

He feels so good in my arms, like they were made to hold him, but I know I have to let him go.

I finally release him and he blinks up at me with wide eyes. "Why are you crying? Are you sad?"

"No." I shake my head, wiping the wetness from my cheeks. "I've never been happier."

"You cry when you're happy? I didn't know that."

"Only if you're *really* happy."

He nods like this makes perfect sense.

Sarah takes my hand and squeezes it. She's a pretty woman, in her forties with a few wrinkles from laughing, and soft brown hair.

"We'll see you soon," she tells me with a smile.

"Mhmm." I nod, close to breaking out into hysterics again.

I watch them leave, and once they're gone, a sob breaks free of my chest.

Jace gathers me into his arms, and I bury my face into his chest.

He rubs my back soothingly, humming softly—I think it's a new song he's been working on.

I rub my face against his shirt, probably leaving behind a streak of mascara tears.

When I finally have a hold on myself, I look up at him. "This was the best day of my life. Thank you—without you, this would've never happened."

"I'd do anything for you, don't you know that by now?"

He glides his fingers down my cheek and my stomach clenches. The amount of love he looks at me with is mind-blowing. I never in a million years thought we'd end up here—together. But somewhere along the way our paths crossed, and then they intersected. Some things are just meant to be, and I think that's the case for us.

epilogue
...

jace

One Month Later

Death isn't something that's easy to accept, even when you know it's coming.

I held my father's hand as he passed away and Nova stood at my side while I cried. I didn't even know why I cried, but I felt like someone should, and if I didn't do it, who would?

My father's last month wasn't an easy one.

Every day he grew weaker until he couldn't get out of the bed.

I went every day to see him, though. In the beginning, I

didn't want to, but by the end I was hoping they'd continue on forever.

I learned more about my father in that month than I did in all of my twenty-three years.

Some days, when the pain was too much, he'd revert to his old self, but most of the time he was kind. He asked me questions about myself that before he never cared to know and even asked me to sing for him.

I was singing to him as he took his last breath.

He died with a smile on his face so he either loved my singing or was glad he didn't have to listen to it anymore.

I fix my tie into place and look in the mirror. My hair is slicked back, my face clean-shaven. My new suit fits me perfectly.

I have to give a eulogy at my father's funeral today.

I meet Nova in the middle of the apartment, my eyes raking over her. The black dress she wears has long sleeves but ends above her knees. The skirt part flairs out at her hips and the top shows off the curve of her breasts.

"If you keep looking at me like that, we're going to be late," she quips.

"Wouldn't be a bad thing." I look her up and down.

She laughs. "Come on."

She ushers me to the door.

The funeral is held in a church twenty minutes away. I find it ironic since I don't think my father set foot once in a church while he was alive.

Nova and I head into the church. Cade, Thea, Xander, and Rae are all already there, so we say hello. Nova stays with them while I go hunt down someone to tell me where the fuck I'm supposed to be.

Eventually, I end up greeting people as they arrive. Pretty much everyone that shows up is someone that he worked with. It's a small crowd, but it's better than nothing, because that was my biggest fear.

When it's time for me to speak, my palms begin to sweat.

I clear my throat and speak into the microphone. "I'm ... uh ... Jacen ... Jace. His son." I point stupidly at the casket. "I'm Heath's son." I pause to take a breath and laugh lightly. "I'm not very good at public speaking—singing in front of people, not a big deal, but this ..." I grasp the podium. "I'm supposed to get up here and tell you what a good man my father was, but I can't lie to you. For most of my life he was horrible, but this last month ... Maybe it was the fact that he knew he was dying but I finally saw some humility in him. He seemed human, for once. I always thought he was a bionic robot or something," I joke. "As twisted as it sounds, I'm kind of selfishly glad he got sick, because it allowed me to see him in a different way. I got to know him in a way I never had before. We didn't have the typical father son relationship, but this past month I got a small taste of what could've been. I wish it had been a lifetime like that, but it wasn't, and so I'm thankful for what I had." I press my lips together, thinking. "That's something I've grown to learn—quality over quantity. I used to think more of something was better—more drinks, more girls, more sex. Then this girl came into my life, with her ever-changing hair color and shook up my whole existence. I suddenly understood *quality over quantity* because she's everything I never knew I needed. Every moment I get to spend with her is one worth remembering. My dad didn't like her, not at first, and she knew that, but by the time he passed he'd grown to love her too. I don't think anyone can't not love Nova." I smile at her in the first pew. "Dad saw too, by the end, that quality over quantity is better, and I hope that's something you all can learn too, before it's too late. Thank you."

I step down and head down to sit with Nova and my friends.

A few more words are said and then I stand to help carry the casket out to the grave. Xander and Cade stand to help me, along with a couple of the men Dad worked with.

We carry the casket outside into the cold, snowy, February air.

The girls huddle close together, trying to stay warm.

His grave is right beside my mom's. I used to hope my dad would go to hell, but now I hope he's wherever Mom is and that they're finally together again.

My father might not have been the best, but I never doubted that he loved my mother in her own way.

I grab a flower from the arrangement on his casket and drop it onto my mother's stone.

Nova loops her arm through mine, laying her head on my shoulder.

I squint at the sun shining through the bare tree branches.

"Confession—I think life works in mysterious ways."

She smiles up at me, her dark brown hair blowing in the

wind. Her nose is red from the cold and she crinkles it, accentuating her freckles.

"It definitely does," she agrees.

If there's anything the last month has taught me, it's that life is always changing. What's true today, might not be true tomorrow. What you feel today, can change in an instant. You have to learn to let things go, and when you do, you become stronger for it.

I know I am.

www.ingramcontent.com/pod-product-compliance
Lightning Source LLC
LaVergne TN
LVHW032047070526
838201LV00085B/4772